Dale Brown

Former US Air Force captain Dale Brown was born in Buffalo, New York, and now lives in Nevada. He graduated from Penn State University with a degree in Western European History and received a US Air Force commission in 1978. While in the Air Force, he was a navigator-bombardier, flying over 2500 hours in tactical and training aircraft and receiving several military decorations and awards.

He was still serving in the Air Force when he wrote his highly acclaimed first novel, *Flight of the Old Dog*. Since then he has written a string of *New York Times* bestsellers, all available from HarperCollins: *Silver Tower*, *Day of the Cheetah*, *Hammerheads*, *Sky Masters*, *Night of the Hawk*, *Chains of Command*, *Storming Heaven*, *Shadows of Steel*, *Fatal Terrain* and *The Tin Man*.

'Undoubtedly my favourite book for some time . . . *The Tin Man* features one of his old heroes, Patrick McLanahan. Dressed in a high-tech suit, he takes on a gang who are terrorising a city. Technical flaws in the suit hold him back, but they only add to the power of the writing and the tension Brown manages to create in his powerful thriller.'   *Oxford Times*

'Dale Brown is a master at mixing technology and action. He puts readers right into the middle of the inferno.'   LARRY BOND

'Brown is a master . . . bringing life to his characters with a few deft strokes.'   *Publishers Weekly*

'A master of the future-shock game.'   *Kirkus Reviews*

BY DALE BROWN

Flight of the Old Dog
Silver Tower
Day of the Cheetah
Hammerheads
Sky Masters
Night of the Hawk
Chains of Command
Storming Heaven
Shadows of Steel
Fatal Terrain
The Tin Man

DALE BROWN

THE TIN MAN

HarperCollins*Publishers*

HarperCollins*Publishers*
77–85 Fulham Palace Road,
Hammersmith, London W6 8JB

www.**fire**and**water**.com

Special overseas edition 1999
This paperback edition 1999
1 3 5 7 9 8 6 4 2

First published in Great Britain by
HarperCollins*Publishers* 1999

First published in the USA by
Bantam Books 1998

Copyright © Target Direct Productions Inc 1998

The Author asserts the moral right to
be identified as the author of this work

ISBN 0 00 651180 5

Set in Meridien

Printed and bound in Great Britain by
Caledonian International Book Manufacturing Ltd, Glasgow

DEDICATION

This novel is dedicated to my wife, my confidante, my best friend, and my lover, Diane; to our son and first child, Hunter; and to my old buddy Saber.

The soul truly has no beginning and no end; I'm glad these three souls touched mine.

It is also dedicated to the memory of Sergeant George Sullivan, University of Nevada-Reno Police Department, brutally killed in the line of duty in January of 1998, and to all the other men and women who wear a badge and put their lives on the line to protect ours. Thank you for your service.

ACKNOWLEDGMENTS

Very special thanks to my wife, retired Sacramento Police Department Narcotics lieutenant Diane Joelson Brown, for her encouragement, support, and technical advice. This book would not have been possible without her patience, insight, and expertise. The mistakes are all mine, but the credit goes to her.

Thanks also to Lieutenant John Kane, disaster-preparedness expert, Sacramento Police Department; Lieutenant Leslie Brown, watch commander, North Patrol, Sacramento County Sheriff's Department; Detective David Cropp, Narcotics investigator and expert, Sacramento Police Department; and Officer Vonda Walker and Corporal Paula Gow, Sacramento Police Department, for their technical assistance.

I also thank retired Sacramento Police Department officer and fellow pilot Bert Sousa for his help in profiling and helping to gather information on outlaw motorcycle gangs. A source of information on biker gangs, which Bert encouraged the author Yves Lavigne to write, was *Hells Angels: Into the Abyss* (New York: HarperCollins Publishers, 1996). Hells Angels is a registered trademark of the Hells Angels Motorcycle Corp.

AUTHOR'S NOTE

This is a work of fiction. Any resemblance to any actual persons or events is purely coincidental and is a product of the author's imagination. Although I endeavor to be as accurate as possible, the use of actual places and organizations is meant only to enhance the authenticity of the story. It is in no way intended to depict, represent, or describe any real-world person, organization, agency, or the procedures they follow.

Similarly, the information regarding the manufacture of methamphetamine has been included to enhance the authenticity of the story. The drugs produced, their by-products, and the compounds used in their manufacture described herein are deadly. Do not attempt to duplicate these procedures.

Your thoughts and opinions about this or any of my works are welcome! Please e-mail your comments to me at:
Readermail@Megafortress.com

or visit my Web site on the Internet at:
http://www.Megafortress.com

Because of the tremendous number of messages I receive, it may take a while for me to reply, but I read every one. Thank you!

Dale Brown
Lake Tahoe, Nevada, USA

REAL-WORLD NEWS EXCERPTS

ARMORED-CAR KILLING PROBED
– *San Francisco Examiner and AP, 11/26/97*
San Ramon, Calif. – Oakland police investigating the shooting death of an armored-car guard and the disappearance of his partner – along with $300,000 – searched a Sacramento motel early Wednesday and recovered 'hundreds of thousands of dollars,' according to Sacramento police.

No one was in the room at the Motel 6 at Richards Boulevard and Jibboom Street in central Sacramento when officers served their search warrant at 3:30 A.M.

Authorities are searching for the missing guard Thomas Franklin Wheelock and consider him the 'prime suspect' in the case.

Oakland police were not immediately available for comment on the motel search.

Investigators suspect the fatal shooting and apparent theft mark the latest case in a troubling new trend: security guards succumbing to the temptation of fast cash.

'To have that one person who you trust to back you up, turn around and take your life is a very scary thought,' said Dan Connolly, chairman of the Independent Car Operators Association. 'It leads more and more to the adage that you trust no one in this business . . .'

4 SUSPECTED OF BREWING DRUG AT MOTEL
– *Los Angeles Times, 11/15/97*
Studio City, Calif. – Four people were arrested on suspicion of running a methamphetamine lab in a motel room by

police who seized two gallons of ingredients and enough equipment to produce thousands of dollars worth of the drug, the Los Angeles Police Department said Friday.

. . . The LAPD's Hazardous Materials section also responded to the scene because of the toxic chemicals used to produce methamphetamine. 'This stuff is so toxic that it penetrates through the walls and carpets,' said Sgt Michael Linder, one of the arresting officers.

. . . Small portable meth labs have become ubiquitous in Los Angeles.

. . . Larger-scale meth production is carried out in rural areas where producers can run electric generators and the noxious fumes can go undetected. 'You have to be pretty brazen to cook in the city because the smell is so strong,' said Linder . . .

TRAFFICKERS HIRE FOREIGNERS TO TRAIN PRIVATE MILITIAS IN FACE OF REFORM EFFORTS, OFFICIALS SAY – *The Washington Post, 10/30/97*

Mexican drug-trafficking organizations are hiring foreign mercenaries to strengthen their paramilitary forces, heightening the threat that traffickers pose to U.S. security interests, senior law-enforcement officials said yesterday.

. . . The Arellano Felix organization 'maintains well-armed and well-trained security forces, described by Mexican enforcement authorities as paramilitary in nature, which include international mercenaries as advisers, trainers, and members . . .'

. . . Knowledgeable sources said the mercenaries are largely from Colombia, Britain, and Israel and are employed to train the militias in the use of more sophisticated explosives and combat techniques.

In the late 1980's, the Medellín cocaine cartel in Colombia hired Israeli mercenaries to train its private army in the use of explosives. The rival Cab cartel then hired about a dozen British and South African mercenaries to kill the leaders of the Medellín organization . . .

LAW TARGETS METHAMPHETAMINE
– *Sacramento Bee, 10/4/96*
Washington – Taking direct aim at a problem hitting California, President Clinton on Thursday signed legislation increasing penalties for the manufacture of methamphetamine and placing new restrictions on the chemicals used to make the illegal drug.

In a White House Rose Garden signing ceremony, Clinton said the new law would stop what primarily is now a West Coast problem from becoming a nationwide epidemic.

'We have to stop meth before it becomes the crack [cocaine] of the 1990's,' Clinton said of a drug that has caused emergency-room admissions to skyrocket in the Sacramento area in recent years. 'This legislation gives us a chance to do it.'

Law-enforcement officials have identified methamphetamine as the fastest-growing drug problem in the country . . .

Prologue

Those in the business call it the pour-and-run method, and it is one of the most dangerous and explosive chemical processes ever practiced. But Bennie the Chef was the master of this dangerous, arcane art:

In a large glass tub, Bennie mixed seventeen pounds of ephedrine – crushed over-the-counter diet pills dissolved in chloroform – with a toxic, corrosive chemical liquid called thionyl chloride. The combination immediately produced toxic sulfur dioxide, corrosive hydrogen chloride gas, and a substance called 1-phenyl-1-chloro-2-methylaminopropane, or chloropseudoephedrine for short. They call it pour-and-run because even in the open air only a full-body antiexposure suit and an industrial-strength ventilator or positive-flow breathing system will save anyone within fifty yards from being asphyxiated by the sulfur dioxide fumes or severely burned by caustic acid. Bennie never used any of this gear, so it became a test to see if he could run at least half the length of a football field while holding his breath. He ran the race with a towel over his face, because if the hydrogen chloride gas touches any water, even the tiny bits of moisture in the eyes or nostrils, it instantly produces hydrochloric acid so corrosive that it will eat away an eyeball in seconds.

If he survived the test, he'd be several thousand dollars

richer. If not, he'd be alive just long enough to taste the blood in his throat as his lungs dissolved, like a sheet of paper thrown into a fire.

Fifty-year-old Bennie, withered and emaciated-looking, was nearly exhausted after his dash to the edge of the trees – but he made it. His mixing tub was under a lean-to facing into the wind, and he could see the poisonous gas streaming out from the tub and collecting under the shelter. Ten minutes later, it was safe to approach the tub, and he began stirring the mixture.

His two guards, both tall, beefy, bearded men with long hair, huge beer bellies, Doc Martens ass-kicker boots, and black leather vests, could never hope to make the run, so they were already a safe distance away, smoking dope and drinking beer. Both were full-fledged Satan's Brotherhood motorcycle gang members, wearing their 'colors' – the leather vests with the Brotherhood logo and the upper rocker that read 'Brotherhood' and the bottom rocker that read 'Oakland' on the back, and Satan's Brotherhood tattoos on their left arms. Most of the gang members were among the most dangerous of America's outlaw bikers, the ones rejected or stripped of their membership in other gangs such as the Hells Angels or the Outlaw Bikers or the Brothers. They were avowed racists, even neo-Nazi; although they dealt drugs to all races and ran black, Asian, and Hispanic women in their whorehouses and strip clubs, they never associated with anyone other than other whites. There were more Satan's Brotherhood members in the United States than Hells Angels or any other biker gang, but fewer of them in prison. The reason for this was simple: They vowed never to be taken alive by the police.

When Bennie finished stirring the mixture, precipitating the chloropseudoephedrine in the bottom of the glass tub, he moved on to the second, even more dangerous step. In a large steel tank he mixed the chloropseudoephedrine with a metallic catalyst called palladium black and a powerful solvent called hexane, then capped the tank and pressurized it with pure, highly explosive hydrogen gas. The hydrogen would bond with the chloropseudoephedrine to form a shiny white crystalline powder called methamphetamine, more commonly referred to as speed, crank, or meth. In a single day a skilled meth 'cooker' like Bennie could produce about twenty-two pounds of methamphetamine worth four to six thousand dollars a pound in its unadulterated form – assuming he survived the cooking process. The Brotherhood sold it by the pound to wholesalers all across the United States, using gang members who carried it on their bikes, or 'mules' who traveled with the bikers but didn't ride motorcycles or hang out with the pack.

Methamphetamine, born of so many dangerous and toxic chemicals that it is impossible to believe it could ever be safely handled, is one of the nation's fastest-growing abused drugs. By the time it has been cut with pyridoxine, or vitamin B_6, available at any health-food store, its street value has jumped to ten to twelve thousand dollars a pound. Ingested – usually mixed with coffee or booze – or snorted, it produces a gradual high and a sense of heightened energy, sexual potency, and awareness that lasts anywhere from two to twelve hours, followed by a very relaxed weariness that continues for one to three days. If smoked or injected, the stimulant effect is sharper and more pronounced, producing the 'rush' that gives the user a sense of enormous power, limitless energy, and a feeling of complete invulnerability. The Brotherhood and other outlaw motorcycle gangs had gotten very rich selling the drug in the western United States.

Bennie used just over two thousand dollars' worth of chemicals in this batch. Most of them are controlled substances in the state of California but readily available in Mexico or other states. Ephedrine, the main component, was the easiest to get. Mexican factories would ship a ton of diet pills, or even truckloads of the ephedrine itself, if he requested it. If the DEA, the federal Drug Enforcement Administration, or the BNE, California's Bureau of Narcotics Enforcement, started to nose around, Bennie simply switched sources. There were mail-order companies in the US that would ship a hundred cases of diet pills to the Brotherhood every week – and for twenty bucks, kids would steal several pounds of diet pills off store shelves in a matter of seconds. In a pinch, in place of ephedrine Bennie could also use phenylalanine, an amino acid sold wholesale in health-food stores at two hundred bucks for forty pounds. He had even synthesized chloropseudoephedrine from mahuang roots sold in Chinese grocery stores; and he was also adept at manufacturing phenyl-2-propanone, a compound similar to ephedrine, from noncontrolled chemicals. These could be used to produce a large quantity of lower-quality meth if other ingredients were hard to get. But they rarely were, and the meth business was thriving.

Bennie made it through this 'cookout,' but his body, including his eyes and lungs, bore the scars of countless cookouts that had gone horribly wrong. Inhaling just a whiff of thionyl chloride can destroy lung tissue, and a drop of it can eat a pea-sized hole in a hand or finger. Ephedrine can cause severe weight loss, heart arrhythmia, or tremors. Chloroform is a known carcinogen. But Bennie never thought about the hazards. He just thought about the money.

Bennie was a survivor. He had been cooking meth

ever since he and a classmate mixed up a batch while working summer jobs as janitors in a chemistry lab at the University of California-Berkeley back in 1973. The batches they made in the lab's big Florence flasks and Graham condensers were only a few ounces, but enough for Bennie and his friends to party with for a couple of weeks. A tiny hit of crank, less than the size of a fingernail, produced mild LSD-like hallucinations, with the added bonus of creating the 'pecker of power,' a hard-on that lasted for hours. With a little crank secretly mixed in her cocktail, his date for the evening would sometimes turn into a sex-starved creature whose wild-animal lust could pull a ten-man 'train' all night.

Bennie left Berkeley in 1974, but not because he got caught cooking meth in the school's labs – in fact, Bennie's younger professors and graduate assistants were some of his best customers. He had been working on his bachelor's degree in philosophy on and off for almost six years, but he was offered a job far more lucrative than teaching or writing: cooking meth for the Oakland chapter of Satan's Brotherhood. Within three years, he had supervised the construction of eleven major meth labs from Oregon to Nevada to Bakersfield, and taught nearly half the Brotherhood in northern California how to cook meth. He was almost single-handedly responsible for filling the Brotherhood's legal war chests with enough money to pay an army of lawyers to fend off dozens of racketeering indictments all throughout the 1980's.

Now, more than twenty years and countless batches later, Bennie still had the knowledge, the patience, the touch – and, more importantly, he could still run – and he was still the best there was at the meth-cooking game. Besides, meth – especially American-made meth, as opposed to cheaper Mexican meth – had never been more valuable than it was today, so it was a thriving business. Bennie was in it to stay.

He carefully checked that all of the fittings and hatches on his reactor were secure – introducing oxygen through the tiniest leak anywhere in the hydrogen gas line to the pressurized reactor tank can produce an explosion and fireball that would look like a small thermonuclear mushroom cloud. Then he checked the pressure inside the reactor. Still dropping, which meant that the chloropseudoephedrine was still accepting hydrogen. Another hour or so, and it would be done. Another few hours to wash the meth with ether, then dry it in a dryer made from a few janitor's buckets and mop squeegees, and he'd have collected about a hundred and twenty thousand dollars' worth of crank. His two bikers were nowhere to be seen – probably sleeping off the beer – so he stepped away from the hydrogenator toward the tree line for a smoke break.

The key to the all-important second step, the hydrogenation process, was the reactor. A commercial Parr half-quart catalytic hydrogenator with heating mantle and agitator cost nearly two thousand dollars and would produce only about a pound of meth; worse, it *looked* like lab equipment, which always caught the attention of the cops. So Bennie built his own meth lab, designed specifically to be portable, not look like a meth lab, and be capable of producing far more meth than commercial reactor units.

The big-time portable meth lab that Bennie had towed out to one of the remote West Coast Satan's Brotherhood ranches scattered throughout California was the best one he'd ever built. The core of the operation was its forty-gallon hydrogenation reactor, made from an old steel coffee roaster, powered by a big gasoline electrical generator and steam pressurization/vacuum device. It was mounted on a trailer and camouflaged with tar to make it look like an asphalt spreader, a disguise guaranteed not to attract any close inspection or curious sniffing. It was several times larger and much better than a Parr reactor, worth almost fifty thousand dollars. It was his pride and . . .

'Hello.'

Bennie whirled. The two men were standing behind him, no more than ten yards away, maybe closer. Jesus, Bennie thought grimly, they move as quietly as jungle cats! The first guy was youngish, lean, and blond, with a patch over one eye but the other a bright shining blue, wearing a long black leather coat. The second guy was huge, like a pro football linebacker, dark-haired and powerful-looking, standing in a definite cover position a few paces behind and to the left of the first . . .

That meant that the gun would come out of the first guy's right pocket or out from under the right side of his coat, while the second guy would cover the left side. Bennie had been around trained gunmen – mostly cops – long enough to know how they stood when entering a dangerous situation.

Bennie was wearing his black leather vest, the one with the Red Bat logo and the black-and-red bottom rocker that said 'Oakland' on the back, the symbols of a Satan's Brotherhood candidate. He didn't ride a bike so would never be a full-fledged Brother, but to most folks it looked like he was wearing no-shit Brotherhood colors. He hoped these guys would see the symbols and get the message: Clear out right now.

'Hello, sir,' said the man again. 'If I might have a moment of your time?' The accent had a definite British cast, the voice slightly sterner now, a bit more steel in it, not quite official like a cop but definitely authoritative, maybe military.

'You're on private property,' Bennie said in his gruffest, unfriendliest voice, mimicking the Brothers he had known from all over the world. Where the hell were his two guards? Why didn't they wake up from their stupor and come running at the sound of his angry tone? 'Get the fuck on outta here before there's trouble.'

The man in the lead held up his hands, palms facing outward, but Bennie noticed that the cover man never moved. Yeah, the Brit's gesture was meant to be conciliatory, but Bennie looked into his eye and saw nothing but danger. This was not a man accustomed to conciliation, let alone surrender.

'We don't want any trouble,' the Brit said apologetically. 'We're here because I have a business proposition for you, one that I'm sure you will find most rewarding.'

'Who are you?'

'Forgive me, Mr Reynolds.' Oh shit, Bennie thought, he knows my name, my *real* name! 'I neglected to introduce myself. My name is Gregory Townsend.'

Old Bennie, who had worked closely with some of the meanest and most psychotic bikers in the world for over twenty years, swallowed a gasp of fear. A couple of years before, the United States had been in the grip of something even more terrifying than today's threat of nuclear war with China or North Korea: An ex-Belgian commando turned international arms smuggler named Henri Cazaux had been flying around the country, dropping high explosives or crashing airliners into several of the largest airports in the United States. The US military was called in and had set up an extensive air defense network of radar planes, fighter jets, and surface-to-air missiles to try to stop him.

Cazaux had seemed invincible, unstoppable, until his body turned up in a West Virginia dump, with seven

Black Talons fired into it from very close range, the superexpanding bullets shredding his body as if his insides had been chopped up in a blender. No other clues were found. The book was thankfully closed on Henri Cazaux and his reign of terror against the United States of America.

Speculation was rampant about the identity of Cazaux's killer – an FBI hit man, the US Marshals Service's Fugitive Investigative Strike Team, even secret CIA counter-espionage groups. But the most likely trigger man was the highest-ranking surviving member of Cazaux's gang: his chief of plans and operations and trusted second in command, Gregory Townsend – a former British SAS commando and a fixture on Interpol's most-wanted-criminal list for many years. And now the motherfucker himself was standing right in front of him.

Don't look nervous! Bennie begged himself. Stay cool. 'So you're Townsend? Bullshit. I heard he was dead, along with his psycho boss, Cazaux. Killed by government hit squads.'

The guy smiled a frightening smile. 'Indeed,' he said. 'Yes, poor Henri. He was quite mad. But I assure you I am Gregory Townsend, and as you can see, I'm alive.'

'You got any proof you're Townsend?'

'Ah. Proof.' The Brit reached into a coat pocket and Bennie thought, Oh, shit, here's where he drills me. But he pulled a photograph out of his pocket. 'I show you this only because I so greatly desire your services, Mr Reynolds.' He flipped the photograph at Bennie. Bennie snatched it in midair, keeping the Brit and his cover guy in sight. Then he glanced at the picture and froze.

It was a photograph of Townsend kneeling in what looked like a garbage dump and supporting a corpse. The corpse's head was partially blown apart at the forehead so the face was unrecognizable, but the upper torso had been stripped bare, revealing a large multicolored tattoo surrounded by bullet holes. The tattoo was that of the Belgian First Para, the 'Red Berets,' Belgium's elite fighting unit, of which Cazaux had once been a member.

The shot was familiar to Bennie. It was almost identical to the one that had been published in several tabloids and magazines, announcing the discovery of Henri Cazaux's bullet-riddled body, though Townsend didn't appear in the published photos. The gun that he held in this one was a 9-millimeter Browning Hi-Power, which was what the FBI had identified as the murder weapon.

'Poor Henri,' Townsend said again. 'We could have been quite wealthy back then, but he was obsessed with attacking the American government. Insane.'

'Jee-*sus*,' Bennie exclaimed. '*You* dusted Henri Cazaux . . .'

'When Cazaux died, of course, his grip of terror on his business associates died as well,' Townsend said matter-of-factly, plucking the photo out of Bennie's frozen fingers and slipping it back into his pocket. 'But our bloody accountant spilled his guts to the FBI and Interpol – just before I blew him to hell – so all of our numbered bank accounts were immediately confiscated. I am now attempting to reassemble the best of what remains of his organization, and I am recruiting new members as well. This is why I am here today. I would like to offer you a top position in my organization.'

Christ Almighty, Bennie realized, the new king of the international crime trade was asking him to join him! Bennie didn't know if this was a con or the opportunity of a lifetime, so experience told him to treat it like a con. 'You're into guns, right?' Bennie asked. 'I don't know nuthin' about the gun-running business.'

Townsend waved a hand dismissively. 'Guns are not quite as lucrative as before, Mr Reynolds,' he said. 'There are so many of them out there now. Even automatic weapons, heavy military artillery, and high-performance aircraft and battle vehicles are commonplace on the open market. No, not guns, Mr Reynolds. At least not our *main* stock in trade.

'I'm talking about methamphetamines, Mr Reynolds. The state of California estimates meth sales are in excess of two hundred million dollars a year in this state alone, almost all pure profit, and with no importation problems. With the right combination of production, distribution, and enforcement, meth sales can easily top a half a billion dollars a year nationwide.

'You are Benjamin Reynolds, known as Bennie the Chef by the Satan's Brotherhood Motorcycle Club. You have been convicted of manufacturing illicit drugs and possessing a controlled substance only once, and received a four-year sentence, that over eight years ago. But you have been cooking meth and instructing the Brotherhood on how to do it for about twenty years. You are obviously highly intelligent and resourceful, and worth far more than whatever you're making from the Brotherhood. I would like you to supervise the setup of a thousand of your portable meth labs. We will become the McDonald's of the meth world. What do you say, Mr Reynolds?'

'*A thousand meth labs?*' Bennie exclaimed. 'A thousand portable meth labs? You've gotta be joking!'

'A thousand labs such as that one is only the *beginning*, my dear sir,' said Townsend, motioning toward Bennie's portable hydrogenator setup. 'I envision a meth lab in every county and province in every country of the civilized world. You shall supervise their construction. I shall . . .'

'It can't be done, Townsend, or whoever the hell you

are,' Bennie interrupted. 'You want war with the Brotherhood? Just try to horn in on their meth business. There will be a bloodbath – probably all yours.'

'I am proposing a *merger* with the Satan's Brotherhood, Mr Reynolds,' Townsend said confidently. 'The northern California chapters of the Brotherhood control four-fifths of the meth production in the United States, most of it generated by *you*. The problem is that the Brotherhood is disorganized, splintered into factions. I propose to unite them. The Brotherhood will produce methamphetamine, methcathinone, and crack cocaine, and will oversee distribution; I and our new allies will oversee collections, security, and enforcement. The Brotherhood needs you to supervise their meth operations. If you agree to join me, I believe the motorcycle gangs will follow.'

'They might – or they might want to blow your shit away,' Bennie said. 'No Brother is going to work with an outsider, especially a foreigner. They'll be fighting you as much as you'll be fighting the feds. Who's gonna stop the Brotherhood from squashing you and your operation? Who's going to keep all the players together? You? You and what army, man?'

'Myself – and some former members of the *German* army,' Townsend replied. He motioned toward the man standing behind him. 'Meet Major Bruno Reingruber. He has assembled a hundred of his finest officers and soldiers and has agreed to join my operation. Major Reingruber, meet Benjamin Reynolds, Bennie the Chef.'

The German snapped to attention, gave Reynolds a straight-arm Hitler salute, clicking his heels together with military precision, and resumed his on-guard stance, scanning the entire area around them. The guy was enormous, Bennie noted, at least six four, pushing three hundred pounds but as solid as a tree. As for the Nazi salute – that was nothing new. Most of the Satan's Brotherhood were hard-core neo-Nazis. It was part of the 'outlaw biker' mystique, the gypsy thing, being wild and free. Biker gangs were big in Holland, England, Germany, even Australia, and a lot of them were neo-Nazi.

But of all the gangs, the Satan's Brotherhood had the biggest, most dangerous reputation. If you survived the initiation process and became a full member of the Brotherhood, you were set for life. All the drugs, buddies, guns, and whores you wanted. All you had to do was ride, hang out with the Brotherhood, and of course kill, intimidate, cook meth, sell drugs, run whorehouses, and maintain the extreme level of fear that was the Satan's Brotherhood tradition.

'Major Reingruber and his men share in the Satan's Brotherhood's belief that racial impurity has infected and diseased society, and they believe in all-out war between the races and with the infected governments,' Townsend said, as if he felt compelled to explain the Heil Hitler salute. 'Many Nazi sympathizers existed after the Cold War ended. They've been repressed by the West German government but the neo-Nazi movement is flourishing, there as well as here. And Major Reingruber and his men are very good at enforcement and security.'

'Then he'll fit in real well with the Brotherhood – if they don't stomp you first,' Bennie said.

'Major Reingruber believes that even the Satan's Brotherhood and the other Aryan groups in the United States have been weakened and divided by the government, victims of the racial-impurity disease they were sworn to eradicate,' Townsend went on. 'We are not offering to help – we intend to take over. We have formed an army. We call ourselves the Aryan Brigade. We are the soldiers of the new antigovernment order. The key to our success is the northern California chapters of the Brotherhood. When that is in place, the Aryan Brigade will demand obedience from all the chapters.'

'Oh yeah? Well, that'll be fun to watch,' Bennie said, trying to sound as matter-of-fact as the notorious terrorist before him. 'What about you, Townsend? You a Nazi too?'

'I'm a soldier, an officer,' Townsend said after a moment's uncomfortable pause. 'My job is to lead armies and plan campaigns. Major Reingruber and his men are my new army. Before long the Satan's Brotherhood and the other Aryan armies in the United States and then the world will be part of my army – or they will be eliminated. So. What do you say, Mr Reynolds? Can I count on your support?'

Since these guys couldn't be intimidated, Bennie decided to try reasoning. 'Look, Townsend, or whoever you are, there are two very big, very mean leg-breakers over there whose job it is to keep trespassers off this property, and they take their job real serious. So I suggest you . . .'

'*Hey! What the fuck?*' came a warning shout behind them. Bennie's two Satan's Brotherhood enforcers had finally woken up. He didn't give these Brothers any credit for brain-power, but they loved to fight and they loved guns. He hoped to hell there wasn't going to be a gunfight around his hydrogenation reactor – the tiniest spark could blow them all sky-high.

The bikers scrambled for their weapons and started to move toward them. The German made a motion toward his coat opening, but Townsend held up his hand. '*Nicht*,' Townsend said in a low voice. 'Tell those bloody bastards to stay where they are,' he warned Bennie. 'Major Reingruber will not allow them to come near us. We will leave, but I need your answer. Yes or no – will you join me?'

'Or else what – I get blown away by you or your Nazi buddy?'

'If you say no, you'll be on the losing end of an inevitable war between the Aryan Brigade and whoever stands in our way, including the Satan's Brotherhood,' Townsend said. 'I'll let you live for now as a sign of good faith if you say no. But if you are not with me in this war, Mr Reynolds, you are against me, and I guarantee that you will die. Do you have an answer for me?'

Bennie had no assurance that anything this guy said was for real, but he did know that his chances of getting shot in the face by either the Brit or the German were better than good. Better to pledge allegiance to whatever flag was put right in front of his nose, Bennie thought, and work out the details later . . .

'All right, all right, I'm in. I don't know how in hell you expect you and a hundred hired guns to go up against five thousand Brothers, but I'm in.' Bennie turned toward the biker leg-breakers: 'Hey, you guys, put 'em down. These guys are . . .'

It lasted only a few seconds, but Bennie saw it all as if in slow motion:

Sure as shit, the bikers pulled their weapons, one a shotgun, the other a pistol. Never mind that Bennie was standing in their line of fire, the assholes! And they were pretty far away for a gunfight, well over thirty yards. If they thought at all, they were probably thinking that they could scare the intruders off with a shotgun blast into the ground or a few pistol rounds over their heads.

The German had the bikers zeroed in long before they leveled their guns. He withdrew a small machine pistol from his coat and pulled the trigger three times. The first three-round burst missed, but it caused both guys to freeze – not flee, not run for cover, not dive for the ground, just freeze. They made easy targets then, and the next two bursts did not miss. The biker with the shotgun pulled the trigger on his weapon seconds before his lifeless body pitched over backward and hit the ground.

The echoes of the brief gun battle were still ringing in Bennie's ears when he opened his eyes and saw Reingruber trot over to the bikers to check whether they were still breathing. Apparently one still was; he was dispatched with a single bullet to the brain. Then the German put a single round into the other one just for insurance. '*Sie sind tot, Herr Oberst*,' Reingruber said.

'*Sehr gut, Major*,' Townsend said wearily. 'I hoped *that* could be avoided.' He had never reached for his own weapon, Bennie noticed. 'Now, then, Mr Reynolds, I suggest we get our fat friends there out of sight before any curious spectators arrive.' A stunned Bennie didn't say a word as he was led over to the gruesome sight. Reingruber's rounds were all neatly centered in each biker's torso, the spread no more than three or four inches. 'I have some men on patrol in the woods,' said Townsend, withdrawing a walkie-talkie from his jacket. 'I'll send them in to . . .'

'Wait!' Bennie yelled. He whirled toward his trailer hydrogenator unit, his eyes bugging out, and grabbed Townsend's left arm. 'Gas! I smell gas! That shotgun blast must've put a hole in the hydrogenator! Run for your goddamn lives!'

The three men ran upwind of the meth cooker until Bennie could run no more. He collapsed behind a tree some two hundred yards away from the hydrogenator. Townsend and Reingruber weren't even winded.

Townsend spat an order in German into his walkie-talkie, warning his other men to stay away from the hydrogenator and take cover, but to keep it in sight at all times. Then he turned back to Bennie. 'That was quite a little jog, Mr Reynolds. What in bloody hell was it all about?'

All three of them were behind sturdy oak trees, but the blast still knocked them off their feet. They felt the searing heat as the hydrogen fireball swept above them. Then they looked up. The grass and the trees around them had been blackened by the intense heat and the fireball – even the hair on the back of Reingruber's head was singed. The truck, the hydrogenator unit, and the two bikers were indistinguishable black lumps in the middle of the charred field. Every standing object for two hundred feet around the hydrogenator had been leveled, even trees with trunks up to three inches in diameter.

'Well then,' said Townsend as he picked himself up off the ground and surveyed the blast area. 'This will be a good place for the helicopter to pick us up.'

'Jeez, my cooker!' Bennie shouted. 'That was my best portable fucking lab, man! That was fifty, sixty grand, up in smoke! My truck, my chemicals, the product! . . .'

'We will have to get you some more working capital, won't we, Mr Reynolds?' Townsend said, as if he had decided to order a nice bottle of wine. 'We should start with at least one million dollars. That should get you under way building the first ten reactors we need, plus provide us with sufficient operating funds.'

'How in hell are you gonna get a million dollars, Townsend?' Bennie shouted. This was crazy. 'You gonna cook up enough speed to raise that kind of cash? It'll take you years, man.'

A helicopter appeared out of nowhere over the trees,

23

swooping down over the blast area in front of them. Townsend waited until the racket died down. 'We will be back in operation within a month, Mr Reynolds,' he replied crisply. 'And you will address me as Colonel or *Oberst* from now on. I run my organization like a military unit, and even my civilian subordinates must comply. Now, the fewer questions you ask from now on, the better. Follow Major Reingruber aboard that helicopter, find a seat, strap yourself in, and keep your damn mouth shut.'

Chapter One

Patrick Shane McLanahan stood at the head of the long table and raised his glass of Cuvée Dom Pérignon. 'A toast.'

He waited patiently as the sexy young waitress, Donna, finished filling all the glasses – she was spending a lot of time at the other end of the table with his brother, Paul, he observed with a smile. When everybody was ready, he continued, 'Ladies and gentlemen, please raise your glasses to our honored graduate, my *little* brother, Paul.' There was a rustle of laughter around the long linen-covered table at Biba's Trattoria in downtown Sacramento. Patrick's 'little' brother, Paul, had seven inches and thirty pounds on him.

The brothers were as different as could be, on the inside as well as the outside. Patrick was of just below average height, thick and muscular, fair-haired, a masculine and worldly version of their soft-spoken, sensitive mother. Patrick had graduated from California State University at Sacramento with a degree in engineering and a commission in the United States Air Force, then was lucky enough to stay in Sacramento for the next eight years, becoming a navigator student, B-52 Stratofortress navigator, radar navigator-bombardier, and instructor radar navigator.

After winning his second consecutive Fairchild Trophy in annual 'Giant Voice' Air Force bombing competitions, confirming his reputation as the best bombardier in the US Air Force, Patrick was selected for a special assignment as a flight-test engineer at a secret Air Force base in central Nevada – and then virtually disappeared. Everyone assumed he had been assigned to test top-secret warplanes at the Air Force's supersecret air base in the deserts of central Nevada, called the High Technology Aerospace Weapons Center, or HAWC, better known by its unclassified nickname, Dreamland. No one really knew exactly what he was up to, where he was assigned, or what he did to get promoted from captain to lieutenant colonel in such a short period of time.

Then, just as suddenly, he was retired and back in Sacramento tending bar at the family pub with his new wife, Wendy, a civilian electronics engineer who had been seriously injured in an aircraft accident – again, there was very little explanation. No one knew exactly what had happened to Patrick or Wendy, or why two such successful and rewarding careers suddenly ended. Patrick said little about it to anyone.

But then, Patrick preferred not to talk about himself or call attention to himself in any way. He was a loner, a book-worm, and the 'go-to' guy everyone wanted on their team, but who never would have been chosen as team captain. He even preferred solo sports and pastimes, like weight lifting, cycling, and reading. Although he was a fit and hearty forty-year-old, he could not bowl a strike or hit a softball to save his life.

Paul McLanahan, on the other hand, could hit a softball a hundred miles. Although he was fifteen years younger than Patrick, in some ways he appeared to be the older brother: tall, dark, and handsome, a more ebullient, electric version of their tough, hard-as-nails father. Paul was the outgoing, gregarious one, the one who enjoyed the company of others, the more the merrier. He had graduated with a degree in management from the University of California-Davis, and with honors from the UC-Davis Law School – then startled everyone by applying to the police academy while waiting for the results of his California bar exams. He surprised everyone even more by deciding to stay in the academy after learning he passed the bar exam on the first try – only twenty percent of all test-takers did – and after taking the oath as a new California attorney.

But anyone who knew Paul would agree that being confined to a cubicle or law library writing briefs, or tongue-lashing some witness on the stand in a courtroom, was not his style. He was a team player all the way, a natural-born leader, a people person. He'd even refused to sit at the head of the table during his own celebration dinner, in the place of honor. Instead he grabbed his chair and moved it from place to place to be with as many of his friends and well-wishers as he could.

Patrick had not been surprised. The toast could wait. But when Paul had finally turned his attention from Donna, the two brothers made eye contact across the table, and both smiled and exchanged wordless salutes.

I could never do what you are about to do, Patrick said to his brother over the telepathic connection that bound them. I wish I could care more about people the way you do.

I could never do what you do, Patrick, Paul silently responded. You know all there is to know about machines and systems that I could never understand in a million years. I wish I could know more about science and technology the way you do.

29

Patrick tipped his champagne flute to his brother in a silent response: I'll teach you, bro. Paul tipped his glass as well: I'll teach you, bro.

'Paul, you're carrying on a tradition of McLanahan cops in the city or county of Sacramento that dates back almost a hundred and fifty years,' Patrick began proudly. 'Back in 1850, our great-great-great-great-grandfather Shane traded in his gold pan, pickax, and pack mule for a lawman's star because he saw his town sliding into lawlessness. He knew he had to do something about it – or maybe he found out that the gold nuggets weren't just lying around in the streets the way everyone back in the old country said. We don't really know.

'Anyway, Grandpa Shane could have kept on panning and maybe would have made enough to buy himself a big ranch in the valley that he could have handed down to us so we'd all be stinking rich today, but he didn't . . .' Patrick paused, then added, 'So why in the heck am I even mentioning *him*?' When the laughter died down, Patrick went on, 'But since Grandpa Shane pinned on that star and became the ninth sworn lawman in the city's history, there have been six consecutive generations of McLanahan lawmen or women in Sacramento. Paul, you represent the first of the seventh generation to join them.

'We all realize, grudgingly, that with your brains or skills or good looks or dumb luck or whatever it is you've got, you could have gone into business, or law, or anything else you desired,' Patrick went on. 'Instead, you decided to go into law enforcement. Someone not as charitable as I am could accuse you of pulling another Grandpa Shane, that if you went into business or law you'd make enough of the really big bucks to support your mother and your dear loving siblings.' His face and tone turned serious: 'We also know the dangers of your decision. The names of two McLanahans, Uncle Mick and Grandpa Kelly, are on the Sacramento Peace Officers Memorial, and we all know the McLanahan families that have had troubles, or have even been destroyed, because of the stresses of the job.

'But we all know that you're following a dream that's been twenty-two years in the making, ever since Dad first let you hit the siren on his old squad car,' Patrick went on proudly. 'We are here to celebrate your decision and wish you the very best. Congratulations for graduating, and congratulations for being awarded the City's Finest Recruit Award for being first in your graduating class in all areas, and for being chosen Most Inspirational Recruit by your fellow grads. Good luck, good hunting, and thanks for making this commitment to your city and your neighbors. Cheers.' The rest of the invited guests and many of the patrons at surrounding tables shouted, 'Cheers!' and they took a deep sip of the champagne.

'And now, with all due respect to our gracious and beautiful hostess, Miss Biba, we will adjourn this social gathering and reconvene at a *proper* establishment, the Shamrock Pub on the waterfront, for the *real* celebration,' Patrick said with a grin. The owner, Biba Caggiano, tried with her generous smile to persuade the partisan crowd to stay, but it was no use. Biba's and the Shamrock were both longtime Sacramento landmarks, but for entirely different reasons – Biba's meant fine food, fine atmosphere, and elegance, and the Shamrock – informally known as McLanahan's – *didn't*.

'The rule at McLanahan's tonight is, as I'm sure every cop in town is well aware,' Patrick reminded them, 'that if you carry a badge, your money's no good – except maybe for the chief, that is.' That remark earned Patrick a raucous round of applause. 'The primary purpose of reconvening this gathering at the Shamrock is to get young Probationary Officer McLanahan accustomed to working the graveyard shift, since that's where he will most likely be for the next several months on the force. So we must all do our part and stay up until dawn with Officer McLanahan and his buddies so they can get a good idea of what it's like to see the sun *rise* at the *end* of the day. Lastly, we meet there to prove the old Irish maxim: God invented liquor so the Irish wouldn't rule the world. It's time to prove how correct that saying can be. Last civilian at the bar buys it!' With a flurry of kisses for Biba, the crowd headed for the waiting taxis that would take them to the second half of the evening's festivities.

Its real name was the Shamrock, but everyone knew it either as McLanahan's or the Sarge's Place, after Patrick's father's rank when he retired as a Sacramento police officer and ran the bar. Whatever its name, it was one of a handful of bar-and-grills in the downtown area that catered to cops, kept cop schedules, and was attuned to what was going on in the law-enforcement community. It was known to sometimes be open at six A.M., right around graveyard-shift change after a particularly busy or bloody night, or on a Sunday evening after a cop's wake. Although it was no longer fully owned by the McLanahan family, Patrick, as de facto head of the clan – their mother, Maureen, was now retired and lived in Scottsdale, Arizona – was tasked to pour the first round of Irish whiskey, and they raised their glasses to the new crop of California peace officers who had graduated earlier that day.

He poured a lot of whiskey that night. Most of the academy grads, and all of them with assignments in the Sacramento area, were there, along with dozens of active, reserve and retired cops from all sorts of agencies, from the Sacramento Unified School District Police to the FBI; and McLanahan's extended its invitation to party to anyone who carried a badge into harm's way or in support of law enforcement – which included a few firemen, parole and probation enforcement officers, dispatchers, and even district attorneys and DA investigators. Everyone was welcome to join in the party – but cops give off a definite air of distrust bordering on hostility to anyone they don't recognize as one of their own, so no outsiders dared venture toward the free drinks. Not that any cop actually *prevented* a civilian from going near the bar; it was simply made clear by the eye signals and body language that the free drinks were for cops only.

As they had been for the past twenty-two weeks, the grads were together at one very large table, passing frosty pitchers of beer around and accepting congratulations and words of encouragement and advice from well-wishers. Although the academy was run by the city of Sacramento, only seven of the fifty-two graduates were going to the Sacramento Police Department: eleven were going to the Sacramento County Sheriff's Department; fifteen others to other California police, sheriff's, and different law-enforcement agencies. The remaining nineteen graduates had no positions waiting for them: They had paid their own way to attend the five-month program, half junior college, half boot-camp academy, hoping to be hired by one of the agencies sometime in the future. Needless to say, they took full advantage of the free drinks and aggressively buttonholed the highest-ranking officers they could find, hoping to meet an influential sergeant or administrator and make a favorable impression.

The target of most of the jokes and abuse that night was the honor grad, Paul Leo McLanahan. Every veteran cop wanted a piece of him, wanted the opportunity to see what the number one grad of the latest crop of 'squeaks' (so named because of the sound of the leather of their brand-new Sam Browne utility belts) was made of. Paul did the one thing that raised the blood pressure of most of his tormentors: He was polite. He called them 'sir' or 'ma'am' or by their rank if he knew it. He gracefully extricated himself if he was in danger of being drawn into an argument – 'So what do you think of the fucking chief?' – a drinking contest – 'Stop sipping that beer, rookie, and have a bourbon with us like a *real* man!' – or an arm-wrestling match – 'Hey, I'll show you a good short guy can take a big guy *any* day!' When Paul entered an argument, it was to pull a friend away from the confrontation or to keep it from getting out of hand; when he walked away, he made it look to everyone as if he was on *their* side.

Paul had come around behind the bar to help Patrick and Wendy wash some mugs and shot glasses, and he saw his big brother grinning at him. 'What?'

'You,' Patrick said. 'Sometimes I can't believe you're the same kid who used to drop out of trees and ambush me or your sisters. You're so laid back, so damned . . . what? Diplomatic.'

'That's the main thing they taught us, Patrick – sometimes what you do in the first few seconds of a conflict, or even *before* you arrive on the scene, will determine the outcome,' Paul said, finishing the glasses and giving his sister-in-law an appreciated shoulder massage. 'Go in pissed off, hard charging, and kick-ass, and everyone rises to the challenge and wants to kick ass too, and before you know it the fight's on. Being polite takes the wind out of most guys' sails – you call a guy "sir" enough times and sound like you mean it, and he'll go away from sheer boredom.'

34

'Nah. I'd just pull out my gun and shoot 'im,' Patrick joked.

'That's the absolute *last* option, bro,' Paul said seriously. 'Dad told me that in thirty-two years on the force, he'd only been involved in a half-dozen shooting incidents, and he regretted firing every bullet even though he used it to protect his life or that of another cop. There are guys on the force who have *never* fired their weapons except at the range. I want to be one of those guys.'

'In this city? I doubt it,' Wendy said dryly. Wendy McLanahan was very close to term, but she didn't show it at all – her belly pooched out only a little, which made it hard for most folks to believe she was due in less than three weeks. She wore preggie slacks and a baggy Victoria's Secret silk blouse, but even without them she carried her baby close under well-conditioned stomach muscles and had no sign of a ponderous or waddling walk. She had let her reddish-brown hair grow long and straight; it curled seductively over her shoulder and nestled between her ample baby-ready breasts. 'I do like your attitude better than your brother's – but you have to remember, he's been trained to drop bombs on folks for years.'

'Yes, I know – the SAC-trained baby-killer,' Paul said with a smile. 'What was it you always said SAC stood for? Your target list, right? – "schools and children." Hey, Cargo.' Paul grabbed a passing uniformed cop. 'Cargo, meet my brother, Patrick, and his wife, Wendy. Patrick, Wendy, this is Craig LaFortier. We call him Cargo.' Patrick could see why – the guy was huge, at least six four and close to three hundred pounds. 'Kicks butt in the Pig Bowl football game every year. He's my FTO.'

Patrick and Wendy shook hands with LaFortier, the cop's hand engulfing theirs. 'I assume an FTO is the guy you'll be riding with for the first few months?' Wendy asked.

'Yep,' said LaFortier in a deep, foghornlike voice. 'It stands for . . .'

'"Fucking training officer,"' Paul interjected.

'*Field* training officer,' LaFortier corrected him, with a scowl fierce enough to darken the entire waterfront. 'And that better be the last time I ever hear that crack, rook, or you'll be *washing* patrol cars at the South Station instead of riding in 'em. Yes, Paul gets a little on-the-job training for six months. We start tomorrow night.'

'*Tomorrow?* You just graduated!' Patrick exclaimed. 'They don't give you an orientation or anything?'

'Normally, yes,' said LaFortier, 'but my shift begins tomorrow, and I have off for Christmas, so instead of waiting two weeks, Paul gets to start right now. He'll come in a couple of hours early and we'll get him a locker, show him how to make coffee the way I like it, all that important stuff. But we need guys on the street.'

'So we heard,' Wendy said worriedly. 'Seems like gangs and drugs are worse than ever here in Sacramento.'

'They're bad everywhere, in every big city in America,' LaFortier responded, 'but this new wave of drug activity has got us back on our heels. The hard stuff is back – LSD, heroin – but now homegrown junk like methamphetamines are exploding on the streets. And the competition between the criminal organizations is increasing too. Northern California is the collision point – it's a natural nexus of white, black, Latino, Asian, and even European gangs. They've all found a home here, and the violence is bound to escalate.'

At the sight of Patrick's face, LaFortier added hastily, 'You don't need to worry about Paul, Mr and Mrs McLanahan. He can handle it. He's the rising star, the guy

36

everyone's watching. And he comes from good stock – the Sarge will be watching over him, I know it. He'll do fine.'

As he was speaking, an eerie hush enveloped the tavern, as if all the air were being sucked out into space. All four of them turned. The chief of police of the city of Sacramento, Arthur Barona, was entering the bar, together with one of the department's captains, Thomas Chandler, the commander of the Special Investigations Division.

Patrick was fascinated. In sixteen-plus years in the US Air Force, he had never seen anything quite like the open hostility that radiated from the street cops in that room. But if Barona noticed it as he made his way to the bar, he wasn't letting on one bit.

He was a tall, powerfully built man in his early fifties, and had been the city's chief of police for five years. He wore a dark suit instead of his chief's uniform, a political judgment that attested to his administrative and political career background, first as a Dade County, Florida, prosecutor, then as a law-enforcement bureaucrat and consultant to a number of governors and to the US Department of Justice. It was no secret to anyone that being the police chief of a major metropolitan city was not Arthur Barona's ultimate career goal. In fact, it was just a stepping-stone, a square-filler, a device to get some practical, on-the-street experience to flesh out his résumé for higher political office.

Barona's energetic personality, his knowledge of the newest trends and philosophies of police-department management techniques, and his nationwide political connections made him popular with city officials and government leaders, but decidedly unpopular with his own rank and file, who generally resented having a politician running their department. The rumor was that

Barona could not even qualify on the police shooting range and had had to be given special permission by the state Department of Justice to carry a firearm in California.

But Arthur Barona moved through the bar with absolute confidence that evening, smiling and greeting everyone as if he were the most-liked man in the state. If he caught an eye that didn't seem actively hostile, he extended a hand and exchanged a pleasantry. He seemed adept at avoiding empty handshakes or unreturned greetings. The academy grads still looking for positions helped break the ice by going up and introducing themselves to Barona, handing over business cards and chatting him up, hoping to stick in the chief's memory when it came hiring time.

'Well, I heard this was the place to find all the grads,' Barona said cheerfully as he finally approached Patrick and Wendy at the bar and put out his hand in greeting. 'I'm Arthur Barona. This is Captain Tom Chandler, one of my boys. We had a late-night meeting and thought we'd swing by to congratulate the graduates.'

They all shook hands. 'I'm Patrick McLanahan, and this is my wife, Wendy,' Patrick said. 'Son of the former owners and honorary bartender tonight. Welcome.'

'Ah yes, another of the Sarge's sons,' Barona said. 'Your father was a legend in this town.'

'*Is* a legend in this town, Chief,' Craig LaFortier interjected, not looking up from his beer.

Barona looked at LaFortier and nodded. 'Hello, Craig,' he said, acknowledging LaFortier but his smile dimming a bit in irritation.

Having been away from Sacramento for so long, Patrick hadn't known about the strained relations between the city, the chief of police, and the rank and file. When he returned earlier that year to run the tavern, he had heard all the crass remarks against the chief, the sour jokes, the not-too-subtle digs, the derogatory and sometimes out-and-out hostile articles in the police officers association's newsletter. But he assumed this was all standard employee-employer ribbing. The chief was accused of siding with the city against the cops in contract negotiations. That was understandable, of course – he reported to the city manager and the mayor – but to the cops on the street, the chief wasn't 'one of us.' He carried a badge under false pretenses, they thought. And, of course, every other problem associated with running a big police department was heaped on Barona's shoulders, with budget and manpower cuts the big points of conflict.

'What'll you have, Chief Barona?' Wendy asked. 'It's on the house. We're toasting the new officers tonight.'

'Just an ice water, please,' the chief replied.

LaFortier snorted his displeasure. 'Can't drink a real drink with the street cops tonight, Chief?' he asked.

'I've still got a deskful of papers to go through, and alcohol just slows me down. It can screw up your judgment and make you say things you wish you hadn't said too,' Barona said. LaFortier just shook his head and took a deep pull at his beer. Barona turned to Paul, held out a hand, and said, 'So this is the new lion on the force. Congratulations on being named honor grad, Officer McLanahan. Fine job.'

'Thank you, Chief,' Paul said, shaking hands. 'I'm anxious to get started.'

'We need tough, smart young troops like you out on the street, Paul,' Barona went on. 'But Captain Chandler and I were remarking earlier that a man with your impressive background, with a law degree and as a member of the bar, might better serve the city in an advisory role at headquarters, or in SID. Plenty of high-profile cases coming through the system – good state and national visibility for a hard-charging guy such as yourself.'

'I appreciate the consideration, sir,' Paul responded, 'but I joined the force to work the streets. My dad said that Patrol was the only place to be.'

'It's true that Patrol is our biggest and most important division, Paul,' Barona said, his face indicating his surprise that Paul wasn't embracing his generous offer. 'But our job is to investigate crime, and that's accomplished in many ways other than in a radio car or walking a beat. We have dwindling resources and manpower, and we can put our most talented young men and women in many different areas where their skills can be put to optimal use . . .'

'So what you're saying, Chief,' LaFortier interjected, still refusing to look up from his glass of beer, 'is that Patrol, which is already only seventy-five percent manned, might lose another good cop to go work for you in your office or get stuck behind a desk in SID on another "task force" or "special project" that some politician in the state house or in Washington cooked up. Do you really think that's such a good plan, Chief?'

Barona was not smiling now. It seemed to Patrick that every cop in the place had moved three paces closer to listen. 'Paul will still have to prove himself on the street, just like any rookie, Craig,' Barona said. 'Alongside you, I'm *positive* he will be a standout. But he was recruited and chosen because of his unique background and education, and with all the necessary and vital programs mandated for us by various government agencies, we need to utilize every member of this department to their fullest extent.'

'These "programs," Chief, are sucking manpower and

resources away from everyday law enforcement and investigations,' LaFortier said, finally facing Barona. 'Every time a new program gets started, another officer or two is pulled out of squads and stuck behind a desk shuffling papers and punching data into a computer. Some city councilman's car gets keyed by some vandals in broad daylight, so we have a truancy task force, with six sworn officers dragging kids out of bed to go to school. You sent four of my guys to Mexico to work in some joint DEA-ATF task force, and they come back and say they sat out on the beach for four days. This so-called "new and improved" community-oriented policing program took three officers off my graveyard shift just so you can . . .'

Chandler tried to lower the temperature. 'Craig, c'mon, ease up.'

'Craig, those task forces are necessary in modern police-force management,' Barona responded, 'and they bring in plenty of state and federal grant money to the department . . .'

'Where *is* all this money, Chief?' LaFortier pressed on forcefully. 'South Station is slated to get only seven new bodies next year, which won't make up for the sixteen we lost this year due to layoffs and early-outs. Half our new radios are still in boxes because we don't have battery chargers for them. We're still using shotguns that didn't pass POST armorers' inspection two years ago; and we still don't have enough automatic rifles for all the shift sergeants, when we should have them for every officer—'

'Corporal LaFortier,' Barona interrupted, a stern edge to his voice, 'now is not the time to go through the entire budget line by line with you. I'll be happy to discuss it anytime during business hours. I came by to congratulate the new officers and wish them well.' He shook hands again with the McLanahans, studiously avoiding LaFortier and the others who had come over to lend him their unspoken support. 'Whenever you get off graveyard shift again, Craig,' the chief said – meaning, Don't ever expect to get off –' come by and we'll discuss your opinions. Good night, all.'

Barona continued his good-byes as he headed toward the door, leaving Captain Chandler with the others at the bar. 'What was that, LaFortier?' Chandler asked when the chief was out of earshot. 'You making a show for the rookies tonight, or what?'

LaFortier looked at Chandler with disgust. Like Paul McLanahan, Tom Chandler had been one of the department's hot young rookies when he came on the force twenty-five years ago. Tall, smart, tough, in excellent physical shape, and with a two-generation cop legacy behind him, Chandler was a fast-burner from the first day. He too had been assigned to LaFortier as a rookie to hone and polish his already-formidable cop instincts. He was promoted through the ranks at breathtaking speed.

But Chandler had lots of outside interests too – namely, Las Vegas, gambling, exotic cars, and especially women. Like most high rollers, he had his good times and bad. When he was hot, he drove to work in a Corvette and wore silk suits; when he was not, he took the bus and wore mail-order polyester.

He was now in his early fifties. Two divorces and seven years after making captain, he was struggling with a new marriage and a stalled career. As far as LaFortier could tell, Chandler's newest tactic to try to jump-start that career and have any chance at all of making deputy chief or chief was to be the new department kiss-butt. 'Since when did you become Barona's doorman, Tom?' LaFortier retorted.

'What do you want, Cargo?' Chandler asked. 'The chief plays the hand he's dealt.'

'Bullshit, Chandler. I want what we were promised, that's all,' LaFortier said, 'and it's his job to get it for us, not get whatever he can for himself. The President promises a hundred thousand more cops on the streets, but after four years Sacramento gets half of what we were promised because the city can't come up with the matching funds. After the North Hollywood shootout, they promise us more automatic weapons, better armor, better communications equipment, more training. We haven't seen shit. My guys handle twenty percent more calls per hour than they did last year, but when I go to headquarters, I see all my guys sitting at desks writing memos or making slides for some presentation the chief is going to make on yet another trip to Washington. It sucks, Tom. Patrol is taking it in the ass again, as usual.'

'"If you ain't Patrol, you ain't shit" – is that what you think, Cargo?' Chandler asked. 'All other police work is a waste, right?'

'No,' LaFortier shot back. 'But sworn officers to work a truancy task force, or a graffiti task force, or a "traffic-signal dodger" task force? Give me a break. I need guys on Patrol, not giving speeches in front of the garden clubs on how we shouldn't try to beat yellow traffic lights. Do away with all the bullshit, Tom, that's all I'm saying.'

'The chief comes down here to congratulate the new rookies, and you gotta dump all this shit on him with the whole place listening in,' Chandler said, shaking his head. 'Real smart. Makes you wonder why the graveyard-shift roster will permanently have your name on it.'

'You better get going, Captain – master's waiting for someone to open the door for him,' LaFortier said acidly.

Chandler shook his head in exasperation. 'Even the

solid cops turn bitter after a while, I guess,' he said, then turned up the collar on his overcoat and left.

LaFortier finished his drink with a quick toss. 'At least my ass is out on the street where it belongs, not sitting in a country club playing footsie with the mayor,' he said half-aloud. To Paul he said, 'Tomorrow evening, be at the South Station by eight, ready for inspection, and we'll go over a few things. Thanks for the party, Mr McLanahan.' LaFortier lumbered off.

'Sheesh, he's a big guy. They make bulletproof vests big enough for him?' Patrick deadpanned.

'Oh yes,' Paul responded. 'He looks like a big blue billboard.' He grinned. '*Mr* McLanahan,' he mimicked. 'Sounds like you're an old fart, bro.'

'I *am* an old fart, bro,' Patrick said. 'But I can still kick your ass.'

'Have another drink, bro – you'll stay in fantasy-land longer,' Paul shot back.

But Wendy's face was serious. 'What do you think about all this going on between the cops and the chief and the city, Paul?' she asked.

'I don't think about it,' Paul replied. 'Budget cuts are a way of life, but officer safety is never being compromised. Tensions will always exist, but the city and the chief always support the troops.' He smiled reassuringly, then put his arms around Wendy's and Patrick's waists. 'It means a lot that you came up here from San Diego. I know the docs probably told you not to travel. You're due next week, aren't you, Wendy?'

'Not for almost three weeks. And unless I was confined to bed, Paul, we weren't going to miss your graduation. Besides, the boss flew into town, so we were able to hop a ride on the corporate jet. We head back tomorrow afternoon.'

'Worked out perfectly then,' Paul said. Wendy gave him a kiss and scooped up more shot glasses and beer mugs. Paul turned to his brother. 'Wendy looks great, and so do you. San Diego must agree with you.'

'Yep, it's great,' Patrick said. 'Seventy-two degrees and mostly sunny every day. We love it.'

'We didn't hear much from you for a while there. It seemed like you dropped off the face of the earth last spring. Lot going on at work?'

'Yes.' Patrick wasn't about to tell his brother that he had been busy flying secret attack missions over the Formosa Strait, trying without success to keep China from devastating Taiwan with nuclear weapons – or that he and Wendy had ejected from an experimental B–52 bomber over central China, were captured, and were part of a prisoner exchange.

'Well, at least can you tell me about this new company you work for? I remember you were forced to retire, because you came back here to work the bar – but then all of a sudden you're gone again, and the next we know you're in San Diego.'

'I can't really talk about the company too much either, Paul,' Patrick said. 'They're involved in a lot of classified stuff for the military.'

'But you're flying again, right?'

Patrick looked puzzled. 'Flying? What makes you think I'm flying again?'

Paul gave his older brother a satisfied grin. Yup, he had guessed right and he knew it. 'I remember your face, your talk, your entire body language when you were flying for the Air Force, bro,' he said. 'You were one supercharged dude back then. You were *groovin'*, I mean, really getting into life! You look that way now. I know you're all excited about having a kid and all, but I remember the only other time you were this – well, hell, *alive*! – was when you were flying, dropping bombs from big-ass bombers or flying some new supersecret plane you could never talk about.'

'What are you talking about? What's all this about secret bombers? I never told you . . .'

'Don't bother denying it – I know it's true,' Paul said. 'You practically salivate when something comes on the news about a war in Europe or the Middle East and the press thinks the Air Force flew a secret mission. Plus, you cut your hair – looks military-regulation length again.'

'Mr Detective here,' Patrick laughed. 'Just graduates from the academy and he thinks he's Columbo. No, I work for Sky Masters, Inc., and that's all I can say.'

'I know you, Patrick,' Paul said. 'This company you work for, they're involved in some real high-tech shit, aren't they? I mean, real twenty-first-century *Star Wars* stuff, right?'

'Paul, I . . .'

'You can't talk about it,' Paul finished for him. 'I know, I know. Someday, though, I'd like to know more about it. I've always been fascinated by all the stuff you could never tell me about, ever since you were flying B-52's.' Paul hesitated, and Patrick felt that old telepathic connection again. It sounded silly, but it was nonetheless true: his brother could tap his head and find out all he wanted to know anytime he wanted. That was reassuring, somehow . . . 'I *know* you had something to do with what happened to that aircraft carrier, and that nuclear attack on Guam,' Paul went on. 'I got the same feeling when I heard those stories about the conflict in Europe between Russia and Lithuania, and earlier with China and the Philippines. You were there both times. You were up to your elbows in it.'

'Someday, maybe I can tell you,' Patrick said with a smile. 'Right now, all I can tell you is this: It's *really* cosmic.'

'Well, be sure to let me know when you invent a phaser and force field for cops on the beat,' Paul said, clapping his brother warmly on the shoulder before heading off to make another circuit of the room. 'I'll be first in line to try them out.'

Her touch was light and soothing, loving and caring – but her hand was warm and moist, and as if a Klaxon had suddenly gone off, Patrick was instantly awake. 'Wendy?'

'I love you, sweetheart,' she answered.

Patrick pushed himself up and peered at the red LED numerals of the clock on the nightstand; it read 5:05 A.M. He turned on his bedside light. Wendy was sitting upright in bed, her right hand still touching him, her left hand gently rubbing her belly. 'Are you okay?' he asked.

'I'm fine.'

But she obviously wasn't fine. 'Are you having contractions?'

'Oh, *yes*,' she replied, and he heard a twinge in her voice. If his wife ever used foul language, he decided, the likelier answer would have been, 'Fucking-A, Sherlock, I'm having contractions!'

'How long?'

'A couple of hours. But no real pattern. Very irregular. It's probably Braxton-Hicks again.'

'Oh. Okay.' It was a lame response, but what else do you say? 'Gee, dear, you're in pain, and I'm really concerned, but it's not *that* pain, the *official* pain, so I'll go back to sleep now'? Braxton-Hicks contractions, sometimes mistaken for real labor pains, had been a regular occurrence for

Wendy all during her pregnancy. So things were stirring, but the action probably wouldn't start for several days. Right? Wendy wasn't due for another three weeks. And first babies were more often late than early – right?

They had left the party downtown right after midnight. They were staying in a suite at the Hyatt Regency Hotel in downtown Sacramento, not far from the tavern. During the ride back to the hotel, he sensed that Wendy seemed a bit more uncomfortable than usual, but that was probably due to fatigue – her normal bedtime was closer to nine P.M.

They probably never should have come to Sacramento at this stage – hers was the definition of a high-risk pregnancy. Wendy Tork McLanahan, an electronics and aeronautical engineer first on contract to the US Air Force and now an executive and chief designer for a small Arkansas-based high-tech aerospace firm, had spent most of the past two years in and out of hospitals after twice ejecting out of experimental military bombers, the latest just last June over the People's Republic of China, along with Patrick and the crew's copilot, Nancy Cheshire. Wendy had just recovered from her injuries from the *first* ejection when she was forced to eject from the second plane.

Thankfully, she did not lose the fetus. After a brief hospital stay and a few weeks to recuperate – and be debriefed by what seemed like every agency in the US government except the Department of Agriculture – Wendy returned to work and kept on with her duties as vice president in charge of advanced avionics design at Sky Masters, Inc. until her maternity leave began two weeks ago.

She was in great shape, the baby was fine, and she had insisted they could not miss Paul's celebration. And after all that had happened over the past two years, Patrick wanted a family life, a *normal* life, more than anything else in the world. He hadn't done much of the family thing for most of the last ten years, and he was anxious to get reacquainted with everyone.

But here they were, four hundred miles away from home, and the baby was obviously headed down the chute very soon. Decisions. Good, bad, who the hell knew? Stop waffling and deal with it *now*, Patrick told himself.

'I'm going to call Dr Linus in San Diego, just in case, get someone standing by,' he told Wendy. Her nod and her touch told Patrick she really didn't think it was false labor this time, so he picked up the telephone. Time to get moving. 'Jon's got the company jet at Mather demoing that electroreactive cargo liner technology,' Patrick reminded her. 'I think we should try to make it back to San Diego.' Dr Jon Masters, their boss and president of Sky Masters, Inc., was at the Aerojet-General rocket plant east of Sacramento, to demonstrate a new lightweight technology he developed for protecting an airliner's cargo compartment from a bomb blast. 'The jet can be fueled up and ready to go in less than two hours, and we can be at Mather in thirty minutes and at the hospital in Coronado in four hours.'

'All right,' Wendy responded. 'I'll get dressed.' She swung her legs out of bed and headed for the bathroom, then stopped halfway. 'Dear?'

'What, sweetheart?' Patrick replied. He turned. Wendy was reaching for a towel – and then he saw the growing bloody puddle on the white tile floor, and leaped out of bed with a speed and agility he thought he had lost long ago.

He knew then that they weren't going to make it back to Coronado.

Rocket-testing facility,
Aerojet-General Corporation,
Rancho Cordova, California
several hours later

'What's the latest on Patrick and Wendy, Helen?' Jonathan Colin Masters, Ph.D, asked by way of a voice check. The boyish-looking chief engineer and president of Sky Masters, Inc. was setting up a small video camera in front of a first-class seat inside a Boeing 727 airliner fuselage.

'What? Jon, are you listening to me at *all*?' his vice president and chairman of the board of directors, Dr Helen Kaddiri, asked through the videoconference link. Kaddiri was several years older than Masters, one of the original founders of the small high-tech aerospace firm that now bore Jon Masters's name. She tolerated his high-school antics and laid-back style of doing business because Jon knew how to build systems that the government wanted, and he knew how to sell them – but this, Kaddiri thought, was going way too far. Worse, Masters didn't even seem to care that he was risking his life just to sell a product. He was nuts.

'Can you hear me? Is this thing working?'

'I hear you fine, Jon,' Kaddiri said.

'I asked, have you heard anything about Wendy since the message that they were heading to the hospital?' Masters repeated.

'Jon, pay attention to what I'm saying to you,' said a frustrated Kaddiri. 'We have other ways of doing this demonstration—'

'Helen, we've been over this a million times,' Masters interrupted. 'I'm doing *this*. Now, is there any word from Patrick and Wendy or not?'

Kaddiri closed her eyes, unable to argue any longer.

Nuts – that was the only logical explanation. Insane. Definition of a death wish, of childlike feelings of invulnerability.

Kaddiri was conducting the technology demonstration briefing at a videoconference center at the Federal Aviation Administration headquarters in Washington, D.C. Several research directors of the FAA, along with aerospace-manufacturer and airline representatives, were outside the conference room awaiting the start of Masters's remote video demonstration, beamed via a two-way datalink using Sky Masters's low-Earth-orbit satellites, called NIRTSats (for Need It Right This Second satellites), specifically launched for this demonstration. Jon was back in California, about to conduct the demonstration itself. He was literally sitting atop a powder keg, as both of them knew, and all he could think about was Patrick and Wendy McLanahan's new arrival.

'Stand by one, Jon,' Kaddiri replied with an exasperated sigh, then turned to her assistant, who made a phone call and came back with an answer a few moments later. 'Wendy McLanahan was admitted to Mercy San Juan Hospital in Citrus Heights, east of Sacramento, this morning around five-thirty. Everyone's doing fine,' Kaddiri responded over the videolink. 'No other word. Happy?'

'She's been in labor since five-thirty?' Masters asked incredulously.

'She's apparently been in labor since *three* A.M., Jon,' Kaddiri corrected him. She could see him wince at the thought of being in pain for that long. If Jon were a woman, she decided, he'd get one contraction and immediately want to reach up inside and yank the kid out himself. 'Everything's going to be fine. Wendy's a tough girl, and they've got some good docs up there.'

'Excellent,' Masters replied, relieved. 'Can't believe

they're going to have a kid. After all they've been through . . .'

'Jon, pay attention to me for once,' Kaddiri said. 'Forget about the McLanahans for a moment – *they're* going to be fine. It's you I'm worried about. This is nothing but a dangerous grandstanding stunt that is likely to get you killed. I know you don't care about yourself or your fellow officers, so think about our company – *your* company. The company would suffer a tremendous loss if you were hurt or killed. Don't do this. Let's put the telemetric mannequin in place the way we originally planned.'

'Helen, you crazy kid, you're really concerned about me,' Masters said as he slipped into the seat, smiling his maddening, cocky grin. 'I'm touched.'

'You *are* touched, Jon – touched in the *head*!' Kaddiri retorted, upset that he appeared to be making fun of her anxiety for him.

Jon Masters was closing in on his fortieth birthday, but in many ways he really was still a teenager – probably because he had bypassed most of his adolescence and teen years and pursued his studies rather than girls. He was a savant, a boy genius. He received his undergraduate degree from Dartmouth College at age thirteen; by age eighteen he had a Ph.D from the Massachusetts Institute of Technology, and by age twenty he held over a hundred patents as a NASA engineer, doing work for the National Strategic Defense Initiative Organization and the Department of Defense.

And today, with billions in government contracts and licenses in the works, Jon Masters now had a little time to kick back and do what he really enjoyed doing – tinkering, experimenting, lab work – and it was as if he had regressed to his childhood when he played with transistors and drew detailed blueprints for rockets instead of playing baseball and drawing pictures of superheroes. But he never lost the cocky attitude he had developed when, as a superintelligent teenager going after his doctorate, he felt he had to break down his professors' amused, smirking self-righteousness about awarding an advanced degree to a kid.

After all the years Kaddiri and Jon had worked together, it was still impossible for her to determine what that punk genius was thinking or feeling. Helen Kaddiri, the American-born daughter of Indian scientist-professor parents, had followed much the same path as Jon, but at a more conventional age and taking a more conventional route getting there – she was eight years older than he was. She started an aerospace company, Sky Sciences Inc., in Tennessee, after being rejected several times for senior-level positions at other companies where she felt her talents were being overlooked because of her gender. Her company was not large or hugely profitable, but it was hers and it was her pride and joy.

But in a surprise move, her own handpicked board of directors voted a young, cocky engineer from NASA onto the board, feeling he would surely help take the little company into the big leagues. The smart little brat took generous stock options instead of a salary, pledging to get rich or go broke along with them, a move that made him even more popular with the board. Jon Masters did indeed take Kaddiri's little company to a higher level – and in the process took over almost all of the company's outstanding stock, then control of her board of directors, then Helen's position, then her authority, and eventually even the company name. Kaddiri made one unsuccessful attempt to wrest back control; her failure made Masters even more popular, even cockier.

She still enjoyed significant wealth, prestige, and authority as chairman of the board and corporate vice president of Sky Masters, Inc. But Helen Kaddiri could not count the times she had resolved to gladly trade it all in and go back to the bad old days as president and chief bottle washer of a company, no matter how dinky, that didn't include Jonathan Colin Masters, B.S., M.S., Ph.D., CEO, RPITA – Royal Pain In The Ass.

Kaddiri clicked open the commlink again and said sternly, 'Jon, you know about the instability problems, those power surges that we couldn't control. The power surges could set off those explosives. Now put the dummy, the *other* dummy, in the seat and get out of there.'

'We did a test with explosives before, Helen . . .'

'But not with three separate chambers spaced so closely together, and not with the amount you've got loaded in there,' Kaddiri argued. 'It's too dangerous. At least have the range safety officers take some of those explosives out. Get out of that thing, Jon, and let's—'

Masters looked at his watch and said quickly, 'Too late, Helen. It's time. We've got the satellite constellation for only another hour, and the FAA wants to reopen this airspace for the afternoon rush into San Francisco and San Jose. Let's bring 'em on in and get this dog and pony show started.' Kaddiri had no choice. She could either tell Masters to go to hell and get out of there before she witnessed a disaster, or comply.

Helen Kaddiri stepped up to the briefer's platform after her audience filed in and the room was secured. She stood before a large rear-projection video screen, which showed the company logo along with video clips of several military technologies in operation – satellite reconnaissance systems, communications satellites, space boosters, and military weapons, all designed by Sky Masters, Inc. 'Good afternoon and welcome, gentlemen,' Kaddiri began. 'I am Dr Helen Kaddiri, vice president and chairman of the board of Sky Masters, Inc. Thank you very much for the invitation to present this technology demonstration program to you. I must remind you all that today's presentation and the information contained in it is copyrighted and patented material, and is also classified under Sky Masters, Inc.'s memorandum of understanding with the Department of Defense concerning weapons-technology information transfer, and is not to be released to anyone outside this room without . . .'

It soon became obvious that the assistant deputy secretary of the Department of Transportation, Edward Fenton, who was the highest ranking government executive at the briefing, was perturbed. Just a few minutes after Kaddiri began, Fenton raised a hand: 'Excuse me, Dr Kaddiri, but I understood that Dr Masters was going to be available to answer questions. Is he available today? If not, it would be best if . . .'

'Yes, Secretary Fenton, he's with us now on a live videoconference hookup from California.'

'A videoconference? From California?' Fenton shook his head in exasperation, then nodded to his assistant, who started to pack up his boss's notebooks. 'Dr Kaddiri, I rearranged my schedule for two entire days to accommodate Dr Masters because he was flying all the way to Washington personally for this presentation. If we were going to do this by videoconference, I wish you'd have told us. I'm sorry, but I'm going to have to . . .'

The screen behind Kaddiri went blank, followed immediately by the videoconference shot of Jon Masters in the cabin of the 727. 'Sheesh, Ed,' Masters said, taking a sip of Pepsi from his ever-present squeeze bottle, 'but you sure know how to spoil a good show. I was all set to do a big entrance.'

Fenton's irritation was quadrupled by being addressed by his first name. Masters noticed this right away and smiled. 'Oh, sorry. I mean, Mr Assistant Deputy Secretary, I wish you hadn't screwed up my entrance. But I'm ready to make our presentation now.'

If Fenton was peeved at being addressed by his first name, it angered him even more that Masters was rubbing his nose in it by sarcastically using the proper title. 'Dr Masters, you've wasted my time and that of all these good folks by not being here for this presentation. You will reschedule this briefing with my staff when you can be here in person, as I requested, and I think you owe us all an apology. Now if you'll excuse me . . .'

'Folks, I'm not being lazy – believe me, this is a better way to do this demonstration. I'm ready to do it right now, and I guarantee I'll blow your socks off.' Masters was addressing everyone in the FAA conference room with a confident smile, but when he saw that Fenton was still packing up, he quickly added, 'American companies should have first dibs, but if I can't get DOT and FAA to sign off on it, I'll go to Europe. Check my prospectus, folks – I've already got Commerce Department clearance to sell overseas. Time is money, guys, and this technology is ready to go *now*. If I don't do this for you now, I'll do it for Airbus tomorrow.'

Fenton could feel all eyes move from the monitor to him at that moment. No one in the aerospace industry or the airlines really liked Jon Masters, the genius with the attitude of a smart-ass seven-year-old, but everyone knew that he represented the cutting edge in aerospace technology. A license for one of Masters's new gadgets could be worth billions. No one liked the Federal Aviation Administration, either. It was an agency that could be tolerated only as long as its authority didn't hamper business.

Masters was being rude and crude as usual, but if Fenton walked out, he'd probably cost all or some of them billions. They all knew that Masters had Commerce Department authority to export this technology, whatever it was, and that fact alone made this presentation important.

Fenton felt their icy stares and silent sit-down commands, scowled at the video monitor, and said angrily, 'We don't like threats, Dr Masters.'

'Sorry, sir,' Masters said. 'But I'm just excited. You know what it's like. I guarantee, you're really going to like this. *Really*.'

The aerospace execs breathed a sigh of relief. If Masters kept up his punk attitude, Fenton would walk. But the apology showed Fenton the proper, if minimum, amount of respect, and Fenton returned to his seat. His aide scrambled to rearrange his papers and notes before him.

'Thanks, Ed,' said Masters. The execs concealed their chuckles. Masters went on: 'Folks, I've been building gadgets for twenty years to help the military find and blow things up, but now I've developed a technology that will help *prevent* something from being blown up. It's called ballistic electro-reactive process, or BERP for short.' Helen Kaddiri swallowed her irritation – it was just like Jon to give his inventions ridiculous names like 'BERP.' 'Let me explain how I discovered this technology.'

Jon Masters held up a square wire frame, then dipped it into a pan of liquid on the seat next to him and held it up to the camera. 'We've all played with soap bubbles as kids, right?' He poked the bubble on the wire frame, and it promptly burst. 'The film is less than three-thousandths the thickness of a human hair. Held together by simple chemical bonds, negligible surface tension. Easy to break – obviously. But while I was experimenting, I touched a couple of hot wires to the frame that a

57

bubble was on, then shined a laser light on it. Here's what I saw.'

The lights in the cabin dimmed, and a beam of green laser light emanated from somewhere just off camera and shined on a new bubble Masters formed in the frame. The surface of the bubble continued to shimmer and undulate. 'Watch.' Masters flipped a switch, then moved his finger against the bubble. The surface of the bubble changed – the undulations and shimmering stopped, replaced by a solid green color. 'See that? All the light refractions and surface eddies on the bubble disappear. Now check this out.' Masters turned the frame horizontally, then carefully placed a paper clip on the bubble. It did not break – the paper clip appeared to float in midair. Masters even waved the wire frame, and the paper clip held fast.

'I know what you're thinking – the paper clip is suspended by a magnetic field formed by the wire frame, or by surface tension. Not so fast, Sherlock!' Masters withdrew a regular wooden pencil from a pocket and dropped it on the bubble – and it too was supported in midair. 'That bubble is three-thousandths the width of a human hair, yet it's supporting millions of times its own weight. Surface tension? Chemical properties of the soap solution? Yes and yes – but properties that were changed by an application of a small electric charge.' The lights in the cabin came on again. Masters flipped the switch beside him, and the paper clip and pencil promptly dropped through the frame into his lap as the bubble burst.

'I call it electro-reactive collimation, a realignment of the molecular structure of the soap solution so that the surface tension of the solution is millions of times stronger than normal,' Masters said. 'Collimation occurs in nature all the time, but it's usually induced by temperature or chemical interactions. I can make it occur with the application of a small electric current. By varying the amperage and frequency of the electric charge, I can also vary the properties of the collimated material.'

'How long have you been working on this process, Doctor?' one of the execs asked.

'Oh, about thirty years,' Masters replied. 'I first discovered it when I was around seven years old. I knew lots of kids who played with soap bubbles, but as far as I know I was the only one who shot an electric current through one. I just hooked up an old six-volt dry cell to the wire frame, and there it was.'

'This is all very fascinating, Doctor,' Fenton said, 'but can we get to the point of this demonstration?'

'Sure, Ed.' He held up a piece of cloth mounted on a frame with wires attached to it. 'It's possible to collimate a whole variety of liquids and colloids – those are substances that have properties of liquids, solids, or gases combined. I can even use seawater to protect ships and submarines from collision or from damage due to water pressure – imagine a submarine that can dive to the deepest depths of the oceans without being crushed, using the seawater around it, the very thing trying to crush the ship, to *protect* it! Of course, it's also possible to *de*-collimate something, or make it *less* dense, without using temperature or without mixing other chemicals in it. When I get that technology working, the applications will be truly *Star Wars*-like – can you say "phaser guns," boys and girls?

'But the really cool application of electro-reactive collimation is in materials science, and it's there that I've had the most fun over the past couple years,' Masters went on, his excitement evident in his voice. 'That's because solids can be collimated just like liquids and gases. Now we start getting into some really neat applications!' He held up another, larger wire frame, this time with a thin, light gray material hung within it. 'This is a piece of one of the BERP materials I've developed. It's lightweight fabric, about as light and flexible as nylon.' He rustled the frame, and the fabric swayed as everyone expected. 'Now check this out.'

Masters picked up a hammer, hefted it, and swung it at the fabric. The observers were stunned to hear a dull thud. They saw Masters drop the wire frame after he hit it with the hammer, but they were still too startled to take any notice. He picked up the frame and shook it again, and the fabric moved as before, like a linen handkerchief – but when he swung the hammer, the fabric again instantly solidified into a hard plate.

He also dropped it again after he hit it, jumping in surprise when the electric shock came, a bit stronger this time. And this time Helen Kaddiri noticed. 'Jon, what's wrong?' she radioed to him via his earset communications unit. 'Why do you keep dropping it?' There was no reply, confirming Helen's worst fear. 'Jon, is that thing shocking you again?'

'It's nothing, Helen,' Masters whispered, loud enough for his voice to be picked up on the private earset link but not loud enough to be heard by those watching the demonstration in Washington. 'I'll just hold it with the pliers, like we planned.'

'But if it's malfunctioning, you've got to terminate the demonstration,' Helen said, horrified. 'It's one thing to shock your hand. But if it lets off a voltage spike next to a hundred pounds of TNT, it could malfunction and blow you to bits!'

'It's not malfunctioning, Helen. Look at these guys – they're mesmerized. It's working perfectly!'

'Terminate this test, Jon. You can't do the demonstration until we figure out why it's doing that.'

In response, Masters picked up the wire frame, this time using an insulated pair of pliers so that the small electric current that built up on the frame each time he hit it wouldn't shock him. He beat on the fabric repeatedly, and each impact was punctuated with that same hollow thud. Then he took the fabric off the frame, folded it, and stuck it in his shirt pocket.

'That's . . . that's unbelievable!' someone in the audience gasped. 'Amazing!'

'The applications for BERP are unlimited,' Masters said. 'I thought about all the possible military uses of the process – protecting vehicles, making punctureproof tires, making bulletproof tents, even creating portable roads resistant to land mines. But there is one use for it that has always stuck in my head: enhancing flight safety for the general public by strengthening the cargo compartments of airliners to protect against terrorist bombs or any other catastrophic explosion destroying an aircraft, such as the fuel tank explosion that brought down TWA Flight 800 a while back. Just a few hundred pounds of BERP and its control equipment per airplane – far less weight and cost than lining an airplane or cargo containers with Kevlar or other armor material – can save hundreds of lives.'

'Now how is this possible, Dr Masters?' Fenton asked incredulously. 'That can't possibly be strong enough to protect against a bomb blast or a fuel tank explosion!'

'Glad you said that, Ed,' Masters said. 'That's why I'm here talking to you on the satellite videoconference from the Aerojet rocket-testing site near Sacramento today – a satellite videoconference, by the way, provided by Sky Masters, Inc.'s NIRTSat small tactical communications and reconnaissance satellite technology specifically for this demonstration.' Jon was never above plugging his own products. 'I'm in the first-class section of a surplus Boeing 727 airliner fuselage.' The shot of Masters changed to an overhead shot of the Boeing 727, minus its wings and engines. 'Located within this fuselage are three suitcases loaded with fifty pounds of TNT apiece. One is inside the cockpit in a large Rollaboard suitcase, such as the flight crew might carry on board; another is located directly underneath the first-class compartment in the cargo hold; and the third is located underneath the coach-class compartment in the baggage space.

'I've placed my BERP material in two places in the plane.' The camera shot changed again, revealing an interior view of the plane's forward cargo compartment. The only baggage in the compartment was a lone crate marked DANGER HIGH EXPLOSIVES. In the background, illuminated by spotlights, the gray BERP fabric could be seen clearly. 'First, I've lined the cargo compartment directly below the first-class section with exactly eighty-three pounds of BERP.'

The camera shot changed again, this time to the airliner's cockpit. Except for removed avionics and upholstery stripped off the seat frames, it looked like an average cockpit. A wheeled suitcase marked DANGER HIGH EXPLOSIVES sat between the pilot's and copilot's seats. 'Second, I took off the headliners in the cockpit and lined the fuselage there with forty-one pounds of BERP, then replaced the headliners. I also put some BERP in the cockpit door leading out to the galley. In addition, I sandwiched some of the BERP fibers into the Lexan cockpit windows on the copilot's side of the cockpit, but not on the pilot's side. This darkens the windows slightly, equivalent to number one ultraviolet tinting. Tinting is not currently allowable on cockpit windscreens in the US, but maybe when you see this, the rules can be modified a little.'

The camera changed back to a shot of Masters, amazingly still sitting in his seat. 'I also made a curtain of BERP material between the coach- and first-class sections of the plane. There is no BERP anywhere else on the plane. I'm leaving the coach section unprotected just to show the kind of damage we're talking about, and also just because I like to see things blow up.' Masters paused, grinning like a kid at the zoo, then put on a set of headphones. 'I will now detonate all three crates of explosives, starting with the cockpit. Here we go . . .'

'*What!*' Fenton and several of the others shouted almost in unison. 'Are you *crazy*, Masters? Do you actually plan on blowing up that plane *with you inside it*? Get the hell out of that plane, right now! . . .'

But the screen had changed to four separate shots: The upper half of the screen showed the overhead satellite view of the airliner; on the lower half, one shot showed Masters in the first-class section; one showed the cargo compartment underneath the first-class section of the plane; and a third showed a shot of the cockpit from outside, right from the nose of the airliner looking through the copilot's windscreen. Masters waved once to the camera and held up a box with three large red switchguards on it.

'Is he serious, Dr Kaddiri?' Fenton asked. Kaddiri didn't know how to respond. They could very well be watching Jonathan Colin Masters's last day on earth, and she was powerless to stop him. 'Is he going to . . .'

As if in response, Masters lifted the first red switchguard, gave a last jovial 'Fire in the hole, folks!' and pressed the button underneath. The entire audience leaped to its feet in shock as the images unfolded before them.

The cockpit was the first to go. It erupted with a bright yellow fireball, but amazingly only the pilot's windows blew out, sending a shaft of fire and smoke sideways out of the plane – the copilot's windows crazed into white spiderwebs but did not break. In the first-class section, Masters jumped in surprise, but there was no other hint that fifty pounds of TNT, enough to bring down a small building, had just exploded less than thirty feet in front of him.

'I'm fine! I'm fine!' he shouted gleefully. 'Perfectly all right! That was a fifty-pound TNT explosion just a few feet away from me, and I'm fine!' The airline executives looked relieved and angry at the same time – relieved that he was all right, and angry that they had been forced to watch such a suicidal display.

'Washington, Washington, this is Range Control,' an excited voice cut in on the closed secure link. 'Helen, I'm picking up a power surge in the BERP circuits. I've set the explosives continuity circuits to safe. Jon, if you can hear me, you better get out of the plane now. That surge could cause the rest of the BERP to malfunction – it could even set off the other explosives.'

Jon touched his earset so he could hear better through the ringing aftermath of the explosion that had erupted right in front of him. 'Negative!' he shouted. 'Don't safe those circuits! I'm all right! We can continue the . . .'

A second later, seen from the overhead satellite view, the entire aft section of the airliner heaved and flopped awkwardly into the air, the cargo section completely blasting apart before it was obscured by smoke and debris. Masters never touched the detonate button – and if he had, it would have had no effect because the range safety officer had terminated the test and disconnected all detonation power from both the arming switch and

64

the explosives. But the surge of energy in the BERP material had discharged through the cabin, grounding on the nearest available object – the fifty-pound case of TNT. The electrical discharge was enough to bypass the safety interlocks, set off the electrically actuated blasting caps, and detonate the TNT.

Masters was thrown back into his seat as the entire interior of the aircraft rocked forward from the concussion, the deck jerked upward as it buckled, and a new gust of smoke forced its way into the first-class section – but again, Masters was unharmed. The entire aft two-thirds of the Boeing 727 was either in pieces or lying crumpled and twisted on the ground, but the forward third was intact. More smoke rushed into the first-class cabin. Helen noticed with horror that the large ventilators designed to keep the air clear had malfunctioned. The surge of power caused by the BERP system had shorted out the ventilators.

'Jon! Can you hear me!' Kaddiri shouted. The airline executives were watching in horror as smoke partially obscured their view of the interior of the first-class cabin inside the test article. 'The ventilators have failed! Get out! Range Safety Control, get Masters out *now*!'

Inside the test plane, Masters jumped again as a third explosion ripped into the plane. The camera shot of the cargo compartment under the first-class section disappeared in a blinding flash of yellow. This time Masters really seemed scared. They could see his eyes bugging out with the first hint of concern and worry about whether this stunt was really a good idea. The floorboards under his feet buckled, a few of the first-class seats broke free and flew through the air, they heard him scream . . . and then the camera went dark. The overhead shot revealed nothing – the first-class cabin appeared to be intact, but huge billows of smoke and occasional tongues of flame began pouring up from underneath the fuselage near the already ripped-up coach-class section.

'Oh my God!' Kaddiri screamed. She picked up the direct-line telephone beside the lectern. 'Jon, come in! Range Control, come in! Is someone there? Answer me, goddammit! . . .'

'What happened?' Fenton shouted. 'What happened? Is Masters . . .'

'I'm okay, I'm okay!' they heard a moment later. The first-class section camera came on again, showing a disheveled but otherwise intact cabin, faintly obscured by a thin haze of smoke. Then Masters's face appeared behind a firefighter's positive-breathing face mask, almost touching the lens. There were some streaks of black under his nostrils from exhaling smoke, and his short-cropped hair appeared to be standing on end, but he looked unhurt. A range-safety fireman was trying to pull Masters to his feet. 'The camera broke free of its mooring – hold on a sec.'

'Is he *insane*?' Fenton shouted. 'That plane is on fire!'

'"Hold on a sec," my ass!' Kaddiri shouted in the telephone. 'Range Control, pull Masters out of that plane right *now*!'

Masters aligned the camera in its original place, straightened his seat, sat back down, took a deep breath from the oxygen mask, then handed it back to the fireman. He looked a bit shaky, his eyes darting around the cabin, his breathing a little rapid, but he was unhurt. 'I'm all right, guys. The explosion ripped the seat rails off the deck, and all the seats went flying. Here.' Masters grabbed the camera and swung it around the cabin, focusing on the floor. 'But see? The deck is still intact. It ballooned up about a half-foot but didn't rupture.' He swung the camera aft toward the coach-class cabin. Smoke was beginning to pour through the curtain, but he lifted it so he could point the camera at the devastation beyond. The cabin was completely destroyed, mangled and blackened. Fire-fighting foam extinguishers had already discharged to cut off the fire. 'All I had was a BERP curtain between me and all that. Awesome.'

'He's crazy, Dr Kaddiri, *crazy*!' Fenton shouted. As if the explosions had been set off in the conference room in Washington rather than a rocket-test site in California, the airline and government execs were scrambling for the door in shock and disgust. 'This is either some kind of trick, a publicity stunt, or the work of a seriously deranged mind. In any case, I'm not going to allow myself or the US government to be manipulated by such antics!'

'What are you saying, Secretary Fenton?' Kaddiri asked in amazement.

'The department will not consider Masters's development request and will block any efforts to utilize that . . . that BERP technology until we can get someone in your organization to present a rational, scientific demonstration and validation program,' Fenton said angrily. 'And if he tries to sell that technology overseas, you'll be sanctioned here in the US, and any foreign aircraft using that technology will be barred from entering US airspace.'

'But – but we proved the technology *works*!' Kaddiri argued. 'I'll admit, Secretary Fenton, that Jon's methods were a little extreme . . .'

'*Extreme!* We could have watched Masters blow himself to *bits*!' Fenton shouted. 'He couldn't place a robot or a dummy in that seat instead of himself?' Fenton massaged his temples, in visible discomfort. 'I still can't get that picture out of my head, Dr Kaddiri – it's like watching images from Vietnam, of Viet Cong prisoners being executed in the streets or Buddhist monks immolating themselves on TV . . .'

'Listen, Ed . . . I mean, Secretary Fenton,' Masters said through the satellite videolink, deciding far too late that he had better be more diplomatic – and fast. By this time, more rescue workers in breathing apparatus had arrived and were hauling him to his feet, trying to hustle him out of the stricken fuselage. He looked like a hunted animal. 'This technology is too important to ignore,' he shouted. 'Forget this demo. No one got hurt. I'll turn over all my test data to you. It's for real, believe me . . .' But the fear and panic over the demonstration overrode his protests. It was too late. Fenton and the others were gone.

Helen Kaddiri plopped down on a nearby chair in the empty conference room, deflated. Years of research, months of preparation – wasted. It would be at least another year, maybe longer, before they'd be allowed to present any information on BERP again. Damn Jon, damn his screwy project names, damn his complete disregard for prudence! It could take a complete change in administrations at the Department of Transportation, even the White House, before they got to present any more projects to the government, to *anyone*!

The range-control phone rang, and Helen picked it up. 'Kaddiri.'

'Helen, it was so *cool*!' Masters shouted gleefully into the range-control officer's speakerphone. 'I mean, it was scary – man, when I saw that deck buckle, I thought I was a goner – but it held! It works!'

'Jon, everyone here is gone . . .'

'Hey, don't worry about the FAA or the airline guys,' Masters said. 'They'll calm down, and when they realize how important this technology is, we'll have another dem-val program set up very soon. We'll—'

'Not "we," Jon,' Helen Kaddiri said bitterly. 'I've had enough of you and your complete disregard for anyone else's feelings or thoughts or opinions. You seem to think this is all a big game, and you don't seem to give a damn how it affects our business.'

Jon looked for the switch to turn off the speakerphone and flipped it but instead turned on the area-wide loudspeakers. Their conversation was broadcast all around the testing area, making it easy for the three dozen range personnel to hear Kaddiri go on: 'I tried to have you removed as president, and I failed, so I'm not going to try it again. I'm resigning as chairman of the board of directors, and I'm leaving. I'm not going to work for a nutcase. If you want to kill yourself, go ahead, but I'm not going to stand by and watch you take the company down from underneath us.'

'Helen, wait a sec. Everything is cool! We'll be fine . . .'

'You are *not* fine, Jon. You're obsessed. You're crazy. You're unstable. I'm not going to work with someone who completely disregards his own safety and the reputation and quality of this company, the company that *I* founded, not *you*. I'm going to trade in and sell my stock options and start Sky Sciences Inc. again, and this time I won't let you or anyone else tell me how to run it, no matter how much of a whiz kid they might be. Good-bye, Jon. I'll see you in the funny papers – or in the obituaries. You're sure to end up in either place.' And she slammed the receiver home.

The slam reverberated through the loudspeakers around the old rocket test site like a 155-millimeter howitzer shot. A sheepish Masters looked at the faces of the stunned and amused technicians around him.

'That crazy kid – she's still in love with me,' he said, though his characteristic boyish grin was strained. He took a swallow of Pepsi from his squeeze bottle and tried to walk nonchalantly back to his mobile control bunker. 'She'll be back – she still loves me,' they could hear him muttering.

He was still in a daze when he entered the bunker, so he didn't even notice the two strangers in black battle-dress uniforms. He went to his little cubicle, put his feet up on the desk, and punched up a digitized video replay of the test, complete with telemetry readouts. But he really wasn't watching the replay – he was thinking about Helen. The two men approached the cubicle, and the first one raised two fingers out of his belt as if drawing a pistol from a holster, aimed it at Masters, and mimicked pulling the trigger. Still no reaction. 'Shee-it, Doc,' said Air Force Lieutenant Colonel Harold Briggs, 'killin' you wouldn't even be no fun.'

Masters whirled around. Standing behind him was a wiry, medium-tall black man wearing a wide grin on his face and a big pearl-handled .45 Colt on his hip. Beside him was a tall, powerfully built white man as dour as Briggs was cheerful, as muscular as Briggs was lean. 'Hal Briggs! Gunnery Sergeant Wohl!' Masters exclaimed. 'What are you guys doing here?'

'Our two Pave Hammer aircraft are getting overhauled up at McClellan Air Force Base north of Sacramento,' Briggs explained. The MV-22 Pave Hammer was a tilt-rotor aircraft that could take off, land, and hover like a helicopter, but had the speed and load-carrying capability of a cargo plane. The Pave Hammer variant of the V-22 Osprey was specially designed for high-risk, low-level flight into enemy territory. 'McClellan is the only facility that has the equipment to service them. They do all the depot-level maintenance for the F-117 Night Hawk stealth fighter-bombers here too, so once the Air Force gets done overhauling and test-flying the stealth fighters, they work on our gear. It's all classified, by the way. Not just ISA, but the F-117's too.

'Anyway, we heard you were nearby doing some kind of demonstration, and of course when we found out what it was we hotfooted over here. Madcap Magician is very interested in BERP. Of course, everyone in ISA thinks BERP is a joke, so they sent me and Gunny.'

Masters realized why Hal Briggs was so chatty – there was no one else in the bunker to overhear them. The ISA – the Intelligence Support Agency – was a subdivision of the Central Intelligence Agency's Directorate of Operations. When a CIA agent in the field gets in trouble, the directorate calls on the ISA to help extract a friend, rescue an agent, create diversions, find targets, neutralize enemy defenses, or engage many other covert actions.

The ISA is broken down into action groups, or cells, comprised of members from military, civilian, and government specialties; the cells are so secret that one ISA cell would not recognize another. Colonel Hal Briggs was the commander of one such cell, code-named Madcap Magician. Composed mostly of former or active-duty Force Recon Marines, Madcap Magician was usually called upon for high-risk operations deep within enemy territory. Jon Masters had worked with the group on many projects. They liked using Sky Masters, Inc.'s gadgets as much as Jon liked making them.

Masters rolled his eyes in exasperation. 'C'mon, Hal,' Masters said. 'I didn't present this project to the military or to any national-security agencies because I know it will go "black," get buried in a top-secret classification for twenty years. No one else will be able to take advantage of this technology. BERP can save thousands of lives, Hal.'

'Looks to me like you barely got away with keeping your own,' Briggs pointed out wryly. He studied the digital replay on the big computer monitor on Masters's desk. 'It works, Doc. Congratulations. You might have a few kinks to iron out, but it works. Very cool.'

'Thanks, Hal,' Masters said. 'But I still don't want—'

'Dr Masters, you've already presented BERP to the industry leaders,' Briggs interrupted. 'The cat's out of the bag. You'll eventually put BERP on every major airliner in the world, and that's cool. But you know your technology can save the lives of ISA agents who put their own lives on the line for our country. All I'm asking is give us a chance to take advantage of your breakthrough.'

'I don't know, Hal,' Masters said. 'I really wanted to make BERP the first thing I built that can preserve lives, not help destroy them.'

'Believe me, I can think of a bunch of ways BERP can help save *my* narrow black ass,' Briggs chuckled. Wohl shook his head in exasperation. He was quite accustomed to his commander's tone and attitude but irked by it too. 'But we're not trying to stop you from deploying your system – we just want you to give us first dibs on it.' When Masters still hesitated, Briggs added slyly, 'Remember, Doc, it's a new fiscal year. ISA has got plenty of bucks to spend. I know the money's not as important to you as public safety, but I'll bet you all the memory chips in Silicon Valley that you could use a little seed money. And you'll be doing my and Gunny's boys a world of good. What d'ya say, Doc?'

Masters had truly not thought about making a profit by deploying BERP; he had actually been thinking of ways to *require* the world's airlines to support placing BERP systems in poorer countries' aircraft, in exchange for his granting free licenses to the technology. But he had no such compunctions when it came to the military or to government agencies like the CIA. They had bucks to spend on whatever sneaky black covert ops they were involved in, and Jon saw it as his duty to his company's shareholders to get as much of that money as possible.

'Well, since I've scared off all the major airplane manufacturers and the FAA,' he said with a shrug, 'I might as well help you out. Exactly how much money are we talking about here, Hal?'

Briggs and Wohl were still watching the replay on the screen. When they saw the aftermath of the explosions and then looked at the man who had sat atop 150 pounds of TNT and *survived*, they were astounded. 'Name it, Doc,' Briggs said, his voice hoarse with excitement. 'Show us a way BERP can help my guys in the field, and you can name your price.'

Jon Masters was smiling broadly now. 'Patrick and Wendy have been working on a few interesting items,' he said. 'Patrick calls it his Ultimate Soldier program. All based around this.' He withdrew the piece of BERP material from his pocket and held it out for Briggs and Wohl.

'This is it?' Chris Wohl asked. 'This is BERP?'

'That's it,' Masters acknowledged. He felt Wohl's black battle-dress uniform and Wohl scowled in irritation. Masters withdrew his hand quickly, as if he had touched a hot stove. 'About the same thickness as your fatigues there, Gunnery Sergeant.'

'It's too shiny, too slick,' Wohl said. 'It'll make noise when you move. Doesn't breathe like cotton either. It'll be hot as hell in a desert environment and cold as hell in cold weather.'

Masters hit the keyboard on his computer, freezing the digital video playback. He pointed to the intact first-class section of the airliner. 'Gunny, we can dull it, and we can build in an environmental unit to keep the wearer comfortable. But can your cotton BDU's save your ass like *this*?'

Briggs and Wohl looked at each other, their minds racing. Then Briggs turned to Masters and said, 'Doc, show us what else you got, and we'll go Christmas shopping. When can we see everything?'

'Patrick runs the program, and he's here in Sacramento,' Masters explained. 'In fact, Wendy's having her baby today.'

'No shit!' Briggs exclaimed. 'I thought she wasn't due to pop for another couple of weeks.'

'It's happening right now, Hal – in fact, it should've already happened,' Masters said. 'We've set up an office here in Sacramento, out at the secure development center at Sacramento-Mather Jetport, and Patrick can demo his stuff for you there. He's got some cosmic stuff that I'm sure he had you guys specifically in mind for.'

Mercy San Juan Hospital,
Citrus Heights, California
several hours later

Paul McLanahan breezed into the hospital room carrying bouquets of flowers and balloons and almost ran smack into the departing doctor. He found Patrick sitting beside the bed, holding Wendy's hand and brushing back her hair from her sweaty forehead. The room was furnished to look more like a regular bedroom than a sterile hospital room – the hospital bed like a bed at home, a comfortable couch and chairs, nice wall decorations, a pleasing dresser.

But the image was spoiled by a cart stacked high with monitoring equipment, plus an IV stand with two large bags of clear fluid on the other side of the bed, the lines leading to Wendy's right arm. The sight made Paul's heart sink. 'Patrick?'

'Paul!' Patrick exclaimed. 'What are you doing here? I thought this was your first night of duty?'

'I'm on my way to the South Station to report in, but I wasn't going to show until I stopped in to see the new baby – except I see he hasn't arrived yet.' Paul was wearing a civilian blue-and-brown Gore-Tex foul-weather jacket, but when he removed it, Patrick saw that he had his uniform on underneath. 'I had a class this afternoon that I had to be at in uniform,' he added, 'but I'm not officially on duty, so I had to cover up.' He wore matching police department patches on both sleeves, a simple brass nametag, and a dark blue turtle-neck shirt under his uniform blouse with the letters *SPD* embroidered on the neck. His shoes were polished to a high gloss. He wasn't wearing a utility belt, but he did have a small semiautomatic pistol in a clip-on holster on his belt. All standard gear, except for a small American-flag pin over his nametag.

Man oh man, Patrick thought, the kid looks good in a uniform! Sacramento Police Department uniforms, especially for rookies, are as plain as can be, but on his little brother it looked as sharp as a tuxedo. Or was that just because his little brother was wearing it?

Of course, Patrick's eyes were drawn to the badge, a large silver seven-pointed star with 'Sacramento Police' and a badge number, 109, in black, probably not much different from the original Gold Rush-era badges of the Sacramento Police Department. Patrick knew the history of badge number 109 – it had been their dad's patrolman badge, and their grandfather's badge, and their great-grandfather's badge, made from silver instead of chrome, as they were now. The first McLanahan cop, Shane, had not worn a badge number, but he was known to be the ninth patrolman recruited in the newly incorporated city. So when they issued badge numbers years later, future McLanahans first inherited number 9, then 109 when the department grew and badge numbers had three digits. It was a source of intense pride for Paul to wear it. Legacy was very important for police officers. In a profession where death can be a moment away, it was reassuring and right for cops to feel a sense of history and continuity, as if the badge made its wearer invincible.

'C'mon in, bro,' Wendy said. Her voice was strained from fatigue and pain, but she wore a welcoming smile and held out her hand. Paul found a place for the flowers and balloons, gave her a kiss, and pulled a chair over to her bedside. 'You look great, Paul,' she said. 'Ready for duty? Your first night on patrol – how exciting!'

'I thought you guys got dressed in the locker room,' said Patrick.

'We do, but I sat in on an MDT class – that's Mobile Data Terminal, the communications terminal in the cars – downtown, and I had to be in uniform for that,' Paul explained. 'The academy doesn't teach the MDT because the various departments use different systems, but I wanted to be up to speed before I hit the streets.

'But forget about me, you guys, what about you? When I got the message this morning that you guys were headed to Mercy, I thought the baby was going to be born in the back of the car. Sheesh, Patrick, maybe you'd better wait outside – he's obviously afraid to come out and face you.' His smile dimmed as he noticed that his brother and sister-in-law weren't sharing his joke. 'Any complications?'

'Wendy's in labor and she's one hundred percent effaced, but not dilated over three centimeters,' Patrick said, reciting the obstetrical lingo he had been hearing for hours now. 'She's been in labor since three A.M. and her water broke at five, but it had blood in it so we came right in. The doc found blood and meconium – baby shit – in the amniotic fluid, so he was worried about infection. They hooked the baby up to a monitor with a probe attached to his scalp, and of course they got Wendy wired for sound and put an IV in at the same time. So no walking around, no relaxing showers – our delivery plan pretty much went out the window fifteen minutes after we arrived here.'

Patrick offered Wendy some crushed ice to keep her hydrated – she initially refused, but relented after a mock stern demand from her husband. He pointed to one of the monitors. 'Here's the baby's vitals, and here's Wendy's uterine monitor . . .' – he watched as the graphing needle started a rapid climb –' . . . and here's another contraction. Deep cleansing breath, sweetie.' Wendy took a deep breath and expelled it all the way out, her eyebrows knotting in concentration as she tried to separate her mind from her pain, as they had taught in Lamaze class. 'Good. About thirty seconds to the peak. Don't hold your breath, hon. Let it out through your teeth if you need to, but don't hold it . . . good. Five seconds . . . that's the peak, hon, you're doing good . . . on the way down, about thirty seconds and it'll be over . . . real good, babe, you did good. Give me another deep cleansing breath. Relax your hands, sweetie, and relax those toes too, you're staying tense when you should be relaxing. You need another calf massage?' He reached over to knead her left calf.

Paul looked at the strip of paper unreeling beneath the monitor – Wendy had obviously been undergoing this same ordeal for a real long time now. His sister-in-law looked as if she had been beaten up and left in a sauna. The sheets were wet with sweat, and her face was ashen from the exertion. 'How much longer, Patrick?' he asked.

'I don't know. I hope things start happening soon. It's kicking Wendy's butt pretty good. They don't want to give her any pain stuff until she's dilated to five centimeters.'

'I'm sure that will be a big relief – I know it will be for *me*,' Paul said, wondering if he could ever be as strong and as together as they were. 'I think I'm having sympathetic abdominal pains.' He hesitated, then asked, 'Do you think they'll do a cesarean if she doesn't dilate any more?'

'We can't do a C-section,' Patrick said. 'Wendy has . . . er . . . has some abdominal injuries. A C-section would be risky. It'll be a normal vaginal delivery. We'll give her something to speed up labor if we need to.'

'Injuries? How did she get injured? What happened?' Then he saw Patrick hesitate, and he held up a hand to stop him. 'I got it, I got it – you can't talk about it. God, I hope everything turns out okay.' He wrote a number down on a slip of paper. 'Here's my pager number. Call when the big event happens and they'll page me.' He kissed Wendy on the forehead, just as another contraction began. 'Deep cleansing breath, sweetheart,' Paul said with a reassuring smile. 'I'll see you soon.' Wendy's smile was contorted by a grimace, but she squeezed his hand in thanks.

Joseph E. Rooney Police Facility, Franklin Boulevard, Sacramento, California
a short time later

Paul met up with LaFortier in the roll call room of the South Sector Substation a few minutes before eight. 'Hold it right there, rook,' the big police corporal said. Paul stopped. 'Stand ready. Let's take a look.' Paul stood at parade rest while LaFortier scanned the uniform. 'Where's your damned badge, rook?'

'On my raingear, sir.' Badges were always worn on the outside of outer garments such as jackets or rain-coats.

'Let's see it.' McLanahan handed over his raingear and hat. He was wearing it properly, all right – and he was wearing *the* badge, the old silver badge. Almost seventy-five years old, it belonged in a museum. Instead, a new cop would be wearing it on the streets of Sacramento, which was as it should be. LaFortier reverently ran his fingers over the heavy silver star for a moment, careful not to get fingerprints on it, then handed the raingear back. 'Lots of history behind that star, rook. You better be up for it.'

'I'm ready, sir.'

'Good. And let's stop with the "sir" stuff unless the LT's around. I'm Craig or Cargo or partner to you. You "sir" or "ma'am" every other superior officer you see, which will be everyone, until he or she tells you not to or buys you a meal, which will never happen, so keep on doing it.' McLanahan nodded. 'Weapon.'

McLanahan unholstered his SIG Sauer P226 semiauto-matic service pistol, careful to keep it pointed at the floor with his finger outside the trigger guard. He walked over to a clearing barrel in a corner of the roll call room – a steel fifty-five-gallon drum half-filled with sand and canted at an angle that provided a safe place to load and unload a weapon. Aiming the gun at the sand inside the barrel, he ejected the magazine, opened and locked the slide, retrieved the bullet ejected from the chamber, checked the chamber, and handed the unloaded weapon over to

LaFortier. As expected, LaFortier found it spotless – they hammered weapon-care lessons hard at the academy. He checked all of McLanahan's magazines to make sure each had the maximum fifteen rounds of 9-millimeter subsonic hollow-point parabellum police-load ammo in them. 'Lock and load,' he told his new rookie partner as he handed the weapon back. McLanahan reloaded his weapon in the barrel, chambered a round, decocked the action, ejected the magazine, put the sixteenth round back in the magazine to fill it completely again, then holstered and secured the weapon.

Jesus, LaFortier thought, it's going to be tough to nail this guy on anything. McLanahan didn't seem to be cocky, but it was always best to nail the rookies on one or two uniform items just to keep them from thinking that their shit didn't stink. 'Handcuffs.'

McLanahan handed over his handcuffs. 'One pair? You only expect to arrest one guy at a time?'

'We're only issued one pair at a time.'

'I know, but I don't care. Get yourself a double carrier and carry two from now on. Go to Property tomorrow and tell them I told you to get a second one.' He touched the inner claw of each side of the cuffs and spun them; they spun easily. They'd obviously been recently graphited. LaFortier handed them back. 'Got a spare handcuff key?' McLanahan reached around behind his back and retrieved a tiny key – in case he was ever handcuffed with his own handcuffs, a hidden spare key could get him out. The Sarge obviously taught his son well, LaFortier thought. 'Good. When you get a few pay-checks in the bank, invest in a good Streamlight. The city's flashlights aren't worth shit. Keys?'

McLanahan undid his Velcro key holder and retrieved his set of keys – cops were issued a whole wad of them for various rooms, lockers, call boxes, and dozens of other things. He had secured his keys with a thick rubber band to keep them from rattling, leaving only the squad-car key outside the band so it could be retrieved easily. Yep, this kid knew his shit and kept his eyes and ears open. The Sarge had probably rubber-banded his toy keys when he was a youngster, LaFortier thought.

'Very good. Now all you have to do is do the same for the next twenty or thirty years, and you'll be in good shape.' He turned serious for a moment. 'Now, what's this I hear about you sitting in on an MDT class this afternoon?'

'Yes, sir, I did,' McLanahan said. 'They didn't give us much MDT training in the academy—'

'I know that,' LaFortier interrupted. 'You'll be scheduled for it soon enough. But you need permission from your sergeant before you can request overtime.'

'I didn't want any overtime – I did it on my own time.'

'For you, there is no "own time," rook,' LaFortier said. 'You work for eight hours and eight hours only, from nine P.M. to five A.M. I had to get permission just to get you in here *one* hour early. Neither the city nor I want dead-tired rookies on the street. Graveyard is tough, McLanahan. You need every hour of sleep you can get. But more importantly, you did something that I didn't know about, something I had to hear about from *my* boss.'

LaFortier leaned forward, getting right in McLanahan's face so his new partner could look nowhere but in his eyes. 'If I don't teach you anything else in the next six months, rook, you will learn this: We must, we *will* communicate with each other. We need to act like *one* out there. I'm not one of those FTO's who'll tell you to just shut up and listen and stay out of the way. We need to be each other's eyes and ears. When one of us is occupied, the other is watching, listening, always on guard. We never work alone. You want something, even if it's trivial or personal or anything, you tell me. You talk, you tell me what's on your mind, and you verbalize. You don't think of yourself, you think of *us*. Understand?'

'I understand, Craig,' Paul responded. 'I was just trying to get pumped up, sir, you know, get a little ahead . . .'

'I know you're gung ho, McLanahan,' LaFortier said. 'All you McLanahans have a reputation of being bulldogs. But reputations don't count for shit until you earn yours. Don't go off freelancing. You got an idea you want to do something, talk to me about it first. I'm your FTO, but I'm also your partner. We work as a unit. Remember that.'

'Yes, sir.'

'Clipboard,' LaFortier said, holding out his hand and taking McLanahan's metal clipboard.

Good job, LaFortier thought as he studied its contents. McLanahan had indeed put himself ahead of his peers by sneaking into that Mobile Data Terminal class. The department usually took weeks to schedule that class, so the rookies had to absorb as much as they could about the complicated system as they went along. It felt good to be riding along with a rookie who wasn't afraid to take some initiative, who knew what he didn't know and went out and got it on his own.

Even the clipboard was put together pretty well. But he could never let McLanahan slide that much, not on the first day. 'You're missing several forms in here, rook,' he said. 'I'll show you what you need to bring. Forms are written in point-five millimeter B lead pencil, not

82

in pen, not in HB lead. And you better have more than one pencil – you'll probably lose at least three a night. Follow me.'

Mercy San Juan Hospital, Citrus Heights, California
several hours later

The obstetrician completed his examination. 'Still only three centimeters – maybe four,' he said.

Wendy McLanahan was too exhausted to register any reaction except to close her eyes as another contraction began. Patrick's jaw dropped open. 'Doc, you said she was three centimeters *eight hours ago*. Wendy has had a contraction every three or four minutes since three P.M.! What's going on?'

'It's a difficult delivery, that's all, Mr McLanahan,' the doctor said. 'We'll go ahead and give her some oxytocin to speed things up. That might help.'

'I'm not on a timetable here, Doc, but she's already exhausted – she's shaking, she's sweating like crazy but she's shaking and white as a ghost and complains of being cold. It looks like she's going into shock. What are we going to do?'

The obstetrician studied the monitor readouts. 'I wouldn't worry too much, Mr McLanahan,' the doctor said. 'Wendy seems strong, and so does the baby. It's important that she not push . . .'

'She's too *exhausted* to push, Doc,' Patrick protested. 'What about an epidural? Something to reduce the pain? . . .'

'Normally we don't do an epidural until she's dilated at least five centimeters,' the doctor said. 'We can give her something to take the edge off, but an epidural at this stage would be asking for trouble. She may not be able to push when the time comes. We'll start the oxytocin – that'll get things moving a little more quickly – and I'll give her a mild painkiller in her IV. As soon as she's at five centimeters, in one or two hours at most, we'll . . .'

'One or two *hours*?' Patrick exclaimed. 'It's almost twenty hours now!'

'I don't think she was in active labor when you brought her in, Mr McLanahan,' the obstetrician said. 'In any case, we have to let things take their course. We want to avoid too much intervention. Accelerating labor is a big enough step. We want to avoid having to do a cesarean if at all possible.'

'We can't do a cesarean at all, Doc,' Patrick said. 'Wendy had wanted this to be as natural a childbirth as possible, with minimum drugs and maximum mobility . . .'

'I know that, Mr McLanahan,' the doctor said, 'but things are obviously not going as planned. We may have no choice . . .'

'Read the records, Doc,' Patrick said. 'She *can't* have a cesarean.'

'I read the records Dr Linus faxed to me, Mr McLanahan, and I read his annotation about abdominal injuries and damage to her circulatory system. I also read that Dr Linus recommended terminating the pregnancy because of the severe risks to Wendy's health if there were complications during delivery.' The doctor saw the guilt that spread across Patrick's face and felt sorry for him. They obviously wanted a child badly enough to risk the life of the mother. He looked at the chart and frowned, then studied Patrick warily. 'I'm a little confused about a few things, Mr McLanahan,' he said. 'I see evidence of scarring, perhaps burns, and damage to her lungs, abdomen, and heart, but no cause listed. How did your wife get injured? A car accident?'

Patrick swallowed hard, obviously conflicted and apprehensive. 'I . . . I can't tell you,' he responded.

'Excuse me?'

'I can't give you any details, Doc,' Patrick said. 'I thought Dr Linus was going to include a note with the medical records explaining . . .'

'There's a note saying something about sensitive and classified government information,' the obstetrician said, 'but I need to know what has happened to your wife before I can treat her and the baby. You're asking me to work in the dark, Mr McLanahan, and that's dangerous. Do you want that for your wife and new baby? Which is more important – national security or the lives of your wife and child?'

'My family, of course,' Patrick said resolutely. 'I'll tell you anything you need to know. What about this oxytocin stuff, about speeding up labor?'

'The drug will supplement, then eventually take over, the frequency and intensity of her contractions – we'll have better control,' the obstetrician said. 'Things will happen fast after that. If they don't, we'll start considering our options . . .'

'Not a cesarean,' Patrick said emphatically.

'If you won't consider a cesarean, then you risk the health, even the life, of the baby . . .'

'I said *no* C-section,' Patrick said, his voice hard, his eyes piercing the doctor's. 'I'm not going to risk Wendy's life. Period.'

The doctor nodded. He saw the pain on Patrick's face. 'All right, I hear you. We'll make that decision later – that probably won't be for a few hours. But first, we need to talk. Sit down . . .'

The complex was called Sacramento Live! and it was the biggest thing to hit the downtown area in years: ten night-clubs and ten movie theaters, all in one location on K Street. Everything was in one place, from quiet, elegant, relaxing steak houses that served fine wine and cigars, to pizza places with games and cartoons for the kids, sports bars, jazz, rock and roll, funk, country-western, and Generation X. Patrons could do one-time parking or take Light Rail right to the mall, see a movie, then spend an evening in one place, or circulate among all of them, and never go outdoors. The place was packed all year long, but during the holidays it was shoulder-to-shoulder, with mall-weary shoppers taking refuge in the movie theaters and then enjoying dinner and a drink before heading home.

The doors closed at midnight. It normally took the small army of cleanup crews less than an hour to straighten up, but during the holiday season they needed extra crews, and it took the seasonal workers longer to do the job of cleaning up the huge complex. The night managers of the clubs were usually finished counting the receipts, checking the time cards, doing a closing inventory, and preparing the books by one A.M., so several cleanup crews were still inside when the day's receipts were boxed up in large locked steel containers by each club's manager and an armed private security officer and wheeled over to the bookkeepers and general manager in the cash room on the second floor of the complex.

Security was tight inside Sacramento Live!, especially when the cash was on the move. Off-duty Sacramento Police Department officers patrolled the complex when it was open, but all but one of them went home at midnight, leaving only private security forces on duty. A private elevator, guarded on the first floor by an armed security officer and controlled by the chief of security from the second floor, took the steel cash bins upstairs to the cash room. Other security officers monitored cameras mounted throughout the complex, keeping watch over the area around the private elevator while the cash bins were in motion. Watchmen armed only with radios and flashlights patrolled inside and outside until all the regular employees had left the building and the cash was secure. The lone off-duty police officer was stationed with the chief of the private security company on the second floor during the receipts transfer; the radio he carried was a standard-issue police radio, linked to Central Dispatch. The private security officers and watchmen were connected to each other via radio, as well as to the chief of security on the second floor.

The elevator could only take three cash bins and their escorts at a time, so five boxes were left waiting on the first floor as the first group of three went upstairs; and three boxes had yet to come out of their respective clubs. The first three boxes had already made it to the second floor when the main lights dimmed, then flickered out. The battery-powered emergency lights immediately snapped on.

'Power failure procedures, power failure procedures,' the chief security officer announced over the emergency public address system. One guard blew a whistle, and the cleanup crews on the first floor instantly stopped what they were doing and headed to the front door, escorted by an armed security guard. He had the easy job. The other guards groaned, because the alarm meant that the elevator was shut down – and that meant they would have to lug the heavy cash bins up the stairs to be secured in the cash room until the main power was restored.

'First floor, all secure?' the chief of security radioed.

'Secure,' came the reply from one of the guards, signaling that the cleanup crews had been escorted outside and the doors were closed, locked, and checked. The chief of security opened the stairwell door on the second floor, which locked behind him, and walked downstairs. The door to the first floor was locked on the other side, so that occupants of the second floor could use the stairwell as a fire escape, but no one on the first floor could walk upstairs unless it was opened by security. The chief security officer knocked on the door three times, received two knocks in response, then gave one more knock before pushing it open. Carlson, one of the newer security officers, was on the other side of the door. 'Okay, boys, the sooner we get these boxes upstairs, the sooner we . . .'

A man in a dark outfit, a military-style helmet, and a dark face mask appeared out of nowhere. The chief of security had just enough time to register his shock before the intruder raised a gun with a thick suppressor fitted to the muzzle to his forehead. There was a bright flash of light, then nothing.

'Security One-Seven.'

The off-duty Sacramento Police Department officer at the desk on the second floor of the complex retrieved his radio from the desk and keyed the mike: 'Security One-Seven, go.'

'Are you 908 yet?'

'Negative,' the officer replied. It was common for off-duty officers to forget to report in to Dispatch when they completed an off-duty assignment, and since it was thirty minutes past his scheduled off time, Dispatch was checking up on him. 'They have a power failure here. It'll be another thirty minutes.'

'Check. You got a call from your sitter. No problems, just a status check. Let us know when you're 908.'

'Roger.'

'KMA 907 clear.'

The exasperated officer tossed the radio on the desk with a thud. His life was heading down the shitter pretty fast these days. As if the holidays weren't bad enough, his old lady had decided she didn't want to be married to a cop anymore – or be a mom, or be a housewife – so she took off for L.A. with her new poke, leaving him with their five-year-old daughter and a mountain of bills. He had already burned out one baby-sitter with all the overtime and off-duty jobs he had signed up for, and he guessed he was going to burn out another one before his folks could come from Montana to help him out. Before she left, his old lady had cleaned out the checking account too, so it looked like the only presents his little girl got this year would be charity stuffed toys normally reserved for the city's homeless kids, or presents from his folks. Merry fucking Christmas.

There were three knocks at the locked stairwell door. The cop circled the security desk and knocked twice in response. There were two knocks in response, the correct reply. He pushed open the door . . . and was dead before he hit the ground.

Sacramento County Main Jail,
651 I Street, Sacramento, California
the same time

In all the years Paul McLanahan had lived in Sacramento, he never even knew exactly where the new county jail was downtown. Now, on his first night on the job, he had been inside it twice. It was said that the new jail looked like a luxury hotel and the Hyatt Regency downtown looked like a jail, but to Paul the place just looked bleak, sterile, and miserable.

He and LaFortier drove into the underground parking garage of the jail under a large steel roll-up door. After securing their weapons in the trunk of their car, they escorted their prisoner to the thick steel-and-glass door of the jail, which was guarded by a sheriff's deputy sitting behind bulletproof glass. Because this prisoner was suspected of carrying drugs, they donned latex gloves, escorted him to a secure bathroom, and conducted a strip search – including the unappealing process of ordering the prisoner to drop his pants, bend over, spread his cheeks, and cough several times so they could look up his anus for any sign of hidden drugs. One look at this guy's ass made Paul want to take a steaming hot shower, and he considered double-gloving if the guy decided to fight. But the ten-block chase they did to catch him – he had started running as soon as he saw LaFortier and McLanahan slow down as they passed him on the street – had obviously taken the fight out of him.

'That law practice is looking better and better all the time, isn't it, rook?' LaFortier asked Paul with a grin. Paul went on shaking out clothes and sneaker inserts.

For Craig LaFortier, booking a prisoner was a chance to meet up with buddies and swap stories, which was what he did while he helped Paul fill out the reports. There were at least three other city police officers in the booking room, along with eight Sacramento County Sheriff's deputies, four California Highway Patrol officers, and a smattering of officers from other agencies that Paul couldn't identify right off. The holding cells were full, so prisoners were handcuffed to benches around the perimeter of the booking room while the arresting officers asked them questions, filled out paperwork, and shot the shit. Since this was Paul's second trip to the jail that night, he fell under the rookie officer's basic on-the-job training schedule: first time, observe; second time, do it; third time, be prepared to teach it to somebody else. The learning curve out here, he decided, was as steep as Mount Everest.

Paul had managed to do much of the paperwork at the scene of the arrest and in the car on the way over to the jail, so he finished it a few minutes later, with the prisoner handcuffed to a nearby bench. LaFortier checked it over. 'Looks pretty good,' he said. 'But only four bindles of low-grade meth, less than a hundred dollars' worth – with the overcrowding they've got here, he'll be released in an hour.'

'But he's got priors, Cargo,' McLanahan said, waving the suspect's computer printout rap sheet. 'He's been convicted before for possession with intent to sell . . .'

'But he wasn't caught with enough to get him on a new intent charge this time,' LaFortier said. 'Four bindles, no payo sheets, no wad of cash, not found in a high-crime area – although he was pursued into an area where his probation says he's not allowed to go. Of course, that'll be *our* fault, not his. He'll get five thousand bail on a felony possession charge, his girlfriend or wife will put up the five hundred bond, and he'll be free. I'll testify as an expert witness that his intent was to sell, but if he's got a good lawyer, they'll plead it down to a misdemeanor possession long before his court date and he'll skate with a slap on the wrist, maybe a month or two in jail for the probation violation . . .'

'Almost doesn't seem worth it,' Paul said.

'Getting a little war-weary already, rook?' LaFortier asked, amused. 'A few hours on the street and you're already feeling frustrated? Welcome to the world. Don't worry about the prosecution – worry about the arrest and the evidence. Cops blow more cases from sloppy field work than DA's blow in court – or at least that's what they like to tell us. Let's get this guy booked and get back on the street.' Paperwork in hand, LaFortier and McLanahan escorted their prisoner through the booking process. The place was packed, so it was a slow business.

First, a nurse did a quick medical examination. Old hypodermic needle track marks were found on the guy's arms, so he had to submit to a blood test for HIV antibodies. After another twenty-minute wait, they escorted him to the booking window, where they presented the arrest and evidence reports to the booking sergeant. The prisoner was booked, strip-searched once again by sheriff's deputies, and placed in a special isolation holding cell to await pictures, prints, and the results of his AIDS test to determine whether he'd be placed in a cell with other prisoners or segregated in a medical isolation cell. With that, LaFortier and McLanahan headed back out to the garage.

'We need to cut that booking time down to less than an hour, rook, and that includes driving time,' LaFortier said. His radio squawked. LaFortier listened, heard a familiar voice say something about a power failure at the Sacramento Live! entertainment complex, and turned his radio volume knob down so he could talk to his partner. 'I'm taking time with you because you need to learn this stuff and do it right and develop good habits and all that shit. But we belong on the street, not in the jail. So we'll be hustling from here on out to get our booking times down.' He noticed a faraway expression on McLanahan. 'You okay, rook?'

'The jail gets me down a little, I guess,' McLanahan

said. 'Hauling them in like bags of garbage, strip searches, paperwork, putting them in the system like rats in a cage . . . it seems so dehumanizing.'

'Never seen the jail before, have you?' Paul shook his head. 'That should be required for every applicant. It gets everybody down, rook. The only alternative to processing them and putting them in the system is putting a bullet in their head when we catch them, and we don't want that, do we, rook?'

'No.'

The big FTO saw that Paul's somber expression didn't change. 'Why'd you join the force, McLanahan?' LaFortier asked. 'You're a damned attorney, for chrissakes. Passed the California bar and everything. We got lots of guys on the force going to Lincoln Law School nights, and lots of guys who have even graduated, but you're the only cop I know who's actually passed the bar exam – and on the first try too. You could be an assistant DA, make more money, wear a decent suit, work in a nice office or do that telecommuting thing, and never have to look up a perp's diseased bunghole. Is it because of your old man? Is it a family thing? Because if it is, you won't make it one more friggin' night on the streets . . .'

'No, it's not,' McLanahan said resolutely.

'Then why? The prestige? The uniform? The famous badge you get to wear? The gun? Certainly not the money. It has to be because of the old man, some sort of responsibility you feel to put another generation of McLanahans on the force because your older brother's not a cop . . .'

'I did it because I want to help, Craig . . .'

'That sounds like academy brainwash propaganda, rook.'

'It's not propaganda, sir,' McLanahan said firmly. 'This is *my* city, my *home* . . .'

'It's that guy's home too, rook,' LaFortier interjected.

'It's all those guys' homes in that jail, even the illegals and the transients. They all have rights, you know. They have a right to do whatever they want . . .'

'They don't have the right to break the law in *my home*,' McLanahan said angrily. 'We follow the law in my home. My family follows the law. My neighbors follow the law. We all depend on the law to help us live in peace. It offends me, it *pisses me off*, when someone breaks the law in my city! . . .'

'All right, all right, be cool, rook.' LaFortier held up his hands in mock surrender. 'You're preaching to the choir here. In my book, there's only one reason for being a cop – it gives you the authority, the responsibility, to protect your city and your neighbors from criminals. You knew that. So I know there's hope for you. All you need to do is *remember* what you just told me. Forget about the diseased A-holes and the rats in a cage and collecting the garbage. You're here, now, tonight, to protect your city. Don't lose sight of that. Got it, rook?'

'Roger that,' Paul said, his energy resurging. The jail was a necessary part of the job, Paul decided, but it wasn't *the* job. Being out on the street, helping those who needed help and nailing the predators was his job. He went around to the passenger side of the car, got in, and strapped in.

'You ready to go, rook?' LaFortier asked.

'Yes, *sir*,' Paul said, his enthusiasm genuine.

'Ready to hit the streets? Ready to nail some more bad guys? Ready to enforce the laws of this fair metropolis?'

Paul registered the rising sarcasm in LaFortier's voice and realized the big FTO was still standing outside the squad car. Then it hit him. Sheepishly, he unstrapped, got out, and walked around to the trunk. LaFortier tossed him the keys, and McLanahan retrieved their weapons.

'Next time, rook, it'll cost you dinner,' LaFortier said, strapping on his sidearm. 'The first time you forget your gun when you're on your own, sure as shit you'll be involved in a bad situation. Don't forget again. *Now* we're ready.'

They drove out of the parking garage, then waited on the ramp for the steel roll-up door to close behind them. 'We'll grab a coffee – at Starbucks, not the shit they serve at the jail or at headquarters – then take a swing past Sacramento Live! before heading back to the south area,' LaFortier said to his partner as they pulled out onto the street.

'Sacramento Live!? Why?'

'A buddy of mine is doing an off-duty gig there, and he told Dispatch something about a power failure. We'll just pop in on him for a minute or two.'

'Did he ask for any assistance?' McLanahan asked. 'I didn't hear the call.'

'No, he didn't ask for assistance, rook,' LaFortier said. 'But I'll tell you right now, and you can take this to the bank: There is nothing that feels better, except maybe for some big-titted brunette sitting naked on your lap, than seeing a squad car pull up to your scene. Even if you're Code Four and didn't ask for backup and are completely in control of your situation, it feels damn good to see another cop out there with you. Same goes for sheriff's deputies, security guards, ambulance drivers, street sweepers, waitresses, and convenience store clerks, anyone who has to work the graveyard shift . . .'

'But how can you do that? You can't be everywhere . . .'

'You listen and you observe and you pay attention to everything,' LaFortier said. 'First of all, when you hear it on the radio, you should pay attention – since we do most of our communicating on the MDT nowadays, a guy using the radio is away from his car, on foot, and usually confronting a suspect, so if you're available and nearby, swing on over to his location. Listen to the cop's voice, his tone – that speaks louder than his words. Listen to background noises – if you hear lots of voices in the background, shouting or crying or screaming, the cop might be outnumbered or up to his eyeballs, and he sure as shit wants a little backup even though he might forget to ask for it, or he might be too afraid of the crowd's reaction if he calls for help. When you see a cop on the street confronting someone, even if it's one-on-one, check it out. Let him Code Four you on your way if he doesn't need help.

'You'll understand all this soon, especially after your probationary period, when you're on the street by yourself,' LaFortier went on. 'This little city can seem awful big and lonely at night, even for the toughest veteran cops. Rusty'll probably ream us out for wasting our time snooping on him, but take my word for it, everyone appreciates the swing-by.'

The obstetrician strode quickly into the room and went directly to Wendy's bedside, checking the readouts on the vital-sign monitors, then beginning a digital exam. Wendy didn't seem to notice him; her head lolled to the side and her dry lips were parted slightly. An extra blanket covered her up to the chin, but she still shivered occasionally.

Although he didn't show it, Patrick was a frazzled mess inside. An alarm on the fetal monitor kept going off, and a nurse would come in, hit the quiet button, and leave. He didn't know whether she was taking any real notice, because it had been going off regularly for at least half an hour and he was afraid she'd gotten desensitized to it by now. He could do little for Wendy. An hour ago an anesthesiologist had finally installed an epidural line into Wendy's spine – it was the only procedure that Patrick was told to leave the room for – so she was no longer in body-numbing pain. Unfortunately, she was also not very responsive. The oxytocin had taken over her contractions now, and she was being racked with one every two or three minutes. There were so many tubes and wires hooked up to her and the baby that she looked like some weird science experiment. This was definitely not the way they wanted to deliver this child.

'What's going on, Doctor?' Patrick asked when the obstetrician had finished his exam.

'It's time to act. The baby's pulse rate is high now and his blood oxygen level is low, and it looks like his head is banging right up against the cervix – but she's still dilated only five centimeters. I'm afraid we don't have any choice – we need to do a cesarean.'

'We talked about that already,' Patrick said angrily. 'Wendy can't do a cesarean, because of her injuries . . .'

'We don't have any choice in the matter, Mr McLanahan,' the doctor said. 'You're going to lose the baby if this keeps up. We can't increase the oxytocin any further. We're coming up on twenty-four hours since her water broke, so the chance of infection is climbing. Any more delay, and we could lose both of them.'

'Then . . .' – Patrick couldn't believe he was going to say this, but he had to – '. . . if the surgery is too risky, we should . . . we *have* to abort the delivery.'

'I've been speaking to Dr Linus since you gave me permission to get details on Wendy's injuries,' the obstetrician said. 'I think she's strong enough to handle a cesarean. Dr Linus and I disagree . . .'

97

'Then we should go with Dr Linus's recommendation.'

'I'm the attending physician now, and I'm here and he's not,' the obstetrician said firmly. 'And I'm the one responsible. I don't know the extent of her injuries, but I don't think Dr Linus does either – apparently you've been playing this secrecy game with him too.' Patrick averted his eyes. It was obvious that he felt the awful pain of having to choose between maintaining some government secret and the health and well-being of his family, and was now discovering that he might have made the wrong choice. Sometimes, the obstetrician thought, these guys play the loyal little tin soldier routine too seriously, forgetting that there are real lives at stake.

'Frankly speaking,' the doctor went on, 'you two took an awful risk by continuing this pregnancy, with the horrendous medical history Wendy has. The chances of mother and baby coming out of this pregnancy in good health were never better than fifty-fifty. You should have been advised of that . . .'

'We were,' Patrick admitted. 'But it was a miracle Wendy got pregnant at all, so we decided to go ahead with it.'

The doctor gave Patrick a faint smile. 'Well, sir, now we all have to live with the consequences of that decision. It's a tribute to her that she stayed in such good health through this pregnancy, and that is a definite plus in her favor – but we're in trouble now. The worst has come true. You need to make a decision, Patrick.'

'All right,' Patrick said, reaching over and taking Wendy's hand. She stirred but did not return his gentle squeeze. 'What are my options?'

'The only way for us to ensure that we'll deliver a healthy baby at this point is to do a cesarean right now,' the obstetrician said. 'The only way to ensure Wendy's health is to terminate the pregnancy. We can wait and hope that Wendy dilates to ten, but we risk injury or death to your baby because his head is pounding against her cervix and he's showing obvious signs of distress, and we also risk the chance of infection for both mother and baby. We can go ahead with a C-section and risk Wendy's health, although I'm fairly confident that she can come out of it all right. Or we terminate the pregnancy to save Wendy. That's about it.'

Patrick looked at his wife, but she was out of it. You have got to help me on this one, sweetie, he told her silently. I can't make this decision on my own.

As if in reply, she opened her eyes and managed a weak smile. She swallowed, took a ragged breath, and said in a low voice, 'You are going to make a great father, lover.'

'Wendy, listen to me. I have to ask you – the baby's in trouble, you're in trouble. I think we need to . . . to abort it, sweetheart.'

Wendy's expression never changed but she raised her chin confidently. 'You won't do that, Patrick,' she said.

'I can't risk your life, Wendy . . .'

'I've had my life already, Patrick,' Wendy said. 'You'd be denying a new life. You won't do that.'

'But we have other options, Wendy,' Patrick said, pleading with her. 'We can adopt. I can't risk losing you . . .'

'Patrick, sweetheart, we have a life right here, right now, that we must decide about,' Wendy said. 'There are no other options. It's us three right now. You know what you have to do.'

Wendy's smile never dimmed as Patrick's eyes filled with tears. He reached down, kissed her on the forehead, pressed her hand, and nodded. She nodded in reply and closed her eyes as another wave of contractions, more painful than the last even through the epidural, washed over her.

Patrick turned to the obstetrician and said, 'Cesarean.'

'All right, let's go,' the doctor said. Nurses came in to get Wendy ready to move to the pre-op area.

'I want to be there,' Patrick said emphatically. 'I want to be with Wendy. I'm not leaving her side.'

'You'll be there,' the doctor said. Patrick was handed a package with a thin plastic surgical gown, cap, and shoe covers. 'Put those on. We'll have you wait outside the pre-op area until she's been taken into surgery, and then we'll bring you in. Don't worry.'

The speed at which the nurses and doctor were working told Patrick that the greatest battle of their lives was just beginning.

LaFortier drove past the main entrance to Sacramento Live!, then parked the car across the street half a block down. LaFortier put the car in park but did not shut off the engine. He sat thinking. 'Why don't we just give the guy a call on the radio and have him let us in?' Paul McLanahan asked.

'It's dark inside,' LaFortier said.

'They had a power failure, Cargo.'

'But the battery-powered emergency lights are off too,' LaFortier pointed out. 'One or two lights out, I can understand – but *all* of the emergency lights malfunctioning at the same time? . . .'

'What are you thinking?'

'I'm thinking that Rusty's probably pretty pissed off right now,' LaFortier said. He picked up the radio. 'Security One-Seven, One John Twenty-One.' No reply. LaFortier tried again; still no reply. 'I'll get Dispatch to beep him.

He might be in the can or something.' LaFortier swung the Mobile Data Terminal toward him and typed, 1JN21 TO POP3 REQ PLZ BEEP SECURITY 17, a request to activate the beeper on the off-duty officer's radio, a loud tone signaling the officer to check in right away.

'Should we get some backup?' McLanahan asked.

'Not just yet – let's see if Rusty checks in,' LaFortier replied. He put the car in drive and rolled farther down the block, out of sight of the front of the building.

'Er bewegt sich in nördlicher Richtung auf der Seventh Street,' the lookout reported. A gunman, fully outfitted with body armor, helmet, and several heavy automatic weapons, was stationed at each entrance, monitoring the outside with night-vision goggles.

'Verstanden,' said the one in the staircase. Three others were taking cover in the staircase, hidden behind the half-open door. Still another was just dragging the body of the off-duty police officer away from the security desk, out of sight of the cash room located just opposite the security desk. The gunport in the door of the cash room was still closed – apparently the men inside hadn't heard the commotion outside yet.

'What is the procedure when they open the door, Mullins?' one of the gunmen asked in heavily accented English.

'They'll call out first on the phone, Major,' said a man in a security guard's outfit. 'Then they'll look out the gunport. The security chief is supposed to stand in plain sight before the door is opened. Then they'll . . .' Just then, a loud beeping sound came from the security desk.

'Is that the call?' asked the gunman identified as the Major, obviously the leader of the group. He was clad in thick Class Three bulletproof Kevlar armor protecting every part of his body except his head; his ballistic Kevlar infantry helmet, which had an integral communications headset, red-lens protective goggles, and a gas mask, was in his hand. His combat harness was arrayed with ammo pouches, grenades, and a large-caliber automatic pistol in a combat thigh rig. He scared the hell out of the security guard.

'No – that's the cop's radio,' the guard replied. 'Dispatch is asking him to check in.'

'Do you know their procedures?' the Major asked. 'Can you respond for the policeman?'

Mullins, the Judas security guard, hesitated. It had been two years since he was kicked off the Oakland police force, caught stealing drugs and guns out of police property rooms. He couldn't get a decent job anywhere in the Bay Area, although he had never been charged with any crime because the department wanted the incident kept quiet. He finally found a job with a private security company in Sacramento. But he was unable to get a gun permit and make the big bucks of an armed security guard, so he made minimum wage as a seasonal-hire watchman at Sacramento Live! and other locations around town. He lived in a filthy fifty-dollar-a-week hotel room near the Greyhound bus terminal in the downtown area.

But Mullins now had additional sources of income. He had always loved motorcycles, and when he got kicked off the Oakland force, this passion turned in a dark direction: He became a Satan's Brotherhood recruit. The Brotherhood paid him well to simply look the other way when the gang wanted to steal some fuel from a refinery, chemicals from a warehouse, or pharmaceuticals from a medical supply store.

His conspiracy activities were no longer for the benefit

of Satan's Brotherhood, however. Two weeks ago, a couple of paramilitary guys with German accents had approached him and offered almost a half-year's worth of wages for one night's work. He readily agreed. All he had to do was brief the head of the group on the security procedures when the cash boxes were being moved, and open a door when instructed. He'd make five thousand dollars on the spot.

But he never expected these guys to be so bloodthirsty. Every private security officer had been executed on the spot, even the unarmed watchmen. And now, instead of being given his money and let go, he had been dragged upstairs by one of the Germans to explain the cash room routine. He hesitated.

'Go, Mullins. Answer them. *Now!*'

'But I don't know this department's codes or procedures . . .'

'Go! It must be answered. Tell them everything is okay.'

Mullins walked up to the security desk and picked up the beeping police radio. Hesitantly, he keyed the mike button. 'Security One-Seven, go ahead.'

'Security One-Seven, roger, One John Two-One is requesting a 940 at your 925.'

Oh shit, he thought – Sacramento uses nine-codes instead of ten-codes. It had been ages since he'd used any radio codes at all. He figured that 925 meant 'location,' but he had no idea what a 940 was. Probably some sort of meeting. 'Ah . . . roger, tell One John Twenty-One that I'll be done here in thirty minutes and I'll meet him at . . .' – he remembered that the county jail was only about three blocks away – '. . . at the jail. Out.'

'Roger, Security One-Seven. KMA clear.'

*   *   *

'That was *not* Rusty Caruthers,' LaFortier said grimly. Paul could see his partner's mind racing, turning scenarios and possibilities and explanations over and over in his head. But after several long moments, all he said was, 'Shit.'

'Maybe it was one of the private security guys, answering Caruthers's radio,' Paul McLanahan offered.

'Then why didn't he say so? Why didn't he say, "The cop's in the bathroom, I'll tell him you want him to call in ASAP," or something,' LaFortier said. 'No. This guy tried to answer the radio *as if* he was Rusty. Something's going on.' He put the car in gear and pulled back onto the street. 'Let's cruise around the complex and take a look.'

'*Ein Polizeiwagen kommt durch die* Seventh Street,' one of the lookouts reported on the radio. '*Der gleiche Wagen wie vorher.*'

'He bought it,' Mullins said nervously.

'*Nein*,' the Major said. Just then, they heard a faint metallic slam – the tiny shuttered steel window on the cash room door had opened, then closed and locked. The Major deployed his men on either side of the door, and he and Mullins took cover behind the security desk.

'Attention in the cash room,' the Major shouted. 'You are surrounded. My men and I have taken your guards and police officers prisoner, and we have already taken the other eight cash bins. You will come out of that room immediately and surrender yourselves. If you come out now, you will not be harmed.'

'We called the police!' a voice called from inside the cash room. 'They're on their way!'

'We have disabled the phone lines, alarms, and power to the entire complex,' the Major said. 'The police were already here, but we convinced them all is well. No help will be arriving. It is advisable you surrender and come out at once. If we become too impatient, we may have no choice but to execute our hostages. The decision is yours.' He turned to Mullins and asked in a low voice, 'Where would the money be kept right now?'

'They're probably locking the uncounted money away in the bins, getting ready to put it all in the safe,' Mullins replied.

'Does the manager have access to the safe once it is locked? Is it on a time lock?'

'I don't know,' said Mullins. The leader looked angry, so he decided he'd better answer with something more than this real fast. 'But I think . . . yes, it is.'

'Then we need to blow that door open at once, before they put the money in the safe,' the Major said. 'The dynamite, right away!' His men moved quickly to set explosive charges on the cash room door.

Patrick McLanahan was still waiting in the hallway outside the surgical suite, dressed in his plastic surgical outfit. It had been more than twenty minutes since the obstetrician, the anesthesiologist, several nurses, and another doctor Patrick did not recognize finished scrubbing and entered the OR.

A nurse came trotting down the hallway with a cart. He held out a hand to get her attention. 'I'm the father,' he said. 'What's happening? I'm supposed to be in there with my wife . . .'

'The doctor will let you know as soon as possible,' she said.

Patrick held the door open after the nurse rushed inside. The scrub area was to the right, separated from the operating room by a curtain. It was pulled aside, and he saw a cart with what he recognized as a defibrillator – a device used to shock an irregularly beating heart back into a normal rhythm – being pushed over to the operating table. Gowned and masked medical personnel surrounded the table. 'What's going on?' Patrick shouted.

Several heads turned in his direction. He heard the obstetrician's voice shout, 'Close those doors!'

'Dammit, tell me what the hell's going on!' Patrick shouted.

'Mr McLanahan, let us do our work now,' the obstetrician said. 'Nurse . . .' The doors to the surgical suite were closed, and a moment later a nurse came out, took Patrick by the arm, and instructed him to remain in the hallway.

'What's happening?' Patrick repeated. 'Is Wendy all right?'

'It's a critical moment, that's all,' the nurse said.

'What in hell does that mean?' Patrick exploded. 'Is she all right?'

'The doctor will let you know as soon as he can,' the nurse said. 'Please wait here.' And she hurried back in without saying anything else.

It was a nightmare, Patrick thought, an absolute nightmare . . .

As expected, they found Caruthers's squad car parked on the K Street Mall itself, on the south side of the Sacramento Live! complex. Off-duty officers were allowed to use city squad cars to transport prisoners if necessary; and although the K Street Mall was a pedestrian mall, off-limits to all vehicles, the K Street Mall shop owners and the public welcomed cops parking there.

Sacramento Live! occupied almost an entire city block, between Sixth and Seventh streets and K and J streets. A long L-shaped alley that snaked around the complex from Seventh Street all the way to J Street cut off the northeast corner of the block. From Seventh, LaFortier shined his searchlight down the alley and saw only Dumpsters. 'Looks okay to me,' McLanahan said.

'The alley curves around back there – we can't see all the way around,' said LaFortier. He pulled the car into the alley. LaFortier aimed the searchlight on the doors along the complex. They all appeared secure. When they made the turn around the curve, they saw a large Step Van delivery truck parked near the loading dock on the east side of the complex.

McLanahan unbuckled his seat belt. 'I'll check it out . . .'

'Stay in your damn seat,' LaFortier ordered. He drove past the truck without stopping or slowing, then exited from the alley on J Street and turned right on the one-way street.

'Aren't we going to check out that truck?' But LaFortier was already typing on the MDT computer terminal – he had memorized the plate number on the drive-by. By the time he turned right back onto Seventh Street, the 913 check reply came in: 'Commercial plates,' McLanahan said, reading off the terminal display. 'Two-ton truck, registered to a rental company in Rancho Cordova . . .'

But LaFortier was also scanning the screen. 'Wrong kind of truck,' he said. 'Wrong make, wrong size. Probably stolen plates.' He stopped the car just north of the entrance to the alleyway on Seventh Street and swung the MDT terminal toward himself. He typed: 1JN21 TO POP3 927 CIRCUMSTANCES SAC LIVE POSS 211, and sent the message through with the urgent-call button, which would send out a loud beep on all other officers' terminals. Seconds later, the terminal came alive with the radio designations, names, and badge numbers of the downtown-sector patrol units. Moments later several units responded to the call with ENRTE, including the downtown-sector sergeant.

Paul could feel his pulse racing and his heart pounding as LaFortier worked the terminal. He knew something was happening, but it was all going on via the computer. 'Talk to me, Cargo,' Paul said.

'Here's what I've got,' LaFortier told him. 'I sent in a 927, "suspicious circumstances," with a possible 211, "robbery in progress," and I sent it with an urgent-call message prefix because we've got an off-duty cop inside who could be in trouble. The urgent-call message causes the MDT to respond with a readout of all of the sector units, and anyone who might be available checks in. Here it says the sector sergeant is en route too – he knows that there's a fellow cop inside, and he knows that Sacramento Live! is a hot location, and he knows from my call sign that I'm not a downtown-sector corporal, so he'll take charge of the scene himself when he arrives. A 211 call always gets a lot of cops' attention too.

'But because I called it in and I'm the senior guy on the scene, it's my job to feed info to the en-route units so they have an idea of what's going on and what to do. I'm going to tell the sergeant that I think Rusty has been kidnapped; I'm going to tell them about the Step Van; I'm going to run down the report of the power failure; and I'm going to recommend we stay off the radios or go to a tactical channel because whoever's got Rusty's radio can monitor us.' LaFortier typed: SUPP 1JN21 POSS 207 SECURITY17 971 VEHICLE CALREG 1734BD21 POSS 503 IN ALLEY N OF K STREET LAST RPT POWER FAILURE SAC LIVE RECOMND MDT OR TAC CHANNEL 6 211 SUSPCTS MAY BE MONITORING FREQ.

'Now what do we do next?' LaFortier asked. It took Paul's whirling mind a moment to catch up. 'C'mon, rook, what's next?'

'We gotta go in and check on Caruthers,' McLanahan finally replied. 'Officer safety first.'

'Very good. Now . . .' At that moment, another squad car, this one with an *S* designation beside the car number, signifying the patrol-sector sergeant's car, pulled up alongside theirs. The windows between the two cars rolled down. LaFortier recognized the downtown graveyard-shift sergeant, Matt Lamont. 'Hey, Matt. This is my trainee, McLanahan. Paul, Sergeant Matt Lamont, downtown patrol.'

'What's going on, Cargo?' Lamont asked. His eyes registered McLanahan but he didn't bother to greet him. 'What are you doing downtown?'

'Was coming from the jail and heard that Rusty was doing an off-duty gig here at Sacramento Live!,' LaFortier replied. 'I was going to stop by and visit, but I couldn't raise him on the radio. I drove around and found a truck in the alley. The plates don't match the vehicle registration. Someone answered Rusty's radio, but it didn't sound like him.'

'Yeah, I heard that too,' Lamont said. He was in charge of all the off-duty officers in his sector as well as the downtown graveyard-shift units. He picked up his radio and keyed the mike: 'Security One-Seven, Edward Ten.' He tried several times; no response. Lamont turned back to LaFortier: 'Where's Rusty's car? On the mall?' LaFortier nodded. 'All right, Cargo. Let's put your rookie in the mall in a cover position next to Rusty's car. Cargo, I want you on the J Street alley exit. I'll stay here and monitor the alley on this end. This'll be a loose perimeter only. Once we're set up and the other units arrive, we'll have a look inside. Let's go.'

LaFortier drove forward to the K Street Mall. 'Okay, Paul, listen up,' he said. 'Your job will be to watch the

K Street Mall exits, report anything you see, and, most importantly, protect yourself. You take cover behind Caruthers's car – behind the engine block, remember, because it gives you more protection. You've got three exits onto the mall, so watch all three as best you can. Stay out of sight. Don't let anyone out of the building unless their hands are up in the air. Call for backup before you do anything. Just stay calm and think before you move. Got it?'

'Got it, Craig.'

'Good. Out you go.'

McLanahan retrieved his nightstick and left the squad car, then trotted across Seventh Street and down the K Street Mall to the empty squad car. He knelt beside the right front fender, oblivious to the rain.

He found his heart racing, his breathing shallow and rapid, and his forehead and neck sweating as if he had just sprinted a hundred yards instead of jogging a hundred feet. He had stationed himself between the right front tire and the right door, with the engine block between himself and the doors across K Street. Visibility was poor in the rain, but he could make out all three Sacramento Live! doorways that emptied out on the K Street Mall.

Paul turned up his radio, but it was silent. Was it working? Were the batteries charged? Did he leave the South Station with dead batteries in his radio? He double-checked that he was on the correct channel, then turned the squelch knob and got a loud rasping rumble of static. Shit! Enough to alert bad guys for three blocks around. He turned the volume down a couple of notches, then turned the squelch knob until the static disappeared. Leave the friggin' radio alone, he told himself.

Now what? Draw his weapon? Why? There was no threat in front of him. What if a wino or a transient wandered onto the mall? Should he break cover and move him, or stay hidden and hope he'd pass? And if he did either, what if the bad guys decided to make a break from the building right then? Or what if the wino was one of the bad guys? . . .

Snap out of it, Paul! he told himself. Stop confusing yourself with endless scenarios. Just pay attention and stay alert.

Paul tried the squad car's door – it was locked, as it should be. He saw that the 12-gauge Remington police-model shotgun was still in the electric quick-release clamp on the front seat, and filed that info away in his head in case he'd need it – he had a set of car keys on his key ring, and all of the department's car doors and trunk locks were common-keyed so he had access to the car if necessary. He scanned the street, looking for escape routes, hazards, and other places for cover and concealment. Not much out here – a couple of concrete traffic barricades, some concrete trash cans, a few directory/advertisement kiosks. There were few places to hide along the mall.

More help would be arriving any minute. Good. Something was bound to happen soon.

'All right, out there!' the general manager of Sacramento Live! shouted from inside the cash room on the second floor. 'We're coming out! We'll open the door, then the guards will toss their guns out, and then we'll be unarmed. Do you hear me? We surrender! We're coming . . .'

The claymore mine blast slammed into the steel door, ripping it from its hinges and hurling it inside the cash room like a two-hundred-pound leaf being tossed around by a tornado. One security guard inside died instantly, crushed by the flying door; the body of a second one shattered as the force of the blast hit him square-on. The third guard was just picking himself up off the floor, leveling his weapon at his attackers, when he was killed by a burst of automatic gunfire from their assault rifles.

The Major now had his helmet on. A grenade launcher was slung over his shoulder and he was carrying an AK-74 combat assault rifle with a laser aiming sight; a small backpack held additional ammunition. He went into the devastated cash room with his heavily armed personal guard and Mullins, the renegade watchman.

The general manager and his three club managers were cowering on the floor, blood seeping from wounds on their faces and hands and from their ruptured eardrums. The Major scanned the room. None of the money bins were visible – apparently they had all been locked away in the safe at the back. He raised his rifle and aimed it at the man in the middle. 'Who is the general manager?' he shouted.

Mullins pointed to the man on the left, who was crouched over the mangled body of one of the guards. 'He is,' he said, praying it would help save these poor bastards' lives.

'*Sie!*' the Major said in a loud voice so they could hear him through his gas mask and through their shattered, blood-filled ears. 'Open the safe now or you will die.'

'I can't,' the general manager said. 'It's on a time lock. It won't open until nine tomorrow morning. Any attempt to open it will trigger an alarm, and it can't be—'

'Liar! Idiot!' The terrorist pulled the trigger of his assault rifle, and the head of one of the club managers burst open like an overripe melon. The general manager, showered with blood and brains, screamed, then stared in horror at the destroyed head.

112

'Open that safe or you will watch the rest of your employees die.'

The general manager was on his feet in an instant, fumbling for keys. He inserted a key into the combination dial with shaking fingers, turned it, entered a combination, turned the key again, completed the combination, and pulled the safe door open.

'*Schweinehund!* You needlessly caused the death of one of your workers to save your profits!' the Major shouted, and shot the general manager point-blank in the groin with a three-round burst from his assault rifle. The burn from the muzzle blast was a full foot in diameter, and the noise in the small cash room was deafening – but not as loud as the agonized screams of the emasculated manager until he finally bled out and died.

'*Schnell!*' the Major shouted, and three more of his men rushed in, as heavily armed as their leader. 'Get the bins to the truck!' They pulled the steel cash bins out of the vault and wheeled them outside. The Major ignored the two surviving club managers, issued more instructions through his radio, then turned to Mullins. 'How will the police deploy outside? Will they use heavy weapons?'

'I don't think . . . no, they won't,' Mullins replied, more afraid than ever of saying he didn't know to a guy who had just killed five men in cold blood right in front of him. 'I haven't heard any reports of a SWAT call-out, and anyway this city's SWAT teams are only on fifteen-minute alert during graveyard shifts – it'll take them at least a half hour to get here. The shift sergeant might have a semiautomatic M-16, but they don't train with it much . . .'

'*Ein einziges Gewehr? One* rifle? What kind of police force does this city have?' The Major laughed. 'A child with a Kalashnikov can do battle with the police in this city and have a good chance of winning! *Kinderpolizei!*'

113

'Hell, only SWAT had M-16's until just a couple months ago – and half the politicians in this city want the cops *completely* disarmed,' Mullins said. He was so glad to actually know something that he was babbling. 'All the other cops only got sidearms or shotguns with double-ought buck. Your only real problem is that the county jail is only three blocks away, and police headquarters is only six. Once the call goes out, lots of help will arrive real fuckin' fast.'

'We will be out of here long before that,' the Major said confidently. 'Kill all the police!' he shouted to his men as they made their way down the stairs to the rear exit, heading toward the alley and the waiting truck: 'I will tolerate no gunfights with them. We hit *hard*, and we hit *first*.'

The explosion from the claymore mine rattled the windows and rippled the glass front doors of Sacramento Live! Paul McLanahan jumped. He dropped the radio, fumbled for it in the darkness, picked it up from the wet pavement, and mashed the mike button: 'I heard explosions! Explosions coming from inside the building!'

'Clear this channel!' came another voice, probably Lamont. 'KMA, Edward Ten, show a 211 and 994 on this location, all downtown units respond Code Three, set up a perimeter on Capitol, Eighth, Fifth, and I streets, bomb explosion inside the Sacramento Live! complex, repeat, bomb explosion inside Sacramento Live! . . . stand by . . . KMA, add a 246 on this location, shots fired . . . Jesus, *more* shots fired . . . requesting SWAT and Star unit call-outs for a 994 and 246 inside Sacramento Live! and request a 940-Sam on my location on Seventh Street.'

'Edward Ten, One Lincoln Ten responding,' came another

radio message. That was from the downtown-sector lieutenant, obviously monitoring the radio. He was the one
who would take charge of the scene when he arrived.

To a supercharged Paul McLanahan, the automatic-rifle
fire from inside the complex sounded even louder than
the explosion. His SIG Sauer P226 was out and leveled at
the front entrance to the Sacramento Live! building before
he realized it. The gunshots seemed so close, so goddamn
loud, that he ducked as if the bullets were pinging off
the walls around him. His gun hand was shaking, and
every little sound, every gust of wind, made the gun
muzzle jump. He felt vulnerable as hell, exposed to the
entire world.

He started running through scenarios again. What do
I do if I see a guy come out of the building? Should I
challenge him? But won't that give away my location
and make me a target? If he's got a gun, should I shoot
first? What if he's got more bombs, or even grenades?

The bulletproof vest he was wearing underneath his
uniform shirt didn't seem nearly as thick and protective
as it did half an hour ago.

Craig LaFortier had the squad car's spotlight aimed right
at the delivery door that swung open behind the Step Van
truck parked in the alley. It lit up the three black-clothed
armed men who came rushing out of the building pushing
the big wheeled bins that LaFortier knew the clubs used
to hold their cash. He saw the hydraulic lift mounted on
the rear of the truck rise to the level of the loading dock.
Two more armed men in black were standing in the back
of the truck, ready to pull the bins inside it.

'Five 211 suspects in the alley on the loading dock!' LaFortier shouted into his portable radio. 'All suspects 417. Request immediate backup!' He reholstered the radio, then took a firm Weaver grip on his service pistol, crouched as low as he could behind the right front fender of his squad car, and shouted, *'Police! Freeze! Drop your weapons! Now!'*

He never expected them to surrender – and they didn't. As soon as he saw one of them unsling a rifle from his shoulder and level it, he opened fire, aiming three rounds each at the five gunmen he could see across the street.

He saw them jerk and jump as the rounds hit, but they didn't go down. Two of them leveled big assault rifles with huge banana magazines at him. Staying low, LaFortier ran up J Street to a nearby parked car and crouched behind the left rear fender, again shielded by the engine block, seconds before the suspects opened fire. They peppered his squad car with heavy-caliber automatic-rifle fire, shattering the windshield and blowing out the two left tires, and stopped shooting only when they finally shot out the searchlight.

'Shots fired, shots fired!' LaFortier shouted into his radio. 'Heavy automatic-rifle fire coming from the alley, two suspects with rifles, possibly all five have automatic rifles. Suspects are wearing body armor too. Go for head shots, repeat, go for head shots!'

'Get out of there, Cargo!' he heard Lamont yell in the radio. 'Clear out east to Seventh or meet up with the unit on Sixth. John Twelve and John Fourteen, John Twenty-One is coming your way. Cover him.'

LaFortier knew that Seventh Street had more units, so he decided to head toward Sixth. 'This is John Twenty-One, I'm headed west down J.' He dropped the magazine from his SIG and immediately slammed home another one. Time to get the hell out . . .

Just then, a cop's worst nightmare appeared before his eyes. A lone gunman, looking as if he was covered in a suit of black armor, marched out of the alley onto J Street with his AK-74 leveled. When he was thirty feet from the abandoned squad car, he shouted, '*Tod allen Polizisten!*' and opened fire, spraying it in a side-to-side sweeping motion on full auto. Then he continued to march forward, raising the rifle up so he could aim it at anything that moved on the other side of the car. His walk was deliberate, no hurry in his steps, no effort to hide himself – just as if he were a pedestrian crossing the street.

LaFortier dropped the radio, aimed, and fired five rounds at the guy's head. He knew he was shooting back toward Seventh, toward Lamont and the other units, but it was a chance he had to take – this guy *had* to go. One of his shots must have hit flesh because the guy went down and LaFortier heard him shout, '*Achtung! Ich bin angeschossen! Ich bin angeschossen!*' as he clutched his neck and began to crawl back toward the alley.

But LaFortier didn't see the second guy until it was too late. The gunman peered out from around the corner of the Sacramento Live! building, took aim at LaFortier with a shoulder-fired antitank missile launcher, and fired. The car Craig LaFortier was hiding behind blew twenty feet in the air and crashed back to earth, a ball of fire and molten metal.

Matt Lamont, who had low-crawled west on J Street up to the alley with his sergeant's-issue M-16 rifle cradled in his arms, was too late to help LaFortier, but he was going to get a piece of this cop-killer if it was the last thing he ever did. He raised the M-16 and fired three rounds at the gunman's head, but all of them missed.

He leaped to his feet, crouched low, and approached the corner of the building next to the alley, determined to shoot at any head that appeared under his sights. At the corner of the building adjacent to the alleyway, he risked a fast peek around the corner. A tremendous volley of automatic-rifle fire rippled the corner of the building. His semiautomatic rifle was no match for at least three automatic assault rifles in the alley. He hotfooted it back to Seventh Street and took cover behind a tree.

'Officer down, officer down!' Lamont shouted into his portable radio. 'Code 900, Code 900, Sacramento Live! complex, heavily armed suspects in alleyway between J and K Streets!'

As he issued the Code 900 – the dire-emergency code, the code guaranteed to get every cop in town headed this way on the double – Lamont was watching the alley for any sign of the suspects. But all he could actually see were the remnants of the burning car across J Street, the one that had protected his friend and fellow cop Craig LaFortier. At least Cargo got one of the bastards before he died, Lamont thought grimly.

'What in hell happened?' Mullins asked nervously. The explosion and the volleys of automatic gunfire outside could be heard throughout the complex – it sounded as if the whole damned area was filled with cops, all out for blood.

The Major was listening for reports through his helmet-mounted headset. 'One of my men in the alley is dead,' he said.

The radio in Mullins's hand began bleeping, the all-points alert. 'They've called a Code 900,' he said. 'Every cop in the county will be here in a matter of minutes.'

'Then it is time we are off,' the Major said calmly, and began issuing instructions to his men via his headset commlink.

'What about me?' Mullins bleated. 'I don't have any armor! They'll cut me down in three seconds!'

'Shall I put you out of your misery now?' asked the Major, leveling his rifle at the turncoat.

'*No!*'

'Then go, get out of my sight. You are on your own. I let you keep your life, since you served us well. But I warn you: If you are caught, and if you even think about revealing anything about myself or my organization, then you had better pray the police kill you first. Because I will see to it that your agony is prolonged over several long days. Now *verschwinde!* Go! My troops and I have work to do.'

Paul McLanahan had been taught about the Code 900 in the academy, listened to the instructors, heard the recordings of actual radio calls. But the main thing he learned was never, *ever* call for one on the radio – it was reserved for someone in a much higher pay grade than himself. He could call for 'backup' or 'cover' or 'officer needs assistance' or 'officer in distress' or even 'HELP!' but could *never* call a Code 900. The only reason to ever call one, the instructors had said seriously, was if the earth was splitting open and all the citizens of hell were flying forth.

But he knew that was exactly what was happening. He saw and heard the rocket explosion on the other side of the complex on J Street, saw the fires, heard the gunshots, heard the heavy machine-gun fire in return. Jesus, Cargo, *please* get on the radio. Say something, man. Say *something* . . .

And when Paul heard the 'officer down' call, he knew it was his partner. And with the sector sergeant calling a Code 900 over the air, he also knew this battle had probably just begun.

There were men shouting over on Seventh Street, the wail of sirens just a few blocks away. The sounds were reassuring to the young rookie, alone and pointing his gun at a darkened building. All he wanted to do right now was be with his partner, cover him, defend him, carry him to safety. But he would never leave his post until given an order to do so, so he was glad that other officers were responding and rushing to help Cargo. He would just have to . . .

An ear-splitting explosion blasted him out of his reverie. The main doors of Sacramento Live! on the K Street Mall blew open, scattering a wall of glass and fire thirty feet away. He felt a hard slap to his head, followed by a gust of super-heated air. His ears were ringing so loud, he thought he might be completely deaf. He found his finger had tightened on the trigger of his SIG, and was afraid he might have accidentally squeezed off a round. Then another explosion rocked the night, and Lamont's squad car burst into flames over on Seventh Street – another rocket had been fired from the alley, destroying the car and sending officers scurrying for cover.

And then they appeared: two columns of four wearing helmets and gas masks, led by a figure dressed completely in thick black body armor who was firing an AK-74 out onto the street as the columns brazenly strode out the shattered front doors of the Sacramento Live! complex. The men behind him fired smaller but still murderous-looking H&K MP-5 submachine guns, sweeping both sides of the street with a hail of gunfire. As the column marched down Seventh Street, the Step Van wheeled out of the alley onto Seventh, moving into position to pick them up.

But they were marching away from Paul, and they didn't see him. He took aim on the closest gunman and fired three rounds at his head. The last man in the right column stumbled, stopped, turned directly at Paul, lifted his visor, saw the squad car parked there, and swept it with a two-second burst of automatic gunfire. Highlighted in the glare of a nearby streetlight, he made an ideal target, and Paul took the shot and hit him square in the face. The man screamed and went down, clutching his face and writhing on the ground.

Paul was lining up another shot when two of the gunmen in the right column wheeled around and opened fire with their MP-5's. He returned fire, pulling the trigger as fast as he could, rather than aiming, in the hope that his attackers might dive for cover or run. But they did neither. They fired again, concentrating their fire now.

They were coming after him, two deadly assailants with submachine guns. Time to get the hell out.

Paul had started to move along the right side of the squad car, getting ready to retreat to his chosen fall-back position, a sturdy-looking information booth a few yards away, when he felt a pain in his right leg. He looked down to see half of his right calf ripped open, just above the top of his boots.

He was a kid from the TV age and had seen plenty of guys get shot on TV. They all had it wrong, he realized. His leg did not fly backward – he never even felt the bullet hit. His leg was not shot off. There was no spurting blood. He felt very little pain – that was the weirdest part. What he could see of the wound – it wasn't much – was big and ugly – obviously a ricochet, the bullet spinning after it hit a wall or the ground, and not a direct hit.

Paul tried to run but then the wound got him – *now* he felt the goddamn pain! He sank down to his right knee. The gunmen were reloading, flipping the big banana magazines upside down to reload from fresh clips taped against the first ones. He aimed and fired again, missing. This time they did not return fire, evidently satisfied that they had gotten him enough so that he was no longer a threat. He saw them head back north on Seventh to catch up with the others, who were still sweeping the streets with volleys of gunfire, covering the Step Van until it could pull up beside them.

No fucking way! Paul McLanahan shouted to himself. You're not getting away, not after killing my partner! But all he had was his 9-millimeter pistol – no match for submachine guns. But something else was.

Paul grabbed for his keys, thankful that he had rubber-banded all but the car key together so he could find it easily. He unlocked Caruthers's squad car from the passenger side, leaned inside, started the engine, and put it in gear. Then he laid himself across the front seat, left hand on the steering wheel, right hand down on the gas pedal, pushed on the accelerator, and shot forward.

The two gunmen who thought they had disposed of him turned, aimed, and fired, but they were too late. Paul mowed both of them down under the squad car, hurling them up, then under the fender like corn stalks under a harvester. More automatic gunfire hit the car. The windshield shattered. Without letting up on the accelerator, Paul shifted the car into reverse. Tires screeched. He was shoved forward under the dash by the momentum, losing his grip on the steering wheel. With the right front tire shot out, the car looped to the right and crashed into the corner of a building on K Street. The engine died. He was trapped.

Paul looked up. There was another attacker less than ten feet away, his submachine gun raised, aiming right at him, moving closer for a cleaner shot.

Paul hit the tiny switch on the radio console and the electro-clamps released on the big Remington 12-gauge shotgun mounted on the dashboard. Now lying on his back in the front seat facing the approaching terrorist, Paul racked the action, leveled the shotgun, aimed for the face and neck, and pulled the trigger.

Nothing but a dull click! Christ, the shotgun wasn't loaded. Caruthers, doing an off-duty job, obviously hadn't thought he needed to bother loading it. In desperation, Paul tossed the shotgun at his assailant. The muzzle caught the assailant right in the middle of his gas-mask lens, shattering it.

'*Ich bin verletz! Helft mir!*' The terrorist screamed something in a foreign language – was it German? Paul didn't know.

The gunman ripped off the broken mask, lifting his helmet off with it. Paul got a good look at a very young, chiseled face, square jaw, close-cropped black curly hair, dark bushy eyebrows, and a nose twisted awkwardly to the right, obviously broken. The guy seemed frozen, paralyzed with fear, as if realizing that Paul could identify him. Paul reached for his SIG Sauer P226 sidearm . . .

. . . but it never cleared leather. Another masked and helmeted figure pushed the unmasked guy aside, shouted, '*Zeit zu schlafen, Schweinehund!*' and opened fire with his MP-5 submachine gun from fifteen feet away, raking the rookie cop with a three-second full-auto burst at point-blank range.

*　　*　　*

'Mr McLanahan!' the nurse shouted from the door of the operating room. 'Come with me! Hurry!'

Patrick felt his heart lurch. 'Is Wendy all right?'

'Put on your mask and follow me,' the nurse ordered.

My God, Patrick thought, what in hell have we done? He didn't hear a baby's cry – what in God's name had happened?

Gowned and masked figures surrounded the operating table. All he could see was Wendy's head. Her eyes were closed, and a large white drape hid her body from his view from the shoulders down. A plastic bonnet covered her hair, and he could see her arms fastened down to the sides of the table with Velcro straps. The anesthesiologist was at the head of the table, his eyes fixed on an array of monitors and several automatic fluid-metering devices. There were two IV stands with empty whole-blood and plasma bags hanging from them. He motioned Patrick to an empty stool next to Wendy's head.

'Mr McLanahan,' the obstetrician began, not looking up from his work, 'this is Dr Jemal, our chief of surgery. I asked him to be here for this delivery.'

'Chief of surgery?' Patrick asked. 'Is Wendy all right, Doc?'

'She suffered a uterine rupture and serious internal bleeding at the beginning of this procedure,' Jemal began. 'The scarring on her abdomen was extensive. She must have been in some degree of pain throughout the entire pregnancy, to have those scars on her belly stretching like they were.'

'But will she be all right?'

The anesthesiologist spoke up: 'Ask her yourself.' Patrick turned and saw Wendy looking up at him, with an expression that said nothing but love.

'Hi, sweetheart,' she said. Her eyes were clear and alert, and her slight smile lit up the room more brightly than all the operating spotlights together.

'Wendy . . . oh God, Wendy, how are you?' Patrick asked, his eyes welling with tears as he bent over to kiss her. He looked over at the obstetrician. 'Dammit, Doc, can you tell me what's going on here?'

'Can't . . . right . . . now . . . Dad,' the doctor said. A startled Patrick saw Jemal standing on a low stool, pressing down on Wendy with all his might. Then the room filled with the glorious sounds of a squalling baby.

'You've got a son, Mr McLanahan, a nice healthy boy.' The obstetrician held the tiny form out for the nurses. 'He's just fine. The bad news is, I think you've lost your uterus, Wendy. We'll have to do a hysterectomy, I'm afraid. But you've made it through okay. Congratulations!'

Patrick watched in fascination as the nurses clamped and cut the cord, briskly rubbed the baby down, suctioned his nose and mouth, and placed him in a small heated booth on a table. He was weighed, footprinted, and had silver nitrate drops placed in his eyes to prevent infection, then swaddled in two blankets and topped off with a white-and-blue knitted cap that covered his head. Then the nurse picked up the little bundle and handed it to Patrick.

Patrick Shane McLanahan had handled four-hundred-thousand-pound warplanes, nuclear devices, and multi-million-dollar weapons. Now, holding the seven-pound bundle that was his son in his arms, he felt helpless, stunned.

He held the baby up so Wendy could see him, and they wept tears of joy together as the baby opened his bright blue eyes, looked first at his mother, then at his father, and started to cry. Patrick nestled him back into his arms and the crying stopped. He bent down and kissed his wife. 'You did it, sweetheart, you did it!' he said proudly. 'Good job.'

'*We* did it, Patrick.' She reached for his hand. 'As soon as we get back in the room, page your brother. I can't wait until he hears the good news.'

From Seventh Street, the Step Van with the gunmen on board sped south to Capitol Avenue, then west to the Tower Bridge. It stopped when it was a third of the way across, and two men got out, set four satchels on the roadway, then ran back to the truck. Seconds after the Step Van had cleared the bridge, the satchel charges blew, sending the entire eastern third of the span down into the Sacramento River and eliminating the major pursuit route out of the city of Sacramento.

The Step Van continued down SR-275, then got onto Interstate 80 and drove westbound on the freeway. The pursuing California Highway Patrol and the Sacramento police thought it was the terrorists' first real mistake. Units from Davis to the west as well as from Sacramento started to converge on the Step Van. Roadblocks near Davis blocked the east- and westbound lanes of I-80, and dozens of units rolled westbound on the freeway, ready to chase the van down.

But the chase did not last long. Reports filtered in that the Step Van had stopped in the middle of the westbound lane on the Yolo Causeway, the two-mile-long section of divided interstate stretching over the farmlands that formed the flood plain west of the Sacramento River before it reached the San Joaquin Delta. The truck was trapped. There was no way off the elevated causeway, and no connectors between the eastbound and westbound lanes. Police units would arrive in a matter of minutes. If the terrorists tried to make a run for it by climbing down off the causeway, they'd be easy to chase down in the flat, marshy rice and barley fields below.

Led by the Highway Patrol, the units converged on the Step Van. Apparently the terrorists had figured out where they were, because they had driven almost to the far western end of the causeway, stopped, then thrown the lumbering truck into reverse and headed back eastbound. Too late. There was no escape now . . .

Several tremendous explosions shook the causeway. Once again, satchel charges had been set, this time at the ends of both lanes of the interstate, effectively sealing off the lanes in both directions. The cops couldn't get to the Step Van but neither could it go anywhere. Before long . . .

Minutes later, the real escape plan became obvious. A military-surplus UH-1 Huey helicopter swooped out of the night sky and touched down in the middle of the causeway. The police watched, helpless, from a mile away, as the paper money was taken out of the cash bins, transferred to duffel bags, and loaded aboard the helicopter. A Sacramento County Sheriff's Department helicopter with two SWAT deputies riding the landing skids and two more inside tried to approach, but the terrorists were prepared. A streak of yellow fire from a Stinger anti-aircraft missile hit the helicopter's engine, sending the aircraft out of control and crashing into the rice fields south of the causeway. One deputy riding the skids was killed by the engine explosion when the missile hit; the other was pulled inside the helicopter as it was falling. The three deputies who survived suffered moderate to severe injuries during the crash landing.

Ten minutes later, the Huey was airborne. It headed

east, flying a few hundred feet above the ground to avoid being tracked by air-traffic-control radar until it reached the foothills of the Sierra Nevada Mountains. Then it vanished.

At Placerville Airport, forty miles east of Sacramento, several trucks were waiting for the chopper when it lit down. Major Bruno Reingruber was the first to step off the helicopter, and he exchanged straight-armed salutes with Colonel Gregory Townsend. '*Willkommen zuhause, Major,*' Townsend said as the terrorists began transferring the duffel bags to the trucks. He counted the men as they emerged, then frowned as four wounded were carried off. 'It did not go well, I take it.'

'They all fought like lions, *Herr Oberst,*' Reingruber said grimly. 'The police fought with desperation, and they were lucky. I promise I will slaughter ten policemen for every one of our soldiers killed.'

'You will get your chance, Major,' Townsend said. 'The city of Sacramento has not yet even begun to bleed. This is a small haul compared to the penalty we will take from this city before we are finished. The city of Sacramento will learn to fear us. They will surrender to us – or the death toll will rise. But remember our ultimate objective. Tearing this city apart is only a means to an end.'

Chapter Two

Over two thousand cops from hundreds of departments
and agencies throughout the United States snapped to
attention and saluted as the three caskets carrying the
two dead Sacramento Police Department officers and one
Sacramento County Sheriff's deputy were carried into
Blessed Sacrament Cathedral in downtown Sacramento
for the memorial service. An estimated one thousand
spectators came out in the blustery cold to join the officers
and watch the solemn procession. Led by two uniformed
officers playing bagpipes, another thousand mourners,
including the governor of the state of California, two
US senators, all the local congressional, state assembly,
and state senate members, and the mayor and the chief
of police of Sacramento, followed behind the caskets and
took seats inside the cathedral as they were placed before
the altar. Each casket was draped with an American flag,
with the officer's service cap, badge, and nightstick placed
on top. The Christmas decorations in the cathedral and
on the route through town offered a strange yet inspiring
contrast to the mournful occasion.

The service had just begun when there was a rustle of
surprised voices in the back of the church. Heads turned to
watch as a heavily bandaged young man in a wheelchair
rolled down the long aisle. The man pushing the chair

positioned it beside the casket on the left, and the young man laid his right hand on the flag. Then he sat quietly, his eyes on the altar.

Amid the rising murmur in the cathedral, the chief of police of the city of Sacramento rose from his seat in a front pew and walked over to the wheelchair. As usual, Arthur Barona was wearing a dark suit rather than his chief's uniform, and like most of the higher-ranking politicians attending the funeral, he had a bulletproof vest underneath his jacket.

'Hold it,' Barona said in a low voice. 'What's going on here?'

The young man in the wheelchair looked up at the chief through swollen eyes. His head, neck, torso, left arm and shoulder, and right leg were wrapped in bandages, but his uniform tunic was draped over his shoulders, with all insignia and devices removed except for the shoulder patches and his silver badge, which had a black band affixed diagonally over it. He saluted the chief, then looked up at the man who had pushed the wheelchair, silently asking him to speak for him.

'Sir, Officer Paul McLanahan requests permission to stay by his partner,' Patrick McLanahan said, his voice almost a whisper.

'His partner? Who is that? Who are you?'

'My name is Patrick McLanahan, Paul's brother, sir,' Patrick responded. 'Corporal LaFortier was Paul's partner, his training officer.'

'He's McLanahan?' the chief sputtered. His face went white as the name registered. 'Wasn't he shot?' He was confused and embarrassed. There were so many wounded, so many press conferences, so much to do trying to track down the suspects, that Barona had not yet visited the hospital to see his injured officers.

'Officer McLanahan, you should be in the hospital,' Barona said.

The murmur of voices in the cathedral grew louder. When Barona looked up he saw a sea of faces looking at him. The sympathy for the officer in the wheelchair was visible on the faces of the VIPs seated in the front of the cathedral – as was the open hostility on the faces of the Sacramento cops toward the back.

'Sir, please –' Patrick started.

Barona put a fatherly hand on Paul McLanahan's right shoulder and bent down to talk to him. 'It's all right, Officer,' Barona said, his voice sympathetic. 'Your partner is in God's hands now. You're relieved of duty for now.'

Patrick was surprised by Barona's response. Why was he denying Paul this simple request? It didn't make sense. 'Sir,' Patrick said, raising his voice so more people could hear him, 'Officer Paul McLanahan respectfully requests permission to stay by his partner.'

'I'm sorry, but I can't allow . . .'

'Chief Barona, please let Paul stay.' It was Craig LaFortier's widow, seated in the front pew directly behind her husband's casket. She stood, bent down to hug Paul gently, gave him a kiss on the cheek, returned to her seat, then reached over to hold his bandaged arm as if prepared to keep him in place should the chief try to pull him away. All eyes were back on him again, Barona realized, as if waiting to see what he was going to do.

What had started out as if it might be some sort of grandstanding demonstration had turned into a scene deeply touching to those in the church, and it appeared as though Chief Barona was trying to prevent it. Patrick – who had objected from the start to his wounded brother's leaving the hospital and, after losing that argument, had insisted that he accompany him to the service – watched

133

Barona as in sequence anger, then confusion, then embarrassment and worry passed across his face. The chief felt very exposed; he had to extricate himself from this scene gracefully – and fast. He put on his best fatherly expression, gave permission with a nod, and laid his hand on Paul's right shoulder again before returning to his seat.

Being the chief of police for the capital of California, a city of almost half a million people, was certainly no popularity contest, Patrick acknowledged, but shouldn't the guy at the least *recognize* one of his own officers, especially one who had been wounded in the line of duty, and not object to his display of loyalty?

The ceremony was designed to move and uplift the listeners. The amplified voice of the bishop of the archdiocese of Sacramento sounded the reassuringly familiar prayers. The music of the organ resonated through the great space. The speakers told of how LaFortier had killed one attacker before he was murdered, and they spoke about the heroic but futile actions of the police and sheriff's units as they tried to stop the heavily armed robbers. Inevitably, politics entered into some of the eulogies. There were appeals for a total confiscation and ban on all assault rifles in the state of California, and calls for more prisons, more executions, and more funding for everything from the police to education to welfare programs – even a call to close the downtown entertainment complex for fear it might attract further violence. Patrick ignored it all. What moved him were not the voices or the prayers or the ceremony or even the organ, but the bagpipes.

When the two uniformed officers, one from the Sacramento Police Department and the other from the Sacramento County Sheriff's Department, played their bagpipes, the keening soared above the utter silence throughout the huge cathedral. There was something about the sound of a bagpipe, Patrick thought, that reached very deep into the soul. The eerie wails were sad yet stirring. Haunting. That was the word. The sound of the bagpipes mesmerized him. Patrick knew that for centuries armies of Scotland, England, and even America had marched into battle with bagpipes blaring, the sound inspiring and terrifying at the same time.

As he looked at the coffins, then at his injured brother in the wheelchair, he felt the anger surge in his chest. The wail of the pipes touched a rage within him, something evil, something angry. He had been away from Sacramento for many years, but it was still his home – and his home was under attack. For US Air Force Brigadier General Patrick McLanahan, the pipes were not a tribute to the fallen police officers – they were a rallying call. The homeland was under siege. It was time to take up arms and defend it.

The ferocity of the assault on the police had startled Patrick. He knew of nothing else on so drastic a scale within the United States. He had fought with ex-military drug smugglers when he flew for the Hammerheads of the US Border Security Force, but Salazar and his former Cuban-military 'Cuchillo' pilots had not dared to venture into America's cities. Henri Cazaux was the only exception, but he had confined his attacks to simple kamikaze-like aerial bombardments of major airports, quickly stopped by federal and military forces. The recent robbery-shootings in Hollywood, in which heavily armed gunmen kept a hundred police at bay for nearly thirty minutes, were little more than a 'suicide by cop' incident – the robbers wanted to shoot up the city, and they wanted the police to kill them.

From press accounts of the shootout, the guys who robbed Sacramento Live! were clearly military. They certainly hadn't used pure military tactics – marching out into the open in columns of two abreast with guns blazing had not been used in combat since the redcoats were kicked out of the Colonies. But their weapons, their armor, and their brazenness meant they knew right from the start that they had the upper hand.

How would the police stop nutcases like these guys? Would cops on the beat now carry automatic rifles? Would armored vehicles replace squad cars to protect against anti-tank rockets? What if the robbers decided to use even heavier weapons? Would the streets of Sacramento eventually turn into a battlefield? Would the National Guard or the regular Army replace the police?

Patrick McLanahan knew military combat strategies. He knew what would be needed to analyze the enemy and plan an offensive. But he had to have information, intelligence, and reconnaissance. He had to find out more. He would get all the information he could from the police and the federal authorities investigating the attack, and then map out a counteroffensive strategy of his own.

Patrick could see that Paul, now white with fatigue, was paying the price for leaving his hospital bed to come to the memorial service. After the ceremony, Patrick allowed him to accompany Craig LaFortier's casket – empty, of course, since the terrorists' brutal attack left no remains – down the aisle and to the outer doors of the church. But as the caskets were borne to the hearses, he turned the chair and wheeled Paul out a side entrance to a waiting police department ambulance, which raced Code Three back to the University of California-Davis Medical Center in downtown Sacramento. Paul, now barely conscious from exhaustion, was quickly taken back to his room.

Patrick stayed next to his brother until a doctor examined him. The doctor ordered complete bed rest and no visitors for the next twenty-four hours. A police officer on duty outside his room was given strict orders not to let anyone inside but medical personnel.

Patrick made his way to a nearby waiting room, got a cup of coffee from the vending machine, and sank wearily into a chair. The TV in the room was set to a local channel and showed aerial shots of the funeral procession, nearly a mile long, as it moved through downtown Sacramento toward City Cemetery. They also showed the Sacramento Peace Officers Memorial in Del Paso Heights, which was getting ready for its own memorial service for the three slain officers. The memorial was ringed by Ionic columns, with a tall stone obelisk in the center of the circle and bronze plaques of Sacramento's slain officers on the outside of the circle. As the sun moved across the sky, the shadow created by the obelisk pointed at each officer's plaque at the precise time he had died. Spotlights on the columns created the same effect at night.

Patrick had been to many formal military funerals. The last one, a secret service in the desert of central Nevada just four short months ago, had been for his friend and superior officer Lieutenant General Bradley James Elliott, who had been killed in a crash of his experimental EB-52 Megafortress bomber while on a top-secret strike mission inside the People's Republic of China. The President of the United States and the president of the newly independent Republic of China on Taiwan attended that service. Brad Elliott was buried in a small graveyard in the Nevada desert near the secret base now named for him, a graveyard reserved for those who died while test-flying America's newest and most top-secret warplanes.

But cop funerals were different. The police usually strive to stay low-key, even anonymous, on a day-to-day basis, but when a cop is killed the display of solidarity and strength is anything but low-key. Was this for the public's benefit, their attempt to show the public that the police might be hurt but they weren't defeated? For the law-enforcement community's benefit, an attempt to rally their strength in the face of death? For the crooks' benefit – again, demonstrating the sheer power, strength, and brotherhood of their adversaries? Patrick couldn't begin to guess.

Hearing a commotion out in the corridor, Patrick got up and headed for the door. To his surprise, he saw Arthur Barona striding down the hallway with a knot of aides, cops, and reporters with microphones, tape recorders, and TV cameras following close behind. At the door to Paul's room the cop on duty, who had been instructed just minutes earlier not to let anyone in, moved out of the way without a word. Barona and another cop with captain's bars on his uniform, whom Patrick recognized as Thomas Chandler, walked right in.

'Hey!' Patrick shouted. 'You can't go in there!' Everyone ignored him. Enraged, he sped down the corridor, pushed past the cop on duty, and stormed inside. Barona was already seated beside Paul's bed, holding his left hand. Paul was awake but clearly groggy – and when Patrick saw his eyes begin to roll up into his head in exhaustion, he exploded. 'Hey, you motherfucker,' he snapped, 'get the hell out of this room! The doctor ordered no visitors!'

Cameras and microphones swung in Patrick's direction, and a couple of reporters fired questions at him while warily staying out of his reach. The cop on duty grabbed him from behind, pinning one arm behind him

138

with a come-along grip, and pressing a finger into the mandibular nerve behind his jaw. Patrick yelled in pain. The cop had him but good – he could go in no direction except straight down at the floor, right in front of all the reporters and cameras.

'Hold it, Officer, hold it,' Barona said quickly. 'Let him go. That's Officer McLanahan's brother.' Patrick fought to keep from swinging back at his attacker. The cameras and microphones were squarely on him now. Barona said, 'I'm very sorry, Mr McLanahan, but the police force is at a very high state of readiness and alert, and anyone can be considered a threat. Now, what was it you had to say to me?'

'The doctor ordered uninterrupted rest, no visitors at all, for twenty-four hours. That order includes family, friends, and chiefs of police and reporters. Look at him. He's totally wiped out. You should have checked with the doctor before barging in like this.'

Barona looked down at Paul as the cameras swung back toward him. He gave his hand a squeeze, patted him on the head, and nodded. 'Let's let this brave officer rest now, guys. Everyone outside.' He led the reporters out of the room, then stood in front of the door as if on guard himself. 'That's one tough rookie cop in there, folks,' he said to the reporters, who had arrayed themselves around him, with Paul visible over Barona's shoulder through the windowed panel in the door. 'He wounded three terrorists in the Sacramento Live! shootout before being gunned down himself. Seriously injured, he still had the toughness and spirit to get up out of that hospital bed and attend his partner's funeral. That's a Sacramento cop for you: the best of the best.' He turned toward the windowed panel, gave a thumbs-up, and said, 'Get well soon, Officer McLanahan. We need more soldiers in blue like you out there protecting our streets.' As he averted his head as if hiding a tear, his aides used the moment to end the photo opportunity, and the reporters were quickly hustled toward the elevators.

When they were well out of range, Barona said to Patrick, 'My staff should have checked first.' He shot a sideways glance at Tom Chandler, as if silently blaming him. Chandler extended a hand, and Patrick took it reluctantly. 'I'm sorry for the intrusion, Mr McLanahan,' Chandler said, 'and I'm sorry for what's happened. I promise you we'll find out who did this.'

Patrick didn't think any more of either apology than he did of the grandstanding in Paul's room, but he let it slide. 'No problem,' he said, and turned to Barona – 'Paul's doing okay. He's tough.' – only to find he had already turned to speak with his aides. He took a step toward him and the aides noticed. 'Excuse me, Chief Barona. I was wondering if I could speak with you for a moment?'

Barona wiped the instant look of irritation off his face – he didn't want to seem impatient with any member of a cop's family. 'Of course, Mr McLanahan,' he answered. They stepped away, far enough to feel as if they were carrying out a private discussion, but near enough to be overheard. Chandler joined them. 'What can I do for you, sir?'

'I was wondering if you could give me any more details of the incident in which Paul was hurt,' Patrick asked. 'Any details about the robbers, where they came from, where they went, who they are – anything that might help to explain how something like this could happen here in Sacramento.'

'It's not just in Sacramento, Mr McLanahan,' Barona responded. 'It's a nationwide problem. The increase in crime, in gang violence, in the use of assault weapons, in the brazenness of the criminal element – it's happening all over the country.'

Christ, a political statement at a time like this. Patrick felt that flush of anger again. 'I understand, Chief, but about the robbers – are you saying they were gang members? As in Crips or Bloods? What kind of gangs? Do you know specifically who did this?'

'We don't have that information yet, Mr McLanahan,' Barona said with an edge of impatience. 'My deputy in charge of public affairs will provide that information when it becomes available. If you'll excuse me, sir, I'd better get back to my office so I can organize the hunt for those bastards that attacked your son . . .'

'My *brother*,' Patrick corrected him curtly. 'Listen, Chief Barona, I want to help with the investigation. From what the press and the speakers at the memorial service said, they were heavily armed military types. I can help track them down and fight them. I'd like to speak with you and your investigators about ways I can help . . .'

Barona again glanced at Chandler, as if asking, Why in hell are you allowing weirdos like this near me? 'What is it you do, Mr McLanahan?' he said.

'I work for a defense contractor in San Diego. We produce communications, surveillance, and space systems for the US military.'

'You mean satellites? I don't see how a satellite can help us. If you'll excuse me . . .'

'We make other things as well, Chief,' Patrick said. 'Weapons. Sensors. We can access information from all over the globe. If you can tell me what you need or what your special objectives might be, I'm sure we can design a system that can help you.'

Barona regarded Patrick with complete exasperation.

'Mr McLanahan, you're not trying to sell me a communications system, are you? Are you a salesman? If you are, this is hardly the time . . .'

'I'm not trying to sell you anything, Chief,' Patrick retorted. 'I'm trying to *give* you something. I can give you any kind of exotic weapon, sensor, or electronics system you might need to help locate and capture the bastards who killed those cops and put my brother in the hospital. I can outfit your officers so they'd never have to enter a building without knowing exactly how many people are inside and where each and every one is. I can give them the ability to paralyze a roomful of criminals with a single shot. I can make it so an officer would never have to fear a bullet ever again. I can give a single officer the power of—'

'Mr McLanahan, please,' Barona interrupted, rubbing his eyes tiredly. 'This all sounds fascinating, but I don't have the time to—'

'Chief Barona, I'm not making any of this up – I can do all of what I'm saying,' Patrick said. 'But it would be better if you gave me some kind of idea about what we're up against . . .'

' "What *we're* up against"?' Barona mimicked. He closed his eyes, then stepped past Patrick, poised to head away. 'Listen to me carefully, Mr McLanahan,' he said. 'Let me caution you about something. Interfering with a police investigation is a crime. This crime will also be investigated by agents of the US military, ATF, FBI, the state police, and by volunteers from agencies all across the West. No one kills a cop anywhere in America without brother officers coming to help. But civilians are not permitted to participate. You'd be needlessly endangering yourself and those around you. You don't have the training and experience it takes to—'

'But I do have the training – and I've got the advice, assistance, and equipment necessary to do the job,' Patrick said. 'Let me talk to you about this in more detail. I can demonstrate technologies that will astound you.'

'No thank you, Mr McLanahan,' Barona said. 'Again, I must warn you – stay away from this investigation. I would hate to punish any family member of a fallen cop, but I will if I must to protect the lives of other cops. Take care of your family and your brother, sir, and leave the investigation to us.' Barona snapped up the collar of his coat, signaling an end to the conversation, and strode off. Chandler nodded to Patrick, looking a little embarrassed by his chief's tone, and followed behind.

Patrick could do nothing more. He went up to Paul's room once more and looked through the door window. His brother was asleep. He could see his slow heartbeat and respiration registering on the monitors near the bed. Nurses had access to the room from an interior door that opened on the central nurses' corridor, and a nurse's aide was busy recording vital signs right now. The officer was back on duty outside the room, and he gave Patrick a look that clearly warned him to stay away. *Now* he's doing his job, thought Patrick bitterly. He nodded to the officer and left.

The drive over to the hospital where Wendy was recuperating was twenty minutes by freeway, and after three days of shuttling back and forth, he could do it in his sleep. It gave him ample time to think.

Barona seemed completely befuddled by this incident. He was good at feeding the press plenty of reassuring and meaningless tidbits, but he seemed more concerned about looking good and engaged and in control rather than actually doing anything to capture the cop-killers. Barona wasn't the one to talk to, Patrick decided. He had to find the guy in charge of the investigation itself. Maybe he'd be more willing to accept some unconventional assistance from a secret source.

When Patrick entered Wendy's room a few minutes later, he found her asleep – and Jon Masters sitting in a chair beside the bassinet, cradling the baby in his arms with an expression of unabashed awe. 'Jon!' Patrick exclaimed. 'What a surprise!'

'Hey, Patrick, look at this little guy,' Jon said, his voice low and a big grin on his face. 'He's great, man, really great. Wendy said it was okay I hold him, and then she fell asleep, so here I am, stuck on baby patrol. Is it okay? You want him back?'

'As long as you don't plan on keeping him, you're welcome to hold him,' Patrick said with a smile. He kissed Wendy gently on the forehead, then took a seat beside Jon in the foldout chair-bed he had been sleeping in over the past few days.

They both gazed at the child as if he were a radiant being – which of course he was, at least in his dad's eyes. He had a mass of soft wavy blond hair with tinges of red all through it, so much of it that it framed his face under his little knitted cap. He had tiny ears, round little shoulders, and solid arms like his father, but a soft, gentle face and a pert little chin like his mother. He opened his eyes when he sensed his father near him, and the two men found themselves looking into the clearest, roundest, most liquid blue eyes either had ever seen. Then he closed them, pursed his lips as if in approval, and fell asleep again.

'What are you going to name him?' Jon asked. 'You know, Jon is always a good name . . .'

'Bradley,' they heard Wendy reply. They turned to see her struggling to sit up in bed. Her stomach muscles were almost useless after the cesarean, so moving was still painful, but she appeared determined to test her muscles more and more every hour. She had gathered her long hair into a ponytail again to keep it in check, and she looked as beautiful and as vibrant as ever. Patrick sat on the bed beside her. 'I think we decided that months ago, whether it was a boy or a girl,' she told Jon, holding her husband's hand. 'And since James was my dad's name . . .'

'Bradley James McLanahan?' Jon Masters exclaimed, rolling his eyes in mock disbelief. 'You gave your son, this cute, innocent, tow-headed little boy, the same name as the scourge of the United States Air Force? Shame on you.' He grinned at them both, then asked, 'What about your brother? How is he?'

'They say his condition is improving,' Patrick replied, 'but of course that was before we sneaked him out of the hospital to go to the memorial service. He was just about unconscious when we got him back there. The doc prescribed bed rest and no visitors, not even family, for twenty-four hours.'

'How bad is he?'

Patrick shrugged. 'He's alive, thank God. He was shot at close range with a nine-millimeter submachine gun on full automatic. The bulletproof vest saved his life, but he's still in very serious condition. He's got a cracked sternum, damaged esophagus, and some internal bleeding in his left lung that might require more surgery. A bullet grazed off his left collarbone and lodged in his larynx, so they had to remove it . . .'

Jon Masters shrugged. 'No sweat. We can replace it.'

Patrick blinked. 'What?'

'His larynx. We can replace it with an electronic one. A lot better than the "buzzers" they use now. All internal microchip design. A pretty good duplication of human

145

speech – he won't sound like a dime-store wind-up robot. What else?'

Patrick looked at Wendy with surprise, and continued: 'Some broken ribs, his left shoulder's gone, his left arm might be destroyed, and his right leg was pretty badly injured . . .'

'We can fix all that too, Patrick,' Jon said confidently. 'Sternum, ribs, scapulas, collarbones – easy. Lightweight fibersteel bone, stronger than steel but lighter than natural bone. Won't set off any X-ray security machines like Brad's stuff did.'

'Sky Masters builds prosthetic devices too, Jon?' Wendy asked.

'Are you kidding? With Brad Elliott on the staff? That was one of his pet projects,' Jon replied. 'In typical Brad Elliott fashion, he buttonholed a bunch of folks on the board and badgered them into giving him a budget – he even got some grant money. He got a bunch of guys in R & D experimenting with prosthetic devices, and they've made a lot of progress. The arm and leg will be the most exciting. The prosthesis Brad Elliott had for his right leg is like a scurvy pirate's peg leg compared to the devices we've got now . . .'

'We're hoping he won't need any prostheses, Jon,' Patrick said. 'The docs can't say for sure, but they're hopeful. His leg isn't that bad – he might get seventy-five percent back. The arm, the shoulder . . . well, it's just too early to tell.'

'What I'm trying to say, guys, is don't worry about Paul,' Jon said. 'All he has to do is hold on to his will to live – and when I heard he actually talked you into putting him in a wheelchair and taking him to the church to be with his partner, I thought, This kid wants to live, all right! But I don't want to hear this "seventy-five percent" crap. Let me help him, and I can make him better than new. Like they said in the TV series, "We can rebuild him. We have the technology."'

'This isn't a TV series, Jon, and this is not an experiment. He's my brother, and it's his life we're talking about,' Patrick said seriously.

'I know, Patrick,' Masters said. 'We'll let the doctors care for him. He'll need surgery, rehabilitation, and time. But if he needs anything more, I just want to let you know that our company's resources are available to help him. I don't want you to worry.'

Patrick nodded in appreciation, though the anger still seething deep within him was almost palpable. 'Thanks, Jon,' he murmured.

They all fell silent, watching the baby sleep. Wendy finally broke the silence: 'Tell us, how did the BERP demonstration go?'

Masters lowered his eyes to the floor, then shrugged. 'No word yet. I thought it went really well. Awesome, in fact. The technology works perfectly.'

'Still got that glitch with the energy discharge through the material?' Patrick asked.

'Uh . . . yes, that problem's still with us,' Jon admitted after a rather lengthy pause. 'But good news: Your buddies Hal Briggs and that big scary Marine stopped by.'

'They did? Where are they?'

'They're out at McClellan. They said something about servicing their aircraft . . .'

'Yep,' Patrick said. 'McClellan does a lot of nondestructive inspection on aircraft, mostly high-value or classified aircraft like the stealth fighter, cruise missiles, stuff like that. Hal Briggs's Madcap Magician cell uses stealth C-130 cargo planes for infiltration and extraction missions, and only McClellan can do maintenance on the stealth skins.'

'It sounds as if their organization is interested in pursuing some of your ideas for additional applications for BERP.'

'Great,' Patrick said. 'But I still agree with you: This technology belongs on the world's airliners. We can sell it to the government or the military later.' Jon looked a bit uncomfortable, but said nothing.

'Where's Helen?' Wendy asked. 'Is she still meeting with the FAA and the airline reps, or is she back in San Diego?' Jon hesitated again. Patrick and Wendy looked at each other quizzically. 'Jon? . . .'

'She . . . she resigned,' Masters said sheepishly.

'She *what*?'

'She resigned. She's going to take her stock and go form her own company again.'

'What happened? Did you have an argument?'

'No!'

'Then what, for God's sake?'

'Oh, she was a little upset because I didn't play kiss-ass with the FAA and didn't show them the proper amount of subservience,' Masters said, a touch of his childish whininess showing in his voice. But he could see that neither Patrick nor Wendy was buying this, so he added, his voice almost a whisper, 'She might have been a little upset at *me* because I stayed on board the test fuselage during the BERP demo.'

'You *what*?' Wendy exclaimed. She looked at her husband, but to her surprise, he didn't seem angry. His expression was more like wonder, like curiosity.

But the baby seemed to register her tension, and started to squawk. She cradled him in her arms. 'I don't believe it!' she said. 'Jon, you could have gotten yourself killed. No wonder Helen was upset! And you televised the whole thing for the folks in Washington – my God, do you realize you could have forced them to watch your death if something had gone wrong? No wonder there's no word from the FAA or the airlines. They probably think we're all a bunch of crazies or scam artists.'

Wendy glanced at Patrick again. He was wearing his one-thousand-yard stare, the look he got when his mind was far away. 'Patrick?'

'I'll talk to Helen, ask her to stay on,' Patrick said, shaking himself from his abstraction. 'Jon, you've got to talk to the board and tell them what happened, then convince all the members to talk to Helen. Not only would we be losing our most valuable designer and engineer, but the information she could take with her might cost the company billions.'

Wendy was disappointed in Patrick's lack of outrage, but she decided to ignore it – he certainly had enough on his mind right now. Besides, Jon seemed genuinely sad and sorry at the prospect of Helen Kaddiri's leaving the company. It had always seemed to Wendy that Jon took delight in tormenting Helen, but perhaps that was just a facade.

Bradley was getting restless; it was time to feed him. Wendy pulled her hospital gown off her shoulders. Jon's mouth dropped open as the baby latched on and hungrily began to nurse. Wendy made no effort to cover herself. 'Whoa,' Jon said, snapping to his feet and looking embarrassed. 'I think that's my cue to exit.'

'It's okay, Jon . . .' But he was out the door in a flash.

Wendy smiled as she cuddled her son against her breast. 'Maybe you should go talk to him, Patrick,' she said. 'He seems pretty confused right now.'

'Good idea. He might have to apologize to Helen in front of the board, and we all know how good Jon is about apologizing – *not*.'

'Thanks,' Wendy said.

Jon Masters was standing in front of the window at the end of the hallway, looking lost. Patrick walked over to him, a slight smile on his face. 'You really didn't have to leave, Jon,' he said. 'She's only feeding the baby.'

'I know.'

Patrick's grin broadened. 'It's not a striptease, Jon.'

'I know, Patrick,' Jon insisted. 'It's just . . . well, I . . . I've never . . .'

'What? Never seen a woman breast-feed a baby before? Women breast-feed in public all the time nowadays.'

'Not that I've noticed.'

'There's nothing to be uncomfortable or embarrassed about. Sheesh, you sound like a prude or a virgin or something.' As soon as the words were out, Patrick regretted it – Jon's face turned beet-red. 'Ah, shit, Jon, I'm sorry. I didn't mean to poke fun at you.' But Patrick kept looking at him, hoping he would elaborate. That made him turn even redder.

'Hey, I've been busy . . .' he protested.

'Jon, you don't owe me or anyone an explanation,' Patrick said. 'If it's right for you, then it's the right thing to do.'

'You're darn right it's right,' Masters said emphatically. 'When it's right for me, it'll be the time. Not before. No matter what anyone says.' But he didn't succeed in convincing even himself. 'Who am I kidding? I'm a geek. Who'd want to go to bed with a geek?'

'Jon, you're not a geek – you're a successful business-man and scientist,' Patrick said. 'You're also good-looking, funny, spontaneous, and easygoing – not to mention stinking rich. All these years you've been too busy – too driven – to think about it. But when you're ready to be with someone, when you feel you want to share what

150

you've got with someone else, they'll come flocking to you, believe me.'

'They will?'

'Yep.'

'How do they know when I'm ready?'

'They don't know,' Patrick said. 'The difference is *you*, not them. They notice all the time, but you don't notice them. It's like when you have a baby – all of a sudden, you see babies everywhere. You *know* all those babies have been out there all this time, but now you notice them all because you're ready to notice them. It's the same with a mate. When you're ready, you start to notice.'

'And then?'

'And then you go about finding the right one.'

'Well, how the heck do I do that? How do I know which one is the right one?'

'You trust your instincts and you be yourself, Jon,' Patrick said after a moment's consideration. 'Like attracts like. If you stay true to yourself, the ones most compatible with you will be drawn to you. After that, you begin the process of discovery. You learn more about them over time. You find yourself thinking about them. You're comfortable with them. You just know. They become more important than anything – work, sleep, eating, everything.'

'I don't get it,' Jon said. 'How? There's gotta be a way you really know . . .'

'There isn't, except you listen to what your head and your heart tell you . . .'

'You mean sex, right?' Jon asked nervously.

'It's not just sex, Jon,' Patrick said. He couldn't believe he was having this discussion with Jon Masters, his boss, for Christ's sake, here on a hospital maternity floor! With all that had happened in the past three days, this was the last conversation Patrick expected to be having. He felt as if he were explaining the facts of life to a teenager – and then he thought, Hey, this is good practice for when I'll have this talk with Bradley a few years from now! 'Sex is great, of course, and it's a big part of the picture, but most of the time, it's not the whole thing. What most guys are looking for is a partner. Someone to share stuff with. You know what I mean?'

'No.'

'I think you do, Jon. You have a lot, but what you really want to do is share it with others. You do it all the time in your work: You invent stuff like BERP or these prosthetic devices, but then you turn around and you want to give it away. Well, it's the same with your life. You want to share your life with someone else – not because they asked for it, or because they need it, but because you want to share, and the other person has something to give that you like and need as well. It's a two-way deal.' Jon nodded, and Patrick could tell that at least some of what he said seemed to be making sense. 'It's about Helen, isn't it, Jon?'

'*Helen?* What about Helen?'

'You like her, don't you, Jon?'

'Helen is, like, maybe eight or ten years older than I am!' Masters retorted. 'What makes you think I like her?'

'Age doesn't matter, and you know it,' Patrick said. 'She's intelligent, she's independent, she's dynamic, and she's cute. I see how you act around her . . .'

'What? What are you talking about?'

'C'mon, Jon,' Patrick said with a reassuring smile. 'You try to play the boss, the head guy, but around Helen it's as if you're trying to impress her with how big a boss you can be. You don't act the same way around me or Wendy or the board of directors – you're either someone's best friend, or you ignore them. Except with Helen. You seem to want to get her attention all the time, prove to her that you're in control, unafraid, confident, and even cocky. If I didn't know better, I'd say you act like a schoolkid trying to impress a girl he's got a crush on.'

'Get outta town, Muck,' Masters said. He turned away from Patrick, scowling – but then his scowl broke into a grin. 'You think Helen's cute?'

'Of course,' Patrick said. 'She's kind of mysterious . . .'

'Yeah. Kinda exotic, forbidding, deep, dark, like those women in the *Kama-sutra* drawings,' Masters said, staring out the window as if he were studying her photograph. 'You know she used to be married?'

'I think I heard that somewhere.'

'Yeah. Married a guy from England after she got her doctorate from Oxford. They broke up after they got to the States. No kids.'

'Well, I'd say you have a problem now, because you made her leave the company and she sounds pretty pissed off at you,' Patrick pointed out. 'If you want to have a chance at telling her how you feel, you'd better . . .'

'Tell her how I feel? You mean, tell her I like her?' Jon asked incredulously. 'Are you nuts?'

'What are you talking about, Jon?' Patrick asked in surprise. 'You have feelings for Helen, but you'd just let her leave without saying anything to her?'

'What am I going to say to her? How can I tell her anything now? She'll punch my lights out! She'll strangle me! . . .'

'Jon, the worst defeat is never having tried to win,' Patrick said earnestly. 'You have got to tell her. Maybe she will punch you out. Maybe she'll still leave. Or maybe she'll surprise you and stay, and even love you back. Who the hell knows? But you've got to try.'

Jon's horror at the notion of even approaching Helen

Kaddiri was changing right before Patrick's eyes. Patrick watched him as he thought of speaking with her, of seeing her again. 'Maybe you're right. I should just go for it. Thanks.'

'Anytime,' Patrick said warmly, clapping him on the shoulder.

'Hey, Muck, you're pretty good at this. You and Paul ever talk like this?'

It was then that Patrick realized that he hadn't thought of his brother for what seemed like a long time, and the reminder brought Paul's awful, ugly situation crashing back. His smile vanished. He turned to look out the window.

'No,' he said somberly. 'He was a kid when I was in college – he was doing his thing, and I was deep into mine. When he was in high school, I was a new Air Force officer, working like crazy to be the best; when he was in college, I was away at Dreamland. Besides, he was always busy with outside activities – class president, sports, parties, always on the go. But it's funny – we hardly ever speak to each other but we know each other pretty well. It's like we're connected somehow.'

'It must be cool to have a brother,' Jon remarked.

'If you ever need a brother, Jon, I volunteer,' Patrick said. 'I was never a very good big brother with Paul, but I do my best.'

'Thanks, Muck. You as my brother – Brigadier General Patrick S. McLanahan, my big brother. Cool. That makes me little Brad's uncle, doesn't it?'

'It sure does.'

'Very cool.' Jon put his arm around Patrick's shoulder, and they stood there for a while, trying to reset their lives and shelter each other from the chaos around them. Jon turned for the elevators. 'I gotta get going. I'll stop in and say good-bye to Wendy and Bradley first . . .'

'One sec, Jon,' Patrick said. 'I want to ask you something.'

'Sure.'

'About the BERP demonstration. You actually sat in the test fuselage when those explosives were set off?'

Jon rolled his eyes. 'Not you too, Muck? Are you going to chew me out too? You think I'm crazy too?'

'No, no, it's not that,' Patrick protested. Jon looked at him, puzzled. Patrick turned away, obviously wrestling with an important question. 'I wanted to know . . .'

'Know what, Patrick?'

Patrick hesitated for a long moment, then asked, 'Were you afraid, Jon? When those explosives went off, were you afraid?'

Masters was surprised – not that the question itself was unusual, but that it was coming from Patrick McLanahan, whom he considered to be one of the bravest and most heroic persons he had ever known. 'Umm . . . actually, Patrick, to tell the truth, no, not at first. I guess I didn't even think about it. I knew BERP would work, and I knew it would impress the FAA and the airline pukes if I stayed inside the test article when we blew it up, to show that BERP works. I thought it would be the ultimate testimonial – I was putting my ass on the line to show that BERP worked.'

He shook his head and his eyes grew wide as he recalled the moment the explosives were set off: 'But I'll tell you, Muck, when that first charge went off – whew, I nearly peed my pants. The second blast, when BERP set off the explosives, was even worse. The third blast – well, I thought I was going to die, plain and simple. That deck rolled up under me like a big carpeted steel bubble. When they say thrown around like a rag doll, boy, I know what they mean by that now!'

'But you weren't scared? You sat in that fuselage with a hundred and fifty pounds of TNT under you, enough to bring down a large building, and you weren't afraid?'

'I know it sounds like BS, Muck – but no, I wasn't afraid,' Jon said. 'I pressed that button with no problem whatsoever. And you know what?'

'You'd do it again,' Patrick interjected. 'You'd do it a hundred times again. You'd sit right on a case of TNT to prove that your technology worked. You felt so strongly about yourself and what you had made that you were ready to risk your neck to prove it.'

'Right on. You understand. That's a relief – man, I was beginning to think I was crazy. If you would have told me how stupid I was for doing what I did, I'd be hurt.'

'Jon, you *were* stupid,' Patrick said. 'But sometimes we know we have to do something dangerous like that to prove a point. It only seems stupid to others.'

Masters nodded, glad to hear those words from Patrick. But there was obviously something more. 'What is it, Muck?' he asked. 'Why are you asking? Why are we talking about this?'

Patrick hesitated, then shook his head. 'Just some stupid ideas I have of my own,' he said. 'It's nuts.'

'Nuts? You? Hardly. You're the most level-headed, intelligent, calculating, no-nonsense, pragmatic guy I've ever known. What do you have in mind?'

'Nothing. Forget about it.'

Jon decided to drop it. 'When I spoke with Hal Briggs and Chris Wohl when they came by after the demo,' he said, 'they said ISA is very interested in some of the BERP applications you've been drawing up – the Ultimate Soldier ideas. They want to see a demonstration as soon as possible. I've spoken to the board, and they approved a development-funding package. You've got your green light.'

'Great!' Patrick exclaimed. 'It'll probably mean BERP goes black, Jon. I know we had other ideas for BERP, much more altruistic ones . . .'

'Hal convinced me there's plenty of time to deploy BERP in the civil markets,' Jon said. 'But the money he's talking about was too difficult to ignore.'

'But BERP going black will create a security nightmare since we've already demoed the process for the airlines and the FAA,' Patrick pointed out.

'Hal promised help there too,' Jon responded. 'His team has got to lay low because of what they did getting the EB-52 Megafortress out of Guam – beating up on those Navy security guys apparently ruffled a lot of feathers. Hal figured having Madcap Magician provide security for us while we put together an Ultimate Soldier prototype will work out well for everyone concerned – we get top-quality security, and they hang out in an out-of-the-way place until the heat blows over.'

'Great,' Patrick said, finding himself enthusiastic for the first time in several days. 'I can get started right away, while I help Wendy with the baby and watch over Paul as he recuperates. I might need a little more personal time, but I don't think I'll need paternity leave . . .'

'Take all the time you need, Patrick. Hell, after all that's happened lately, I'd approve a year's leave if you asked for it.'

'I don't need that much – only some leeway if I think Wendy, Paul, or Bradley needs me,' Patrick said. 'But thank you. It means a lot. We might consider moving the program office to McClellan Air Force Base or to our facility at Mather . . .'

'Way ahead of you, Patrick,' Masters said. 'I've already got that approved. We take over the old alert facility at Mather this week. The Ultimate Soldier program office will be set up there, with full security.' Then he hesitated. He could see that Patrick's mind was elsewhere again, some kind of scenario or plan being developed, analyzed, changed, and tested in his head at warp speed. 'You're going to start something, aren't you, Patrick? You're going to go out looking for some ass to kick.'

Patrick looked at Jon with his cold steel-blue eyes and said, 'I want to destroy those bastards who killed those cops and hurt Paul, Jon. I don't want to arrest them or defeat them or punish them. I want to annihilate them. I know we have the weapons and the technology to crush them, and *I want to do it*. Tomorrow. Right now.'

Jon felt as if Patrick had been screaming at him, although his voice had been no more than a deep, dangerous-sounding whisper. 'Jeez, Muck, this doesn't sound like you. Usually you're the one who wants to hold back, look at the situation, formulate a strategy, you know, all that "Plan the flight then fly the plan" shit you always say.'

'Not this time,' Patrick said. 'I want to find the men who did this to my brother, to my police force, to my city – to my damned home – and I want to crush them like insects. I'm going to use every bit of technology and firepower I can gather to do it. I'm going to do it whether or not I cooperate with the police or the city or the FBI or whoever else is involved.'

Jon looked at his friend, stunned. He had never seen Patrick so angry, so determined, so . . . bloodthirsty. He had seen him after crises that had ended in tragedy, yet he had never come unglued. Now, he seemed *possessed*.

'What do you want me to do?' Masters asked. 'What do you want from me?'

'Everything,' Patrick said. 'Access to everything. All your reconnaissance and surveillance gear. All your computers, your networks, your communications systems, your aircraft, your satellites. All of your weapons, your sensors, your prototypes, your manufacturing facilities. Most of all, access to you. These bastards who attacked in the city were soldiers, not ordinary robbers. I'm going to need every bit of modern weapons technology I can get to bring them down.'

Jon swallowed hard. 'You can't have it,' he told Patrick, shaking his head.

Patrick nodded, hurt in his eyes but steely determination on his face. 'I understand, Jon—'

'Let me finish, Muck,' Masters interjected. 'You can't have any of it unless I can help you.'

'*What?*'

'*I* want to help you,' Masters repeated. 'I always feel left out when the fighting starts, by Washington or the Pentagon or whoever's in charge. I don't want to be left out this time. If we fight, we fight together. You tell me what you need and I'll get it for you – but I want to be there with you when the shooting starts. A piece of the action. That's all I want.'

Patrick hesitated. What he had in mind was outrageous enough for him to question whether *he* could take it on, much less involve Jon Masters in it. Jon had no idea how dangerous it could be – hell, Patrick had no idea how dangerous it could be.

But the call to battle was still sounding in his ears; he could still hear the twin bagpipes at a triple cop funeral. Patrick had no idea what was calling Jon Masters or what danger awaited them both, but nothing was going to stop him now.

'Agreed,' Patrick said, holding out his hand. 'We work

together. I'm not even going to tell you how dangerous this will be. But whatever happens, we do it together.'

Instead of shaking hands, Jon embraced his new brother. 'Very, very cool. When do we start?'

'We start immediately,' Patrick said. 'It's time we collect some intel on the enemy.'

Special Investigations Division Headquarters, Bercut Drive, Sacramento, California Friday, 26 December 1997, 1832 PT

The sign on the outside of the cluster of one-story warehouselike buildings said City of Sacramento Public Works, Department of Highways, but Patrick knew that there were other offices located there. At six-thirty that evening, there was only one other car in the parking area outside the building, and it was farther down on the north side. The occupied space had a sign that read Reserved – No Parking.

Patrick got out of his car just as a man was leaving the building. 'Captain Chandler?' he called out from several paces away. The man watched Patrick approach him but must have decided he was no threat – his right hand stayed casually tucked in his pants pocket as he walked toward his car. But when Patrick got closer, he could see under the glare of a nearby streetlight that Chandler had pulled his suit jacket back, allowing free access to the pistol on his belt. He reached the passenger side of his car as Patrick came up, with the car between them. But he simply unlocked his passenger-side door and threw his briefcase on the right front seat, casual but cautious.

Things were clearly still very tense in Sacramento.

Every cop in town acted as if he had a big red bull's-eye painted on his forehead.

Captain Tom Chandler was wearing a very nice brown double-breasted suit and tasseled loafers – a clean-cut, professional-looking guy, more high-powered executive than street cop. 'What can I do you for, sir?' Then he recognized Patrick. 'You're McLanahan, aren't you? Paul's brother? I met you at the Sarge's Place the night of the shooting, and at the hospital when you got in the chief's face.'

'That's right,' Patrick said. 'I want to talk to you.'

'Concerning?'

'The attack on my brother. Who was responsible for it. I want some information on the investigation, and I want it now.'

'You're *demanding* information?' Who the hell did this guy think he was? Chandler tried to put a brake on his rising anger. 'I'm afraid there's nothing I can give you, Mr McLanahan.'

'But you're the commander in charge of the Special Investigations Division,' Patrick said. 'I heard SID would be in charge of the investigation.'

Chandler looked worried – clearly he didn't like Patrick's knowing he was the man in charge of SID. The Special Investigations Division of the Sacramento Police Department was the most prized, the most high-profile, and the most secretive in the entire department, second only to the Patrol Division in importance. SID encompassed three permanent offices – Intelligence, Narcotics, and Vice – along with several task forces that were assigned it as funding and necessity dictated, such as Asset Forfeiture, Interdiction, Counterinsurgency, Antiterrorism, and Gangs. Although Chandler officially reported to the deputy chief in charge of the Investigations Division, he

161

frequently met directly with the chief of police, the city manager, the city council, and the mayor, giving him extraordinary power and access. Being the commander of SID was generally regarded as an essential stepping-stone to the chief's office.

Then Chandler figured it out: the Sarge's Place. That's where McLanahan must have picked it up. He decided to be affable. 'Ah yes, the Sarge's Place,' he said. 'I used to go there when I was a sergeant. We used to bullshit about ongoing investigations all the time over a few brews. I'll bet that place is full of cops ready to give you all kinds of information about the shootings.' He had guessed right. A couple of hours ago at the Shamrock, a dozen cops had come in after first swing's shift change, congratulated Patrick on chewing out the chief on local TV, and volunteered information on the Sacramento Live! shootings. 'Unfortunately, I can't offer you any information, and I caution you on relying on rumors and guesses you might hear at the bar.'

'Yeah. Everyone's "cautioning" me but no one's telling me anything,' Patrick said. 'My brother is in critical condition in the hospital after being shot with a damned MP-5 along with three other cops, and three guys are dead. But none of the families have been told a thing. Is this the way the city is going to handle this situation? How would it look for me to go to the TV stations and tell them the city isn't briefing the families on the status of the investigation, that you're leaving us completely in the dark?'

Chandler slammed the car door, walked around to the other side, and got right in Patrick's face. 'I respond well to threats, Mr McLanahan, but I guarantee you it won't be a response in your favor. In fact, I get downright disagreeable. Tell me, sir, is that what you want right now?'

Chandler saw McLanahan tighten his jaw and square his body toward him. Was he going to get into a fight with this guy? His mind was turning over scenarios in rapid-fire succession when, to his surprise, McLanahan just . . . crumpled. His shoulders sagged, his arms went limp, his head drooped, and his knees looked rubbery. Was this some kind of sucker-punch ruse? An astonished Chandler, ready to defend himself, heard the guy sobbing! Here was this guy, short – probably no more than five eight – maybe two hundred pounds, but solidly built, like a wrestler or rugby player – and shit, he was actually crying! Paul McLanahan had quickly gotten a reputation of being a tiger who could handle any situation with calm and control – he certainly proved himself at the Sacramento Live! shootout – but obviously his guts didn't run in the family.

'Jesus – c'mon, Mr McLanahan, it's all right,' Chandler said soothingly, but not moving any closer. This might still be a sucker punch, although the guy really looked like he was losing it big-time.

'I'm sorry, I'm sorry!' McLanahan said hoarsely through his muffled sobs. 'Nothing like this has ever happened before. After my father's death, I was so afraid that Paul would be next. Our mother's had to be sedated, she was so upset. Paul could lose his arm. Oh God, I don't know what to do! I don't know what I'm going to tell our mother . . .' He was babbling, his conflict and fears pouring out all at once. Chandler thought the guy was going to collapse right on the hood of his car. For crying out loud, mister, get a grip!

Well, he couldn't very well leave him sobbing like a baby in the parking lot. 'Come with me, Mr McLanahan,' Chandler said. He led him to the side door, which had a sign on it that said No Admittance – Door Blocked – Use

Main Entrance and an arrow pointing toward the Highway Department door. Chandler unlocked the door, then stood in the doorway and blocked it until he could shut off the burglar alarm, using the keypad. Inside was a reception area furnished with a couple of desks, several file cabinets, and what looked like a communications center setup; there were two banks of radios, computer terminals, and several recharger stations for handheld radios.

McLanahan followed Chandler past the reception area and down a hallway. They passed an empty conference room with a sign on the open door reading Classified Briefing In Progress – No Admittance, continued past some more doors and a break room/exercise room, and finally came to a door marked Captain. Chandler punched a code into a CypherLock keypad, unlocked the door, asked McLanahan inside, and offered him a seat. Patrick rested his elbows on his knees and hung his head while Chandler crossed behind his desk and sat down.

'I'm sorry to be keeping you like this . . .'

'Forget it,' Chandler said. 'Can I get you something? A soda? Iced tea?' From the odor he detected, McLanahan had already had a few pops before he came over here – he'd obviously needed something to ratchet up his courage enough to mouth off at a cop. What was it with these burnouts? Past glories gone, living vicariously through their smarter, more successful siblings. Good example of white trash.

'You cops don't keep anything stronger in the desk?' McLanahan asked, trying to sound jokey but coming across as hopeful.

'I'm afraid a bottle of rotgut in the desk drawer went out with Philip Marlowe and *Kojak*,' Chandler replied, his disgust with Officer McLanahan's brother growing by the minute.

'A soda would be fine then,' McLanahan said. Chandler went out to the break room. When he came back a half minute later, McLanahan had an elbow on the desk, one hand hiding his eyes and his other hand wrapped around his mid-section as if he was going to be ill.

Chandler returned to his seat behind the desk. 'I'm sorry, Mr McLanahan, but there's very little I can tell you about the investigation concerning the shootout,' he said. He prayed McLanahan wouldn't get sick in his office or start crying again. 'I wish there *were*.'

'Have you made any arrests yet?'

'No, not yet,' Chandler replied. 'But we have some strong leads. The helicopter the gang used to make their getaway from the Yolo Causeway was seen at Placerville Airport shortly after the incident, so we're concentrating our search in the foothills. This is highly confidential information, Mr McLanahan. Please don't share it with anyone, not even your mother.'

'All right,' McLanahan said. His voice sounded as if it was going to break again. 'I'm afraid we won't have the money to care for Paul. The doctors say he could lose his left arm, that he might not ever be able to talk again . . .'

'If it's any comfort to you and your family, Paul will receive full medical benefits,' Chandler said. 'If he can't return to work, he'll receive full disability benefits. That's his entire base salary, tax-free, for the rest of his life.'

'Disability?' McLanahan gasped. Chandler saw the guy's face grow pale, then green. 'You mean, they'll classify him as disabled?'

'I didn't say that, Mr McLanahan . . .'

McLanahan abruptly got to his feet. 'I . . . I think I'm going to be sick,' he gasped.

Oh, for Christ's sake, Chandler cursed to himself. This

165

guy is a total wussie. 'Out the door, to your left, make a right, three doors on the left, men's room.' McLanahan nodded, clutched his midsection as if he had a cramp, then rushed out of the office. He was gone for several minutes. Chandler finished a cigarette, then got up to find out if the guy was all right. He ran headlong into him coming back to the office. 'Are you all right, Mr McLanahan?'

'I . . . I'm so sorry . . . jeez, I'm so embarrassed,' McLanahan said. 'This whole horrible tragedy has got me all tied up in knots.'

'Perhaps you'd be better off if you cut back on the booze a little,' Chandler told him sternly. 'Your family could use your support, and you're in no condition to give it to them like this. Go home. We'll keep you posted on the progress of the investigation.'

'Can I visit you again? Can I get some regular updates? Anything?'

Oh *please*, Chandler thought – the last thing he needed was this guy hanging around the SID offices. Although the location of SID headquarters was hardly super-secret-classified information – the radio station about a block away used to make joke announcements when the Narcotics officers were mounting up and getting ready to go on a search-warrant operation – no one who worked here wanted civilians hanging around. Especially boozehounds like this guy.

'Look, Mr McLanahan,' Chandler said patiently, 'you're the brother of a member of this department. I'd hate to turn you away, but I will if you insist on stopping by here often and asking a lot of questions that no one except the chief can answer.'

'But why?' McLanahan whined.

'Because if any unofficial, inaccurate information got out about those killers, it could create a panic in this city,'

Chandler explained. 'If you call first, and promise not to take advantage of the privilege, you can come down and I'll give you any information I can, which I can tell you won't be much due to the sensitive nature of this case. Do you understand?'

'Yes,' McLanahan said in a low voice.

'You might actually get all the information you need from the press,' Chandler said.

'But it would really help if I—'

'I think your time would be better spent with Paul and your family,' Chandler said sternly, hoping McLanahan would wuss out again. But it looked as though he was standing fast on his request, so Chandler added, 'But if it'll make you and your mother feel better, give me a call before you come down, and we'll meet and talk. Fair enough?'

'Yes,' McLanahan said. He extended a shaky hand; Chandler found it cold and clammy. 'Thank you. I'll get out of your hair now. And I promise I won't bother you unless it's absolutely necessary.'

'Fine. Good night.' Chandler couldn't wait to hustle this guy out the door. He watched him until he climbed into his car and drove off. He probably shouldn't have let the guy drive, and he prayed he didn't get into an accident.

Paul McLanahan lived in a roomy three-bedroom apartment over the Shamrock Pub on the waterfront in Old Sacramento, the one in which Patrick and Wendy had lived earlier that year, before they moved to San Diego. Patrick had decided to move his family into the apartment until Paul was out of the hospital. He had already converted the second bedroom into young Bradley's nursery, complete with crib, changing table, and a chest of drawers filled with baby supplies and clothes, and he had fixed up the master bedroom for Wendy and himself. He wanted to duplicate their Coronado apartment as best he could so she would feel as much at home as possible. When Paul was closer to being discharged from the hospital, they'd move into a short-term executive apartment, and once he was on his feet, they would go home to San Diego.

The third bedroom, Paul's office, had been converted too – into a command center. That was where Patrick found Jon Masters when he arrived back from the meeting with Chandler. 'How's it sound, Jon?' Patrick asked.

'Loud and clear,' Masters replied. 'Good job. Where did you plant them?'

'Captain's office, break room, bathroom, and conference room,' Patrick replied.

'Good. Listen.'

Jon hit a button on a tape recorder on the desk, and they heard Tom Chandler's voice, a little scratchy but clear enough, talking on the phone to his wife: 'I'm on my way now, hon. I was going to be home twenty minutes ago, but the brother of that rookie cop that was hurt in the shootout? He showed up in the parking lot . . . yeah, that's the guy, the one on TV. Big tough guy on TV, right? He demands information, and then when I tell him where to stick it, he starts blubbering all over me. What a baby. I think he was drinking too. So I sat him down and held his hand for a few minutes. Then he almost blows lunch in my office. I finally told him to go home and sleep it off. So I'm on my way home . . . okay . . . great . . . sure, I'll pick it up on my way back. See you in a few, hon. Bye.' And the line went dead.

'I caught another few minutes of Chandler making basketball and Super Bowl bets with a bookie – that information might come in handy someday,' Jon added.

'Kinda dumb, making bets on an office phone that's probably being monitored, but I guess you don't need to be a genius to be a police captain.' He shut off the tape recorder, rewound the tape, then set it to auto, which would automatically record any conversations picked up by the electronic eavesdroppers. 'You should be an actor, Muck,' Jon remarked with a smile.

'I thought I was going to barf after swishing that whiskey in my mouth,' Patrick said. 'What's the range of this system?'

'Only a couple of miles,' Masters said. 'We're at the extreme range limit now. I want to put up a relay on a nearby building – the one adjacent to his would be the best, but it can be anywhere within a half mile of the bugs. The relay will increase the range to about ten miles. Then we can pick up the transmissions from anywhere. Maybe we can launch a NIRTSat constellation and get the taps downloaded to us anywhere on the continent.'

'I don't think we'll need to do that,' Patrick said with a wry smile. He knew Jon Masters's appetite for technological overkill; he'd do it with the least bit of encouragement. 'Will they be able to detect the bugs?'

'They might,' Jon admitted. 'They're voice-actuated, which means they don't activate unless there's sound in the room. Most times when security teams sweep a room for bugs, they try not to make any noise, so the bugs should be undetectable, but they do carry a very low power level all the time in standby mode so there's still a chance a bug sweeper might detect it. The bugs store information in packets, then microburst the packets out in irregular intervals to try to confuse a passive detection system. So it'll be harder to detect the bugs when they transmit too.'

Masters paused, then added, 'But it's usually not bug

169

detectors that find the bugs, Patrick. Most times it's just plain ol' good counterintelligence work. Someone will eventually realize information is getting out. A local PD might not have sophisticated detection or backtracing gear, but all they need to do is plant false information to try to ferret out a snooper. Once you start using the information you get, your days of bugging offices will be numbered. They'll just swoop down on you one day and it'll all be over. Might be hours, might be days.'

But Patrick wasn't listening. 'Thanks, Jon,' he said. 'I'll start monitoring the taps, and I'll talk to you after we get some worthwhile information. Once we find out who the enemy is, we'll plan our next move.'

Masters nodded. Patrick McLanahan always knew what he was doing. 'Wendy called while you were out,' he said. 'They're going to keep her in the hospital for another few days to be safe. They'll discharge her on the thirtieth.'

'Good,' Patrick responded.

Jon was startled. '"Good"?'

'That'll give us more time to come up with a plan,' Patrick said. 'I want to move before the police do. I want first shot at these dirtbags.'

'Are you trying to hide this from Wendy?' Jon asked incredulously. 'You're not going to tell her what you're doing?'

'Not now,' Patrick said. 'Not right away. I want to formulate a plan of action before I tell her. I'm hoping they'll catch the terrorists before too long, and if I tell Wendy about this, it'll upset her for no reason.' Jon shook his head at this backward logic, but decided not to argue the point. 'I'm off to Mercy San Juan. I'll be back later.'

He knows what he's doing, Jon Masters told himself for the third or fourth time that evening. It's Patrick

McLanahan. He always has a plan. He always knows what he's doing. Always . . .

'Here's what we have so far, Chief,' Captain Tom Chandler began. He was giving an update briefing to the chief of police, Arthur Barona, as well as to the deputy chief of investigations and the deputy chief of operations of the city of Sacramento. 'It's not much:

'The private security company for the Sacramento Live! complex has still not heard from one of the guards who was on duty the night of the shootout, Joshua Mullins. He's being sought as a material witness, but we're looking at him as an accomplice to the robbery. Mullins is ex-Oakland PD, resigned while under suspension. Lived in an apartment downtown, but the place was cleared out. He has some ties to local biker gangs, so we did some interviews in some of his hangouts. No one's seen him.'

'I want him,' Barona said. 'Send out his description on the wire to all state agencies. He's probably headed back to the Bay Area.'

'Already out,' Chandler said. 'We're setting up surveillance on local biker bars – the Bobby John Club, Sutter Walk, Posties, a few others, as much as manpower allows. Sacramento County is cooperating with us in setting up surveillance on biker bars in the county, and we're working with Yolo, Sutter, Alameda, San Francisco, and Placer County DA's to gather intelligence on biker bars in their jurisdictions.

'Our informants are giving us information on a guy

171

that Mullins may have been in contact with who goes by the name of the Major. No information yet on who he is, where he comes from, what he's up to, or why he might have wanted Mullins. The sergeant in charge at the Sacramento Live! shootout says he thinks he might have heard one of the gunmen shouting in German or some other language after being hit, so we might be looking at a foreign terrorist group. I've been in contact with the FBI and Interpol, but we don't have much to go on except their outfits, weapons, and MO. All of the gunmen hit during the shootout were carried off.'

Chandler stopped. Barona looked at him in surprise. 'That's it, Chandler? That's all you have?'

''Fraid so, Chief.'

'Tom, that's completely unacceptable,' Barona said angrily. 'It's been over a week and we haven't got an arrest in sight. We need to get some action going on this case or the city's going to eat all of our lunches for us. Now get me some arrests.' The chief stormed out of the conference room.

Chandler ran his fingers through his hair in exasperation. 'Anything else I can frustrate you gents with today?' he asked.

'We know you're stretched to the limit, Tom,' said one of the deputy chiefs. 'Put everybody you got on finding this Mullins guy. We'll see about tossing some uniforms your way to ease the workload. What do you have in mind?'

'I've already wasted the next two months' overtime budget,' Chandler said. 'Any more and I trash the entire next quarter's budget almost before it starts. I've got enough manpower for round-the-clocks at just two places. Posties and Sutter Walk are private clubs; Bobby John's is public. Mullins's more likely to turn up at one of the private clubs.'

'Then put your surveillance units there,' the deputy chief said. 'Then as soon as you can, get someone on the Bobby John Club too. We'll send out a notice to watch sergeants to circulate Mullins's description to their patrols. But if he has any brains at all, he's long gone out of this town. We'll try to juggle some money around for overtime, but don't count on it. Do the best you can, Tom.'

'Do the best you can,' he says,' Patrick McLanahan mused as the recording fell silent. 'How can he? Every one of those cops in the entire division is already working twelve-hour shifts.'

'Yeah. We've heard talk about that "Major" guy before. He's starting to sound like the mastermind of that robbery.'

'Sure does,' Patrick agreed. He paused for a moment, then added: 'We need to bug the Bobby John Club. No telling how long it'll take for SID to start up surveillance there.'

'Sounds good to me,' Masters said. 'You know anything about the place?'

'Just enough to stay away from it,' Patrick replied. 'Having a drink or shooting pool with the bikers at the Bobby John Club used to be the cool thing to do in high school, but I never went. They certainly were never any competition for the Sarge's Place's business.'

'Well, Chandler said it was a public bar,' Jon pointed out. 'I suppose you have as much right as anyone to go in there. If there's a million motorcycles parked out front, we'll just go in another time.'

Bobby John's had been around a long time in the Del Paso Heights neighborhood of Sacramento. Several big Harleys were parked out front. The wind had kicked up, and it felt raw and blustery, heightening the sudden sense of dread Patrick felt as he opened the door and stepped inside, four surveillance bugs tucked away and ready to go.

Although his family had run a bar for years, Patrick never liked going into them – especially strange bars, in lousy parts of town, at night, and alone. Even when it's dark outside, there's always a time after walking into a bar when your eyes aren't adjusted to the gloom within. Patrick felt vulnerable: Everyone inside could see him, but he couldn't see them – or danger coming. Tables and people were shadows. He felt on display, naked, a stranger invading unknown territory – it was like walking into a cave knowing there were bears lurking inside. He could run headlong into the guy he was looking for and never recognize him.

Patrick decided to withstand the heads turning toward him, the stares, and the muffled comments, and just wait in the doorway until his eyes adapted. If his target tried to leave, at least he'd have a chance to intercept him. Standing there, he realized that to the hostile watchers he must look like some kind of Wild West gunfighter, but there was no other solution.

As his eyes adjusted, the details of the place grew clearer. It was small and narrow. The bar stretched almost the entire length of the wall to the right. Two pool tables dominated the room to the left, with a few tables and chairs scattered around. At the far side of the bar, a dark hallway led to the back of the building. Patrick could hear loud voices from back there – more patrons, he guessed. A biker was leaning against the hallway wall; he appeared to be guarding a private room. Patrick saw a shaft of light briefly illuminate the hallway and guessed there was a back door at the end leading to the alley-way in the rear.

The walls were covered with posters of naked biker women, motorcycles, and other typical barroom art, plus some not very typical stuff: a collection of Confederate States, Third Reich, neo-Nazi, White Power, and Ku Klux Klan flags and posters. Patrick even recognized several national flags, including Russia, the Afrikaner flag of South Africa, the flags of the old East Germany, the Ukraine, and Belarus. No doubt about the theme of this place.

Just plant the bugs and get the hell out, Patrick told himself. One at the bar – it should be able to pick up male voices for ten to twenty feet in all directions – one at a pool table, one in the bathroom, and one in the meeting room in back if he could get there.

There was no place open at the bar, so Patrick stood at the waitresses' pickup station. The bartender ignored him. He could make out the faces in the bar now. Some glared at him with undisguised hostility. To his surprise, a few others seemed to be looking at him with fear, as if he might be a cop coming to arrest them or a leg-breaker coming to collect a debt. Most paid no attention. It was dim enough for no one to notice as he attached the first listening device under the edge of the counter.

But his luck didn't last for long. The huge, fat, bearded biker on the stool nearest him looked up from his beer. 'Hey, sweet cheeks, the faggot bar's down the street,' he growled drunkenly. Patrick ignored him, enraging the biker. He reached out and gave Patrick a shove hard enough to push him back a few feet. 'I said, the faggot bar's down the street, rump ranger. Hit the fucking road.' Patrick decided he'd better move to a table back behind the pool tables, but the biker looked as if he wasn't going to let him go.

'Hey, Rod, knock it off,' the bartender ordered. He put another beer in front of the guy, who promptly forgot about McLanahan. The bartender scowled at Patrick. 'This ain't no tourist stop, sport,' he said. 'What do you want?'

'Use your bathroom?'

'The john's only for paying customers.'

'I'll take a beer.'

'Five dollars.'

'Five?'

'You just bought Rod there a beer too.'

Patrick put a five on the bar. 'Where's your bathroom?'

'Coffee shop two blocks down,' the bartender snapped. 'Now get the fuck out.'

Patrick tried to keep his voice steady. He had dealt with a few badasses at the Shamrock Pub, mostly college kids after a few too many or lowlifes trying to pick a fight with a cop. He'd thought he could handle this one. Nevertheless, he was already starting to feel events spinning out of control, and he had been here only a few moments. 'I'll take that beer and then hit the road,' Patrick said.

The bartender reached down to the cooler behind the bar, pulled out a bottle of beer, and put it on the bar. But before Patrick could take it, a gloved hand reached past him and picked it up. Patrick turned and saw a guy not much taller than he was, with long brown hair, a beard, a leather jacket, and dark, dead-looking eyes, standing right beside him. Another biker, this one with a shaved head and a goatee, had crossed behind the guy and was standing to Patrick's right.

'Who are you, asshole?' the first guy asked, taking a swig of beer.

'I'm nobody,' Patrick replied. 'Just came in to get a beer and take a piss.'

As the guy nodded, Patrick's world exploded right in his face. A boot kicked the side of his left knee, sending him crashing against the bar in pain and buckling him halfway to the floor. He heard the sound of shattering glass, and a second later felt the jagged edge of a broken beer bottle against his throat, drawing blood. A hand with the grip of a steel vise clamped around the back of his neck, hauling him up tightly against the bar. Several more bikers had come over, surrounding them.

'You know, you're one stupid motherfucker coming in here like this,' the guy with the beer bottle said. 'You think you can just march in here and feed us a line of crap? Who the fuck are you, pretty boy?'

'I'm nobody,' Patrick repeated. 'I came in for a lousy beer!'

'Fucking liar!' the biker shouted. By now, Patrick was looking for the first opportunity to make a run for the door, but the hand squeezing his neck tightened still more, and he cried out in pain. 'Talk!'

'I'm the brother of one of the cops that got shot downtown,' Patrick said through the sheet of pain slicing through his head.

'What in hell do you want?' Patrick kept his mouth shut. The grip tightened even more, and he thought he was going to pass out. 'You better talk, candy-ass, or I'll snap your neck in two!'

'Mullins,' Patrick murmured against the pain and terror. 'Mullins set up that robbery. I want him.'

The grip on his neck didn't subside, but Patrick was relieved to hear some laughter behind him. 'What do you want to do with him?' asked a different voice.

'I want to question him about the Major, about who staged that robbery,' Patrick gasped out, trying to struggle free. 'And then I want to kick his fucking ass.'

There was another round of laughter. 'Hey, pretty boy, that's good,' the guy with the broken beer bottle said. 'But today's not your lucky day. Because Mullins's got hold of your neck right now, and in a minute he's going to take you in back. If you're lucky, he might just fuck your white-bread ass and carve his initials in your face. But if he takes what you just said personally, you're going to end up in a garbage truck on your way to the dump.'

Patrick strained to see over his shoulder. The guy holding his neck was the biker with the shaved head and the goatee. He didn't look like the police intelligence description at all. Even his eyebrows were different; he had colored them with mascara, like the goatee. 'Hey, cop-killer,' Patrick said. 'You and me, motherfucker. Let's see how tough you are without your army.'

Mullins laughed in his face, then shoved his head down onto the bar. Patrick turned his head just in time to avoid a smashed nose. 'Killing those cops was business, asshole,' Mullins said. 'But fucking you up is going to be personal.'

'The cops have this place under surveillance,' Patrick said through clenched teeth, his voice shaking. He couldn't believe how scared he felt right now. 'They've photographed everyone coming in and out of this place. If I turn up dead, all of you'll be murder suspects.'

'Maybe so, asswipe,' said the guy with the bottle. Patrick

felt hands going through his pockets. They took his wallet and some cash, but thankfully missed the tiny quarter-sized listening devices. 'But you'll still be fuckin' dead. Now you're going to tell me how you found out about Mullins and the Major, and you'd better talk or I'll—'

'Hey! Look at this!' A different biker ripped something from Patrick's clenched right hand. He held up a tiny object – what looked like a short, thick cylinder, white, with a round rubber tip. Patrick's arms were twisted behind his back, and his head was jerked upward.

'What is this, asswipe?' the guy with the beer bottle yelled, holding the object up to Patrick's face. 'This looks like a rubber bullet, or some kind of shotgun shell. You better tell me, asshole, or Mullins there will twist your fucking head off!'

'Let me go!' Patrick shouted. The tiny shell was his last hope, Patrick thought grimly, his only chance to escape. He had hesitated to use it and he was going to pay for it now. 'I'll get out of here. I won't come near this place again. Just let me go.'

The guy with the beer bottle gave Patrick a backhanded swat across the face, drawing blood from a cut lip. 'I guess I'm just going to have to beat it out of you, sport . . .'

'It's a nerve-gas grenade!' someone said in a loud voice. They turned to see a figure standing in the doorway in front of the rear hallway. Jon Masters was holding up an object like the one taken from Patrick. 'Just like this one. Twenty-five-millimeter cartridge, filled with a half a milliliter of Novichok, a V-class anticholinesterase agent that will paralyze you in about eight seconds. It uses a nitrogen propellant so it will spray the gas through the entire room and easily disable just about everyone here. Here – catch!' And he threw the grenade as hard as he could across the bar and against the wall.

The grenade burst with a loud *pop!* and exploded into a thick white cloud of gas that spread throughout the entire room with astonishing speed. It looked like an instant fog. It tasted of acidity, like sulfur, burning the eyes and throat.

The bikers scattered. Patrick dropped to the floor – but not because of the gas. It burned and it tasted funny, but it wasn't disabling. He was free! 'Jon!'

'Here, Muck, he—!'

As Patrick looked up, the biker with the beard ran headlong into Masters coming toward him and grabbed him. The broken beer bottle flashed in the foggy air. 'Jon!' Patrick screamed. He struggled to his feet, trying to catch the biker's arm as it lashed out, but he was far too late. 'Jon!' he screamed again.

Masters's jacket was ripped open across the chest, and Patrick saw blood spilling out of the wound. Jon's hands clutched at it ineffectually, blood seeping through his fingers. 'Patrick?' he said weakly.

'C'mon, Jon, let's get out of here!' But he was frozen in place. Patrick grabbed him around the waist and half-pulled, half-dragged him outside. He felt someone clutch at him from behind, and in a fit of rage he swung back with his right hand. He connected with thin bone and tissue, and they heard the assailant yelp as he let go.

With Patrick half-carrying Jon, the two men made their way down Del Paso Boulevard to a Safeway supermarket parking lot, where a rented Dodge Durango sport-utility vehicle was waiting for them. 'Okay, we can slow down now,' Patrick said, pulling Jon back.

They turned around. Half a dozen motorcycles were roaring down Del Paso Boulevard, and they saw men running down the street. 'We gotta get out of here now, Patrick!'

180

'Calm down,' Patrick said, wiping blood from Jon's jacket front. 'Running will only attract attention now. Try to stay upright, Jon. Just a few more steps. Hang in there, brother.'

'I . . . I need help here, Patrick . . .'

'C'mon, let's keep going. You'll be okay.' They forced themselves to walk casually toward the car. Patrick was out of breath by now, gasping from the effort of supporting Jon and the aftereffects of the adrenaline pumping through his veins. When police cars zoomed past, the two of them stopped to watch, just like normally curious onlookers.

Patrick helped Jon into the passenger seat and examined his wound under the dome light. It was a deep cut, but it was not bubbling or pumping, which meant that it had not pierced a lung or a major blood vessel. He eased off Jon's jacket, pressed it against his chest, used the seat-belt shoulder harness to anchor it tightly in place, then got into the driver's seat and started the engine. They pulled out onto the street. More police cars were racing in toward Bobby John's, and fire trucks too, but there was no sign of pursuit. They drove away from the scene, careful not to speed. They got on the Interstate 5 freeway through the downtown area, then merged onto the Highway 50 freeway heading east, away from the city.

Neither man spoke for a long time. The enormity of what happened had silenced them. Finally, Patrick said, 'Thanks for getting me out of there.'

'You're welcome, Muck,' Jon answered. 'But it's your contingency plan that did it – those wireless mikes so I could listen in and carrying those practice bomblet target markers.' Patrick pressed Jon's hand against his chest to staunch the bleeding further. This was one contingency he hadn't planned on.

'Man, that was a close call,' he said shakily. 'Jesus, was I scared. I thought I was going to die. All I could think about was Wendy, and Bradley, and how we would die in the middle of a filthy beer-soaked barroom floor. God, Jon, I'm so sorry . . .'

'It's not your fault, Muck,' Masters said. 'It was a good plan.'

'But I didn't mean for you to get hurt . . .'

'Hey, c'mon, Patrick. I'm not an innocent bystander or your blind, faithful sidekick. If I didn't think I could stay safe, I wouldn't have gone in there.'

'But you could've been killed . . .'

'Nah. They were just trying to scare us. But we don't scare that easy, do we, General?' But Patrick could see through all the bravado that Jon was badly shaken. God, when he saw that blood spurt out of Jon's wound . . . Patrick had seen death before, had even *caused* death before, but not at this close range, and never so personally as this.

He wasn't going to allow him to ever go into harm's way like that again, Patrick decided. Jonathan Colin Masters was more than one of America's truly great scientists and engineers, he was his newfound brother. There was no way he could allow him to risk his life in Patrick's personal vendetta.

Sky Masters, Inc. had rented office and hangar space at Sacramento-Mather Jetport when it was obvious that the McLanahans were going to be in town for a while, and they had planned that it would be their destination after the bugging operation. They took the Mather Field Road exit from eastbound Highway 50 a few minutes later and drove around the east end of Mather's eleven-thousand-foot runway to the former Strategic Air Command alert facility, now converted into a secure research and development site. The facility still had its twelve-foot-high chain-link fences topped with barbed wire and fitted with cameras and intrusion sensors; the vehicle entrapment and inspection area; the two-story underground building, complete with offices, conference halls, and a kitchen; and the alert-aircraft parking area, now with two large jumbo-jet-sized hangars at the south and west sides. A right turn past the deserted weapon-storage area, down a long road, past the alert-crew picnic grounds, and they were at the front gate of the old B-52 bomber alert facility, where B-52 bombers and KC-135 aerial refueling tankers once sat nuclear ground alert, ready at any time to fight World War III.

Sky Masters security personnel were on duty, and one of them, Ed Montague, confronted Masters and McLanahan at the vehicle entrapment gate. 'Evening, Dr Masters, General McLanahan. How's Dr McLanahan and the new . . .' He stopped short when he saw Jon's blood-soaked jacket. 'My God!' He looked at Masters, whose face was as white as a ghost. 'What the hell happened, sir?' He waved to the guard shack, and they admitted the Durango into the entrapment area.

'Ed, we're going to need a first-aid kit,' Patrick said. Montague retrieved a large kit from his office, and administered first aid while the vehicle and Patrick were searched. Once inside, they brought Jon to the security office, where they spent the next twenty minutes cleaning and dressing the six-inch gash that the biker had carved in Jon's chest.

'Want me to call the sheriff's department, General?' Montague asked.

'No thanks, Ed,' Patrick replied as he put a clean shirt on. 'But we do need that industrial-medicine doctor we hired, Dr Heinrich I think his name is, to look at Jon. Get him on the phone and get him out here, and make sure he brings a surgical kit.'

'I'm fine, Muck,' Jon protested.

'It doesn't look too bad, but I want him to look you over anyway,' Patrick said.

'Doc's on the way,' Montague reported a few moments later.

'Good,' Patrick said. 'If he releases you, Jon, Ed will take us back to Paul's apartment in a security vehicle. Ed, then I want you to get the Durango cleaned up and turn it back in to the rental company first thing in the morning. I want you to take care of it personally.' The security officer nodded that he understood.

They met the doctor twenty minutes later. He was needed. Heinrich, who had been hired as a consultant and to over-see safety and medical operations at the temporary Mather operations plant, put a total of forty stitches in Jon Masters's chest, fifteen of them internal dissolving sutures. Despite plenty of local painkillers Jon passed out three times during the procedure – the first time when he saw the doctor threading the first needle. He was like a little kid at the doctor's office, flinching at the slightest touch and muffling a cry whenever the needle pierced his skin.

Not that he didn't have good reason. The bottle had cut about a quarter of an inch into his chest at the initial blade-impact point, piercing two inches of muscle, and then slashed another four inches of skin across to his shoulder, leaving bits of glass along the hideous gash. The doctor had to lay open the deepest part of the wound to work on it from the inside out. To Patrick, watching and at times assisting Heinrich, the wound looked so deep and so red that he swore he could see down to Jon's lungs. Heinrich prescribed antibiotics, a mild painkiller, and bed rest for the next three days, and sent them home.

Patrick felt devastated. Even worse than the hell of watching it was the recognition that he alone was responsible for the assault.

With Montague at the wheel, they headed for Paul's apartment downtown; it would be easier to watch over Jon there than in his hotel room. Police cruisers were all over the downtown area when they reached there half an hour later – it looked as if martial law had been imposed on the city. They were stopped at the intersection of I and Second streets. A sign read DUI Checkpoint – All Vehicles Must Stop. Two Sacramento police officers surrounded the car.

'Good evening, folks. We're conducting a routine check of all vehicles for compliance with underage – and impaired-driving laws,' the officer on the driver's side said as if reading off a cue card. The other officer shined a flashlight into the two faces in the backseat, the powerful beam easily penetrating the tinted windows. 'We won't take up any more of your time than is necessary. Where are you folks coming from tonight?'

Patrick noticed that the officer who spoke to Montague didn't stick his head right down close to his face so he could sniff for alcohol on the driver's breath, as was usual at most DUI checkpoints Patrick had encountered. Ed Montague noticed it too. Sensing the tension, he showed his retired-police-officer and licensed-private-investigator identification, including his concealed-carry permit. 'We're coming from Mather Jetport,' he explained. 'I'm escorting Dr Masters and General McLanahan home.'

The officer heard the name 'McLanahan' and stopped at once, recognizing Patrick in the backseat. 'Sorry to have bothered you, sir,' he said, and nodded to his partner to stop his flashlight probe. 'Have a good night.'

'No problem at all, officer,' Patrick said. 'What's going on?'

'Couldn't tell you, sir. Where are you folks headed?'

'Old Sac. Front and L.'

'The Sarge's Place.' The officer obviously recognized the address. 'I'll call ahead and make sure you're not bothered again – we have checkpoints set up all over. Have a good evening.'

The other checkpoint they encountered did a cursory inspection, probably so it wouldn't seem as if they were exempting anyone, then waved them through. Ed helped Jon into the apartment, then wished them good night and departed. Jon was moving about fairly well, but Patrick was close at hand to help him as he undressed and got ready for bed.

'Jon, I am so sorry for this,' Patrick said for the umpteenth time. 'I promise you, this will never happen again. Never.'

'Never? As in, you're going to stop this scheme of yours?' Jon asked. Patrick's eyes fell to the floor. Jon went on: 'Patrick, you know I agree one hundred percent with what you're feeling, with your hurt and pain and desire for revenge. I sure as heck would want a piece of that biker guy, especially now that he's given me forty stitches and messed up my good looks.'

Patrick smiled at his boss, new brother, and friend.

'But taking on these guys is crazy,' Jon continued. 'You have no choice but to turn just as dirty, as low-down, and as psychotic as the worst of those jerks in order to beat them. Is that what you really want?'

'What I want is to destroy the punks who killed those cops and tried to kill Paul,' Patrick said.

'How, Patrick? We carried some fake nerve-gas grenades tonight, hoping we could scare our way out of trouble. But these guys don't scare too damned easy.' To hear Jon Masters say even a mild cuss word told Patrick

186

how upset he was. 'What do we carry next time? A gun? I'll bet every guy in that bar had a gun. Do we carry bigger guns? Machine guns? Bazookas? What? How far do we take it?'

Patrick chose not to answer the question. 'If you want to help, I'll plan it so you won't have to come into a place or situation like that again,' he said. 'You'll be support only from now on. I don't want you in the line of fire.'

Jon looked bone-weary at that, as well as scared, but he nodded resolutely. 'I'll still help you, Muck,' he said. 'I agreed to help, and I will.'

Patrick sank into a chair in the corner of the bedroom, rubbed his eyes, and tested his nose, cheekbones, and jaw for any signs of fractures. 'Jon, I'm not going to hold you to that,' he said. 'I feel like I'm out of control, like I'm on a roller coaster. I can't control what I'm feeling. I want to lash out at those guys. I feel I have the power and the ability to do it. I don't want to sit by and watch while others fight my battles for me, especially the cops in this city that are hamstrung by politicians and bleeding hearts.

'But I'm doing it *wrong*, dammit! I'm not afraid for myself. I'm like you in that airplane fuselage – I know the danger, but I've got to do it. But then I think of Wendy and young Bradley, and how my son would grow up without a father if I died in that hellhole of a bar, trying to stop scum of the earth who can probably never be stopped.' He stopped and buried his face in his hands. 'Oh God, I don't know what the hell to do.'

The ring of the doorbell startled Patrick. I ought to have a gun, he thought. He went to the door. 'Who is it?' he called.

'Mr McLanahan? This is Captain Chandler, Sac PD.

I'd like to speak with you.' Patrick looked through the peephole and saw Tom Chandler holding his gold badge up to the lens.

A thrill of panic ran through Patrick. Had he been discovered already? He opened the door and let Chandler inside. He had no other officers with him. 'You're up late tonight,' Chandler said.

'We were working late, out at Mather.'

'You and another gentleman, right? Average height, thin build, short hair, looks like a teenager?'

'What's going on, Captain?'

'You know what's going on, Mr McLanahan,' Chandler replied angrily. 'You were at the Bobby John Club tonight, you and some other guy. Is he here?' Patrick was silent. 'You better answer me, Mr McLanahan, because in about three seconds I'm ready to bring the wrath of God down around your ears.'

'Yes, he's here,' Patrick answered.

'Is he hurt?'

'Yes, but he'll be all right. We had a doctor look at him.'

Chandler breathed a sigh of relief. 'You have any idea how stupid that move was, McLanahan? Do you? What were you two doing at that bar tonight?'

'Trying to get answers,' Patrick said. He decided to try his desperate-burnout-older-brother routine again. 'I'm just trying to find the ones who hurt Paul. I was just there to look around, listen, try to learn anything I could.'

'With a gas grenade?'

Patrick shrugged, averting his eyes. 'Hey, I'm not into guns or pepper spray. I had to do *something*.'

Chandler took a step closer and pointed a finger at Patrick's face. 'If I find out you're doing anything else on the streets in connection with the robbery, Mr McLanahan, I will toss your ass in jail for obstruction and interfering with a police investigation,' he said. 'No more, do you understand?'

'Yes. I understand.'

'You'd better.' Chandler paused for a moment, then said, 'Listen. For what it's worth – and only because your brother's a fellow cop – I'm going to tell you this. You will not repeat this to anyone, or I *will* lock you up. I wanted to let you know that two men who allegedly were involved in the Sacramento Live! shootout with the police downtown have been arrested. A third was found dead.'

'That . . . that sounds like great news, Captain,' Patrick said. 'Thanks for telling me. Do you expect more arrests soon?'

'Yes,' Chandler said. 'We'll let you know of any further developments. I'm going to remind you again that all this is classified information. I'm telling you this as a courtesy. Don't disappoint me.'

'I understand, Captain.' Chandler nodded and headed out the door.

Patrick went back to the bedroom and found Jon asleep; the painkiller had kicked in. Back in the living room he got out the listening-device recorder, eager to hear what had gone on at SID headquarters in the past couple of hours. The news was astounding. Two men had been arrested after showing up at a north-area clinic with broken legs and internal injuries, professedly from an auto accident. Both were German nationals and held valid work permits for Canada, but their injuries were not fresh and their story made the clinic staff uneasy enough to call the police. The nature of the injuries suggested they might have been the ones hit by Paul in the off-duty cop's squad car during the Sacramento Live! shootout, and the arrests followed.

The second part of the news was even more startling: Joshua Mullins had been found dead in the Sacramento River – shot execution-style. Patrick went back to the bedroom and woke up Masters. 'Well, it looks like Mullins's dead,' he told him, 'and two of the holdup men were arrested when they tried to get medical treatment.'

'Mullins? The guy that nearly killed you tonight is *dead*?' Jon looked very pleased. 'That sounds like good news to me, brother. Looks like the cops were on the warpath after all.'

Patrick nodded.

'So?' Jon went on hopefully, 'Does this change your plans now? What are you going to do?'

'I think, brother,' Patrick said with a satisfied smile, 'that I am going to bring my wife and son home from the hospital, then see to it that my brother Paul gets all the help and care he needs. And then I'm going to get on with my life and leave the police work to the police. I've seen enough to know I'm outgunned, outclassed, and just about completely clueless.' He got to his feet and stretched, relaxed and satisfied. 'Good night, Jon. I'm sorry for what I got you into tonight.'

'Don't be, Patrick. I'll be fine.'

'I'll take care of you, and then we'll get back to work,' Patrick said. 'We've got to get Helen back, go schmooze the FAA and the airlines into getting that BERP-development deal going again, and then knock Hal and Gunny Wohl's eyes out with the Ultimate Soldier system. I can't wait to get started.'

And he went out to the sofa bed in the living room and slept. Despite the pain from the battering he had taken, Patrick slept soundly for the first time in many days.

'I don't understand any of this,' said Bennie 'the Chef' Reynolds. 'First you send two of the Major's men to the hospital – and then you execute another one? What's the sense in that?'

Townsend smiled but did not reply. Bennie, Gregory Townsend, the former German soldier Bruno Reingruber, and several of Reingruber's men were at one of the Aryan Brigade's hideouts in the rural area of Sacramento County about thirty miles south of the city. The ranch house was in the center of a forty-acre parcel of land, surrounded by multiple fence lines and electronic security monitoring; police couldn't get within a quarter mile of the house in any direction without being spotted. It looked like a typical stucco house common in the hot, dry Sacramento Valley, but in reality it was a small fortress. The doors, hinges, and frames had been reinforced with steel to prevent all but a vehicle-mounted ram from breaking them down; booby traps were set up all around the ranch to warn of intruders; and the place had caches of weapons, equipment, and supplies enough for an extended siege or to equip a very potent strike team. Inside, it was more of a command center than a farmhouse. The kitchen had been set up as a communications center, and the dining room transformed into a conference room.

'It is simple, Mr Reynolds,' Townsend said. 'Major Reingruber's men fought with courage and skill and were wounded in battle. As distasteful as it is to turn any of our men over to the enemy, civilian medical facilities are far superior to our field hospitals and it became necessary that they receive the care they deserve.

'Mullins, on the other hand, disobeyed a direct order to

stay out of establishments and areas designated off-limits by myself and the staff. He was especially ordered not to make contact with any Satan's Brotherhood members or frequent any of their so-called clubhouses. He violated all of these directives. His capture could have jeopardized our entire operation. There was only one penalty suitable for his dereliction of duty and gross insubordination – death.'

Well, that certainly followed the pattern of this organization, Bennie said to himself. Townsend and Reingruber were ruthless when it came time to discipline their men. Reingruber's sergeants dispensed that discipline swiftly and painfully. Bennie had seen the German soldiers accept punishment like automatons, standing at attention while taking a blow to the stomach or a cattle-prod to the back. And if they failed to stay standing at attention or were a little slow recovering from their punishment, they got more of the same. Reingruber and sometimes Townsend himself presided over the discipline sessions, and always spelled out to the other soldiers the exact nature of the transgression for which the punishment was being administered. The converse was true too: If a soldier did well, even in a small way, they offered praise and congratulations almost to the point of effusiveness. Bennie hated to admit it, but it was challenging and rewarding to serve under these two. Their men were paid well, ate well, and trained and worked hard . . .

. . . Too bad they were murderous bastards who would kill any or every one of them if they felt the need.

Several minutes later, a lookout reported that pickup trucks were on the property. The announcements were followed by electronic warnings picked up by motion and seismic sensors – and woe to any sentry, Bennie knew, who didn't report an approaching intruder to Townsend or Reingruber before the sensors went off.

'Pickup trucks. Brotherhood,' a sergeant reported. 'Five in all.' Townsend and Reingruber nodded. A few minutes later, five Satan's Brotherhood members were admitted into the ranch house. They were thoroughly searched, manually as well as electronically, and a boxful's worth of weapons taken away from three of them. Typical Brotherhood, thought Bennie. Either the bikers actually thought Townsend wouldn't check them for weapons, or they thought that once he had found one or two, he'd stop looking.

The leader of the Brotherhood, Donald Lancett, did not show. Bennie had warned Townsend he wouldn't. In his place, Lancett had sent one of the local chapter heads, Rancho Cordova president Joey 'Sandman' Harrison, to represent the Brotherhood. If there was a right choice for this meeting, Harrison was not it. Sandman had been ousted as the president of the Oakland chapter of another outlaw motorcycle club, kicked out because he was so mean, so murderous, and spent so much time in prison. He hated the role of representative, envoy, or message boy; he hated foreigners; and he hated anyone who even considered trying to move in on his very lucrative east Sacramento drug territory. Clearly, Lancett had chosen him for today's meeting in order to get in Townsend's face and stay there.

Harrison's beady eyes scanned the room. He noticed the big bottle of Jack Daniel's sitting on a table in the corner, went over, opened it, and took a big swig. Townsend watched him with an ironic grin. 'Help yourself to a drink, Mr Harrison,' he said. Harrison belched, walked over to Townsend, and sent his hand down to Townsend's right hip. The holster he found hidden under the jacket was empty. 'I requested no weapons, Mr Harrison,' said Townsend. 'I kept my part of the bargain.'

'Good thing you did,' Harrison grunted. He took another pull at the bottle. 'So you're Townsend, huh? You the one who had to pull Cazaux's plug, right? You probably think you're hot shit now.' He turned to look at Bruno Reingruber. 'This the fucking German?'

'Major Bruno Reingruber, my deputy commander and senior officer.' Reingruber stood at parade rest beside and slightly behind Townsend, his square jaw held high, his chest inflated. When he heard his name, he snapped to attention and gave a Nazi salute.

'Heil fucking Hitler,' Harrison said, his voice filled with disgust. 'You guys are pretty, real fuckin' pretty. You must all be pretty stupid dumb-asses too.' Then Harrison's eyes rested on Reynolds. 'Hey Bennie, you tell your friends that if I ever catch your ass out on my streets again, you're dead.'

'I advise you to listen to these guys, Sandman,' Bennie said. 'They mean business.'

'Oh, I'm sure they do,' Harrison said, talking to Bennie but facing Townsend. 'I'm sure the Angels, the Riders, the wetbacks, and the slopes meant business too. But they're not in control around here either. The Brotherhood is in control of this state.' He shook his head. 'You're a piece of work, limey. First you kill two of our brothers and steal our chemist, then you off one of our recruits, then you set up meetings and want to be the big boss. We don't need no foreigners trying to muscle in on our operation.'

'You are going to produce more methamphetamine in one month than you previously could in a year, Mr Harrison,' Townsend said. 'Easy, safe, and guaranteed to make us all rich in a very short period of time.'

'And this deal includes hosing off a couple of cops, Townsend?' Harrison asked angrily. 'You cost us plenty with that holdup of yours.'

'I see Mr Mullins felt free to talk about our operation with you,' Townsend said, his confident smile dimmer. 'It seems our decision to terminate Mr Mullins's miserable life was a sound one.'

'Mullins was a Brotherhood recruit, asshole,' Harrison said. 'He was one of ours, and you knew it. He gave us plenty of access to businesses, warehouses, and events. Killing him was like attacking all of Satan's Brotherhood. You owe us.'

'Mullins was a weasel who would sell his mother to make a dollar,' Townsend said angrily. 'He did the Sacramento Live! job for five thousand lousy dollars. How much was he supposed to pay you out of that?'

At Harrison's blank face, Townsend added, 'Or perhaps you didn't even know he was doing this inside job? The latter, I suspect. So Mullins was cutting the Brotherhood out of your share of his action. He was a lying, cheating bastard. You should have had him killed long ago.'

'Maybe so, Townsend. But I got one message for you shitheads: Get out of town now, and stay out, or we'll fuck you over real bad. Capish?'

'Aren't you even interested in my proposal?' Townsend asked.

'Does it involve you making or selling meth?'

'Fortunately, no,' Townsend said dryly. 'Manufacturing drugs, especially methamphetamine, seems to be a very hazardous undertaking, best left to you and the Mexicans.'

'If I find out you doin' any deals with the fuckin' Mexicans, asshole,' Harrison said, 'I'll kill every last one of you myself. Your hard-ass German friends won't be able to help you one fucking bit.'

'Major Reingruber would like nothing better than to go to war with you, the Mexican cartels, the police, and anyone else who opposes us,' Townsend said sternly, affixing his one good eye squarely on Harrison. 'But I prefer cooperation to war. Since we have somewhat similar political and cultural views, shall we say, we prefer to work with you.'

'But you got Bennie the Chef,' Harrison argued. 'That means you're cooking. You cook crank in Brotherhood territory, you die.'

'Mr Reynolds is serving as my technical expert and adviser to streamline methamphetamine production,' Townsend said. 'We have devised a means to manufacture meth in vast quantities with safety, security, and profitability in mind – but we do not wish to do it ourselves. We will leave that up to you. Care to see what we have in mind?'

By this time, Harrison's curiosity had taken over. He nodded his assent. Townsend led the way into the barn behind the house, which was guarded by four heavily armed soldiers. There, lined up like barrels in a brewery, were twenty black steel drums, mounted on small trailers. 'What the hell's this, Townsend?' Harrison asked. 'This your idea of a joke?'

'This is the core of my new operation, Mr Harrison,' Townsend replied. 'These are meth hydrogenators.'

'Say what?'

'Hydrogenators,' Townsend repeated. 'Thirty gallons each, with built-in agitators, pressure monitoring, leak detection, air filtration, and product-purification apparatus. The trailer contains a power unit and vacuum-pressurization equipment.'

Harrison still looked confused, so Bennie clarified it for him. 'Big bucks, Sandman. We're talking two, three hundred thousand dollars a day from each one of 'em. Fully portable, fully self-contained – you can practically set one of these things up in your backyard next to your barbecue grill and no one would know you're cooking. It's as easy to use as a Suzy fuckin' Homemaker oven.'

That kind of information Harrison understood. He walked over to one of the units and ran his hand over the dull black steel surface. 'Cool. I'll take 'em. How much?'

'They're not for sale, Mr Harrison,' Townsend said. 'But you can have them. All of them, if you like.'

Bennie looked thunderstruck. Harrison's bearded face broke into a wide grin. 'Wrap 'em up, limey.'

'All I ask is that you pay my organization a modest sum of one thousand dollars a pound for every pound you produce,' Townsend said. Harrison's grin vanished as he tried to do the math in his head, so Townsend did it for him: 'That's twenty percent of the wholesale price but only eight percent of the retail price per pound. You can buy the chemicals and catalysts from us if you wish, or you can supply your own. We even provide the security for each unit, courtesy of the Aryan Brigade.'

'But I get the cookers for free?' Harrison asked incredulously.

'Absolutely free,' Townsend said. 'Each unit reports every time a hydrogenation cycle is completed.'

'Does this asshole ever speak plain English, Bennie?' Harrison complained.

'What he means, Sandman, is that the unit can tell us when somebody cooks up a batch,' Bennie said, falling back into his prerehearsed script even though he was still in a state of shock. 'The colonel gets paid by the pound you cook up. Just so everyone stays on the up-and-up, the unit tells us how much you cook.'

'Precisely,' Townsend replied. 'The unit can tell us how much was made, and when. Each cycle can produce up to thirty pounds of product. You pay us thirty thousand dollars every time you make a full batch, and whatever else you earn is yours to keep. We even provide maintenance for the units – if they ever break down, we will fix them without charge. We will become the Microsoft of the methamphetamine trade.'

'The what?' Harrison grunted, still running his hands lovingly across the surface of the hydrogenator.

'Never mind,' Townsend said. 'Is it a deal, then?'

Harrison was clearly impressed. 'I'll take this deal to the chief,' he said. 'I think he'll like it.'

'Good,' Townsend said. 'Then you'll be off.' Again Harrison looked at Townsend as if he were speaking a foreign language, but when Townsend headed for the door, he understood the tour was over.

Bennie Reynolds was absolutely speechless. When the five Brotherhood bikers had left, he turned on Townsend and asked, 'What the hell are you doing? You're going to *give away* thirty hydrogenator units? We just spent a quarter of a million dollars building these things! They're worth millions of dollars a month!'

Townsend shrugged off the protests. 'It's a good deal for us as well as the Brotherhood,' he said. 'Of course, we'll give a few to the Mexican gangs and a few of the other biker gangs as well. After all, Satan's Brotherhood isn't the only gang in the West.'

'You're going to do this deal with other gangs? That's suicide! If the Brotherhood finds out, they'll go to war.'

'I don't think there'll be a war, Bennie,' Townsend said with a confident smile. 'There's too much money to be made. We have another ten hydrogenators to build, and then we can start scheduling training sessions for each chapter that will get one. My plan is to distribute and train all of the Brotherhood and Mexican-gang chapters in one night, all throughout California, Nevada, and Oregon. Let's get started, shall we?'

Helen Kaddiri glanced briefly at the good-looking guy who opened the hotel door for her before she walked out toward the docks. She had been born and raised in San Diego, but she hadn't been down to the waterfront in years. It was much more crowded than she remembered, but still just as beautiful. The weather was perfect, dry and mild, with just enough of a breeze to bring in the salt air but not enough to require a coat.

She allowed herself to enjoy the weather and the scenery for a moment before her mind returned to the situation at hand: Namely, what in hell did Jon Masters want? His phone call the day before yesterday was the first she had heard from him since the BERP demonstration up in Sacramento. The rest of the board of directors and every one of the senior officers and managers had either spoken or met with her, pleading for her to return – everyone but Jon Masters. Pig-headed as usual.

She had tossed a grenade on their picnic by having her attorney draw up a proposed three-million-dollar settlement agreement. The deal included cashing in some of her preferred-class stock, converting the rest into common stock, and transferring ownership of some of the patents and other technologies still in development that rightfully belonged to her. She wasn't looking to gut the company, although she certainly could if she wanted.

'Helen?' She turned. To her astonishment, she realized that the young, nicely dressed man who had held the door open for her was Jon Masters. It was practically the first time she had ever seen him in anything but jeans and tennis shoes. His hair was neatly trimmed and combed in place, and – this was almost too much to believe – he was wearing a *necktie*! She never imagined he would even own one, much less wear one!

'I . . . I'm sorry, Jon,' she said, completely taken off guard. 'I didn't recognize you. You look so . . . so . . .'

'Normal?'

Helen smiled. 'Something like that, yes.' That was unusual too – Jon never made fun of himself. Just the opposite, in fact – he thought he was God's gift to the Western world. Helen looked down at her slacks, casual blouse, and plain jacket. 'I feel underdressed standing next to you, Jon, and that's certainly something I never thought I'd say. It feels weird.'

'I'm very glad you're here, Helen,' Jon said. He held out a bouquet of red roses. 'Happy Valentine's Day,' he said, looking into her eyes.

A puff of wind could have knocked Helen Kaddiri over. She accepted the flowers with a stunned expression. The most he had ever given her in the past was a hard time. 'Thank you,' she said in a tiny voice. 'I'm flattered. Now tell me: Who are you, and what have you done with the real Dr Jonathan Colin Masters?'

'No, it's me, all right,' Jon said. 'We're this way.' He motioned toward the marina.

'We're not meeting in the hotel?' said Helen. 'I've asked my attorney to join us. He'll be here in a few minutes.' Jon looked confused. 'I assumed this was in response to my settlement agreement, Jon.'

'No. I hadn't planned on bringing any lawyers,' Jon said. 'You can bring him if you want, but it might spoil . . .'

'Spoil what?'

'Spoil . . . the mood,' he said, a little embarrassed.

'The *mood*?' Helen retorted. She had been intrigued at first, even titillated by what Jon was doing; now she was getting angry. This sounded like yet another Masters prank. But it wasn't the fact that he was pulling another prank that made her angry – it was her sense that this *wasn't* a prank, and then realizing that she had deluded herself. 'Jon, what is this? What's going on? If this is some kind of gag, so help me, I'll brain you!'

'It's not a joke, Helen,' Jon said. 'Follow me.'

'Where are we going?'

'It's a surprise,' Jon said. He led her down the steps to the hotel marina. A man in a white waiter's outfit smiled, bowed, and opened the wharf security gate for them. 'I'd ask you to close your eyes,' Jon said, 'but the thought of *you* closing your eyes on this dock makes *me* dizzy.'

'Jon, where are we going?' Helen asked irritably. 'This is crazy. If we can't discuss our differences like rational human beings, we should just . . .'

'Here we are,' Jon said. He had stopped beside the most beautiful yacht Helen had ever seen. It had to be sixty-five feet in length – it looked as big as a house. A waiter in crisp white was standing in the aft cockpit, ready to help them board, and opposite him was a violin player. Up a short ladder was the covered aft deck, on which Helen could see a table laid with a gleaming white tablecloth and place settings for two. The yacht's engines were running, and dock crews were holding the lines, ready to get under way.

'Jon, what in the world are you up to?' Helen asked.

'We'll talk on board,' Jon said. 'Let's go.'

'Where are we going?'

'Oh, I thought we'd go to Catalina for the weekend,' Jon said. 'Depends on the weather. Or we can go to Dana Point, or Mexico . . .'

'*Mexico?*' Helen asked. 'Jon, what *is* all this?'

'Helen, we can talk on board,' Jon said again. He looked up and down the wharf. Attracted by the soft violin music, a small crowd of gawkers had stopped to watch, which was making Jon uncomfortable. 'Your chariot awaits, madame.'

'We're not going anywhere until you answer me,' Helen demanded. 'What's going on? Is this another one of your elaborate pranks? If it is, I haven't got time for any of it.'

'This is no prank, Helen,' Jon said. His face was beginning to show the dejection of someone realizing his grand plan maybe wasn't going to work. 'This is a night out for both of us. A chance to be together, to talk, to have a nice dinner, to see the coast at night.'

'No one else?'

'No one else.'

'What makes you think I'd fall for any of this, Jon?' Helen asked.

'"Fall" for this? There's nothing to "fall for," Helen,' Jon responded. 'We have a lot to talk about. There's so much I want to tell you . . .'

'This isn't about the settlement agreement, about the buyout?'

'No, it's not about any of that,' Jon replied.

'Well, what then?'

'It's about . . . it's about you and me, Helen. About us.'

'Us? There is no "us," Jon.'

'I want there to be an "us," Helen,' Jon said sincerely. 'Can't we go on board?'

'Talk to me right now, Jon,' Helen insisted. 'What are you saying?'

Thankfully, the crowd had started to go on its way. The violin player stepped inside but continued to play. 'Helen, I sensed something in you during the BERP demonstration up in Sacramento,' Jon said. 'I don't know if I'm right or not, but I know what I sensed. And when I thought about it, thought about *you*, I felt really good.'

'You mean . . . you mean, you like me?' Helen asked, sounding perhaps a bit more incredulous than she meant. 'As in, *romantically* like me?'

Jon took her hands in his. 'Yes, Helen. Romantically. I want to see if there's anything there, you know?'

Helen paused, looking into Jon's eyes. This was too much to believe, too much even to grasp. Was this really happening? She became acutely aware that he was holding her hands, and she took them away.

'Jon . . . Jon, this is very nice,' Helen said awkwardly. 'I've never been treated to anything like this before. But . . .'

'But what?'

'We are in the middle of a multimillion-dollar buyout negotiation, Jon,' Helen said. 'You're paying three thousand dollars a day in legal fees to resolve our differences . . .'

'Well, that's over,' Jon said. 'Whatever you want, you can have. Full rights to the patents, full ownership of the unpatented designs you created, full market value of the stock, and your stake in the underlying Dun & Bradstreet value of the company in cash or in percentage of profits. You deserve it; you should have it.'

Helen Kaddiri was flabbergasted. 'Two months of legal negotiations ended just like that?' she asked. 'What's the catch?'

'There is no catch,' Jon said.

'I don't have to go on this boat with you? I don't have to have dinner with you? I don't have to sleep with you?'

Jon gave her a mischievous grin and shrugged. 'Well . . .'

'You are a piece of work, Jon, you really are,' Helen said angrily. 'You can't browbeat me with a bunch of lawyers, so you decided you're going to try to woo me to sign your buyout deal?'

'No! That's not it at all!' Jon said. 'The deal's already

been done. I signed your last counteroffer four hours ago.'

'You did?'

'Yes,' Jon said. He took her hands again. 'So maybe we can consider this a celebration cruise, or perhaps a reconciliation cruise?'

Helen looked at Jon, at the yacht, then back into his eyes. 'Are you serious, Jon?' she asked. 'You just . . . want to spend time with me?'

'Yes,' Jon said. 'Maybe more, in the future, if you want. But let's make this the first step, shall we? I've got so much to tell you, so much I want to share with you.'

'Oh, Jon,' Helen said disapprovingly. She let his hands drop again, not as sharply as before but still a rejection. 'I guess I'm just not a dinner-on-a-yacht girl.'

Jon motioned to the upper deck, where a small rigid-hulled inflatable boat was waiting on davits. 'They've got a cool little Nouverania up there we can use.'

'It's not that,' Helen said after a little laugh that made Jon's heart do a somersault with hope. 'Jon, after all we've been through together, this is just not the way I imagined it ever happening. I never expected to be . . . courted, I guess. And I certainly never expected to be . . . to be swept off my feet. Especially by Jonathan Colin Masters.'

'Well, believe it,' Jon said. 'C'mon, Helen. You know me. I'm a kid trapped in a man's body. I don't know how anything is *supposed* to work. I know how it works in my head, and I just do it. I follow my head and my heart because I don't know any other way. A yacht ride to Catalina . . . well, that seemed to be the way to do it.'

'Not with me, I guess, Jon,' Helen said. 'Thank you. But I can't go. I can't do this. You and me, we have too many bouts under our belts. It would be hard for me to believe that this cruise would be anything else but a prelude to . . . heck, I don't know. Throwing me overboard.'

'Helen, give me a chance,' Jon said. 'I've finally realized that I'm happier with you, that I care about what you think and feel about me, that I want to be with you. I don't know if there's anyone else in your life right now, but I definitely know that I want to be in it. I . . .'

Helen shook her head to stop him. 'I'm sorry, Jon. You've given me a lot to think about. I wish I could go with you. But I can't. Good-bye.'

All sound seemed to evaporate as Jon watched Helen turn and walk down that wharf. The gentle throbbing of the twin diesels was gone, the soothing sounds of the violin, the soft creaking of nearby boats straining on their lines. The only thing he could hear were her quickly fading footsteps, walking out of his life for good.

Sacramento-Mather Jetport, Rancho Cordova, California Wednesday, 25 February 1998, 0717 PT

Jon Masters stepped into the middle of the largest hangar inside the security development center at the old alert facility. It was empty except for those looking on: Lieutenant Colonel Hal Briggs, Gunnery Sergeant Chris Wohl, and Dr Carlson Heinrich, Sky Masters, Inc.'s staff project medical consultant. Briggs and Wohl were dressed in their typical black battle-dress uniforms, each with sidearms, but the others were in business suits. Masters and Heinrich were both wearing wireless earset commlinks so they could talk with the test subject.

Briggs looked a little puzzled. 'We still on for the test, guys?' he asked. 'ISA wants a report yesterday. Where's Patrick? This is his show, right?'

'We're ready, Hal,' Jon said. 'Patrick is standing by.' He folded his hands in front of him, suddenly looking like a schoolboy giving a talk about his summer vacation to his classmates.

'It is believed,' Masters began, 'that gunpowder was invented by the Chinese in the seventh century A.D. When it was brought to Europe in the fourteenth century, it changed the face of an entire continent, an entire society. The first man-portable gun used in anger was used in the fourteenth century by Arabs in North Africa. It too changed the face of the entire planet – that first gunshot truly was 'the shot heard round the world.'

'Despite all of the technological advances we've made in the past seven hundred years, the gun, and the tiny pieces of metal it propels, continues to change lives, change humankind. It is simple technology hundreds of years old, but still deadly, still lethal. When you think about it, it's pretty frustrating: Our company builds all kinds of cool weapons technology, but the best-equipped soldier is usually killed by essentially the same weapon used by a nomadic guerrilla desert-fighter centuries ago.

'The soldier of the twentieth century may have better training, better education, and better equipment, but when it comes right down to it, the infantryman of the fourteenth century would probably immediately recognize him,' Masters went on. 'Their tactics, their mind-set, their methods for attack, defense, cover, concealment, movement, and assessment all remain the same. All that, guys, changes right now. Colonel, Gunny: Meet the soldier of the twenty-first century.'

They heard a tiny *woosh!* of compressed gas echo inside the empty hangar – and then, as if out of nowhere, a figure appeared before them, dropping out of the air from the shadows in a corner of the hangar. The figure landed on its feet and bent into a crouched position, then slowly rose and stood silently before them.

It wore a simple dark gray bodysuit, resembling a diver's three-mil wetsuit; a large, thick helmet; thick gauntlets and boots; and a thin, wide backpack. A helmet covered the entire face and head, molding smoothly out to the shoulders. It had a wide visor, with extensions over the visor containing other visual sensors that could slide into place over the eyes. The helmet appeared tightly sealed from the outside; a breathing apparatus was obviously necessary.

For a long moment, all of them stood and looked at the dark-clothed figure, saying not a word. The figure made one turn, showing itself from all sides, then stood quietly. 'He looks like that dude from *Sea Hunt*,' Hal Briggs finally quipped, 'except shorter and chubbier. Brigadier General McLanahan, I presume?'

Patrick nodded stiffly. 'That's right, Hal,' came an electronically enhanced voice.

'You sound like the voice coming through the clown's head at the drive-up window of a fast-food joint,' Hal said with a grin.

On a secondary comm channel, one that Briggs and Wohl could not hear, Patrick said, 'Jon, I felt that power surge again when I landed.'

'Then I recommend we terminate the test,' Dr Heinrich responded immediately on the commlink. 'The problem hasn't been fixed.'

'Patrick?' Masters asked. 'It's your project, and you're wearing the gear. What do you say?'

Patrick McLanahan hesitated, but only for a moment: 'Let's go on,' he said. 'The shock wasn't too bad, and I feel fine now.'

'I recommend against it,' Heinrich said.

'We're on schedule and on budget right now,' Patrick snapped, his voice much more impatient, even agitated. 'Any delays would be costly. We go on.'

'So how do you take a dump or a piss in that getup, Patrick?' Briggs asked.

'You finish the mission and go home,' Patrick responded flatly.

'Touchy, touchy,' Hal said. 'I don't mean to crack wise, guys, but it's not exactly what we were expecting. How did you fly in here like that?'

'A short burst of air compressed at three thousand psi,' Jon replied proudly. 'The soldier of the future doesn't run or march into combat anymore – he *jumps* in. The soldier can jump about twenty to thirty feet vertically and a hundred and fifty feet horizontally. The power unit he wears can recharge the gas generators in about fifteen seconds.'

'It'd be fun to watch a squad of these dudes *hopping* into battle,' Briggs commented. 'How long does the power unit last?'

'The specs you gave us called for durable man-portable power units to last a minimum of six hours – ours can last eight,' Jon Masters replied. 'Ours can be recharged by any power source available – a twelve-volt car battery, a home electrical outlet, a commercial two-twenty line, an aircraft auxiliary-power unit, or even by solar photo-voltaic cells mounted on the back. If all power is lost, just drop the backpack, and the suit becomes a standard combat-ready insulated suit and battle-ready helmet. Patrick?'

To demonstrate, Patrick reached up to hidden clips on his shoulders and unfastened the backpack power unit, then passed it around to Briggs and Wohl. It resembled an oval turtle shell, contoured to match the body; it was about an inch thick and weighed about twenty pounds. The helmet's oxygen visor automatically dropped open when the power unit was detached. Patrick pressed a tiny switch under the left edge of his helmet, and the helmet unlocked and popped open; he took it off and let Briggs and Wohl look it over.

Briggs was interested in the design and features of the helmet but Chris Wohl was more interested in Patrick. He looked at him carefully and asked, 'Hot in that getup, sir?'

'A bit.' Patrick was sweating, and his face looked a little red, like a football player who had just finished a difficult series of plays and run in from the field. Heinrich handed Patrick a squeeze bottle of ice water, trying to check him over discreetly at the same time. Wohl's face showed uncertainty, but he remained silent. When the helmet and backpack power unit were handed back to him, Patrick put them on, slipping on the backpack and fastening the attach points on his shoulders. It automatically snapped into place, locked, and energized . . .

. . . and, unnoticed and unheard by Briggs and Wohl, Patrick let out a barely audible moan through the commlink.

'Patrick? Was that you? Are you all right?' Dr Heinrich radioed.

'I . . . I felt that shock again when . . . when I put the fucking backpack on,' Patrick answered, clearly in pain.

'Terminate the test and get that power unit off *now*!' Heinrich radioed.

'*No!*' Patrick shouted.

This time everyone heard him. Hal's impressed smile dimmed a bit. Chris Wohl, the veteran infantryman and commando, was clearly concerned now. 'You all right in there, sir?' he asked. 'You don't sound too good.'

'The system's environment is completely controlled,' Masters explained quickly. 'He can withstand heat to three hundred degrees, cold to minus twenty, and can even stay under ice-cold water, all for up to an hour. The suit uses a positive pressure breathing system, so it is even capable of being used in a chemical- or biological-warfare environment.'

Wohl stepped over to Patrick and looked at the suit carefully. If he looked closely, he could see his eyes through the tinted visor in the helmet. The helmet appeared to be fitted with several sensors pointing in different directions, as well as different visors that slid into place over his eyes. Wohl could see that Patrick had an oxygen mask fitted inside the helmet, plus a microphone and several tiny sensors aimed at his eyeballs. 'I see infrared sensors, microphone – what else have you got in there, sir?'

'Complete communications system – secure tactical FM, secure VHF, secure UHF, even a secure cellphone,' Patrick replied. 'I have an omnidirectional microphone that can pick up whispers at three hundred feet. The helmet visor has data readouts and small laser-projected virtual screens that show menus to change the various functions in the system; the menu items are selected by an eyeball pointing system. Miniature infrared warning systems mounted on the helmet warn of movement in any direction.'

'Is that right?' Wohl remarked. He took a step back away from Patrick. 'How does it feel? Can you move around all right, sir?'

'It's a little stiff,' Patrick said, experimentally flexing his shoulders and knees, 'but I can . . .'

Wohl suddenly reached out and, to everyone's surprise, gave McLanahan a firm push. Patrick toppled over, landing on his back with a hard *thud!* on the concrete hangar floor.

'You look like a soft, bloated, overbaked Pillsbury Dough-boy, sir!' Wohl said angrily, almost shouting. 'You look ridiculous! You can't move, you can't run, you can hardly stand up, and you look like you're either going to pass out or sweat to death inside that thing! Do you expect us to spend all that friggin' money on a soldier my *grandmother* can push over? And where's your damned weapon?'

Patrick struggled to his feet, very much like a diver in a wetsuit trying to get out of the surf. He seemed a little shaky at first, as if the fall had knocked some wind out of him, but he was up in fairly short order. Masters replied, 'He doesn't have any weapons, Gunny.'

'Say *what*? No weapons? You're trying to tell me the soldier of the twenty-first century doesn't have any weapons? You've got to be *shitting me*!'

'No, we're not shitting you,' Patrick said, the anger in his voice coming through even in the distortion of the electronic speaker. He was on his feet, feet apart, arms away from his sides, facing Wohl in a challenging stance. 'We're going to develop a new infantry combat system, then have the soldier fire bullets? Get your head out of your ass, Wohl!'

Patrick's defiant words inflamed Wohl even more. 'This is bull, sir,' he said. 'Part of the specs on this project included a new series of area and point offensive weapons. I don't see shit. What is all this? I've trained men in seventy degrees below zero without the wetsuit or power unit, and we've used helmet-mounted sensors and miniaturized comm gear for years. What's so special about this system? Because you've got compressed air in your boots?'

211

Patrick held out his left hand, and Jon Masters put a four-foot piece of one-inch galvanized steel pipe in it. Patrick tossed the pipe to Wohl, who caught it easily in one hand. 'Take your best shot, Gunny,' Patrick said.

'Excuse me, sir? You mean, hit you?'

'That's right, Gunny. As hard as you can.'

'Hey, I'm not going to be part of your testing program, sir,' Wohl said. 'I came here to see a demonstration, not to get you hurt or injured while Dr Masters takes readings. Get someone else to . . .'

At that instant, Patrick leaped off the floor with a sharp hiss of compressed air and slammed into Wohl full force in a flying body tackle. He landed on all fours and got back up to his feet after taking a moment to get his bearings, but Wohl sailed over backward like a small wide receiver hit by a speeding linebacker. 'I said hit me, dammit!' Patrick's electronic voice shouted. 'Just do as you're goddamn told!'

Chris Wohl got on his feet like an enraged grizzly bear. He picked up the steel pipe and swung it with all his might, hitting Patrick squarely in the left shoulder. They all heard the dull thud and Patrick reeled, stumbled slightly over to the right, but did not go down. Wohl swung again. The pipe landed on Patrick's left rib cage. Again, no effect. He blocked two even harder blows with his forearms. The next blow, weaker now that Wohl was winded, landed right on his head, across his right temple. His head jerked to the left from the impact, but he remained standing. Then, as if from the depths of a wild-boar pit, Patrick cried out, a loud, almost animal-like cry, and clutched his head in pain.

'Patrick!' Masters shouted. 'Are you all right? Doc, help him!'

Carlson Heinrich ran over to Patrick, ready to get him

out of the suit and administer first aid, but Patrick swung his left arm and swatted Heinrich away. One of Heinrich's ribs cracked loud enough for everyone in the hangar to hear it.

As Wohl looked at him in amazement, Patrick stepped over to him and rammed his left hand into his chest. The blow felt like a sledgehammer. The wind gushed out of Wohl's lungs, and he fell to his knees, grasping his midriff in pain. Then Patrick reached down, picked up the steel pipe – and hit him square on the side of the head with a tremendous swinging blow. Wohl's head snapped over to the right in a cloud of blood. He landed flat on his face and lay still, blood oozing from his ears, his mouth, his eyes. Then, with another growl, Patrick raised the pipe over the fallen man, aiming one end of it at his skull . . .

'*What the fuck!*' Hal Briggs shouted in shock. Patrick McLanahan, their friend and colleague, was going to *kill* Chris Wohl! He ran over and body-tackled Patrick. They both fell over onto the concrete floor, Briggs on top. 'Patrick, what the hell are you doing, man?' He intended just to hold Patrick, to calm him down – but both of Patrick's arms swung up and hit him in the jaw. Briggs felt as if a steel girder had hit him – the force was no different from being hit by a man, but it didn't feel like arms striking him; they felt like huge steel rods, completely unyielding. Briggs's head snapped upward, blood spattering from a chomped tongue and broken nose, teeth flying.

Shouting like a madman, Patrick struggled to his feet, again clutching his helmeted head. He picked up the steel pipe and turned on the first person he saw: the prone Chris Wohl. He raised the pipe like a woodsman getting ready to split a log and . . .

'*No!*' Briggs shouted. He pulled his .45 Colt from his holster, aimed, and fired three rounds, hitting Patrick twice in the back and once in the helmet. Patrick screamed, the electronically distorted voice sounding like the squealing brakes of a locomotive against the rails, metal on metal. He dropped the steel pipe and again clutched his head, writhing in pain – but still on his feet. He turned toward Briggs, screamed again, and charged.

'Patrick, *stop!*' Briggs fired five more rounds, emptying his Colt. Patrick fell to his knees after the last slug hit him. The air was filled with blue smoke and the walls echoed from the gunshots. The scene was surreal: a costumed figure howling like an animal, writhing in pain, crouched on the concrete floor.

But he still wasn't down. Patrick crawled to his feet, his chest heaving, his electronically amplified breathing heavy and labored. Briggs couldn't believe his eyes. Patrick had just taken eight slugs from a .45-caliber automatic from no more than twenty feet away and he was still alive. Or was he *really* alive? Was this some kind of sick, homicidal automaton? Briggs dropped the empty magazine, pounded a full one home, and took aim . . .

'Wait!' Masters shouted. He ran over to Patrick with Heinrich, plowing into him from the right side and tackling him back to the floor. Patrick swung an arm, clubbing Heinrich painfully on the right arm. Heinrich cried out in pain and rolled free, clutching a broken arm, but it gave Masters enough time to touch a tiny hidden switch under the left edge of Patrick's helmet. An invisible seam appeared, and the helmet popped open and clattered to the concrete hangar floor.

What they saw made their blood turn cold. Patrick's face was contorted in agony. His eyes were bulging, his mouth wide open. The veins on his head and neck protruded so much that they looked ready to burst through his skin, and his neck muscles were horribly swollen. His maddened eyes rested on Briggs. He scrambled drunkenly to his feet, ready to pounce again, ready to rip Briggs's heart out, ready to spill his blood. Briggs aimed for the contorted head and closed his eyes . . .

'Don't, Hal,' Jon Masters said in a remarkably calm voice, holding up both hands. 'He'll be all right now. The power in the suit is deactivated. Just stay away from him.' He stooped to help Heinrich, who was clutching his fractured arm against his body. Patrick got to his feet and charged, but Briggs sidestepped him easily, pushing him away to keep clear of those pile-driver arms.

He watched the way Patrick's eyes darted from side to side; he'd clutch his head and then they'd flash sideways again. He stumbled about, trying to regain his footing, before finally collapsing to his knees on the floor. 'What's he doing?' Briggs asked. 'Why are his eyes doing that?'

'He's trying to activate the eyeball sensors,' Masters explained. 'Trying to activate the systems in the suit. He still thinks he has his helmet on. Don't touch him, Hal. The effect will wear off, but you might set him off again. Look after Chris.'

Keeping a wary eye on Patrick, Briggs went over to Chris Wohl. The big Marine commando was moaning in pain, trying feebly to raise a hand to his head. He looked in very bad shape. 'I think Patrick fractured his skull,' said Briggs, 'but he's conscious – though barely. He needs an ambulance.'

'I . . . I already called for an ambulance,' they heard Patrick say. His breathing had returned almost to normal. He was still on his knees, his head listing to one side as if he couldn't hold it upright. 'As soon as I hit him, I got on the

VHF radio and called the security office for an ambulance. It'll be here any second now.'

'What the hell were you trying to do, Patrick?' Briggs spat. 'What got into you, man?'

'I . . . I don't know, Hal,' Patrick said weakly. 'It was as if I were . . . I don't know, on speed or something. When Chris pushed me, I felt – I just felt like I had to kill him. He was the enemy. I could see everything so clearly, as if I were watching myself. When those bullets hit me, I wanted to rip something apart – anything. I wanted to kill you, kill Chris, kill anyone who came near me. I knew what was happening. I knew who you were, I knew where I was – and I also knew I had to kill all of you.'

'Jesus. I think that suit messed up your head,' Briggs said. 'Jon, help Patrick out of here before the ambulance comes. I'll stay with the doc and Chris.' Masters helped Patrick to his feet and supported him to an adjacent office. When the ambulance arrived, he went back to see Wohl safely loaded in, issued instructions to the security crews, and returned to look after Patrick.

He found him where he had left him, sitting on a bench with his elbows resting on his knees, looking down at the floor. He had opened the top of the suit so he wouldn't pass out from the heat. Jon disconnected the backpack power unit, then helped him strip off the suit. Soon Patrick was sitting in a chair, wearing only a sweat-soaked light cotton undergarment. He was staring straight ahead, his lips parted, the expression on his face suggesting he was replaying the past twenty terrible minutes in his mind's eye.

Jon sat down in front of him. Blood vessels had popped around Patrick's eyes, and the muscles on his neck, shoulder, chest, and arms looked thick and chiseled, as if he had just finished a weight-lifting workout. He began to weep.

'Don't worry about it,' Jon said. 'I think they're all going to be all right.'

'I was afraid I killed Chris. Are they on their way to the hospital? How are they?'

'Chris is hurt pretty bad,' Jon said, 'but he was conscious when they took him away. Carl has a broken arm and rib. Hal has some broken teeth and a cut tongue, but he'll be okay. He's staying with Chris.' The two men sat quietly for a long moment, overwhelmed by what had happened. Then Jon cleared his throat and asked, 'Patrick . . . Patrick, what did it feel like?'

'What?'

'Come on, Patrick, you've got to tell me. You got hit over the head with a *steel pipe*. My God, you were shot in the head and in the back by a big-ass forty-five automatic from point-blank range! The gun blasts almost knocked *me* over!'

'I . . . I don't want to talk about it.'

'You've got to, Patrick!' Masters retorted. 'You know as well as I do that this program is dead. It failed with the airlines and the FAA, and after this neither ISA nor any other government agency will come anywhere near BERP. It's over.

'But you experienced it, Patrick. You know what it's like to survive something like that. I'd never have the guts to put that thing on and have a Hal Briggs fire live forty-five-caliber rounds at me! You're the only one who will ever know what it felt like to be . . .' He paused, then went ahead and said it, '. . . be invulnerable, like Superman. What was it like? How did it feel?'

Patrick whispered something too low to be audible, then began to weep again.

'Never mind,' Jon said reassuringly, putting a hand on his shoulder. 'It's over. We'll destroy the suit. I promise it'll never hurt anyone else again.'

'Jon . . . dammit, Jon, it felt *great*, it felt *wonderful*!' Patrick exclaimed, his tears now more shame than pain. 'When I felt that energy rush through the suit, I felt more alive than I've felt in months. The power is incredible, Jon, enormous. It's like a drug, like a shot of adrenaline jammed right into the heart. But the energy surge did something else too – it made me a little crazy, like a berserker. Everything was running in slow motion. The gunshots felt like ocean waves hitting you – you get pushed around, and you can feel the force behind them, but then the impact is gone and you're still left standing.'

'Did it hurt? Did the energy surges hurt you?'

Patrick laughed. 'Oh God, yes,' he said. Jon looked at him as if he had gone off his rocker. 'The pain was . . . exquisite. That's the only way I can describe it. Exquisite. It was what I always imagined slow death would be like, once you accepted the fact that you were going to die. I felt liberated, powerful, *free*. My whole body felt as if it were on fire. Every nerve was alive, jangling my brain. The incredible pain made me feel . . .' He shook his head, shrugged, and said, '. . . immortal. I was dying, but I felt immortal. It felt . . . *good*.'

'I'm destroying that damned suit, Patrick,' Jon said firmly. 'Apart from what it made you feel like doing, even if it protected you from Hal's bullets the suit itself could have killed you. It's not worth it. No government contract or big breakthrough is worth it.'

But Patrick didn't seem to be listening anymore. He looked totally wiped out. 'I'll call Wendy too . . .'

'No,' Patrick said. 'I'll tell her.'

The first thing Patrick did, after visiting Chris Wohl and

Carl Heinrich in the hospital, was go home and hug his wife and child. But he said nothing. He simply held them close and let their warmth wash away the memories of that terrible morning.

University of California-Davis Medical Center, Stockton Boulevard and Forty-Second Street, Sacramento, California
the next morning

When Patrick arrived at the UC-Davis Medical Center the next morning, he was startled to find a crowd of reporters and TV cameras at the entrance. 'Mr McLanahan!' they shouted. 'Over here, Mr McLanahan! What do you think of the court's decision?'

Patrick always tried to avoid the media, but they were everywhere this time, and he could not hide the confusion on his face. 'Mr McLanahan, you heard about the appeals court's decision, didn't you?'

'No, I haven't,' Patrick responded, curious now.

'A judge in the state appeals court has overturned the superior court's no-bail ruling for the two defendants charged with murder in the Sacramento Live! shootout,' the reporter said. 'He said there's insufficient evidence to hold them on an attempted-murder charge.'

Patrick gasped. '*What?*' he exclaimed. 'No – that can't be!' The reporters circled him like sharks around a wounded marlin. He knew he shouldn't react, should conceal the horror he felt, but he couldn't contain his disbelief. This can't be, he said to himself. The best, the only opportunity to discover more about who had attacked Paul and killed the two Sacramento police officers seemed to be slipping out of their fingers.

In a daze, Patrick pushed his way through the knot of reporters and into the entrance. There were more of them at the nurses' station on Paul's floor but the policeman on duty cleared a path for him as he made his way to the room.

Jon Masters was already there, together with a technician who worked with Carlson Heinrich. Paul was sitting up in bed looking apprehensive, on his lap the ever-present notepad he used for communicating. A lot of the bandages and dressings had been removed from his neck and throat. The most horrible parts were his shoulder and left arm. Despite three separate surgeries, the shoulder, unprotected by his bullet-proof vest, could not be repaired, and the damage to the left bicep and elbow was too extensive. A month ago, the decision had finally been made to amputate the arm. Paul had taken the news stoically, but the nurses told Patrick in private that they had seen him silently weeping when he was alone at night, and more than once he had buzzed them for something to alleviate the pain in the arm that was no longer there.

'You hear about the court decision?' Jon asked.

'Just did, from the reporters outside,' Patrick said, sitting down beside the bed and clasping his brother's right hand, 'but no details. What in hell happened?'

'The appeals court said there wasn't enough evidence that the suspects had anything to do with the shooting.'

'Then they must know who they are,' Patrick said. 'Did they say?'

'They're former German soldiers,' Jon said.

Patrick nodded – he had figured that professional soldiers were involved in the attack. 'Let me guess: They work for some mercenary group or drug gang, and they sneaked into the country and planned the robbery . . .'

'Nope. What Chandler said that night on the tape is true; they have valid Canadian entry and work visas, and a valid Canadian residence and employer. All verified. They said they were visiting friends in Sacramento and didn't know they needed a visa to visit here from Canada.'

'That's bullshit! It's gotta be bullshit!' Patrick exclaimed. 'Didn't the police check out their stories? Where were they staying? What were they doing? Where were they going?'

'They claim they were walking down some road, the Garden Highway I think they said, heading from the riverfront to the apartment complex where they're staying, and got hit by a truck,' Jon responded. Patrick's mind flashed to what he remembered of the Garden Highway. It paralleled the Sacramento River and was very desolate in spots. The Northgate section of town, just off Northgate Boulevard and the Garden Highway, had a large German-immigrant population, so large that it was known as Little Berlin. There were numerous immigrants from Eastern Europe in some of the other apartment complexes in the area too; and with several families often occupying a single apartment unit, it was almost impossible to keep track of the residents.

'They said someone picked them up after the accident and brought them back to the apartment,' Jon went on. 'No one reported it because they were afraid they or their friends might be deported. But when their injuries turned out to be so serious, they were dropped off at the hospital by an anonymous Good Samaritan who didn't want to be identified because he's an illegal immigrant too.'

'But all the media reports of their arrest said their injuries were consistent with their being struck by the police car,' Patrick protested. 'The broken bones in their legs and rib cages matched perfectly with the dimensions of the squad car Paul was driving . . .'

'Yeah – well, apparently the press folks were talking through their asses,' Jon said disgustedly. 'It turns out the police can't *prove* anything. The injuries are consistent with their getting hit by some vehicle, but they can't say for sure it was a police car.

'So the appeals court's decided the murder and attempted-murder charges are unsupported and they've thrown the case out of court. The only charge that's sticking is violation of immigration laws. The worst that will happen to them is they'll be put on a plane and flown back to Canada, or back to Germany if Canada won't take them back – that is, if the city or county can afford to deport them. In the meantime, the county of Sacramento will pick up all their hospital bills.'

Patrick shook his head. 'It's a nightmare,' he said, his voice reflecting his anger and frustration. 'A goddamn nightmare. I thought for sure they were involved in the shootout.' Apparently Masters heard something in Patrick's tone that made him flash back to the previous day, because he looked worried, even scared. Patrick noticed. He gave Jon a nod, a silent 'I'm okay. Don't worry.'

Paul noticed too. 'Everything okay, bro?' came a voice. 'You sound pissed off enough to kill someone.'

Stunned, Patrick stared at his brother. 'Paul? Was that *you*?'

'Damn straight!' Paul smiled proudly.

Patrick's face glowed with wonder. 'The electronic larynx works! You did it, Jon! How does it work?'

'Sensors in the trachea attached to the muscles that normally control the vocal cords activate lasers that duplicate the actions of the vocal cords,' Masters explained.

'The laser pickups activate an electronic voice-box that translates the vibrations of laser light into speech-pattern sounds, then broadcasts the sounds through the throat, mouth, and nasal passages. We can very nearly duplicate Paul's natural voice because the sound still emanates from his mouth, just like normal speech. Fitting the hardware was the easy part – it's tuning the system to closely match his natural voice that's been hard.'

'Incredible,' said Patrick. 'Just incredible. Congratulations!'

'I wish Dr Heinrich were here to hear this,' Paul said. As he spoke, the technician put a device up to his throat and made some fine adjustments. The results were even more startling – Paul's voice, although obviously artificial, sounded remarkably lifelike, like a medium-quality tape recording of his natural voice. 'Dr Masters said you had an accident yesterday?'

Patrick kept his eyes averted. 'Another experiment that didn't go as well as we wanted,' he said. Paul didn't press; he could see they weren't volunteering more. But when Patrick looked up, he found his brother staring at him, and knew he had sensed what he needed to know.

While the technician went on working on the electronic larynx, a nurse brought in a stack of mail. In the first weeks after the shootout, letters had come in by the bagful; they had only recently dwindled down to a handful a day. The letter on top had been delivered by messenger, the nurse said, and Paul signaled Patrick to read it for him. Patrick's mouth dropped open. All eyes were on him. The technician stopped his adjustments. 'Patrick? What is it?' Paul asked.

'It's from the department – the personnel office,' Patrick said blankly. 'Paul . . . you've been retired.'

'Retired?'

'It says they considered light duty, but after consulting with the doctors, your injuries have been considered too serious. You will receive full pay and benefits for two months after you leave the hospital, then go on full medical retirement. Full medical and survivors' benefits, half your base salary tax-free for life. Your personal gear has been sent to your home.'

Paul fell back against the pillow. 'They cleaned out my locker already?' he exclaimed. 'I only used it *once*!' He turned his head away, fighting back tears. 'Man, I can't believe this. Not in person or even by phone – they sent me a *letter* telling me I'm out.'

The room was silent for a long time. Then Masters broke the strain: 'This is good, Paul, because now we have time to work on the second phase. The next project, if you're ready for it, is to start work on your shoulder and arm. I don't think we'll be able to do much here. We should consider transferring you to our facility in San Diego.' Paul said nothing. 'Problem, Paul?' Masters asked.

'I don't know,' Paul said. 'Leaving Sacramento, getting a . . .' He moved his good right arm, then glanced at the emptiness to his left.

'It's a little intimidating, I know,' Jon said. 'But check this out.' He reached into his briefcase, withdrew a videocassette, inserted it into the VCR in the television set, and closed the curtain over the door panel so no one in the corridor could peer in. 'It's yours if you want it.'

What they saw on the screen astounded them. It was a human arm, or at least it looked and moved like one – but it was mounted on a metal stand. It was extraordinary in its detail, with a realistic human shape, dark hair on the forearm, a normal-looking hand with healthily pink fingernails. As they watched, the arm reached down and picked up a pen sitting on an adjacent desk, held it between the thumb and fingers, and began to 'write' in midair.

'It's amazing,' Paul said. 'It looks so – so *real*.'

'It took three months of work just to get the mechanics down to pick up a pen,' Masters said proudly. 'Almost two years of research and development. It contains over three hundred individual microhydraulic actuators ranging in size from twenty-five millimeters in diameter to less than two millimeters. The joints and fittings – the artificial cartilage and tendons – are fibersteel. The arm, hand, and fingers have a much greater range of motion than normal appendages, but it would take a conscious act to make it perform unnaturally. Same with physical strength. The actuators are hydraulic, so they're many times more powerful than human muscles, but we didn't design the system to give you superhuman strength.'

Masters went on with more of the arm's features until he realized Paul was staring into space. He shut off the TV, rewound his tape, took it out of the VCR, and put it back in his briefcase. 'Maybe you want to think about it some more,' he said, nodding to the technician to wind up his adjustments. 'Give me a call when you're ready to talk. See you later.'

When they were gone, the two brothers sat in silence. Patrick saw the tears in Paul's eyes. 'It's going to be all right, bro,' he said.

'What is happening to me?' Paul asked, his electronically synthesized voice a startling reflection of the sadness in his heart. 'I don't feel human anymore.' He looked at his older brother and added, 'And you . . . you don't feel human either. What is happening to *us*?'

'Paul, all you have to worry about is getting well,' Patrick said. 'Everything else is . . .'

'Don't give me that *bullshit*, Patrick!' Paul exploded.

225

'You've been treating me like your kid brother for too long now. You don't have to protect me or spare me any grief. You told me everything was going to be okay when Dad died; you told me everything was going to be okay when you left Sacramento and I hardly ever saw you again; and I get my arm and my throat shot to shit and you're still telling me everything's going to be okay. Everything is still a secret with you, Patrick. I can feel the pain you're feeling, bro, but you're still shutting me out.'

His face turned dark. 'I am turning out to be the thing I most hate, Patrick. I am turning into a machine! I have lasers for vocal cords, microchips for a larynx, and now Jon wants to give me hydraulic actuators for muscles and fibersteel for bones. I am turning into the thing I hate most in the world.'

He scanned Patrick's face with a strange mixture of sadness and pity, and went on: 'But the worst part, bro, is that I feel like I'm in danger of turning into *you*. I feel like my soul is being replaced by a machine. And the only thing I get from you is, "Don't worry. Accept it. Everything will be all right."

'I'm scared, dammit! I'm scared because I'm turning into a damned contraption, a collection of composites and microchips, and when I reach out to you for support and guidance and love, all I sense is another machine, an even more terrible machine, sucking me down even more.' He stopped, waiting for his brother to speak, but there was only silence. 'Talk to me, goddamn you! Talk to me or get the hell out.'

'Paul, I *can't* talk about it,' Patrick said. 'It's all . . .'

'Don't tell me "It's classified" or "It's top-secret" or any of that nonsense,' Paul shot back. 'Something is driving us apart. We want to be together, connected, supportive, but we can't. We're both hurting. I know what hurt *me*,

Patrick. What in hell has hurt *you*?' He closed his eyes, fiercely trying to establish the psychic connection that had once bound the brothers tightly together through vast differences in time and distance. Then he shook his head in resignation. 'All I get from you is a ghost, Patrick, a gray ghost. *Talk to me*, Patrick! What happened? What's going on?'

There was still no reply. Paul threw his head back on the pillow. 'God, first my real family splits up; and then my new family, the police department, kicks me out. Now you're pushing me away. Happy fucking New Year!'

It would have felt so good, Patrick thought, so *right*, to tell Paul everything. Not only about bugging the SID offices, or trying to find Mullins in the Bobby John Club, or about his failure with the Ultimate Soldier project. Everything, going way back: starting with Brad Elliott and Dreamland, the secret bombing missions, the top-secret projects, all the times the world almost went to war and his role in preventing it.

But most of all, he wanted to tell Paul about the people, all those souls he'd encountered, good and bad, over the past eleven years. So many times, so many battles, so many lives that touched his and then were gone forever, while he lived on. He wanted to tell him everything . . .

'I'm sorry, Paul,' he heard himself say. 'I can't tell you. I wish I could but I can't.' Paul turned away. 'Believe me, bro, everything is okay. The most important thing is for you to get better. Get some rest, and later I'll . . .'

'Save it, bro. I'll be fine. Go and do whatever the hell it is you do.'

Patrick stepped toward Paul, reaching out to him . . . but the connection was severed. The person in the hospital bed before him might as well have been a stranger.

He turned and left the room, pushing his way through

the reporters swarming around him clamoring for a statement. He'd had enough of this damn town. Time to take his family and go home.

Wilton, California
the same time

The next meeting between Gregory Townsend and Sandman Harrison and his Brotherhood bikers was brief and to the point: 'The chief says yes,' the Sandman said. 'Thirty meth cookers, ten grand each, charged against our first payments. You provide the training and keep 'em running and we pay one grand per pound. How will it happen?'

'Good,' said Townsend. 'Next week, barring any unforeseen complications, we will deliver a hydrogenation unit to a location that you will advise me of while en route, in order to preserve total security. Each time, your men will pick up the unit, at which time a deposit of one hundred thousand dollars on each will be collected by myself or Major Reingruber.

'Your men will take the hydrogenation units to your clubhouses or safe houses or whatever you call them,' Townsend went on. 'One of my men will accompany each unit. Once at the clubhouse, my man will instruct your chapter members present on the operation of the unit. After the instruction period, you will deliver two hundred thousand dollars as our final advance deposit, to be applied against our share of the first batches prepared by each chapter. Agreed?'

'What about the chemicals?' Harrison asked.

Bennie the Chef answered this. 'The units will have enough chemicals on board for the first test batch, a little over twenty-five pounds. The colonel is supplying the chemicals just for the test batch. You want more, come to us.'

'Like hell we will,' Harrison said. 'We got our own connections.'

'We only guarantee the purity of the product and the safety and efficiency of the hydrogenators if you use our chemicals,' Townsend said. 'If you use inferior ingredients, we cannot be responsible for the outcome.'

'The cookers better work, asshole, or we'll use them as coffins for you and your men – after we get through chopping your sorry asses into little pieces,' Harrison snapped. His angry glare rested on Reynolds, then Townsend, then Reingruber. 'Don't fuck with us, Townsend. You say your cookers need certain chemicals in certain amounts and concentrations, fine. Tell us what they are, and we'll get them. If we need to buy from you, we will, but you sell at cost – you're already making a shitload of cash on this deal and you're not taking any of the risks.'

Townsend spread his hands and nodded. 'Very well. Chemicals at cost. Bennie will supply you with all the specifications you need for the chemicals. If you fail to follow the specifications, of course, the risks are entirely your own.'

'You just hold up your end of the bargain, limey, and we'll take care of the rest,' Harrison said. Townsend held out a hand to seal the deal with a handshake, but Harrison ignored him. 'Have the cookers ready to go next Friday night, and we'll call and tell you where to go.'

As Harrison and the bikers headed for the door, one of them glanced into the kitchen-turned-communications-center, where several TV sets were tuned to the morning news on the major Sacramento-area stations. He stopped in his tracks and pointed to one of the screens. 'That's him!' he shouted. 'It's him!'

'Who in bloody hell are you talking about?' Townsend asked.

'The guy in the bar, dammit!' the gangster said. 'The guy who said he was looking for Mullins.'

'Did he say why?' Townsend asked.

'He said he wanted to ask Mullins about the Major,' the biker said. 'He said the cops were watchin' us. He said he was the brother of one of the cops that got shot and he wanted to kick Mullins's ass.'

His face stern, Townsend turned to Harrison. 'It would seem that you have a leak in your organization, Mr Harrison,' he said. 'Either you have an informant in it, or the police targeted one of your members for special surveillance.'

'Mullins,' Harrison said. 'It had to be fuckin' Mullins.'

'For your sake, you had better hope it was Mullins. I tolerate no security breaches in my organization.'

'Screw you, Townsend,' Harrison said. 'My boys know if they rat on the Brotherhood, they're dead.'

'Good. Be sure it stays that way.'

Gregory Townsend shook his head as he watched the Satan's Brotherhood gangsters drive off. 'Bloody bastards,' he said under his breath. 'They don't deserve this deal. They don't deserve my time one bit.'

'If you want a piece of the meth trade, Colonel,' Bennie Reynolds said, 'you gotta deal with Harrison and Lancett. But once you got them in place, they'll fight night and day to keep the business going.'

'Bloody unlikely,' Townsend remarked. He turned toward the back of the room and saw Bruno Reingruber watching the television screens. He was writing something down on a piece of paper. '*Was ist es*, Major?'

'McLanahan,' Reingruber read from the paper, then went on in German: 'The TV has identified the police officer who wounded my men with his car. McLanahan. He is still in the hospital, *alive*. Not dead, as Sergeant Chernenkov reported. He *survived*.'

'And his brother was in the bar seeking revenge on his attacker. How touching,' Townsend answered him. 'Never mind him, Major. This is not important. We concentrate on setting up delivery of the hydrogenators.'

'I lost four men in the robbery – during *your* robbery,' Reingruber protested. 'You hired Mullins, and he turned on us. Two of my men were killed and two have been under arrest. It says on the TV they are being freed from jail, but what if this McLanahan can identify Corporal Schneider and they arrest him again? To kill a policeman is an automatic death penalty in this state. This is unacceptable. McLanahan must be killed *immediately*!'

Though Bennie did not understand German, there was no mistaking the sense of that fierce '*sofort!*' Townsend chose to ignore it. 'Major, we are not going to expend our energy and talent on making war against one or two insignificant individuals,' he said. 'Forget about McLanahan.'

'Please consider my request, *Herr Oberst*,' Reingruber answered. 'We pledged together to begin a reign of terror in this country not seen since Henri Cazaux, your former commander and mentor. Let us begin that reign of terror now. Our target must be McLanahan. The police officer injured two of our soldiers. His brother dared to track us down, pursue us, and even threaten us. We cannot be seen to tolerate this. My men will fight to the death to avenge their own.'

Townsend considered Reingruber's proposal. He had not planned on a full frontal assault in this city. Eventually, he knew, the police would be augmented by stronger and stronger forces, too much even for Reingruber's well-trained and fierce troops. By that time, they had to have this state in a firm grip of terror if they had any hope of surviving. But he also knew that Reingruber was right about his men's total commitment to vengeance.

'Very well, Major,' Townsend said. 'Present a plan of action for me, including complete surveillance and intelligence reports, and we shall see. But this operation had better be much more than just a killing, Major. If it does not advance our plans to dominate this state, then it will not happen.'

'Ich verstehe, Herr Oberst. Vielen Dank,' Reingruber said with a satisfied smile, clicking his heels together and bowing his head in thanks. 'You will not be disappointed.'

UC-Davis Medical Center,
Stockton Boulevard and Forty-Second Street,
Sacramento, California
Friday, 6 March 1998, 1027 PT

A police sketch artist can usually tell when the composite drawing begins to match the witness's recollection. The witness's eyes narrow, the lips pinch, the body tenses, and the skin turns pale when that critical nuance appears on the sketch. Finally, and usually suddenly, the sketch seems to leap to life, bringing suppressed memories to the fore, painting images of the incident across the face of the witness. And that was what the Sacramento Police Department's sketch artist saw as he put the finishing touches on the computerized composite drawing.

'That's him,' Paul McLanahan said. 'That's the guy I hit with the shotgun.'

SID Captain Thomas Chandler got up from his seat in the corner of the hospital room and took a look at the laptop computer screen. Patrick McLanahan came closer to take a look too, hoping that the sketch matched one of the men he had seen in the Bobby John Club. It did not, and he moved away. Chandler scowled at him. He didn't like Paul McLanahan's brother, and he disliked him even more today. 'You sure, Officer McLanahan?'

'Positive,' Paul replied. 'He was illuminated perfectly in the streetlight.' Chandler nodded – his investigators had been out to the scene of the shooting several times, and the positioning of the lights along the K Street Mall would have made them shine directly on the attacker.

'Any chance at all you can identify any of the assailants you hit with your car, or the one who shot you?' Chandler asked.

'Sorry, Captain,' Paul replied. 'They all had gas masks. I might be able to estimate height and weight, but not enough to make an arrest. A good defense attorney could blast me off the witness stand with ease.'

'You let us worry about the trial – let's get as many of these creeps as possible behind bars first,' Chandler said. He remembered that Paul McLanahan was an attorney as well as a policeman, and he was now thinking more like a lawyer. 'But you're absolutely positive about the guy in this sketch?'

'Yes, sir,' Paul said. 'Absolutely positive.'

'Good,' Chandler said, nodding to the sketch artist. 'We'll circulate the composite and send it to the FBI and Interpol. We'll also bring in more mug books for you to look at. We might get lucky.' He turned to Patrick to include him in the discussion. 'Now explain to me where you're going again?'

'A private hospital on Coronado,' Patrick responded, 'near San Diego . . .'

'I know where the hell Coronado is,' Chandler snapped. 'Explain why.'

233

'I already did,' Patrick said. 'My company is going to do reconstructive surgery on Paul's left shoulder . . .'

'You mean he's going to get an artificial arm, a prosthesis?'

'Yes.'

'Now explain why that can't be done in Sacramento, where he stays under protective custody.'

'Because our medical facility is standing by ready for Paul,' Patrick said. 'It would take too long, be too expensive, and not help Paul one bit for us to move our surgical staff and facilities up here.'

'You realize the danger you're placing your brother in, don't you?' Chandler asked. 'He's under twenty-four-hour guard here.'

'He'll be under careful guard down there too,' Patrick said. 'I'll see to that personally.'

'The city won't pay for this surgery. Paul has to accept all the risks involved – and that means he's in danger of losing his survivor's benefits and medical retirement if something goes wrong.'

'I know that, Captain,' Paul said.

'The city has made Paul, me, and almost every employee of my company sign affidavits agreeing to all that,' Patrick said. 'My company is accepting all the responsibility.' He paused, looking carefully at Chandler, then asked, 'What's the real reason you're bringing all this up again, Captain? You getting a little pressure from the chief?'

Chandler scowled again at Patrick. This was certainly not the same whining Milquetoast that had come into his office a blubbering wreck back after the shooting. Maybe the shooting shook this guy up, made him get off the sauce and take some responsibility for his family. But it was also possible he hadn't changed, and that he was giving Paul some bad advice by taking him out of

Sacramento. Chandler took a deep breath in resignation and said, 'It would look real bad if Paul was hurt . . .'

'Look bad for the city and the chief, you mean.'

'It would look like we weren't there to protect him,' Chandler said. 'The chief is already under pressure for what these gangs have been doing in Sacramento. If we leave Paul's safety in the hands of a private, non-law-enforcement company and they get to Paul, every-body loses.'

'The chief gets embarrassed, the city looks bad – but Paul gets dead,' Patrick said. 'Don't expect me to feel sorry for *you*.'

'I could get a judge to order Paul to stay in protective custody,' Chandler said angrily. 'It would be for his own safety. If there was an arrest and a trial, Paul would be a key witness, and it would be up to the city to protect him so he could testify. We can compel Paul to stay . . .'

'We're going to fit Paul for an artificial limb – you think a judge is going to deny that, especially if you haven't made an arrest yet?' Patrick asked. 'Exactly how long would you and the chief and the city plan on denying my brother a new left arm?'

'Give me a break, Mr McLanahan!'

'Shut up, both of you!' Paul shouted, his electronically synthesized voice raised for the first time. 'Captain, I'll return to Sacramento any time it's necessary to do a lineup or testify in court. I trust my brother and his company to keep me safe until I return.'

'Well, I don't,' Chandler said. 'Paul, what do you know about this Sky Masters, Inc.? We did a check on them. Their corporate headquarters are in a little Podunk town in Arkansas. We can't get any financial records off the computers. We can't verify any income, get tax returns, or even positively verify that the company is a real business entity. We get no responses on our inquiries from the FBI, the Commerce, Treasury, Labor, or Defense departments . . .'

'Captain Chandler, the decision's been made,' Patrick said resolutely. 'If the city is going to try to force Paul to stay, go ahead – we'll see you in front of any judge in the state. Otherwise, we have an ambulance waiting downstairs. What's it going to be?'

Chandler had no option. McLanahan was right: Chandler's office had already talked to a judge about compelling Paul to stay, and had been denied. 'Then your decoy ambulance and the car that will carry Paul will have motorcycle escorts to block off the intersections. You can't say no to that.'

'Not the car,' Patrick insisted. 'The Suburban is armored, and we'll have armed security officers inside.'

'Those robbers had anti-tank weapons,' Chandler pointed out. 'Even an armored car won't have a chance.'

'This one will,' Patrick said.

'You're making a big mistake.' Chandler jabbed a finger at Patrick. 'You're endangering yourself and Paul needlessly.' No response. He was still shaking his head as he departed with the computer sketch artist.

Soon afterward, under police guard, a heavily disguised man in a wheelchair – with a bulletproof vest under his hospital gown – was brought down a service elevator to the underground parking facility and quickly transferred to a waiting Suburban utility vehicle. It looked ordinary, but it was armored with Kevlar, the windows were bulletproof Lexan, and it rode on run-flat reinforced tires. A private ambulance was parked directly in front of the Suburban. Its lights flashing, with two California Highway Patrol motorcycle officers escorting it front and rear, the ambulance sped out of the parking garage and onto Stockton Boulevard. The Suburban followed a moment later, a Sacramento Police Department motorcycle officer behind it.

Just as the Suburban pulled onto Stockton Boulevard, shots rang out and tires exploded on both vehicles. The ambulance screeched to a stop on shredded tires. The Suburban's driver gunned his engine to escape, but a large blue Step Van delivery truck pulled out of a side street right in front of it, blocking its path. Before the Suburban could pull into reverse, four armed men, each wearing body armor, helmets, and black combat outfits, raced out of the Step Van. The motorcycle officers laid down their bikes and dived for cover as the assailants opened fire on the two vehicles. The ambulance driver and his assistant leaped out the passenger-side door away from the gunfire and ran for their lives.

One of the terrorists lifted a short rocket launcher to his shoulder, shouted, 'Die, McLanahan!' and fired an anti-tank rocket into the ambulance, which exploded in a ball of fire. Then all four assailants ran to inspect the Suburban. They found a driver, unconscious but alive, in the front seat – and a headless mannequin, dressed in a hospital gown, in the backseat. The vehicle had taken a point-blank hit from an anti-tank rocket yet was undamaged. Swearing hotly in German, all four ran off to waiting escape vehicles nearby and disappeared.

The wheelchair was just reaching the private helicopter waiting on the roof of the Wells Fargo Building, several blocks west of the UC-Davis Medical Center, when the first reports of the attack came in. 'Holy shit!' Hal Briggs shouted. 'Both the decoy ambulance and the decoy car were ambushed!' With his .45-caliber Colt automatic in his hands, he checked in with his security team on the rooftop and stationed around the building, and received an all clear. 'The ambulance drivers made it out okay; the Suburban driver is hurt but he'll be okay,' Briggs said to Patrick McLanahan as he received more updates. 'That BERP stuff you put on the Suburban saved his life.'

While Paul and the other security men were being loaded aboard, Patrick turned to Briggs and shouted over the roar of the idling helicopter, 'What about the security units at the apartment? Have they checked in?' Members of Hal Briggs's ISA action team were stationed at Paul McLanahan's apartment in Old Sacramento, where Patrick, Wendy, and their baby had been staying. Hal keyed his microphone, ordering all his security units to check in.

All the teams checked in except one.

Hal Briggs and two of his Madcap Magician commandos, both of them experienced US Marine Corps Special Operations Capable soldiers, moved as one through the stairwell and hallways of the third floor of the Harman Building in Old Sacramento, above the Shamrock Pub. Patrick followed, carrying a SIG Sauer P226 9-millimeter handgun, which looked like a popgun compared to the commandos' Uzis and MP-5 submachine guns.

There was no sign of the commandos assigned to guard the third floor and the apartment itself. They reached the front door and Briggs tried it silently. It was unlocked. Patrick had briefed the team on the layout, so they were all familiar with the traps inside the apartment: lots of big closets and cabinets, lots of windows on the river side, a large porch on the west side, thin walls, multiple doors to many of the rooms.

Briggs slid a flat fiber-optic camera beneath the door and activated the TV monitor. He gave hand signals to his commandos of what could be seen within: two hostages, one target visible, straight ahead in the living room. Nothing else visible. Open doorways all along the hallway on both sides – an almost impossible gauntlet. Bad guys could pop out of half a dozen doorways the minute they entered.

Briggs's mind was racing, trying to formulate a plan, when the front door swung open. Guns snapped up to the ready, safeties flicked off . . .

'Only McLanahan may enter,' the astonished commandos heard, in a British-accented voice. 'If anyone else tries to enter, Mrs McLanahan and the child die.'

'Shit,' Briggs whispered. He looked around the entryway as if expecting to spot the wireless TV camera or microphone the intruders used to see them coming. He adjusted his earset commlink and . . .

'Don't,' Patrick McLanahan whispered, touching Hal's shoulder. 'I'll go in. Alone.'

'It's suicide, Patrick.'

'If he wanted to kill us, I think we'd already be dead by now,' Patrick said. He stood, the P226 in his right hand. He raised it, imitated Hal Briggs's Weaver pistol grip as best he could, and entered. The sight before him made his blood turn cold. Wendy was seated on a dining room chair, holding the baby, duct-taped in place with more duct tape over her eyes and mouth – both of them covered in blood. Blood was everywhere – down the hallway, splattered across the walls, all over the floor. 'Jesus, Hal,' he whispered over his earset commlink. 'Wendy, Bradley . . . my God, I think they're already dead.'

'Oh Christ!' Briggs cursed. 'God, no . . .'

Patrick continued forward, past the hall closet – empty – past the open door to the first bedroom on the left – empty – and then to the kitchen on the right. There he saw the two Madcap Magician commandos, their throats slit, staring lifelessly into space. The floor was slippery with their blood. On the left the guest bathroom was empty, as was the . . .

'Please put the gun down, General McLanahan,' the British voice said.

Patrick spun toward the dining room to the right – empty. But as he turned, he felt the barrel of a gun on the back of his head. The guy was *behind* him, dammit! – I'm dead! . . .

'Please don't do anything rash, General, or more will be hurt needlessly. Decock your weapon, and keep your hands extended.' Patrick thumbed the decock lever on the SIG Sauer P226, which dropped the hammer without firing the weapon. 'Very good. Now hold still or you will die.' A gloved left hand reached out and, as the muzzle of the gun continued to press into his head, closed over Patrick's SIG and plucked it from his hands. 'Thank you. Fine weapon. Step forward, hands behind your neck . . . stop right there.'

Patrick was facing the dining room, but out of the corner of his eye he could see his wife and baby. The hatred and anger bubbled up from his chest and came out in a low growl. 'You bastard!' he said. 'First a cop-killer, then a baby-killer. You had better kill me now, because if you don't, I'll dedicate the rest of my life to hunting you down and killing *you*.'

'Give me a bit more credit than that, General McLanahan,' the voice answered. 'I would never purposely kill non-combatants, especially women and babies. Your wife and beautiful child are alive and sleeping – sedated. I set up this little display for you in case I was not here to greet you upon your return. But I promise I will kill you without hesitation if those men in the hallway try to enter the apartment. I would hate to have noncombatants hurt in a gunfight.' Patrick closed his eyes and said a silent prayer.

'Let me go and check my wife and child.'

'All in good time, General,' the terrorist said. 'I have a proposition for you first.'

'Who are you?'

'My name is not important, although I have a feeling you or your associates in the hallway will soon match a name with the voice. You seem to be a very resource-ful man.'

'What in hell do you want?' Patrick barked. 'You already killed my brother . . .'

'Nice try, General. I wish that were true,' the terrorist said, 'but my men report that we missed. Two decoy vehicles – very clever, very effective. I believed you would not use more than one. And the actual escape was not from the hospital heliport, which we had covered as well. This company you work for, this Sky Masters, Incorporated, appears to be serving you well.

'But the men you had stationed here to guard your family were obviously professional soldiers, highly trained and well-equipped, although young and inexperienced,' the voice went on. 'So you appear to still have some connection to the military. Curiouser and curiouser, as they say.'

'Why don't you just leave us alone?'

'I would be most happy to leave you and your beautiful family alone and conduct my business,' said the Brit, 'but you apparently chose to personally involve yourself *in* my

241

business when you showed up at the Bobby John Club, asking questions about the Sacramento Live! incident.

'We could have passed that little episode off as the deranged, futile efforts of a vengeful sibling, and left it at that. But once we found out who you were, we performed with our usual due diligence and began to discover some very unusual and interesting facts about you – or, to be precise, even more interesting was what we did *not* find out about you. Such fascinating tidbits of information, like the colorful pieces of a jigsaw puzzle. One source claims you are an ex-military man working for a military contractor, but other sources say you are an Air Force one-star general. But what one-star general does not have a command of his own? You apparently do not, at least not one that my sources can identify. But here we find these obviously military or ex-military men, guarding your family – and more soldiers outside ready to burst in. Very curious.'

'What do you want?'

'A simple request, General McLanahan: We form a partnership. You obviously have special military contacts, far more extensive and secretive than I could ascertain in a short period of time. All you need to do is sell some weapons or information to me. I guarantee to make it worth a great deal to you.'

'What in hell makes you think I have access to anything of value to you?'

'An educated assumption on my part,' said the voice. 'But I have learned that general officers typically have access to things that sometimes even they are not aware of. My network is vast and growing quickly, and your access combined with others all over the world may prove very valuable. I would be willing to share the profits of our association with you, a fifty-fifty split, if you agree to join me. I can guarantee that you will make hundreds of thousands of dollars a month – in fact, I am so sure of it that I am prepared to advance that amount to you. I can offer you safe havens anywhere in the world, a new identity, a place of safety for your family and your brother.'

'You can take your offers and shove them up your ass.'

'I expected you to say no less, General – few men of worth decide right away to turn against their country and their uniform,' the terrorist said. 'As a professional courtesy, one military man to another, I will give you three days to think about my offer. Take your brother, your wife, and your son, go to your company's headquarters in San Diego or wherever your secret command is located, and consider my offer. Formulate any questions you wish and ask me when I contact you again.

'But if you refuse, you and I are at war, and I will hunt you and everyone in your family down and slaughter them. This is your one and only warning. If you go to the authorities, I will assume that you have chosen to do battle with me, and then you and yours will all be considered combatants and will be executed. That includes your mother in Arizona, your sister in Texas, and your other sister in New York. Do you understand, General?'

'Yes.'

'Very good. Now, General, down on your face, hands behind your neck.'

Patrick reluctantly did as he was told, realizing now that he should have risked shooting the bastard when he had the chance. The earset was plucked out of his ear, and he felt an object being set on his back. 'Attention in the hallway,' the terrorist said into the earset. 'I will be taking my leave now. I suggest you hold your position and do not interfere. I have left an explosive device with the general. It is battery-powered and can be set off either by remote control, if the general moves, or if the device's sensor detects anyone approaching it. It will certainly kill everyone in this room, including the general and his lovely family. If it is not disturbed, it will deactivate itself in about thirty minutes. I think you know what to do. Good day.'

It was a huge relief for Patrick to realize that the man had departed. His greatest fear now was that Wendy or the baby might wake up and set off the explosive. It seemed like only minutes later that he felt a touch on his side, then a crawling sensation up his right thigh. Christ, a rat or a cat or something, he thought in panic. An animal could probably set off the explosive! He fought hard to control his breathing and muscle tremors. The . . . the *thing*, or whatever it was, had moved right up onto his back – oh *shit*, he realized, it was actually sniffing around the object sitting on his back . . .

'*Go! Go!*' came a shout seconds later. But before he could even move, Hal Briggs was pulling Patrick to his feet.

'Jesus!' Patrick shouted. 'Hal, what are you *doing*?'

'It's clear, Patrick, it's clear,' Hal Briggs said. One commando was checking the rest of the apartment, while the other was checking out the window and covering the front, trying to determine the terrorist's escape route. 'There's no bomb in here.'

'What the hell was that crawling around on my back?' Patrick said as he shot over to his wife and son.

'My little Rover,' Briggs said. 'He comes complete with an explosives-detection sensor.' He held up a tiny device the size of a small mouse, trailing a length of thread-thin optic cable. 'Rover' had a pinhole camera and micro-phone, and had little legs so it could crawl up furniture and even walls. 'Sorry, but I had to take the chance.'

Patrick raced over to Wendy and the baby, heard the soft sound of their breathing, and began to gently pull off the duct tape. He realized that it was tomato sauce covering them. 'Jesus, it's not blood, thank God!' he cried to Briggs. 'That bastard is a fucking monster! What was it he planted on my back?'

'This,' Hal replied grimly. He held up a hand-lettered note that read, DON'T FORGET OUR DEAL, GENERAL, and then – oh God! – a tiny baby index finger. It looked as if it had been cut free with a pair of scissors.

'*No!*' Patrick shouted, frantically feeling Bradley's little hands for the wound, tears flooding his eyes.

'Patrick! Patrick, it's all right!' Briggs shouted. 'It's fake! It's plastic!' The baby's hands were fine. 'My God, what a son of a bitch.'

Patrick pulled off the last of the duct tape, freeing his still-sleeping wife and child. Moments later, after a quick check to make sure they hadn't been booby-trapped or wired with a tracking or eavesdropping device, he carried them in his arms out of the grisly apartment and into a waiting car, Briggs and the two Madcap Magician commandos with them.

The car sped toward Sacramento-Mather Jetport. 'We'll have you airborne and out of here in ten minutes, Patrick,' Briggs told him.

'Change the plane's routing,' Patrick said, his arm tight around his wife and child.

'Change it? To where?'

'Arkansas,' Patrick said. 'I want Wendy, Paul, and Bradley out of this state. As far away and as fast as possible.'

Briggs nodded. 'You got it, Patrick.' He couldn't blame Patrick one bit for wanting to get his family as far away as he could from the madness and mayhem in Sacramento.

Behind Toby's Market, E Street, Rio Linda, California that night

It was the only all-night convenience store for miles around. Despite being in one of the highest-crime-rate areas in all of northern California, however, Toby's Market had experienced virtually no robberies or burglaries in over twenty years. The reason was simple: No one in his right mind would dare mess with a Satan's Brotherhood establishment.

Behind the store and down a hundred-yard-long dirt driveway was a small, scruffy farm, with a ramshackle five-room house, several large storage sheds, and a small barn scattered around the property. Even though the market was in the middle of a semirural residential neighborhood, bikers could drive up to the market, grab a six-pack or bottle, then discreetly drive around back to the house without being noticed – assuming anyone even bothered to take notice. That night, more than a hundred motorcycles and another two dozen cars were parked around the farm behind the market. A special meeting of the Rio Linda chapter of the Satan's Brotherhood Motorcycle Club was under way.

Almost two hundred members, pledge members, and guests of the Brotherhood gathered in the barn and looked on as the big German ex-commando explained the operation of the portable hydrogenator in halting English. The device was disguised as a typical covered eight-foot

U-Haul trailer, complete with an authentic paint job and logos. A gasoline-powered generator had been detached from the trailer and set up thirty feet away.

'Is very simple,' the soldier explained. 'You not touch any chemicals. You attach chemical tanks here and here . . . attach power plug here . . .' He worked the controls as he explained the hookup procedures, while a dozen senior Brotherhood members, highly experienced in cooking methamphetamine, stood right beside him watching every step. They would be the ones who would teach the other chapter members how to use the device. They marveled at its cleanliness, efficiency, and safety.

An hour later the tank was opened up, and the specialists examined the result of the first stage of the process. Inside the mixing tank were more than thirty pounds of clean, pure chloropseudoephedrine. 'Is ready for hydrogenation,' the Aryan Brigade soldier said. 'We leave inside. No touch, no filter, no dry. The machine, it do everything.' The Brotherhood cookers couldn't believe it – thirty pounds of absolutely pure chloropseudoephedrine in the tank ready for hydrogenation, and they didn't have to race against deadly sulfur dioxide or risk being burned by hydrochloric-acid gas. There was no smell, no residue outside the tank, nothing. The waste byproducts of the first reaction were collected inside a separate tank, ready for burial.

Even as the second step of the process was begun, discussions started about how the batch was going to be distributed, how much would go to each designated member, and how the money was going to be paid. Thirty pounds of almost-ready methamphetamine was worth between two and three hundred thousand dollars, maybe more, and every one of the members and pledges was arguing about getting his fair share – plenty of customers were out there waiting. As the hydrogenator was being sealed up and pressurized, money was already being collected.

'I wait here,' the German commando said. 'We inspect product together. I am responsible for unit until you pay.'

'We want you to wait outside, Himmler,' said the president of the Brotherhood chapter. 'We don't need you listening in on our distribution plans.'

'*Ich gehe nicht!* I not leave until product is inspected!'

'You leave *now* because I tell you to leave!' the biker ordered. The unarmed German had no option. They gave him a bottle of whiskey and the woman of his choice to keep him company, then escorted him to the propane-refill station in front of Toby's and told him to wait until summoned. A Brotherhood pledge was assigned to guard him.

While the commando and his guard took a seat on a picnic bench behind the propane tank, the biker woman went into Toby's to pee, buy a pack of cigarettes, and chat with the clerk. She was gone no more than ten minutes, but when she came back, she found the Brotherhood pledge dead and the German gone. In panic, she dashed back to the barn to tell the Brotherhood members.

Just as she reached the barn, the world dissolved into a ball of blue-yellow fire and a searing blast of heat that she felt for a fraction of a second before she was vaporized. The mile-wide fireball consumed the barn, the farmhouse, Toby's Market, the propane tank, and thirty houses and businesses surrounding the blast site. The column of fire stretched two thousand feet up into the night sky. The concussion shattered windows and awoke people from their sleep for miles around.

But that was not the only such blast. Throughout the

248

night, in sites all over the state of California, enormous mushroom-cloud-like fireballs erupted without warning. In locations as far north as Chico, as far south as Los Angeles, as far east as Death Valley, and as far west as Oakland and San Francisco, huge explosions ripped the night sky, instantly killing hordes of drug cookers and dealers and not only wiping out members of the Satan's Brotherhood, but devastating other biker gangs as well. In several areas, the methamphetamine hydrogenators were located in the basements of apartment complexes and in the middle of crowded urban areas. Hundreds of innocent bystanders and residents died in the blasts.

In a few short hours, the Satan's Brotherhood Motorcycle Club, as well as much of the membership of several other biker gangs and many Mexican and Asian methamphetamine gangs, had virtually ceased to exist.

Chapter Three

In times of emergency anywhere in the city or county, the Sacramento Convention Center in the heart of the city was transformed into a crisis command center. In a matter of hours, telephone and radio networks were set up in several of the hospitality suites, with the brain trusts of the city and county administration in a command suite and other staff and support agencies in the others, all of them connected by phone, runners, and the Central Dispatch communications center. As the crisis grew, additional suites were commandeered. All the rooms were tied in to the various safety, maintenance, welfare, and administration offices throughout the county, each with its own command center in place. Representatives from outside state and federal agencies also came to the command suite as summoned.

The mayor of the city of Sacramento, Edward Servantez, strode into the side entrance of the convention center, escorted by a plainclothes police officer who had been assigned to him, as to most other major city officials, after the Sacramento Live! shooting. Servantez, a short, dark, handsome lawyer and former state legislator in his late fifties, was accustomed to starting his day early. Accompanying him this morning was one of his aides; the chief of police, Arthur Barona; and the city manager.

Servantez was in his third and last term as mayor of Sacramento, and as such he had been through several crisis-management-team exercises and a few real ones, mostly for natural disasters such as the devastating floods of 1986 and 1997. But no matter how many times he and his staff practiced or implemented the crisis-management plan, it always seemed to turn into a barely controlled bedlam. During the exercises, the staff would often call time-outs to discuss what they were doing wrong and how to get back on track, but it never helped. And during real emergencies, of course, there was no such thing as a time-out.

Servantez removed his jacket, loosened his tie, and took his seat at the center of the head table, situated on a raised platform at the rear of the suite. To his right were the other city representatives – the deputy mayor, city manager, city attorney, fire chief, director of public works, city council representative, and Barona. To his left were the chairman of the county board of supervisors, Madeleine Adams; the sheriff and undersheriff; the district attorney; the county fire chief; and the county commissioner for public works. Places were also reserved at the head table for representatives from the California Office of Emergency Services, the governor's office, the California Highway Patrol, the National Guard, the state attorney general, the FBI, and other state and federal agencies. A briefer's podium, rear-projection screen, and PA system were set up opposite the head table. There were two tables of staff members to the right of the table, and a communication center and refreshment table on the left.

All the necessary players were now present, so Servantez said to Chairman Adams, 'Let's get started, shall we? Can we please get a situation and update briefing?'

'Yes, Mr Mayor.' She nodded to the Sacramento County undersheriff and he stepped up to the lectern. A map of Sacramento, El Dorado, Placer, and Yolo counties came up on the large rear-projection screen. 'At ten-thirty-seven last night an explosion and fire was reported in the area around E Street and Market in Rio Linda,' the undersheriff began. 'The first fire units on the scene reported several homes and businesses on fire or heavily damaged by an explosion, and the call was upgraded to four alarms. Four square city blocks were affected by the blast. Upon further investigation, firefighters discovered remnants of precursor chemicals used in the manufacture of methamphetamines . . .'

'Precursor chemicals?' the city public works director asked. 'What's that?'

'In simple terms, they're the intermediate chemicals that are produced before making the final product,' the undersheriff explained. 'It's a felony to make or possess these precursor chemicals, just as it is to make or possess meth itself.

'The fire captain called in both county HAZMAT teams and sheriff's narcotics investigators, who took command of the scene,' the undersheriff went on. 'The death toll appears to be quite high: Investigators estimate over a hundred deaths and several dozen injuries as a result of this one blast.'

'Are you suggesting this was basically a narcotics case?' Mayor Servantez interjected. 'That's a staggering loss of life.'

Captain Tom Chandler of the police department's Special Investigations Division stepped up to the lectern to respond. 'No, Mr Mayor; we don't believe so, because approximately twenty minutes later, a similar large-scale explosion occurred in the Oak Park section of the city. It was of comparable intensity, destroying homes within one block of the blast and damaging every structure within four square blocks. The casualty count was similarly high – in this case, over one hundred and forty deaths and almost a hundred injuries. Then there was another explosion in the Northgate and Levee Road section of the city just a few minutes later. This one occurred in a storage room under a multifamily apartment building. The death toll is expected to exceed two hundred.'

'My God,' Servantez breathed, shaken by the numbers. 'What do we have here? A serial bomber?'

'Perhaps, sir,' Chandler replied, 'but it doesn't quite fit the pattern. The blasts were close together time-wise but spread out in terms of distance. Serial bombers, even a group of bombers, usually strike targets close together but spread out time-wise.'

'Then what? A gang war? Clumsy drug chemists?'

'Perhaps all of the above, Mr Mayor,' Chandler replied. 'These were not the only explosions that occurred last night. In all, there were four blasts in the city, six in the county, and seven more in El Dorado, Placer, and Yolo counties. Similar explosions have been reported in San Francisco, Oakland, Stockton, Bakersfield, and Los Angeles – a total of almost thirty powerful explosions, with death tolls ranging from a few dozen to over three hundred, and extensive injuries.'

'So what the hell have you found out?'

'All of the explosions have two things in common: traces of methamphetamine precursor chemicals found at the blast scene, and a large number of gang members at each location, usually members of biker gangs,' Chandler said. 'The large numbers of gang members indicate a gang chapter meeting, maybe even an instructional meeting on how to cook methamphetamines. The pattern of the deaths at each location suggests that there was very little or no warning, possibly ruling out intentional explosions or an attack by outside forces. Those killed in the blasts seemed to be very close to the blast center, as if observing or guarding the site.

'At the very least, it appears likely that everyone at the blast scenes *wanted* to be there – these do not seem to be executions or assassinations,' Chandler concluded. 'And while this or any other particular blast could have been a booby trap or experiment gone wrong, the similarity to other explosions throughout the state does seem to rule out an accident. One or two such blasts in one night could be a coincidence. Almost thirty of them, even if spread out in terms of distance, is no coincidence.'

'We've had meth-lab explosions in the past,' the county fire chief pointed out. 'But compared to any others, these blasts are enormous.'

'That's right,' Chandler said. 'A regular-size meth-lab explosion might substantially damage or set fire to a two-bedroom house or typical barn, or destroy a storage shed. These explosions destroyed entire city blocks, perhaps eighteen homes, and damaged many more. This means that the labs in question are many times larger than the usual labs we've seen. Plus, there are a lot more of them. So someone is making large meth-labs, big enough to destroy or damage almost two dozen homes at a time but disguised well enough to escape notice. It's a very serious development. We're wondering how many labs like these *didn't* blow up.'

'Any estimate on how much meth these labs can make?' the mayor asked.

'Hard to say, sir,' Chandler said. 'We're guessing as

much as twenty pounds or even more – that's at least a quarter of a million dollars' worth at a time. The power of the explosions suggests that the meth cookers are using hydrogen gas as part of the cooking process, which is highly explosive when mixed with oxygen. A small meth lab might use a few cubic feet of hydrogen pressurized to thirty or forty psi – pounds per square inch. These labs must have been using perhaps two or three *hundred* times that amount. And the quality of the drug produced by the hydrogenation method is very good – the product can be cut several times to increase its value and distribution tremendously.'

'So what's the situation now?' the county commissioner asked.

'Critical,' the undersheriff replied. 'We've called for this crisis team because our resources, both city and county, are stretched beyond the limit. Both the city and the county have split up our narcotics-investigation teams and made them primaries on pieced-together narcotics-investigation teams, augmented by other detectives and patrol officers. We're using firemen and reservists to secure crime scenes, and because every blast scene involves hazardous materials, these untrained personnel are in great danger. We can't borrow Narcotics officers from neighboring counties because most of them are involved with investigating their *own* meth-lab explosions. And all of the area hospitals are clogged with casualties. We've got a real emergency situation here, Mr Mayor, Madam Chairman.'

Adams spread her hands and looked at the city officials to her right. 'It sounds to me like we need some help in handling the emergency,' she said. 'Undersheriff Wilkins, what are you specifically requesting?'

'We need immediate help in securing and investigating

258

the crime scenes and getting as many of our cops back on patrol as possible,' the undersheriff replied. 'Since the California Bureau of Narcotics Enforcement is likely to be busy investigating all the lab explosions statewide, we should request immediate support from the Drug Enforcement Agency, the FBI, and Alcohol, Tobacco, and Firearms – and we should ask the governor to mobilize the National Guard. We're requesting that the Infrastructure Protection and Security Plan be implemented immediately, and we simply don't have the manpower. All of our communications and utilities could be shut down.'

'Excuse me, Chairman Adams, Undersheriff Wilkins, but I disagree,' Chief Barona interjected. 'I don't think it's necessary to get a lot of federal agencies involved quite yet, and certainly not the National Guard. At least not until we're sure what we're up against.'

Almost everyone in the room looked at Barona in surprise – the most surprised of them the head of SID, Tom Chandler. He was ready to speak up but Servantez beat him to it: 'Excuse me, Chief?' Servantez exclaimed. 'You *don't* want any help in responding to this situation? Did you hear the same briefing I did?'

'Of course, Mr Mayor,' Barona said. 'But we shouldn't bring in a lot of unnecessary outside help until we're sure exactly what we're up against and what we need.'

'We *could* use help on the investigation of those explosions, Chief,' Chandler said. 'We usually call Alcohol, Tobacco, and Firearms on any explosives investigations.'

'Only for bomb explosions, Captain, not lab explosions,' Barona said. 'We have four narcotics-investigation teams and four explosions. We can handle our own emergencies.'

The various officials began to talk urgently among themselves, and Chandler took advantage of the break to go over to Barona. Kneeling behind him, he whispered, 'Chief, my teams are already up to their eyeballs in cases – we have half as many guys in SID as we did just three years ago. Plus some of the teams out working these explosions are federal or state grant positions – they're already committed to other projects outside the division . . .'

'I'm recalling them – they stay on the investigations, Captain,' Barona said. 'Besides, if these explosions did wipe out a bunch of drug gangs, your division's caseload probably took a big cut.'

'But we also usually request help from BNE and nearby counties with big cases,' Chandler argued, 'and they're so swamped too that it's not likely we're going to get any help from them. The feds and the National Guard would help . . .'

'I am *not* going to go to the governor and request that he send troops onto the streets of Sacramento with M-16's to do something that your units should be able to handle well enough on their own,' Barona snapped sotto voce. 'I won't give the bastard the satisfaction. That's *all*. Sit down.'

Chandler returned to his seat, taking a deep breath to try to mask his feelings. He hated to go along blindly with the rumor mill or the department gossipmongers, but the only possible explanation he could fathom for why Barona would refuse outside help was that he didn't want to spoil his political aspirations by appearing not to be in full control.

The meeting pulled itself back to order. 'That's well and good for you, Arthur,' the Sacramento County sheriff said wryly, picking up on Barona's last statement, 'but I've only got three narcotics-investigation teams to investigate *six* lab explosions. I could use the help.' To the head table he said, 'I'd like to put in a request for state Bureau of Narcotics Enforcement narcotics investigators, ATF hazardous-materials investigators, and FBI crime-scene investigator support, ma'am. As many as we can get, as soon as we can get them. And if the National Guard has any HAZMAT-qualified engineer units handy, we could use them to help in the cleanup too.'

'I'll put in the request, and I'll mark it "urgent",' Chairman Adams said, making a note and passing it along to her staff. 'Mr Servantez, if you want to amend my request, you're welcome to do so. Might save you a little time.' When she noticed Barona's icy glare and saw Servantez's hesitation, she leaned over to the mayor so Barona couldn't hear. 'It could cause a problem, Edward,' she said in a low voice. 'The governor might be reluctant to call out the Guard if one government agency asks but another doesn't. We should be united on this.'

'I've got to back up my chief of police and my city council, Madeleine,' Servantez answered. 'Calling in the Guard and the federal agencies takes control of the emergency out of our hands – we burn resources but we don't get any benefit from it. We can ask for plenty of free advice, but I prefer to wait and see exactly what we'll need before we push the panic button.'

'I think you're wrong, Edward,' Adams said. 'Put your name on the request and let's get a handle on this thing early. A little more force on the streets will be much better than too little and having this crisis reignite. I'm sure your chief is competent, but let's not get pride – or arrogance – in the way of handling this emergency.'

Servantez nodded reluctantly. Avoiding Barona's accusing glare, he said, 'After consulting with Chairman Adams, in the spirit of cooperation and conservation of resources, I recommend that the city join the county in asking the governor for assistance from the National Guard and assistance from state and federal investigation agencies.'

Tom Chandler breathed a sigh of relief, thankful that Servantez kept his backbone straight on this one. Barona was as mad as a wet hen. Well, screw him. He'd be proclaiming how great he was right up until the time the gang-bangers and anarchists kicked open his office door.

In any case, Chandler knew his troops and the entire force would be running full bore for the next few weeks.

Wilton, South Sacramento County, California
later that day

Unless Townsend or one of the others needed him for something, Bennie the Chef usually slept in until noon. It had been a very late night, and he had every intention of letting his growling stomach awaken him whenever. But for some reason he'd woken up early, and something made him get up and flip on the TV around seven A.M. What he saw horrified him. Meth-lab explosions. Dozens of them. *Huge* explosions, killing enormous numbers of people and damaging or destroying entire city blocks.

It could only be his portable hydrogenators, Bennie thought. The explosive power of one of those units was tremendous. And he realized the location of each explosion corresponded to a Satan's Brotherhood chapter site – the exact places that Townsend was going to send each unit.

Bennie got in his car and drove to the ranch of the Aryan Brigade brain trust in Wilton. Throughout the drive he listened to his car radio broadcasting reports of the explosions all around the state – it reminded him of the news coverage of the Persian Gulf War, when that too took over the radio. The devastation caused by the explosions was enormous. It was no wonder. Nine cubic feet of hydrogen gas mixed with oxygen and detonated with a spark was enough to blow up a two-story house. Put in enough hydrogen gas under forty psi of pressure, and the explosive effect was multiplied forty times. The steel hydrogenation unit would contain some of the blast, but the net effect would be similar to a four- or five-thousand-pound bomb.

He found Townsend, Reingruber, and several of the organization's top sergeants conducting firearms training in one of the wooden barns. Townsend's weapon of choice was a small 9-millimeter Calico automatic, a short, sleek pistol with a huge cylindrical ammo drum on top. Townsend seemed adept at shooting it either one- or two-handed, with either hand, on full-auto or single-shot.

'What happened?' Bennie shouted as the guards let him approach. Townsend ignored him. Forgetting who he was dealing with in his agitation, Bennie grabbed Townsend by the shoulder. 'I asked you, *what happened*, Townsend?'

Gregory Townsend shrugged off the hand without turning around and finished his target practice – only one round went astray with the distraction; the others were dead-on – then removed his eye protection and ear defenders. 'We didn't expect you up so early, Bennie. I had a driver arranged to pick you up later.'

For a moment Bennie was relieved – Townsend didn't appear to be blaming him for the explosions. Then he felt scared, for exactly the same reason. If Townsend wasn't angry or upset about the explosions, then he must've known about them all along. He looked at Townsend in horror. 'You *planned* this?'

Townsend unclipped the cylindrical drum from the top

of his weapon, clipped a fresh one in its place, and said coolly, 'We had two strikes against us from the very beginning, Bennie: We were dealing with drugs, and we were dealing with the Satan's Brotherhood. Yes, there's lots of money in manufacturing and selling illegal drugs, but the people you deal with in the drug business – very unsavory characters.'

Talk about ironic, Bennie thought grimly – Gregory Townsend calling the Satan's Brotherhood unsavory.

'Did you know that four of my men were killed and one seriously wounded when the Brotherhood's chapter members turned on them while they were delivering the hydrogenators?' Townsend went on. 'I abhor anyone who cannot stick to his part of a bargain. Major Reingruber and his men are going to hunt down the surviving Brotherhood members and teach them a lesson.'

'You didn't *expect* some of the Brotherhood to try to rip you off?' Bennie asked incredulously. 'You blew up all the hydrogenators and wasted a chance to make hundreds of thousands of dollars a day because a few of the chapter guys killed your troops?'

'Of course not, Bennie,' Townsend replied. 'I was going to kill them all anyway.' The way he said it, so casual and so businesslike, made the hairs stand up on the back of Bennie's scrawny neck. 'Actually, I was quite relieved that the death toll on our side was so small. We were at a considerable disadvantage.' Townsend smiled at the shock on his face. 'Bennie, you're an intelligent man. Tell me: What would have happened to the price of methamphetamine in the state of California if there were over a thousand extra pounds of pure uncut meth on the street *per day*? That would equate to approximately one hundred thousand pounds of cut meth each day.'

'The price would drop,' Bennie said.

'"Plummet" is the term you Americans use, I believe.'

'But so what?' Bennie asked. 'Your deal with the Brotherhood was a thousand dollars per pound produced, no matter what the street price was.'

'But if the street price dropped to, say, two thousand dollars a pound rather than eight to ten thousand dollars,' Townsend asked, 'what do you think the Brotherhood's reaction would be?'

'They'd . . . they'd try to renegotiate the deal.'

'Bennie, Bennie, please don't delude yourself like this, not with me,' Townsend scolded him. 'You know as well as I that the Brotherhood would first renege on the deal, then go to war with us to try to cancel it – by killing every last one of us and keeping the hydrogenators for themselves. It was a no-win situation for us right from the start, Bennie. But now answer this: Has California's appetite for methamphetamine been affected by these explosions?'

'Hell no. Why should it?'

'Precisely,' Townsend said. 'So with the market for methamphetamine the same, and with almost every Satan's Brotherhood chapter in the state of California closed or substantially downsized, shall we say, and with the surviving members scattered or eventually hunted down by Major Reingruber and his men, what do you suppose will happen to the price of a pound of methamphetamine that makes it to the street now?' There was a glimmer in Bennie's eyes as he answered the question in his head, and Townsend saw it.

'So you have your answer, Bennie. Now, as we all know, the Mexicans and those remaining in the biker gangs will rush to fill the void left by the Satan's Brotherhood,' Townsend pointed out. 'So the window of opportunity for whoever becomes California's premier meth cooker would be very small, although incredibly lucrative. After a period of time, however, the battle for control of the meth trade in the West will heat up all over again. Meth cookers will be killing each other over a few dollars or a few ounces of white crystals. That will be the time to pack up and take our leave.'

'I don't get it,' Bennie said, shaking his head. 'Are you offering *me* the meth dealership?'

'I am offering you much more than that,' Townsend said. 'I'm offering you protection and distribution assistance as well.'

'All for the price of . . .'

'Just three thousand dollars a pound, plus chemicals at our cost plus ten percent,' Townsend said. 'For a substance that can sell from between ten and thirty thousand dollars a pound or more, I think it's an offer too good to pass up.'

'Three thousand a pound? Why so little?' Bennie asked. 'It's worth two or three times that much.'

'It is more important for us that we maintain a good working relationship with you, Bennie,' Townsend said with an expression that made the little hairs on the back of Bennie's neck stand up all over again. 'Frankly speaking, you know quite a bit about my organization and recent activities. Since killing you would be akin to killing the golden goose, as it were, I find it better to deal fairly with you rather than go to war. Do we have a deal?'

'I can cook anything I want, anywhere, anytime?'

'Supervised by my men, yes,' Townsend said. 'I presume you are not planning to use the hydrogenation method to produce methamphetamine this time?'

'Hell no,' Bennie said. 'The law will be all over the dude who tries to buy thionyl chloride or a tank of hydrogen now. If I can get my hands on some five-gallon drums of phosphorus-3-iodide, some condensers, and what's left of the ephedrine that's stored out here, I can whip up a couple of dozen pounds in one day. We can restart thionyl chloride synthesization later, when the heat subsides.'

'Do you need a hydrogenator or special apparatus for this method?'

'Nope – just the phosphorus, the ephedrine, some water, and a condensing unit,' Bennie replied. 'It's a faster and much safer process than hydrogenation, but it produces forty percent less meth for the same cost. But if the street price for meth takes a jump like I think it will, it'll be worth it. This would give us a nest egg to set up a few more labs in just a couple of weeks.'

'Very well,' Townsend said. 'But we must be very careful now. I am not so naive as to think that our headquarters, labs, warehouses, and meeting places are free from police scrutiny. I must assume that the ranch and the dozen or so other properties I own throughout the state are under some kind of surveillance. I've been fortunate thus far in not encountering any police inter-rogations, but after this past night all bets are off.

'The police may receive some special powers to arrest or conduct investigations in the interest of public safety – but more likely, they'll simply barge in wherever they like and the Constitution be damned,' Townsend went on. 'You are a known methamphetamine cooker. Almost thirty meth labs just blew up all across the state. The police will want to question you. We want to try to avoid all official inquiries on us at this point. If the police find a connection between you, us, and our two men who were just released from custody, and tie us in to the downtown Sacramento shootings, our operation could unravel very quickly. The police will not rest until the ones responsible for killing their own are found and punished – or eliminated.'

Bennie nodded that he understood. 'Okay, Colonel, okay. No way they'll connect me with you,' he assured Townsend. The guy was like a chess master, Bennie thought, always thinking several moves ahead. 'And I'll get to work right away.'

'Very good,' Townsend said. 'We'll get you your chemicals so you can start producing as soon as possible.'

Bennie had that same damn sensation again – the feeling of a long, slow slide into doom. Dealing with a guy like Townsend had to be like dealing with the devil himself. But the money – Jesus, with most all of the Satan's Brotherhood out of the way, it would be raining and pouring meth money. And the level of fear would be so high that no one, not even the Mexicans, would dare get into the meth trade in California for a few months at least. Bennie would be raking in money. And clearly Townsend and his army weren't interested in cooking.

Bennie held out his hand. 'You got a deal, Colonel,' he said.

Townsend smiled that awful smile again, holding up the Calico as he switched it to his left hand so Bennie could not fail to see it – and shook Bennie's hand. 'Very good. Let's get to work, shall we?'

As Bennie moved off to supervise the startup of his new lab, Reingruber came over to Townsend. 'I am weary of these greedy idiots, *Herr Oberst*. We risk all we have to transport some chemicals so we can make a few dollars, when the real money is sitting there waiting for us to take it.'

'Patience, Major,' Townsend replied. 'The city is not yet in a sufficient panic for our purposes. Continue to monitor the target and report if there is any movement. If the local authorities do not act a bit more decisively soon, we may need to implement Phase Three of our plan. But I have a suspicion that, as the Americans are so fond of saying, "The shit will hit the fan" by itself very soon.'

Captain Tom Chandler stepped into the conference room a few minutes after the morning briefing began and took a seat in a corner. Shielding his face behind his FBI National Academy coffee mug, he surveyed the division members present and his heart sank.

His guys and gals looked whipped. After ten days of twelve-hour shifts, weekends included, they were ashen and exhausted. Everyone was chugging coffee to try to stay awake. Personnel assigned to SID could dress casually – it was an all-undercover unit – but most of them looked as if they had been sleeping in their clothes, which was probably not far from the truth. Hats, apparently hiding unwashed hair, were everywhere.

The lieutenant in charge of operations, Deanna Wyler, was giving the morning briefing. She normally dressed like a high-powered executive around the office, emulating the captain; but today she wore black BDU's, a rangemaster's cap, and combat boots, and had her sidearm strapped to her waist with a black web belt. Wyler, who was normally responsible for administration, training, and liaison with other divisions in the department, had probably been to more crime scenes and labs in the past week than she had in the entire six months before.

Chandler had heard through the rumor mill that Wyler was a couple of months pregnant. Selfishly, he had not ordered her to stay away from labs or explosion scenes

269

because he desperately needed the manpower out on the street. She hadn't told him she was pregnant, so officially she wasn't – which meant that in effect, she was accepting part of the responsibility for any damage, illness, or birth defects . . .

Fuck that, Chandler yelled at himself. If anything happened to that child because it was exposed in utero to any drugs or precursor chemicals at one of those lab scenes, it would haunt him for the rest of his life. He would never *ever* forgive himself.

'We have the preliminary investigation report on the explosions ready to go to City Hall and the chief's office,' Wyler began, distributing folders to each officer with the investigation summaries. 'What we had was a total of twenty-five meth-lab explosions, all occurring within eight hours of one another. The labs all appear to be similar: They were all thionyl chloride hydrogenation reactors, approximately twenty to forty gallons' capacity each.'

'Twenty to forty *gallons*?' someone exclaimed. 'You mean liters, don't you?'

'I mean *gallons*,' Wyler repeated. 'We're talking a thionyl chloride reactor capable of producing close to forty pounds of pure crystal meth at a time.' That was probably the one piece of news that could animate this bone-tired audience. The thought of a single lab making that much methamphetamine was astounding all by itself – to think that there were twenty-five of them set up out there at one time, and possibly more, was almost too much to believe.

'Want some more unbelievable stuff?' Wyler went on. 'How about very few signs of precursor chemical stores? No chemical dumps, no storage sheds full of chemicals, no hijacked trucks nearby. When those labs went up, the explosion took out all but traces of precursor chemicals.

Now with that much pressurized hydrogen in the reactor, you know the fire-ball it produces is going to be big and hot. But in the past we've always found huge dumps full of precursors nearby, and an aboveground explosion wouldn't wipe out a below-ground dump or burial site. Some of the sites had chemical dumps nearby, but they hadn't been recently used.

'Now, either the cooks were extraordinarily neat and tidy and cleaned up their precursors before starting to cook – very unlikely – or the chemicals came with the labs,' Wyler said. 'We did find remnants of trailers and hitches and stuff like that at a few of the sites, but that's not uncommon and we didn't think much of it at the time. We think it's a vital clue now. We now feel we're talking about a large, portable, self-contained reactor unit, mounted on a trailer and possibly disguised as a U-Haul or a home-built trailer.'

Wyler let that information sink in a moment, then continued: 'Now, as to the victims. With the exception of a relatively small but nonetheless unfortunate number of civilian casualties, it looks like the right folks got dead in those explosions. Get this: Of those identified so far, about seventy percent of the fatalities were Satan's Brotherhood members or associates. Over a thousand identified casualties. And all these DOA's were found well outside ground zero of the blasts, farther than fifty yards or so. That means anyone within fifty yards was probably Crispy Critters the nanosecond that lab went up. Although we'll probably have no way of knowing for sure for several months, if ever, it's safe to say that most of the Brotherhood members were closer than fifty yards to ground zero, and that the current Brotherhood death toll is just a fraction of the actual number. We could be talking about three, four, even five thousand casualties, guys – maybe up to *eighty percent* of the total known Satan's Brotherhood membership in the state of California.'

'Hol-ee shit,' someone exclaimed.

'Well, what are we sitting around here for?' said someone else, exchanging high fives with the detectives around him. 'Let's get the hell out of here and go to Sammy's for some breakfast. Or better yet, I think I saw McLanahan's open for the graveyard shift. Let's go and get us a few pops and celebrate! ... .'

Tom Chandler rose to his feet. 'Seventy-three children were killed in those explosions – you want to invite the parents of those kids to McLanahan's to celebrate with you?' he asked. The celebrating agents fell silent. 'Whoever did this didn't kill all those Brotherhood bikers for *our* benefit – whatever they got planned for this city has got to be far worse than what the Brotherhood could do to us. Keep your damn minds on the task at hand: Let's find whoever did this and put his ass in jail, *soonest*.'

'We didn't mean any disrespect, Captain,' one of the sergeants said. 'But we been workin' twelve-, sixteen-, some of us even twenty-hour shifts. We're burned out.'

'The chief is counting on us to get a handle on this,' Chandler said.

A moan of resignation went up from the cops in the conference room. Police Chief Barona was currently in Washington, D.C., testifying to some Senate subcommittee on law enforcement about the need for more federal funding for law-enforcement programs for cities, citing the statewide meth-lab explosions as perfect examples of a crime rate almost out of control. If he did get any funding, it would probably be for yet another federal grant research study or education program, not for more cops. And it was a sure bet that the chief wasn't manning a command post or sifting through bags of body parts at three A.M. looking for clues.

'All right, that's enough of the whining,' Chandler said. 'You'll all have one hour for Code Seven after this meeting – and I mean one hour, not an hour and a half, and not at home either – and then I want your butts back out on the street. Start hitting up your informants . . .'

'The CI's have scattered, Captain,' one of the officers said. 'The streets are empty.'

'I don't need excuses, I need results,' Chandler said irritably. 'Find out where your CI's have gone and go talk to them. Bump up the cash offers, but get some solid info from your informants. And update me on the status of your surveillance operations. Obviously the Brotherhood surveillance ops went bye-bye, but find out which surveillance jobs are still standing, and why. If a Brotherhood lab site or hangout or a lab site in a Brotherhood area of town didn't blow up, I want a surveillance set up there.

'Don't forget to call up BNE and any of the surrounding agencies and get the flow of information going again. I know there's been no exchange of information while the crime-scene investigations were being conducted, but now that agencies are wrapping up the crime scenes and starting the investigations, I want that information now. Everyone got that?' Nods all around. 'Anything for me?'

'Yeah,' said one of the sergeants. 'There's a rumor going around that overtime is being cut. What's the story, Captain?'

Chandler took a deep breath, then looked directly at his troops. 'Rumor looks like it'll be true this time. We blew through the first two quarters' overtime budget like it was nobody's business, and emergency procedures went into effect. Starting tomorrow, mandatory flex time up to forty hours, then mandatory comp time. No overtime will be authorized beyond that, so don't ask and don't put it on your time cards. All personnel may have to go on staggered twelve-hour shifts if this keeps up much longer. Until further notice.'

'No overtime!' the cops wailed, almost in unison. 'The sheriff's department gets feds to help them with their investigation, and we get sixteen-hour shifts with no overtime? That sucks, Captain!'

'Listen, everybody has to sacrifice until we get a handle on whoever planned these meth-lab booby traps,' Chandler said wearily. 'This is an emergency situation. Update your surveillances, beat the bushes for your CI's, gather some tight info, and make some arrests. Pronto.' He knew it was not much of a pep talk, but right now Thomas Chandler wasn't feeling too peppy himself. 'Anything else for me?' There were no replies this time, just exasperated expressions. Chandler turned and left, feeling the icy pinpricks of his troops' anger jabbing at his back.

Deanna Wyler rubbed her eyes as she waited for the muttering to die down. 'Okay, listen up,' she said, opening up her notes. 'I looked through all your recent surveillance reports and cross-checked them with the locations of those lab explosions. Two glaring holes: the new Rosalee suspected lab, and the Bobby John Club. Intelligence has filled in a couple of holes for us and I think it's time to revisit those two locations. If someone was going to target Brotherhood labs or hangouts, I'd have thought it would've been those two places. Both are still standing, right?' The sergeants nodded.

'I know we had a surveillance set up on the Rosalee location before, but we terminated it before the explosions because we needed the manpower elsewhere and because we were starting to see more normal activity there – kids, yard work, pet dogs that weren't guard dogs, et cetera. Intelligence says there's a pit bull in the yard again, and they haven't seen the kids that were playing there. They may be cooking and dealing again. Restart that surveillance again tonight.

'Let's restart surveillance on the Bobby John Club too,' Wyler went on. 'We stopped it after that weird bar-fight incident where someone set off a gas grenade, because the place has been nearly deserted. But informants tell us it's open for business again. I'd think that any surviving Brotherhood members would steer way clear of it in case whoever set up the booby-trapped portable labs goes hunting for survivors, but no one ever gave the Brotherhood a lot of credit for brains. I want to know who goes in and out of there; I want to know which Brotherhood members are still breathing, and I want them brought in for questioning.

'I don't think we'll have any trouble getting wiretap warrants, so write 'em up and I'll help you get them signed,' Wyler said. 'I've got some retired folks and some volunteers who are going to come in and help us write up warrants and help around the office too, and we've even got retired judges resworn in and volunteering to sign warrants. So at least a little help is on the way.'

Wyler then stepped closer to the table and laid her best warning glare on them all. 'One more thing, guys and gals: Stop the hangdog poor-overworked-me bullshit. I'm sure the captain will be happy to compare duty hours with yours any day, and he doesn't get flex time, CTO, or overtime, and he doesn't have a union to go cry to if he works too hard. We're all tired. The whole city, the whole fucking *county* is tired. Think about the innocent victims killed or hurt in those explosions the next time you start bellyaching about getting time and a half, CTO,

275

or flex time, while those poor folks are out burying their children and sleeping in a shelter or on the street because their apartment complex was destroyed.

'If you still feel like you're being abused and mistreated, just let me know and I'll be happy to reassign you to Patrol, where I'm sure you'll feel more appreciated. Manning a checkpoint in Oak Park or guarding an explosion site in Alkali Flats on foot at three in the morning might appeal to you. Does everyone get my drift?' There was no response – nor would one have been tolerated. 'Sergeants, I want to see your surveillance operations plans on my desk by two. Everyone: Remember why you chose to put on a badge, and remember your city is in trouble. Now get the hell out of here.'

Bobby John Club
Del Paso Boulevard,
Sacramento, California
Saturday, 21 March 1998, 0145 PT

The night air was fairly warm for this time of year, a first taste of the mild springtime evening temperatures that were right around the corner. The back door to the Bobby John Club, on the alley between Del Paso Boulevard and Anne Street, was open, and the bouncer assigned to the door had been told to move his bar stool out into the alley.

The bouncer saw the figure coming down the alleyway from about a block away. It was a guy wearing a full set of leathers, carrying his motorcycle helmet. He had on a plain dark watch cap, so the bouncer couldn't see much else of his face.

Neither could the police surveillance team parked on

Anne Street, across the alley from the rear entrance to the club. The police had installed a surveillance camera on a light post across Del Paso Boulevard to cover the front of the club, but still had to use a two-man surveillance van to cover the rear. Cameras snapped as the newcomer came up to the door, and the surveillance crew adjusted the 'big-ear' directional microphone to hear the conversation better.

'Where's your ride?' the bouncer asked as the guy approached.

'Broke down, back on Calvados Street,' the stranger replied. 'Gonna use the phone.'

As the stranger started to walk through the door, the bouncer stuck out a finger and placed it against the guy's chest in a clear order to stop. 'I seen you around before, sport?'

'Sure. I been around.'

The bouncer noticed that the leather jacket was fairly new and hardly worn. It certainly didn't look like it had been worn by anyone riding a motorcycle during a wet, sloppy Sacramento winter – it didn't even smell worn, in fact it smelled crisp and new, right off the rack – and there were no colors or logos on it. It looked like the guy could've picked up the jacket at the mall earlier in the day. He wasn't wearing leather chaps or pants either, but some kind of dark gray coveralls. 'You flying any colors, bro?'

'No.'

'Then use the phone at the Safeway back where you came from. Club's closed.'

'Phone's broke.'

'Ours is broke too. Hit the fucking road.'

The stranger turned as if he was going to leave, then stopped and turned back to the bouncer. 'Okay,' he said, 'my motorcycle didn't break down. In fact, I don't have a motorcycle. Never rode one in my life.'

'Like I give a shit. Beat it.'

'The actual truth is this,' the stranger said. 'I'm going to ask you some questions about Joshua Mullins.' He saw the sudden tenseness in the bouncer's face. 'Good. You know who I'm talking about.'

'Fuck off, bozo.'

'Mullins was Brotherhood,' the stranger went on. 'He was also part of a holdup gang that did the Sacramento Live! shootout . . .'

The bouncer could move fast for a guy his size. He shoved the stranger away from the door, then reached inside the doorway for a piece of galvanized steel pipe used to bar the rear entrance when it was shut. The stranger flew backward, landing hard on his back and side, though from his dazed expression it looked more as if he'd hit his head. 'You're trespassing, buster,' the bouncer yelled. 'You get lost, or you get hurt.'

'That guy's gotta be a 5150,' one of the officers in the police surveillance van said with a chuckle as they listened to the interchange. A 5150 was the radio code for a mental patient. Recent events around Sacramento had brought out a lot of weirdos who thought they could clean up the town all by themselves. 'Or probably another stupid cop wanna-be.'

'He's gonna get his head smashed in if he doesn't run like hell,' his partner said. 'Think we should call a Patrol unit before this guy gets hurt – or dead?'

'Yeah. Better get a black-and-white heading this way,' said the other cop. 'We can always Code-ten him if the 5150 beats feet.' He got on his portable radio and called

278

Central Dispatch, requesting that a Patrol unit swing by and shine its spotlight down the alley. 'It'll take a few minutes to get here,' the cop said. 'That'll be enough time to give the 5150 a good healthy scare – hopefully.'

'If the bouncer starts beating on him, we'll have to do something.'

'Relax and wait for the Patrol unit.'

The other cop lowered his binoculars, his mind racing. 'Intel did speculate that Mullins was one of the guys that did that robbery, right? He was the one they found dead a few days later, right?'

'I think so.'

'Did that ever come out in the papers?'

'About Mullins? Yeah. He was a security guard or watchman at Sacramento Live!, one of the missing guards.'

'Yeah, but did it ever come out that he was a Satan's Brotherhood member, or that he might have been *involved* in the robbery?'

'Yeah, sure . . . at least I think so,' the other cop said, not much interested in the subject.

'I don't think it did,' his partner said.

'So?'

'So if it didn't come out in the papers, then how could this guy know that Mullins was Brotherhood and involved in the heist? Not many cops know about that, only guys in Intelligence or Gangs. How could a buff know?'

'How the hell should I know?' his partner said irritably. 'Just take the pictures, okay? I got enough to think about.'

The stranger got himself up to a kneeling position, his chest heaving as if he was having difficulty breathing. 'Here's the deal,' he said. 'You tell me everything I want

279

to know about Mullins and I go away. If you don't, I'll break your head, and then I'll go inside, break some more heads, and destroy the place.'

'Listen, shithead, you got one more chance,' the bouncer said. 'Get up and get your fat ass outta here or I'll bend this pipe around your fucking head.'

The stranger got up, retrieved his helmet, and took a couple paces right toward the bouncer. 'Last chance for you,' he said. 'Mullins was working for a guy called the Major. The word is that Mullins met the Major or one of his men here about a week before the robbery. Tell me about him. Who was he? Did he have a German accent? What did he look like?'

'Not as bad as you're gonna look, asshole,' the bouncer said – and swung the pipe. He faked a head shot, brought the pipe back, and swung it at the side of the stranger's left knee. The blow would've put a two-inch dent in the side of a car. He gaped as the pipe ricocheted off the guy's leg as if he'd hit a concrete post.

'What did he say about Germans?' the second surveillance officer asked. 'Did he say "the Major" was a German?'

'Yeah – I heard about the Major but that never got in the papers either. And I never heard about no tie-in between him and any Germans. What makes him think the Major was . . . Ohhh, shit, he hit him, right in the fucking knees! Better get that Patrol unit over here fast. Looks like the bouncer just tried to break that turkey's knees.'

'They're on their . . .' Both cops stopped to watch. The guy was still standing after being clubbed in the knees. No set of biker leathers would protect him against a shot like that. 'He must've missed, trying to scare him? . . .'

'He hit 'im,' the first officer said, sounding unsure whether or not he saw what he saw. 'That pipe didn't faze him. He must be wearing full body armor, but it sure doesn't look like it.'

His partner put down his light-intensifying binoculars. 'I'm going over there and talk to this guy,' he said.

'You *what*? You'll blow our surveillance, man . . .'

'The guy knew about the Major, and he knew about the meeting here between him and Mullins,' the second cop said, rolling open the sliding door of the van. 'He knows a lot more than any civilian should know. If he's a cop, then he's trying to pull some kind of off-duty or vigilante shakedown thing, and we gotta stop him before he sets this city on fire. Besides, I want to figure out how he can take a hit from a steel pipe and keep on standing. Tell the black-and-white I'm 940.'

The second blow was sheer rage. It was hard, fast, and overhead, aimed right at the head. Patrick McLanahan deflected it with ease with his left arm, cracking the pipe. The surge of electricity from the arm to the rest of his body mixed with the surge of energy he had felt from the blow to his leg, and the two power waves seemed to meet right at his heart, sending an explosive stream of energy through the rest of his body.

Patrick screamed through a wicked-looking smile. They hadn't fixed the problem with the energy surge through the suit but he didn't care. In fact, he was glad. It was like a drug – and he was hooked on it.

It all happened as if in slow motion. The bouncer stared at Patrick as though he were a swamp monster, then grasped the pipe in both hands and tried a major-league home-run swing at his head. Patrick never let it happen.

He simply stepped forward and drove his right fist into the bouncer's chest.

The guy was wearing a bulletproof vest, which attenuated some of the impact and probably saved his life. His sternum and left rib cage shattered, collapsing his left lung. Blood spurted from his mouth and nose and he crumpled to the ground. Patrick was close enough to be showered with blood, but instead of sickening him, it further fueled his anger and thirst for . . .

. . . for what? Patrick wasn't sure *what* he wanted: revenge, information? No, just to take out his frustration and bitterness on whoever was inside. To hurt someone. To make *them* afraid, the way he and his family were afraid. He was going to . . .

'Stop! Police!' Patrick turned. A plainclothes man with a badge on a chain around his neck was galloping across the alleyway from Anne Street. His right hand was behind his back, probably hiding a gun. He held up his gold detective's badge. 'Hold it right there! I want to talk to you.'

Patrick tossed away the watch cap and put on his helmet. The instant the final component of the suit was in place and activated, he felt the extra surge of energy course through his body. He had bypassed the safety system that deactivated the suit when the helmet was removed, which allowed him to take it off but still be protected by the rest of the system. Now that he had put it back on, and the environmental system was fully functional and data was streaming in on his heads-up display and headphones, he felt utterly alive, utterly powerful.

'Take the helmet off *now*!' the detective ordered. Patrick stood there, unmoving. The cop's gun came up. 'I said, take off the helmet, then put your hands on top of your head and turn around!'

'I'm unarmed,' Patrick answered, his voice now electronically amplified through the helmet.

'Do it, buster. Helmet off, hands on top of your head. *Now!*' To his surprise, the guy simply turned around and headed inside the rear door of the Bobby John Club.

He holstered his gun – the guy *was* unarmed, and he couldn't shoot an unarmed man, especially in the back. If he had killed the bouncer, he was a murder suspect and could legally be detained by any means necessary, including shooting him – but if the guy didn't have a weapon it would still be hard to justify using deadly force. 'Jesus, Dave, get over here and give me a hand,' the cop said to his partner, who was listening on the directional mike. 'Better call in a 245 and possible 187, get some backup, and roll an ambulance – I think the bastard killed the bouncer.'

As Patrick came into the hallway, a biker appeared from the kitchen area, rushing him. Patrick solidified his entire left arm and straight-armed him in the face; it was as if the biker had run headlong into a steel girder. The door Patrick was looking for, the one that was closed and guarded the last time he was here, was on the right, locked. He stepped back into the kitchen and ran at the door, using his shoulders as a battering ram. The door splintered and came off its flimsy hinges.

Two bikers were inside, with several partially dressed girls. Patrick recognized one of them as the same guy who had confronted him with the broken beer bottle, the same one who cut Jon Masters – and the one who knew about Mullins and the Major. One girl was kneeling between his legs; the others scurried around the room at Patrick's entrance, grabbing for their clothes. Several lines of a white powder, crank or cocaine, were laid out on a serving tray on the table.

'Who the fuck are you?' the biker shouted.

'I want the Major,' Patrick said, his voice eerie through the helmet. 'Tell me where the Major is and I'll let you live tonight.'

The biker reached over to where his pants were on the floor beside his chair and pulled out a 9-millimeter Glock. 'I never killed anyone while getting a blow job before,' he said with a laugh. He yanked the woman's head back into his crotch, smiled, and pulled the trigger. At the same moment, the other biker pulled a shotgun from out of the corner of the room and fired. Patrick tumbled over backward, crashing into the opposite corner.

The first biker grinned as the invader hit the floor. 'Damn, that felt *good*,' he said, firing another round into him just for good measure. He yanked the woman off his cock by the hair and shoved her aside. 'Get dressed, bitch – the cops are going to be swarming over this place any minute. Clean up that coke and take the tray into the kitchen and get it in the sink. It was self-defense. All you bitches remember that. The guy busted in here and threatened to . . .'

'*Holy shit!*' the other biker yelled. They all turned in horror to see the helmeted invader picking himself off the floor. There was not a single hole in him. A shotgun blast from less than twenty feet away should've put a hole the size of a softball in his chest.

'*I want the Major!*' Patrick said again. The girls grabbed whatever clothes they could and fled, screaming, from this . . . apparition. The second biker racked the action on his shotgun and fired again, but he was shaking so hard from the sight of this guy still standing, walking, and talking, that he missed from fifteen feet away. He dropped the shotgun and ran.

'Hey, asshole!' the other biker screamed futilely, 'get

back here and nail this guy!' He swore, aimed, and fired his Glock. The invader reeled, hit right in the chest – but this time he did not go down. Another shot and another, from ten feet away and less. Still standing. It was clear he had been hit, because he stopped in his tracks and howled, as if ready to collapse from pain or shock, but then he straightened up and kept right on coming.

Patrick grabbed the biker by the right wrist, then chopped his forearm with his hand. There was the sound of bone snapping, and the Glock dropped to the floor. Then he lashed out with his right hand, hitting the biker square on the left collarbone. Bone snapped again, and the biker sank to his knees, screaming like a child. 'I want the Major,' said Patrick. 'Tell me where he is or I'll kill you.'

'I don't know where he is, man, I swear . . .'

Patrick's hand jerked out again, breaking the other collarbone. 'Next, I'm going to break your sternum,' Patrick said, jabbing a finger into the guy's chest. 'Then I'm going to break your neck, and then your skull. You'll be a vegetable for the rest of your life. Now talk. Where's the Major?'

'I swear I don't know,' the biker gasped, his face contorted in pain.

'Who contacted Mullins? Who met Mullins here?'

'I never seen him. One of his guys, one of his lieutenants, came here, but I didn't see him. Mullins told me he was going to meet the Major at a ranch in Wilton. I don't know where, I swear to God! . . .'

'Were they Germans?'

The biker nodded. 'Yeah . . . yeah, Mullins said he didn't want to deal with no krauts, but they paid him good.'

'Where was this ranch in Wilton? What road?' No response. Patrick forced the biker's head between his left arm and his side and squeezed. 'I'll pop your head right off your damned shoulders if you don't talk!' But the guy had fainted. Patrick let him drop in a heap on the floor and headed for the bar. He knew that the patrons had probably scattered like rats in a fire when they heard the gunshots, but he had to find that other biker. If he was this guy's friend, he might know more about . . .

'*Police! Freeze!*' Patrick turned. Two plainclothes cops with gold badges hanging from their necks were taking cover just outside the back door, aiming what looked like very large automatic pistols at him. 'Hands up! Turn and face the wall! Now!'

Patrick ran a system self-test. Battery levels were still in the green, but down to less than two hours' endurance. He had only had the suit on for less than an hour – must be a problem with the power-reserve indicators. Taking all those gun blasts certainly didn't help. He could probably withstand these cops emptying their guns on him, but he couldn't take the chance of more cops showing up and his power draining down into the reserves or to emergency levels. He would then have no choice but to surrender.

'I'm unarmed,' Patrick told the cops. He raised his hands, palms out, so they could see they were empty. 'I'm leaving now. Don't shoot me. I might hurt you if you shoot, and I don't want to hurt the police.'

'Shut up, turn, and face the wall!' one of the cops yelled. Patrick started walking out the door, hands raised.

'Oh shit,' the second cop muttered, 'he's not going to stop. I heard gunshots in there – do we shoot this asshole?'

'He doesn't have a gun, dammit,' said the first cop. 'I don't see any weapons.' He shouted again for the guy to freeze, but he kept on coming.

286

'Fuck,' said his partner, holstering his weapon. He shouted, 'Cover me!' and ran full speed into Patrick like a charging linebacker.

The first cop heard a dull *clunk* when the two bodies collided. The guy was knocked backward into the wall by the flying tackle, but his buddy lay facedown on the floor and wasn't moving. The guy simply got on his feet, took a second, as if regaining his balance, raised his hands again, and started for the door, careful not to step on the unconscious cop.

'Freeze!' the first cop shouted again, aiming his 9-millimeter SIG. 'Stop right there or I'll shoot!' He had made the decision to shoot; his partner was down. At Patrick's next step, he fired three rounds – two in the chest, one in the head. He heard the scream as Patrick collapsed on his back.

The cop grabbed his portable radio and keyed the mike with a shaking hand, keeping his gun aimed. 'KMA, Sam One-Niner, shots fired, officer down, officer down, one suspect down, send cover and an ambu—'

He broke off in midword, gaping as the guy in the helmet crawled to his feet, held on to the wall for support for a moment, then walked toward the door.

This time the shot hit somewhere in the torso, but after reeling back against the wall as before, the guy pulled himself up, pushed the cop out of the way, and stumbled out into the alley. The arm that shoved him felt like a steel bar, but by now he was so stunned, the guy could've used a feather.

'Mother of God!' the cop muttered. He followed the guy outside, his smoking pistol still leveled at him, but a small crowd had formed out in the alley, so he had to lower the gun and decock it. The crowd let the guy trot past them and down the alley, his gait improving with every step until he was sprinting by the time he vanished out of sight.

Torn between pursuit and his downed partner, the cop retrieved his radio and mashed the mike button: 'KMA, Sam One-Niner, the 245 suspect . . .' Shit, how in hell was this going to sound on the radio? He'd just reported that the suspect was down – now he was running down the street? . . . 'Suspect is on foot heading west down the alley behind the Bobby John Club, heading toward Fairfield Street. All units be advised, the 245 suspect is wearing a black leather jacket, dark coveralls, some kind of backpack, and a full-face motorcycle helmet. Suspect . . . shit, suspect does not appear to be armed but should be considered dangerous.'

At Del Paso Boulevard, Patrick ran left onto Fairfield Street. Using the thrusters in his boots, he leaped to the second-story roof of an abandoned printing shop, then paused to do another system self-test. Battery levels were already in the emergency reserve range. The emergency reserves were for escaping and survival, not for fighting. If he encountered any police now, he'd have no choice but to surrender.

Patrick called up and interrogated the discrete global positioning satellite search function on the heads-up display inside his helmet. A tiny red blip appeared, with a direction and range to the target. The red blip was Jon Masters, riding inside a specially equipped AMC Hummer they were using as a mobile support vehicle. Both Patrick's suit and the Hummer carried satellite navigation transponders, for each of them to see and track the other's location. Masters was now less than two-tenths of a mile away, cruising around the target area and trying to look as inconspicuous as a six-thousand-pound Hummer wagon could look on a city street in the middle of the night.

Using the thrusters, Patrick hopped from roof to roof along Fairfield and Forrest streets until he got to Arden Way. He waited on the roof of an apartment building until he saw the Hummer moving closer. Then he leaped off the roof, landing on a patch of lawn – right beside a startled guy just getting out of his car in the parking lot not forty feet away. Patrick ignored him. Fifteen seconds later, when the thrusters had recharged, he made another leap across the parking lot and lit down a few feet away from the Hummer as it slowly cruised down Arden Way. He pulled open the door as it stopped; then Jon hit the gas and sped away as fast as the big all-terrain vehicle could take them.

After they crossed the river and headed down Sixteenth Street south toward the downtown area, Jon finally asked, 'How did it go?'

'Great! It went great!' Patrick said, removing the helmet. Remembering his awful visage when he had taken off the helmet after the demonstration, Jon had been afraid of what he might see this time, but Patrick looked pretty normal. 'Everything worked great!'

They had installed a portable gasoline-powered generator in the back of the Hummer, and Patrick started it up with a push of a button, then brought a cable around and plugged it into a receptacle on a bottom corner of his backpack. Although he couldn't monitor the power levels without the helmet on, he knew from testing that it would take thirty to sixty minutes to recharge the backpack power unit.

'We're done for the night, right?' Jon asked hopefully. 'You got what you were looking for?'

'Hell no – we do it the way we planned!' Patrick

answered. 'I got a lot of good information, but I need more. The next stop might give us the rest of what we need to bust these guys.'

'There seemed to be a lot of cops around . . .'

'We'll do it the way we planned, Jon,' Patrick repeated. 'We'll go to a wider radius to keep this vehicle away from the next location. If all else fails, I'll meet you at Sac Executive Airport, at our rendezvous point. I can hide in the hangar or up on the tower.'

Jon fell silent. It had to be played out . . .

**Rosalee Subdivision,
Elder Creek neighborhood,
Sacramento, California
A short time later**

Sometimes it took days to find the best location for parking a surveillance van. Ideally, the crew wanted a spot a block or so down the street from the target address, close enough to see and photograph everyone entering or leaving the premises with a medium telephoto lens or to look inside an open garage, but not so close as to attract attention to itself or the target. Even in better neighborhoods, the van had to be moved periodically so it didn't attract attention or become a target for thieves or vandals.

Although it only involved sitting, waiting, watching, and listening, doing a surveillance was tough, uncomfortable, tiring work. Depending on the neighborhood and the nature of the operation, the cops doing the surveillance could sometimes switch with other officers for food or relief breaks. But a lot of times they were stuck inside the van for the entire eight-hour shift, forced to use 'piddle packs,' portable toilets, garbage bags, or soft drink cans to do their thing.

But the worst part of a surveillance, even after only a couple of days, was the godawful smell. Thankfully, few cops smoked inside the van anymore, but a closed-up surveillance van quickly collected a variety of odors – fast food of every conceivable kind, sweat mixed with various deodorants and perfumes, fumes from a leaky exhaust, and other, more unmentionable, smells. Leaving the van actually made it worse. The cops grew accustomed to the smell after a couple of hours, no matter how bad it was, and if they then left the van to grab a bite or take a piss, the fresh air made getting back into the stinky, stifling, claustrophobic vehicle that much worse.

The Rosalee subdivision, between Sixty-fifth Street and Stockton Boulevard north of Elder Creek Road, was one of the predominantly white areas of the Elder Creek section of town, with lower- to middle-class homes on generally nice suburban or semirural streets. Go a few blocks in any direction around Elder Creek, however, and it was very different territory. Some houses showed pride of ownership, with clean yards, neat landscaping, and fresh paint; but most were rentals, subrentals, sub-subrentals, or squatter-occupied, and no handyman or can of paint had come near them in years. The area was a melting pot of races and ethnic backgrounds: whites, blacks, Hispanics, Asians, plus every possible mix.

The house just north of the target address on the corner was a very nice single-family property with a decent-looking lawn, well-trimmed shrubs still wrapped in burlap to protect them against the winter frost, plenty of lights surrounding the place, and a For Sale sign in the yard. The reason for the sale was probably the ramshackle house next door, a one-story frame structure of rotted wood and cracking stucco set in a dirt yard covered with patches of brown grass. It was surrounded by a mangled, rusting chain-link fence, and a huge pit bull terrier prowled the yard, barking fiercely at the slightest provocation. Some of the windows were boarded up, and others caged in steel bars bolted onto the outside of the house.

Usually it's the dirtbag traffic around a house that gets cops' attention, but this time it was the dog that had roused the interest of Intelligence and Narcotics again. When the occupants of the house were first busted, they had a fierce rottweiler guarding the place; after the bust, the dog was gone. The new occupants had a dog too, but it was small, a beagle or something like it, just as noisy but no killer guard dog. Drug dealers rarely used beagles as watchdogs. A few kids' toys in the yard, a morning newspaper, and pizza boxes in the trash cans were more indications that maybe the occupants weren't dealing or cooking meth.

But a few weeks later, all these domestic touches began to disappear. The foot traffic increased, the toys vanished, the take-out food containers were gone – meth users never ate very much – and the beagle was replaced by a pit bull. It definitely attracted attention.

The objective of this surveillance was to observe and look for opportunities. It had been suspected that the Satan's Brotherhood was using this house for selling or distributing crank, but Narcotics had never been able to get enough solid evidence to prove it. They had tried every trick in the book: making traffic stops of vehicles that had recently been to the place, hoping to find some crank inside so they'd have probable cause to get a warrant to search the house; tailing frequent visitors, hoping to catch someone on possession with enough stuff to go after the house itself. None of this ever panned out. Neighbors were too terrified of the Brotherhood to cooperate with the police, and there was simply not enough weight moving into or out of the place to attract serious manpower. Surveillance on the house had been spotty at best, and it was finally terminated because the police couldn't justify the cost or time to the captain, or the probable-cause circumstances to a judge who would be asked to sign a search warrant.

But the house was definitely Brotherhood and probably a meth lab – and it had survived the recent bombings. Even on lean days, the place probably turned several thousand dollars' worth of methamphetamine a week – if someone was going to wipe out the Brotherhood's drug outlets, this certainly would have been on the list. That was enough information for Deanna Wyler to order surveillance restarted.

The last three hours of this twelve-hour shift were the real dog part. This was when all the coffee in the thermos was cold and the burgers sat like lead weights in the gut, slowing down blood circulation and acting like a big sleeping pill. The van was cold, the seats smelled musty, and the rubber-covered eyepiece in the 180-millimeter telephoto camera was slimy from all the oily eyes that had touched it.

A few subjects had approached the house this evening, but they had been scared away by the pit bull. One visitor did bring out an occupant of the house; the surveillance teams got some good snapshots of a big biker-looking guy with long, stringy dark hair, a beard, and a leather vest over a bare torso, but little else. The big-ear directional microphone picked up an argument between the two. 'What you got, man?' the visitor had asked, his voice coarse and cracking.

'What you need? You need a snort, man? I got what you need.' They had met at the chain-link fence, but it was obvious that the occupant didn't want to be out in the open too long.

'What the hell is this, man?' the buyer asked angrily. 'That ain't no line.'

'Where you been, muthafucker? There ain't no shit on the street. The Brotherhood's fucked. This is it, man. You want it?'

'You rippin' me off, man.'

The surveillance officer eyeing them through the one-way window scowled. 'They could be talking about buying Girl Scout cookies, for chrissakes,' he muttered. He knew there was nothing in their conversation so far to hold up in court. 'C'mon, boys, do the deal.'

An exchange was made, and the officers got pictures. The twenty-dollar bag of a white crystalline powder looked like a speck of white paint, a fraction of the normal size of a hit of meth. 'They'd laugh that buy right out of the courthouse,' the surveillance officer said. 'We need some weight, boys. These mouse-shit-size buys aren't going to cut it.'

'There's hardly any dope on the streets,' another officer said resignedly. 'Everyone's scared to be holding any weight. They think whoever took out the Brotherhood might go after them.'

'We should give this thing another week, when the brave cookers start gearing up,' said another officer as the buyer moved off and the seller went back inside. 'Nothing worthwhile is happening now.'

'Politics,' the officer watching the front door said. 'The chief and the mayor want something for their press conferences, something so they can show folks they're in control. Election day is coming, and . . .'

'We got another guy,' the officer with the camera interjected. 'Sheesh, I must be getting tired. I didn't even see
him walk up.' He looked up from the eyepiece, rubbed
his eyes, then went back on it: 'Medium height, about
five-nine; husky build . . . looks like he's wearing a full
set of leathers, jacket and pants. How the hell can those
guys wear those things? He's wearing his helmet too. One
of those full-face jobs.'

'I didn't hear a Harley,' the other officer remarked.
'Usually you can hear those things three blocks away.'

'I don't see a bike.'

'No bike, huh?' Now they were all interested. 'What's
he doing?'

'He's . . . uh-oh, he just walked right through the front
gate. That pit bull's going to have him for breakfast – I
don't care how much leather he's wearing.'

'This oughta be good.' The second officer lifted a set of
binoculars and peered through the one-way mirror. 'Here
comes doggie booking around the house.' They could hear
the angry barks and growls. 'The guy must be a regular.
The dog must know him.'

'That dog's still on the hunt . . . oh shit, looks like he's
going to pounce! Better hop the fence, dude!'

The pit bull pounced, all right, jaws extended, teeth
flashing in the light of the front porch, going right for
the newcomer's left wrist – then let go as soon as he
clamped on. They watched the dog shake his head, bark,
growl again, and then leap for the stranger's left ankle.
The same thing happened – the dog bit but did not hold
on. At this angle they could see that the guy was holding
a small backpack in his right hand. A third leap, and this
time the dog clamped down hard on the fingers of the
guy's left hand. The force of the bite jerked him around to
the left and downward – but then, as casually as swatting

a mosquito, the stranger slapped the dog on the side of his head. They heard him yelp in pain and saw him knocked to the ground as if he'd been hit with a baseball bat. Weird. The slap didn't look that forceful.

'And the dog is down!' one of the surveillance officers proclaimed. 'Ha! Never saw a pit bull run with its tail between its legs like that before! What'd he use on the dog – a Vulcan nerve pinch or something?'

'Mace, probably,' said another officer.

'I didn't see him spray. Anyway, sometimes badass dogs like pit bulls aren't affected by pepper spray. He's a lucky bastard, though. He might be cranked up already, and the pain is going to hit him full force when the dope wears off. Hope the crank is worth it. Maybe we can just go and pick this guy up and see how his hand is doing, and ask him what he did to that dog.'

'I don't really give a shit,' said the head surveillance officer. 'Wonder what he's got in the backpack? He just set another bag down by the front door. His hands are clear. Maybe this is a delivery.'

'Through the front door? Yeah, like Domino's or something – your crank delivered in thirty minutes or less or it's—'

A huge explosion rocked the van. The cops' heads flew back as if they had been stabbed in the eyes, the brilliant flash temporarily blinding them. 'Shit, what the hell was that?' one officer shouted, trying to rub the flash out of his eyes. 'He set off a bomb?'

'Sure as hell did!' said another officer. 'Looks like he tried to plant it, but it went off before he could get away.' He scrambled for his handheld radio, hoping it was set to the right channel because he couldn't see the selector knob if it wasn't. 'KMA, Special Unit Four-Four, roll backup, fire and bomb squad on our location for a nine-two-seven bomb explosion. Notify all units of nine-nine-four circumstances, repeat, nine-nine-four circumstances.' The sergeant in charge of the south area sector got on the radio and repeated the 994 call, reminding everyone responding to the call to use bomb threat procedures: no radio, MDT, or cellphone calls within two blocks of the scene.

It took several long moments before the cops in the van could get the use of their eyes back. When they finally peered through their telephoto lenses, they could see the stranger lying on his back, blown about ten feet away by the force of the blast. 'Looks like the biker got a faceful,' one officer said. 'I hope the ambulance guys bring spatulas – they're gonna need . . .'

He stopped, and his jaw dropped in disbelief. The stranger who had planted the bomb and looked as if he had been smashed flat by the explosion struggled to his feet and a moment later was standing in the blown-apart doorway of the crank house.

Patrick heard the dog's bark through his sound amplification system and he even picked up the sound of its pads racing across the muddy grass from the backyard, but he didn't actually notice the pit bull until it grabbed his wrist, then his ankle, then leaped for the fingers of his left hand. There was no pain, but the sight of the big dog latched onto his hand frightened him. All he'd meant to do was dislodge the jaws, but the sound he heard when his other hand hit the poor creature's head was sickening. The dog yelped and dropped to the ground, blood oozing from his ears.

Sons of *bitches*, Patrick cursed into his helmet, sending a dog out to fight their battles! He fought to suppress the anger spreading through his head but he was furious. He hurled the backpack full of explosives against the door, selected the short-range FM channel to the detonator, and keyed the transmit switch.

At the explosion just a few feet in front of him, the light-sensitive visor in the helmet instantly dimmed so the flash wouldn't blind him, and the environmental system inside the suit began circulating more coolant to drench the blast of heat. But the blast pushed him back and off his feet, and when he opened his eyes, the rage that had seared into his head was burning red-hot throughout his body. He moved his arms, then legs, then torso – everything worked fine, no pain anywhere. A quick systems check: battery already down by half, to four hours remaining. It had been at six hours just before he approached the door, so the blast must've sapped a lot of juice. Everything else reported normal.

The explosion had blown open the door, taken out some of the wall to the left and right of it, and cut off all power in the house, but there was enough light from outside for Patrick to realize he was in a living room, with the kitchen visible beyond. The place was a pigsty – the explosion didn't help, of course, but it had to have been unfit for human habitation before that. Garbage was scattered everywhere, and he could make out spray-painted graffiti on the walls.

A tall, lean figure dressed like a commando or special-operations infantryman in a black combat suit, balaclava, and combat harness rounded the corner of the hallway to the left, leveled a small automatic machine pistol at Patrick, and fired. He rocked backward as the triple-round burst hit him, more from surprise than pain or the impact of the bullets, since all he felt were the powerful electric shocks coursing all across his body. Damn, Patrick swore, I thought that problem was fixed! The electric current blurred his vision, and when he rocked back, he stumbled against a piece of debris and sank down against the wall.

'*Stirb, du Teufel!*' he heard the commando shout. He pointed the gun right at Patrick's head and fired again.

This time, Patrick felt the impact of the blast against the helmet – but it was a love tap compared to the surge of electricity that shot through his body. The pain was exquisite, as if every nerve ending was firing like the spark plugs in a race car – but most of all it felt so goddamn *good* . . .

The commando looked as though he were seeing a ghost rise out of a gravesite. '*Wer bist du?*' he shouted.

Patrick charged, forearms up. The commando screamed and fell backward into the tiny kitchen. In rage, Patrick bent over him, grabbed his face in his left hand, and pushed his head against the floor. His fingers felt like steel spikes. He ripped off the balaclava and saw a young, fair, chiseled face staring at him in terror. 'The drugs,' Patrick said through his electronic helmet. 'Where did you get the drugs?'

'*Drogen? Ich weiss nichts!*' the soldier cried. '*Lass mich los!*'

'Who the hell are you?' Patrick demanded. 'Are you a German? *Deutsch?*' There was no answer. 'Who *are* you? Do you work for the Major? *Kommandeur? Der Major?*'

The look on the soldier's face gave him his answer. He had struck home at last.

'Where is the Major?' Patrick racked his brain for remnants of his German – it had been years since he'd used it. '*Vere* . . . no, shit, *wo ist der Major*, asshole?'

'I will not answer!' the soldier said in broken English, and in a flash pulled a knife from a boot sheath with his left hand and shot it toward Patrick's chest. Patrick caught his wrist, but not in time to stop the thrust, only slow it . . .

. . . and the knife blade inched toward the suit, touched it, then pierced it.

A warning tone sounded in the helmet. Cooling fluid from the environmental control system spurted out, and then the knife pierced the thin cotton lining of the suit and touched flesh. At the pulse of electricity discharging through the suit, and his panic, Patrick cried out and rolled away. The soldier leaped to his feet and scrambled for the rear door beyond the kitchen.

The suit didn't work – the knife had penetrated it! Patrick felt for the breach. It was small, a slit less than an inch long – how in the hell could the BERP suit protect him against bomb blasts and gunshots but not protect him against a simple knife jab?

Patrick did a systems self-test. He would lose all of his coolant in a few minutes, and after that the sealed-up suit would probably become too uncomfortable to wear. But he was relieved to see that the system integrity was still intact – a cut in the BERP fabric didn't render the entire system inoperative. He still had a couple of hours of power left.

He was going to catch the German, torture the hell out of him until he told what he knew about the Major. He activated the low-light sensor in his helmet and stopped in his tracks at the entrance to the kitchen. A body was lying on the blood-soaked floor – a big guy with long, stringy hair, his arms and shoulders covered in tattoos, bullet holes in his head. From the commando's gun? What was a German commando or soldier doing here in a known Satan's Brotherhood house? The Major was German too. A connection? Could be that the terrorists who had engineered the bomb blasts throughout the

Sacramento area were mopping up the remnants of the Brotherhood they'd missed. It felt like a clue at last.

He heard a sound in the back of the house and went down the hallway. It was coming from the vicinity of a small bedroom on the right, which had a smell even the suit's environmental systems couldn't filter out – but all he could see was debris and garbage, and evidence of some strong chemicals too, probably from cooking drugs. Then he spotted a little nest of soiled blankets and a filthy pillow, with some empty fast-food containers next to it. It looked as if a small child had been sleeping there. Fucking animals, Patrick said to himself. Allowing a child to live like this . . . it's subhuman.

The bathroom on the left had been partially blown in by the explosion, and he realized this was where the heart-wrenching sounds of a child's sobs were coming from. When he pushed open the broken door, he found a tiny little girl inside, half covered in debris from the blast. She couldn't have been more than two or three, and she was a waif, skinny as a straw, and as dirty and as uncared-for as the house. He could make out bloody cuts on her head; she must have been in there when the explosion hit.

'Easy, sweetheart,' Patrick said softly. 'I'll help you out of here.' But the child began to scream, a long, wild, piercing scream, and he saw her eyes bug out and her little body shake in terror. She tried frantically to claw her way out of the debris, but only succeeded in bringing more of it down around her. Patrick ignored the screams, eased her free, and gently laid her down on the threadbare carpeting in the hallway.

Using his laser holographic heads-up display, he selected the VHF frequency of the UC-Davis Medical Center emergency dispatch center, which he had discovered while with

Paul in the hospital. 'Davis Dispatch, have an ambulance respond to the residence at Sixty-fifth and Rosalee Heights,' he radioed. 'Victim is a female child, approximately age two, with lacerations on the back and head and possible head trauma. How copy? Over.'

'Unidentified caller, this is Davis Medical Dispatch Center, this channel is for official use only. If you require emergency medical assistance, please clear this channel and dial 911 on any telephone.'

'Listen, Dispatch, I'm in a drug flophouse in Rosalee with a dead drug dealer and a young girl who's been hurt in an explosion and is probably going into shock,' Patrick radioed back. 'The police are on their way. Send an ambulance *right now*.' Patrick terminated the call and turned to the now unconscious child. He had to try to give her first aid until the medics got there.

Suddenly Patrick heard a cry, *'You bastard! Get out!'* and something hit his helmet. A half-naked woman was standing at the end of the hall, clutching an aluminum softball bat. He couldn't guess her age – she might have been young and maybe even pretty, but the drugs had left her ravaged face seamed, gaunt, and covered with sores, and her hair hung thin and lifeless. 'Fucking cops! Leave us alone!' she shouted, and swung the bat again. Patrick let it bounce harmlessly off his right shoulder.

'Is this your daughter?' he asked. 'Is this your child?'

'Fuck you!'

'How can you let your own child live in a place like this?' Patrick shouted at her. 'How can you let her sleep in a room where you cook drugs?'

'You want her, you take her!' the woman yelled. 'She does nothing but cry and throw up all day anyway! Just get the hell out!' She moved in closer to take another swat at him, and Patrick swung his left shoulder and hit her square in the face. She bounced off him as if she had been hit by a truck, screamed, scrambled to her feet clutching a bloody broken nose, and retreated back into the bedroom.

Patrick carried the unconscious child to the living room. He found some clothes piled in a corner and tucked them around the frail little body as best he could. Her breathing seemed normal, thank God – maybe it was fright that had knocked her out and she wasn't going into shock. He hunted for pillows to cradle her head . . .

'*Sacramento Police Department! Freeze!*' Patrick turned around. Two guys in jeans, sneakers, and jackets stood in the shattered doorway, aiming automatics at him.

'Do as he says, mister,' said another voice. Two more cops, these in uniform, were taking cover behind the door leading to the kitchen.

Patrick faced them, hands along his side but palms facing outward to show they were empty. 'The child's hurt,' he said. 'I've called an ambulance. Someone get a first-aid kit.'

'I said, stand still and get your hands up where I can see them,' the first cop ordered.

'I'm unarmed. I'm trying to help this child. She was caught in the explosion . . .'

'Turn around, face the wall, with your hands up and your feet spread. Do it! *Now!*'

Patrick felt as if he was in a daze. He turned and faced the wall. Despite his anger at the guys like Chandler and Barona, obeying the police was in his blood. He'd been taught from childhood to cooperate with them, do everything they told him. They were doing an important job. They were there to help the innocent . . .

'One dead over here,' one of the uniformed cops called out, waving a flashlight. He must have found the dead biker in the kitchen. 'Multiple gunshots and knife wounds.'

One of the plainclothes cops saw the blood on Patrick's body. 'Did you kill him?' he asked.

'No,' Patrick replied. 'There was a man here before me, a guy that looked like a soldier or commando, speaking German. There's a woman in the back bedroom too. I don't know how many more are back there.'

'We'll check it out.' The two uniformed officers headed toward the bedrooms with guns drawn, and the first plainclothes cop asked, 'Did you plant a bomb in that doorway to blow that door open?'

'Yes.'

'You're under arrest. You have the right to remain silent.'

'You had this place under surveillance,' Patrick said angrily. 'Why didn't you raid it? Why were you just sitting out there?'

'How do you know we had it under surveillance?'

Patrick looked at the cops. 'You saw a drug deal go down right in front of you, and you . . .'

'*Face the wall!*' the cop yelled, pushing Patrick's helmeted head hard against the wall.

'That's him!' they heard. It was the woman, her nose still bleeding, being led out of the back room, handcuffed and with a blanket over her shoulders. 'That's the cop that beat me up and tried to rape me! When I fought back, he took my daughter and said he was going to kill her!'

When she reached the living room, she caught sight of the man lying on the kitchen floor. She screamed. 'Oh God, that's my husband! He killed my husband! That murdering bastard, he killed my man!'

'Don't worry, lady,' said one of the uniformed officers. 'We've got him. He's under arrest.'

One of the cops grabbed Patrick's left wrist and twisted it down and back. Patrick tried to fight back, and realized that, like the knife attack, the BERP suit couldn't resist a gradual application of force. As long as the force wasn't sharp or powerful, it would not activate.

'Relax your arm, pal,' the cop ordered. 'Don't resist or we might have to hurt you.' Another cop pushed his fingers under Patrick's jaw, pressing the nerve. The sharp pain made him see stars. Another tried unsuccessfully to kick the backs of his knees to get him down, which would give them more leverage. He realized they were easily overpowering him, and in a moment they'd have the handcuffs on him.

'Don't touch me,' Patrick said, fighting to keep his voice steady and his emotions under control. 'I don't want to hurt you. I'll come along peacefully, but don't try to hurt me.'

'Then stop resisting and put your hands behind your back,' an officer ordered.

'You don't need handcuffs on me!' Patrick shouted. 'I'll come along peacefully. Let me loose!' They almost had him – one man was on each arm, and he was tiring quickly.

'That's not how it works, buddy. The handcuffs are for our protection. We'll take 'em off as soon as we're sure you'll cooperate with us. They won't be on long, and they won't hurt as long as you don't try to resist. Relax, bud. We put cuffs on everyone. It's routine. Don't panic over it. Before you know it it'll be over with. No one wants to get hurt . . .'

'Then let me go and I'll do whatever you—'

'*Dump him!*' someone shouted. Pepper spray hit the front of his helmet. The environmental system only allowed a whiff of it to enter the helmet, but the irritation muddled his thinking. He was scared. All four cops were on top of him now, dragging him backward. He landed flat on his back with a hard thump. A forearm was pressed against his throat, a knee was shoved in his groin, and they were trying to pull the helmet off . . .

. . . and when Patrick hit the floor, the electrical surges that had been quiescent for the past several minutes shot back with full force. Patrick screamed, a deep-throated, electronically amplified howl. The uniformed cop with his knee in Patrick's groin got an armored knee to his midriff and was saved from a broken left rib cage only by his Kevlar bulletproof vest. He cried out but kept on fighting until the second knee crashed in. The two plainclothes cops had hold of Patrick's arms, pinning them down with the full weight of their bodies so he couldn't move – but his head was free. Using his legs for leverage, he head-butted one cop, then the other. Blood spattered, but they held firm until Patrick was able to work his right hand free. That was enough – a simple swat at one of their faces made the guy feel as though he'd been hit with an iron skillet. The last cop landed a couple of blows to Patrick's head and rammed his knees into his rib cage, but every blow was like hitting a brick wall, and he finally let go of his prisoner. Both he and Patrick rolled to their feet.

The cop drew his sidearm and aimed it at Patrick. '*Freeze, asshole!*' he shouted. 'Don't move!'

Patrick held up his hands again. He did another system self-test and noticed he now had a problem. Power was discharging more quickly now – the levels were down to one hour remaining, and it had only been minutes since he checked it last. There was no way of telling if the suit would protect him against more gunshots. Time to get out of here.

'All right, listen,' Patrick said. 'I am telling you guys the truth. I am on your side. I blew the door in and came in here because I knew you were doing a surveillance on the place but couldn't enter unless you had probable cause or saw a crime actually take place. I'm not going to hurt you unless you try to arrest me.'

'All right, all right, we won't touch you,' one of the plainclothes cops said. He still had his gun drawn, but held out his left hand as a sign of good faith. 'If you say you're on our side, that's good. We won't try to hurt you either. Just answer a few questions for us, how about that? I gotta remind you that you have the right to remain silent, the right to an attorney, and the right not to answer questions unless your attorney's present. Do you understand what I've just said?'

'Yes.'

'Good,' the cop said. 'There's no reason why anyone has to get hurt. We're just doing our jobs. If you're innocent, if it was justifiable, everything will be fine here. But you gotta cooperate with us. Why don't you start by taking off the helmet?'

'The hell I will,' said Patrick. 'You're trying to delay me until more backup units arrive.' He scanned the police channels accessible through the new VHF system in his helmet comm system. 'Two units, the sergeant, and a fire unit are on the way now. I'll be long gone before then . . .'

'Don't you try to leave, buddy,' the cop said. 'You're a murder suspect. You look like you're carrying a weapon in that backpack, and you hit one of my officers and almost knocked him cold, so you've got a weapon hidden on you. If you try to run, we can shoot to stop you. We'll kill you if we have to, but we don't want to do that. Just stay put. Don't move.'

Patrick made another systems check: power down to forty minutes remaining, much less than he hoped for but still plenty to get him out of this. 'I'll tell you once more,' he said. 'I'm not your enemy. Don't fight me. These guys who set off all the explosions all over the state are the enemies, not me. We need to work together.'

'Don't move,' the cop warned again. 'You're under arrest. Don't move or I'll shoot!'

He had to get out of there before the reinforcements arrived. He fired his boot thrusters, aiming for the shattered front door. Gunshots – this time hitting on his right shoulder, each impact like an electric cattle-prod to his head and his heart. He hit the broken right side of the door and spun around, landing hard just outside.

A small crowd had collected outside the house. A woman screamed. 'Police!' he heard behind him from inside the house. 'Everyone, clear the street! *You! Freeze! Hold it right there!*' And in front of him, no more than fifteen feet away, was another uniformed cop, crouching behind his open squad-car door, lights flashing, headlights dead on him. Patrick dodged left to go around the car. The officer fired two shots. The crowd cried out in horror when Patrick went down, but that was a whisper compared to the reaction when he got back up on his feet.

Warning advisories flashed in the heads-up display inside his helmet. My God! he realized, he was on emergency power. The emergency power setting was for emergencies only – for escaping and surviving, not doing battle. The system was supposed to provide an hour of reserve power, a warning to recharge or leave the battlefield, before reaching into emergency power. He'd never received a reserve power warning, or else it had drained right through that level with one gunshot. His power indicators said he had another thirty minutes of emergency power remaining, but at the rate it was draining with every shot, he knew it would only last a few more minutes.

'Freeze!' called the uniformed cop who had just shot him. 'Get down on the ground! Get down now or I'll shoot!'

There was a sudden soft *whoosh!* and a short blast of compressed air – and Patrick vanished.

'There he is!' someone shouted. Everyone turned. He had reappeared next to a fire truck responding to the scene almost a half-block away. He got up, turned, ran down Sixty-fifth Street, then disappeared again. Police vehicles gave chase, together with a responding sheriff's-department air unit, but it was no use. The suspect had disappeared.

Santo Porte, California
that same time

'It appears you were correct, Colonel,' Reingruber said as Gregory Townsend rushed into the command center at the hideout in the Sierra Nevada foothills near Santo Porte after being awakened by his excited deputy. 'We are receiving news reports from Sacramento about some invasion-style assaults on drug houses and Satan's Brotherhood locations in the city.'

'Is it any of our men?' Townsend asked. 'Are your men accounted for, Major?'

'*Ja, Herr Oberst,*' Reingruber replied. 'All of my strike teams reported in and are returning. It is not any of my men.'

'Any indication on who's behind these attacks?' Townsend asked as he sat down in front of the bank of television sets. 'Is it the Mexican drug gangs? Rival biker gangs?'

'There are no specific reports, sir,' Reingruber replied. 'Reports of a few bikers injured, one casualty. Indications are that police had brief gunfights with the intruders, but there were no reports of arrests. However, one team reported contact with a lone, strangely outfitted unidentified police officer or military security officer. One of my men was seriously injured in a scuffle with him.'

'Was he a National Guard soldier?' Townsend asked. 'A police SWAT officer?'

'He could not verify exactly who it was, sir,' Reingruber said. 'He did manage to wound him, but he reports that the unidentified man's uniform had some unusual characteristics. In addition, reports we have heard on police frequencies indicate that this was the same figure involved in the invasion-style attacks, and that the outfit the unidentified officer was wearing is like full-body bullet-resistant armor.'

Townsend was intrigued. 'A new military technology, in use by National Guard troops but deployed on the street in a civil mission?' he mused. 'I must get as many details as possible on this armor. Where are your men who encountered this man?'

'It will be several hours before the teams return, *Herr Oberst*. They are executing full evasion procedures in enemy territory.'

'I want to talk with that team as soon as it arrives,' Townsend said. He thought for a moment. 'This is a good sign. I see frustrated and maybe even fearful police, perhaps rival gangs trying to move in on the drug trade in the city or vigilantes or militia taking to the streets, and angry citizens demanding that something be done. It is beginning to look as though the city is starting to rip itself apart, Major. Any reports from the target area?'

'Still normal activity, sir,' Reingruber replied. 'Departure appears to be within the week.'

'They will soon have no choice but to accelerate their

departure,' Townsend said. 'It will happen in the next few days. Get your men ready to move.'

Patrick McLanahan was hiding between two Dumpsters behind a minimall just off Stockton Boulevard when Jon Masters pulled up in the Hummer. He had driven there when he noticed on the satellite tracking system that Patrick had not moved in several minutes. Patrick unfastened his helmet, then slid into the backseat. 'How did it go?' Jon asked. Patrick did not reply. 'The tracking device in the suit worked perfectly. I had a map of your every move. The undegraded GPS signals pinpointed you within six feet.' Still no response. 'Lots of police around,' Jon added. 'I thought we'd head the opposite way, east, toward Florin-Perkins Road.'

'Just get us out of here,' Patrick said.

'Patrick, there are police everywhere . . .'

'I've been monitoring the police frequency,' Patrick said. 'The police are setting up a perimeter in the Rosalee subdivision between Stockton Boulevard and Sixty-fifth Street. Head west on Thirty-seventh Avenue and we should miss the outer-perimeter roadblocks on Stockton Boulevard and Lemon Hill Avenue.' Patrick was filled with a burning rage. 'Man, I knew Sacramento had problems, but I never dreamed it was this bad,' he went on. 'The drugs, the abuse, the violence – they're beyond belief. It's like a battle zone.'

'I'm just glad you're in one piece, bro,' Masters said. 'I was worried.' He went south on Stockton Boulevard. They could see a knot of headlights and blue flashing lights up ahead and guessed it was the first police road-block. Jon made a right onto Thirty-seventh Avenue and Patrick steered him through neighborhood streets, hoping the turn hadn't attracted attention. Before long they were safely headed northbound toward downtown Sacramento. 'How did it go, Patrick?' Jon repeated. 'Why didn't you rendezvous with me?'

Patrick started the generator in the back of the Hummer, then retrieved the power cord from the generator and plugged it in. But the backpack power unit was not charging, and the environmental system was completely shut down. 'The suit's damaged,' he replied. 'A knife cut it. I lost the environmental control system and power drained out at three to four times the normal rate. I was lucky to get out of there.' Patrick took a deep breath and leaned back against the headrest. 'I think I hurt a little girl too,' he said.

'*What?* Oh no, Patrick! Christ – how did it happen?'

'The bomb,' Patrick explained. 'The bomb I used to bust open the front door destroyed part of the bathroom where the little girl was.'

'They had a child in there, where they sell and make drugs? How badly was she hurt? Did you call an ambulance?'

'Yes,' Patrick responded. 'She was bleeding, a little shocky – but she screamed pure holy terror when she saw me.' Jon was relieved; a child's death would have been unendurable. 'Jon, you should have seen that house. It was filthy. The child, she was sleeping in a bedroom that they used to make drugs. I could smell the chemicals. She was sleeping on garbage, eating leftovers off the floor, breathing fumes that would've knocked out an adult. It was horrible . . .'

'Patrick, it's all right,' Masters said. 'For all you know, you might have saved her life by doing that raid. You didn't put a child in harm's way. *They* did.' He paused, unsure whether to ask Patrick what he wanted to know;

then: 'What happened with the suit? How was it damaged?'

'It was a knife attack,' Patrick replied. 'I was struggling with this guy who looked like a commando, complete with face mask, combat harness, the works. He pulled a knife. I grabbed his arm, but I couldn't stop him, he was too strong. The blade touched the suit and just went right on through. Power levels dropped off sharply after that, but the system remained intact. But I also discovered that the cops could wrestle with me and win. Any slow action and the suit couldn't activate. I barely got out of there without being handcuffed.'

'It must be the nature of the BERP process,' Jon surmised. 'We never tested the system with a soft or slowly penetrating force, only a sharp impact. The same characteristic of the suit that allows you to move freely means that a slowly penetrating force won't activate the electro-reactive collimation.'

'So a bomb blast won't kill me,' Patrick said, 'but a knitting needle pushed in slowly will go through my heart with ease?'

'We should be able to fix that,' Jon said, cringing at the image. 'We might be able to have you selectively harden sections of the suit. What about the power levels?'

'Dropped way down after the cut in the suit,' Patrick said again, 'especially after being hit repeatedly.'

'Hit?'

'Hit . . . as in shot,' Patrick said.

Jon's gulp was audible. 'How many times were you shot, Patrick?'

Patrick took a moment to count. 'About a dozen times in the space of six minutes. Plus I got hit by a baseball bat a couple of times and bitten by a pit bull – I nearly killed it too.' He said all this so matter-of-factly, Jon noticed, that he could have been a piece of stone relating what had happened.

'So we need to bump up the power reserves a bit, and reprogram the power-monitoring logarithms,' Masters said. 'We still haven't cured those discharges inside the suit, have we?' No reply. 'Patrick, are you sure you're okay?'

Patrick's tone changed a bit as he went on: 'You know what I did, Jon? When I planted that charge by the door, I didn't take cover. I just stood there and let it rip. It was almost as if I was thinking, If this bomb kills me, fine. If I survive, fine, I'll do this mission. I survived. I don't know why I did that. Maybe I thought it was like a test or something, a validation, proof that what I was doing was the right thing.' Patrick was quiet for a long moment, but Jon could actually feel the tension, the rage building in the backseat. 'Those sonofabitches,' Patrick went on in a low, angry voice. 'They kill, they terrorize, they poison others, they abuse their children – I want to kill every last one of them!'

Then he added, 'I got some information on where the Major might be hiding. There was a German-speaking commando already inside that house when I arrived. I think he was there to take out the surviving Satan's Brotherhood members. Another biker gave me information on a hideout in Wilton. I want to go there. Tonight. Right *now*.'

'Patrick, you can't and you know it,' Jon said. 'The reason we were successful today is because we did pretty good intelligence work and planning. We don't have another target planned right now. You have some initial intel on a potential target. Fine. Let's build on that. But now is not the time to do it. Your suit is damaged, it's not taking a charge, and there are cops and National Guard troops everywhere. The only reason we haven't been bothered so far is because there are already so many Hummers on the streets right now that we blend in.'

Patrick thought for a long moment. 'You're right,' he said at last. 'And we've got to get the cops involved in this too. I realize I'm fighting the cops even more than I'm fighting the bad guys. That's no good. Let's get the suit fixed, and then we'll plan our next move.'

Special Investigations Division Headquarters, Bercut Drive, Sacramento, California
a short time later

'What in the *hell* is going on?' Arthur Barona thundered as he strode into Tom Chandler's office at Special Investigations Division headquarters. His suit was rumpled; he had clearly dressed in a hurry. Chandler was on the phone, trying to listen to the information being passed to him and to the bellowing chief of police at the same time. 'I just got tossed out of bed by the damned mayor himself,' Barona went on. 'He's been getting calls about a *rogue Narcotics cop* killing civilians and busting up people's homes and businesses? I want answers, and I want them *now*!' He stormed out of the office to the conference room across the hall.

Chandler put the phone down and went to join Barona. 'That was Deputy Chief Ohrman, Chief,' he said. 'He's ordered Homicide to take over the investigation.'

'What in hell is going on?' Barona repeated. 'Reports of an officer in body armor and full riot gear blowing up somebody's home, killing the occupant and nearly killing a youngster? Another cop in riot gear breaking into the Bobby John Club, nearly killing three patrons?

Cops not trying to apprehend the suspect as he flees on foot? . . .'

'That's inaccurate information, Chief,' Chandler said. He started from the beginning, detailing the two incidents of the strange invader in body armor who appeared to be rushing around the city in a Hummer going after drug dealers and biker-gang members. 'That's all we know right now,' he ended.

'What about this Hummer?'

'A witness reported the suspect getting into a Hummer on Arden Way shortly after the Bobby John Club incident.'

'Arden? That's several blocks from Del Paso Boulevard.'

'The guy moves fast,' Chandler said. 'He's got some kind of jet thing in his boots that lets him jump . . .'

'Or there's more than one of them,' the chief said. 'It's not any of your men, is it?'

'I've started a telephone recall of the entire division and ordered Property to do a full inventory of our property rooms,' Chandler replied. 'I don't think it's any of my men, but I'm going to do a full accounting just in case. Every man has to account for his whereabouts tonight. But I can tell you, it's not any of them.'

'What about you?' Barona asked. 'Where have you been tonight?'

'At home with my wife, Chief,' Chandler replied irritably. That wasn't entirely accurate – until about eleven-thirty, he was with a woman friend up near Folsom Lake. But his wife would vouch for him if anyone bothered to check. She was accustomed to putting up with his antics. 'Yeah, DC Ohrman thinks I was the guy, as if I've got nothing better to do these days than to run around in tights busting heads. That's bullshit. I was home.'

'All right, Tom, all right,' Barona said. 'What else? What about the witnesses?'

'Witnesses and officers on the scene describe an individual, probably male, five eight or five nine, medium build, wearing what appeared to be a dark gray tight-fitting outfit similar to a wetsuit, stiff but flexible; a strange high-tech-looking helmet that altered and amplified the suspect's voice; and a thin backpack, similar in size and shape to a sport-jumping parachute but thinner,' Chandler answered, checking his notes. He paused, then added, 'Our officers at both the Del Paso Heights and Elder Creek scenes report that the outfit worn by the suspect was probably some sort of new lightweight body armor. Several officers reported discharging their weapons at the suspect and hitting him, but the suspect appeared unhurt or only slightly injured.'

The chief asked something, but Chandler's mind had drifted off momentarily. High-tech, high-tech . . . it reminded him of a conversation he'd had with someone not too long ago. Who was it? Chandler couldn't remember . . .

'*Chandler!* What about weapons?'

Chandler shook himself from his reverie. 'No weapons reported, Chief, except my surveillance officers said the suspect planted a satchel charge at the door of a known meth house in the Rosalee section of Elder Creek that was under surveillance at the time.'

'So what it looks like is that we have a vigilante or some well-equipped militia type with explosives roaming the streets,' said Barona, 'taking out the last of the Satan's Brotherhood with more explosives – this time delivered in person by a soldier in body armor. Sounds like whoever booby-trapped those drug machines is looking to finish the job by picking off the survivors one by one.'

'Looks that way to me too, Chief,' Chandler said absently. He was still trying to tease out that memory. Revenge . . . high-tech . . . soldier . . . what in hell was it?

'And the DC is turning this over to Homicide?' Chandler nodded. He couldn't tell whether Barona was perturbed by this news or not. 'Okay, but I still want you working with them. I want to know the results of your division internal investigation too. We might have to do the entire department. We've got to make sure this wasn't a rogue cop.'

'I can guarantee it wasn't,' Chandler said. 'And if it was a cop, he's a pretty stupid, sloppy one – he'll get caught soon enough.'

'Better make that happen, Chandler,' Barona said. 'Find him and throw his ass in jail. Whoever this guy is, I want him hung out to dry.'

Good for you, Chief, Chandler said to himself as Barona stalked out. You bust my hump even though I've been taken off the case – and you'll proudly take all the credit for busting the guy if you have the chance.

Chandler looked over the notes of his conversations with his surveillance teams. It seemed incredible – too incredible to tell the chief: a guy who seemed invulnerable to bullets. A guy who had an outfit that moved like nylon but could instantly harden into a suit of armor. A guy who could leap fifty feet away and twenty feet up. It was a vigilante or militiaman, all right – but a vigilante unlike anyone ever seen before. Either this was some kind of joke, a ploy by his officers in the field to cover for the work of a vigilante or militia group, or it was a science-fiction movie come true.

And if it was true, this guy could be the ultimate police officer, the ultimate weapon in the hands of law enforcement – or the ultimate nightmare for them.

Women. Can't live with 'em, can't live without 'em – can't shoot 'em.

After all the shit that happened in the past couple of months, Tom Chandler thought, and just when it seemed as if he'd be able to come up for air – hell, now Kay wanted a commitment from him, wanted to stop sneaking around, wanted him to divorce his wife. Shit.

He had come to his girlfriend's house to get away from the craziness and relax. Some welcome. They had a good thing going here. Why'd Kay want to screw it up by wanting a commitment? Of course, that still didn't stop them from dropping down and doing it doggie-style right on the living room floor, but Chandler was glad to get the hell out.

It was a long, dark drive from Kay's place overlooking Folsom Lake to Douglas Boulevard, which would take him back toward the interstate and home. The heavy runoff from the deep snows in the Sierra Nevada Mountains, combined with nearly forty straight days of rain, filled Folsom Lake, a one-million-acre man-made reservoir thirty miles east of Sacramento, almost to capacity. They were releasing water from four of the eight big steel gates on the dam, but the water level in the lake was still rising. It was an annual balancing act for water officials in this area: measure releases from the dam to keep the reservoir full to supply the fast-growing Sacramento Valley with water through the upcoming long, dry summer; release enough water to keep the forty-year-old dam from rupturing; but don't release so much as to cause flooding down the American River and inundate the city of Sacramento. State and federal water officials were not always successful keeping all three properly balanced.

Folsom Lake had always been special for Chandler. As a kid, he used to skip school, ride his bike more than twenty miles, and hang out at the lake, trying to stay one step ahead of the truant officers. He lost his virginity at Folsom Lake; he met his first two wives at Folsom Lake. It could look like a raging ocean, as it did now; in four months it could look like a desert wadi with a little stream running down the middle, as it did the year one of the gates on the dam broke and three-quarters of the lake spilled out. It didn't matter to Tom Chandler – he would always be drawn to it.

Chandler was on a shoulderless, unlit road just west of the lake when he heard a loud bang, felt his steering wheel jerk to the right, and heard the sickening *flopflopflop* of a flat tire. *Shit!* He hadn't changed a flat tire in forever, but it would take at least half an hour for a wrecker to get out here. It was a department vehicle and the city would pay for the call, but he didn't want anyone to find out he was taking a city car out to his girlfriend's house. Still swearing, he pulled off to the side of the road, stopped the car, got a Stinger flashlight from his glove compartment, and got out to inspect the damage.

He had just stooped down to look at the flat when he was clubbed over the head with a thick rubber baton. He did not lose consciousness, but he saw stars and he couldn't make his hands and feet work right. As he tried to cover up his sidearm, someone pinned his hands behind his back and the gun was snatched out of his holster. Then gloved hands dragged him off the road into the low brush and sand dunes, and dropped him facedown. A boot pressed down on the back of his neck.

'Good evening, Captain Chandler,' said a cheerful British voice.

'Who the hell are you?' Chandler shouted. 'I'm a fucking cop! Get off me!'

'Who I am is irrelevant and unimportant, Captain Chandler,' the voice said. '*What* I am is your salvation.'

'My what?'

'Your salvation,' the voice repeated. 'I am here to help all your problems go away. Stop struggling and I will be happy to explain. Continue to resist, and I will be forced to end your police career – not to mention your life – sooner than I'm sure you desire.' Chandler realized he had no choice: No one except Kay knew where he was, and she wouldn't try to contact him for at least a day. His wife didn't really care if he was dead or alive. He stopped trying to free himself.

'Thank you so much,' said the Brit, and the boot lifted off his neck. Chandler sat up in the damp sand. There was a figure standing in front of him, but a flashlight was shining in his face, blocking out the man's features.

'I must say, Captain, you are a nasty man,' the Brit said with mock disapproval. 'I don't mean to sound judgmental, but you do seem to be letting your vices get the better of you. Although I truly believe that the true measure of any man is evident in his appetites, it seems you are allowing your appetites to destroy you.'

'I never got slugged in the head by that little voice on my shoulder before,' Chandler said sardonically.

'Indeed,' the Brit replied, all humor gone. 'After some extremely cursory inquiries, I find you are several thousand dollars in debt; you owe several thousand dollars more to a variety of loan sharks and bookies; and you just cannot seem to – how shall I put it? – keep it zipped up.'

'Who the hell are you? The morality police? The church's strike force?'

'I am the man who can make your problems go away, at least in part,' the Brit said. 'What you do with your zipper is up to you. But your gambling debts can disappear tonight.'

'And what do I have to do for you?'

'A simple matter – information. Everything you have on the strange costumed man who has been running about this city. Everything you have on the suit he wears. I understand that suit has certain special properties that are of great interest to me.'

'I don't know squat about a suit,' Chandler said, 'and whoever told you about "certain special properties" has been yanking your chain.'

The rubber baton came down on the back of his head again, not as hard as before but enough to make him cry out. 'Stop being flippant, Captain, or I'll terminate this offer to you right now, *permanently*,' the Brit said angrily. 'I've monitored the police radio reports. Your men said this individual jumped twenty feet in the air and almost a half a city block in one leap. Your reports said not only was he bulletproof, but that his suit was like solid metal armor one moment and then like ordinary fabric the next. This is not conventional body armor. Whatever it is, Captain, I want it.'

'Hey, asshole, I'm not in charge of the case – it's been turned over to Homicide,' Chandler said. 'But listen, maybe we can trade some information. You wouldn't happen to know anything about any German-speaking terrorists in this area, would you? Maybe one called the Major?'

The rubber baton was pressed around his neck so hard that he thought his windpipe would crack. 'I am offering you help with your financial problems, Captain – I'm not interested in becoming your snitch,' the Brit said, coming closer. 'I have made you a very generous offer. Cooperate with me, and you'll live to gamble, screw, and piss your career away as you choose. Cross me, and I'll see to it that you witness the deaths of your wife and your girlfriends before you die yourself. I'm not precisely sure what it is in your pitiful life that you value the most, but I assure you I'm very good at finding out and taking it away from you in a very gruesome manner. When I next get in touch with you, sir, you had better have some information for me, or it will all end for you.'

The choke hold let up just before Chandler thought he was going to pass out from lack of oxygen. He collapsed on the sand, trying not to panic as he took a long, thin breath through his constricted throat.

At least now I've got a good excuse why I'm late getting home, he thought to himself.

Research and Development Facility,
Sacramento-Mather Jetport,
Rancho Cordova, California
Friday, 27 March 1998, 0052 PT

Sacramento-Mather Jetport has two runways, one eleven thousand feet in length, the other six thousand, both one hundred and fifty feet wide. The old Strategic Air Command alert-aircraft 'Christmas tree' parking area – so named because from the air it somewhat resembled a tree – was only two thousand feet long from the end of the ramp to where the throat of the taxiway joined Runway 22 Left. It wasn't even a proper runway, because there was a steep drop from the alert ramp down to the runway. But it was more than adequate for this particular aircraft.

Its nickname was Skywalker. Carried in three sections on board one of Sky Masters, Inc.'s transport aircraft from the company's production facility in Arkansas, together with its self-contained control module, it was delivered to Mather Jetport and reassembled by two men inside one of the hangars at the research and development facility Sky Masters had leased. Skywalker resembled a manta ray, with long, thin, tapered forward-swept wings and a large oblong fuselage. Its skin was fibersteel, a composite material stronger than steel but non-radar-reflective, so it was invisible to radar. It had two small, efficient propjet engines and enough fuel to fly for several hours.

Skywalker's other nickname was HEARSE, which stood for High Endurance Aerial Reconnaissance and Surveillance Equipment. It carried almost half a ton of sophisticated all-weather sensors and communications equipment. It could photograph an object the size of a rabbit from thousands of feet in the air in any weather, and beam the pictures in real time to a ground station or command aircraft.

Under cover of darkness and a light springtime drizzle, Skywalker's engines were started up and it was taxied to the end of the alert parking ramp. A push of a button activated its preprogrammed flight plan and it zoomed down the parking ramp, airborne before it reached the end of the throat. It made a steep left turn away from the buildings over the airport and continued its climb southwestbound. The aircraft had a small transmitter, similar to a light plane's transponder, that would send out a '1200' code to allow air traffic controllers to 'see' it and help any aircraft flying in the area avoid it. To anyone on the ground, however, the plane was invisible.

This was Skywalker's third flight since arriving at Mather Jetport earlier in the week. In its first six-hour flight alone, it had photographed the majority of south Sacramento County, about six hundred square miles. The second flight was used to pinpoint specific locations and to provide comparison photographs that would show activity at any of the targeted locations.

This third flight was not designed for reconnaissance – it was designed for surveillance. The target had been pinpointed. Skywalker would now be used to watch over the target area as tonight's mission got under way.

Special Investigations Division Headquarters, Bercut Drive, Sacramento, California the same time

The side door rattled, clunked awkwardly, then closed. It sounded as though yet another surveillance team was coming in to do its debrief before heading home. Tom Chandler thought he'd sit in on the debrief, show the troops that the old man was still on the job, then go home and get some rack time before beginning the shit all over again in about six hours. Just as he was getting up there was a knock on his door. 'Come.'

The door swung open. Chandler nearly jumped out of his skin. There, standing before him, was the guy. The vigilante. The . . . whoever it was. It was *him*. He fit the description provided by Chandler's Narcotics officers exactly: dark gray outfit resembling a wetsuit, full-face high-tech helmet, backpack, the works.

He entered the office and closed the door behind him. Chandler drew his SIG Sauer P226 automatic from his shoulder holster and aimed it at the apparition. Neither spoke for a moment. Then Chandler said, 'Well, well, if it isn't the Tin Man. You know, that's what the guys in my division are calling you now. We've been looking for you. Who the hell are you?'

'A friend,' the intruder replied in an electronically altered voice.

'What do you want?'

'To give you information.'

Chandler blinked in surprise, but kept the gun level. 'Why the outfit? Why the disguise?'

'A German-speaking commando was at the Rosalee drug house last week,' the guy said, ignoring Chandler's question. 'He was the one who murdered the biker, not me. And a biker at the Bobby John Club told me that Mullins was hired by a German-speaking gang to help in the Sacramento Live! robbery. Those two guys with the broken legs that you let go – they were Germans. That's the tie-in you were looking for . . .'

But Chandler wasn't interested in the Tin Man's theories. 'You're under arrest, bub,' he said. 'You're wanted for the murder of that biker, plus attempted murder of my police officers and a couple of civilians, for breaking and entering, assault, battery, malicious mayhem, and trespassing.'

'I won't allow you to arrest me,' the guy said matter-of-factly. 'Your officers tried. You can shoot me if you like. It won't hurt me. But as I told your officers: I didn't kill that sonofabitch biker. Although after I saw what kind of conditions he kept that kid in, I wish I had.'

'Is that so?' Chandler asked. 'Listen, mister, you can tell all that to the judge. You're under arrest. Turn and face the wall, hands behind your back.'

'Chandler, you will not be able to arrest me,' the Tin Man said. 'I'm telling you the truth. I don't want to

326

fight you – I'm trying to assist you. I'll do anything I need to do to prove I'm on your side. But you can't arrest me.'

'Bullshit,' Chandler said, holstering his weapon. 'My guys told me you can be had.' He reached out and grabbed the guy's right wrist with a come-along hold. He had been practicing various holds just in case he ever encountered him.

But the guy simply reached over with his left hand and, as though he were swatting a mosquito, smacked Chandler's hand. It was only a tap, but it felt as though the hand had been sandwiched between the bumpers of two crashing cars. He jerked it away in pain. 'Motherfucker!' He drew the gun and aimed it again, stepping back so the guy couldn't reach it. 'No more shitting around, asshole! Turn around, hands behind your back!'

'Don't waste your bullets, Chandler,' the Tin Man said. He picked up a letter opener from the desk, held it in both hands, and plunged it into his chest. The blade bent, then snapped. He picked up a silver pen and jabbed it into his arm, and it broke in two. 'You tell me when you're convinced you won't be able to hurt me, Chandler,' the guy said.

'All right, all right!' Chandler said. 'Don't wreck everything on my desk.' He started running through the suspect identification and memorization checklist in his head: height, weight, build, age, voice, other distinguishing characteristics. The guy sounded white, male, maybe late thirties, but it was almost impossible to tell much with the electronically altered voice. The suit might have increased his height and weight, so maybe five seven to five eight and medium build. Keep him here until help arrives . . .

'Now what, big shot? Are you going to break my head and my shoulder bones like you did those bikers'?'

327

'No,' the Tin Man said. 'I came here to deliver my information, and to tell you I'm going after the ones responsible for the violence in this city. I can do it without your help, but I prefer to work *with* you.'

'Who are you to think you're the one to take this on? What makes your information worth anything? Because you wear this high-tech wetsuit and bust some bad guys' heads?'

'You don't have to believe me,' the guy said. 'I'm just informing you of what I'm going to do. We can work together on it. You give me the information I'm looking for, and I'll do what I have to do, what the Constitution prohibits you from doing.'

'I've got a newsflash for you, bub,' Chandler said, praying that one of his patrols showed up soon. 'The Constitution prohibits you from doing it too. It's called breaking the law. You do this, and you'll be just as much a dirtbag as the bums you're going after.'

'Except the *real* dirtbags will be off the street, and I'll go home and stay out of the way,' the intruder said.

'The problem with you vigilantes is that you never go home,' Chandler said. 'The rush you get by breaking heads stays with you, and soon you spin out of control. You think you can just take the law into your own hands like this? What gives you the right to break into people's homes and businesses and tear them up?'

'I don't care if you or anyone else thinks it's right or wrong, Chandler,' the intruder said. 'I've got the power to do it. Are we going to work together, or will you just hear about it on the radio and pick up the pieces afterward?'

'Work together? What the hell do you mean, work together?' Chandler asked. He lowered the gun but kept it in his hand. 'How the hell can you see me working with you? And if I did, who's your first target, hotshot?'

'One of the bikers said Mullins was going to report to a ranch in Wilton,' the intruder said. 'I think that's where we'll find the German terrorists. I'm looking for a British-sounding terrorist who may be working with them too.'

Chandler's throat turned as dry as sand. Shit, he knows about the Brit too? Was it some incredible coincidence, or was it possible that they could be hunting the same guy? And if they were, *could* it be possible to join forces with this guy, the Tin Man, and maybe take on the Brit and his German terrorists together? Perhaps . . . but face it, this character was as much a wild card as the Brit.

'There's only about a dozen suspected labs and possible hideouts in Wilton,' Chandler said. 'You going to hit them all?'

'I was hoping you'd give me a clue.'

'We don't have the foggiest idea,' Chandler said. That wasn't entirely true. But surveillance was extremely difficult because the ranches were so big and the houses were so far off the road. 'Besides, that's Sacramento County, not the city. You got any targets in the city?'

'Why don't you give me a couple?' the intruder asked.

'Because I'm not sure I want to risk losing my badge and my career to help you,' Chandler said. 'Giving you information so you can go out and commit a crime is conspiracy and aiding and abetting. For all I know, this is some kind of elaborate setup.'

'You're a little paranoid, aren't you? I'll go out and find my own targets. See you in the funny papers, Chandler.'

'Wait!' Chandler shouted. Shit, where *were* those guys? . . . 'How can I get in contact with you?'

'Don't call me – I'll call you.'

Chandler followed the guy to the side door – and to his relief, saw headlights turning into the parking area. His cops were finally back.

The Tin Man saw them at the same time, heading for the main entrance. Chandler noticed that the front door had been smashed in and realized his guys saw it too. Within seconds, three of them were approaching it with their guns drawn. Two others came around to the side door. Chandler raised his weapon again. 'You're surrounded, mister. Surrender right now.'

The intruder raised his hands. 'I'm unarmed,' he said through the electronic mask.

'That's him!' one of the officers shouted. 'He's the Tin Man! That's the guy who was at the Bobby John Club!'

'Chandler, your officers won't be able to take me,' the Tin Man said calmly, 'and if they open fire in here or try to tackle me like they did before, someone can get hurt. I'm asking you to call your officers off. I won't hurt anyone if they leave me alone.'

'Captain, he's a murder suspect,' one of the officers said. 'He's wanted for the murder at the Rosalee stakeout – and he put a uniform in the hospital too.'

'I know, dammit, I know!' Chandler shouted to his men. 'But you saw what he can do. Do you think it's realistic to think we can take him?'

The cops were silent. They got the point, recognized they'd need a lot more help or a lot more firepower – but they didn't want to admit it.

'Let him go,' said Chandler.

'But Captain—'

'I said, let him go. We have no choice. Until we can figure out how to shut him off, leave him alone.'

The cops stood there and listened as the Tin Man turned to Chandler. 'Thank you, Captain,' he said. 'I do want to work with you, not fight you. You need to believe I'm on your side – I'll prove it to you. Just wait. I'll be in touch.'

Then Tin Man calmly walked outside. They watched as

he ran northbound across the parking lot, leaped over the low one-story buildings, and vanished. 'Christ Almighty!' said one of the shaken officers. 'I've never seen anything like that! Who the hell *is* he?'

Chandler ordered his men back inside headquarters and had them write out statements detailing everything they knew or had heard about the guy they called the Tin Man. While they were at work, he slipped back into his office. Holding his broken letter opener in his hand, he dialed a tollfree voice-mail number. He had already checked it out; it was a dead phone drop, a computerized voice-mail service, paid for with cash with a PO box as the customer's address. He dared not check further – the Brit was bound to find out.

'The subject was just here,' Chandler spoke into the digital message service. 'He says he's found one of your hideouts and he's heading your way. I think he's heading toward Wilton, sometime soon if not tonight. Catch him yourself if you can. And I want my money, mother-fucker.'

Wilton, California
later that night

'Heading two-three-zero . . . area's clear . . . go,' Jon radioed to Patrick on the secure VHF channel. He was in the Hummer command post, a few miles from Skywalker's target position, watching the blip Patrick made on the screen. The terminal in the Hummer showed a composite picture of infrared and light-intensified surveillance images from the reconnaissance aircraft and the satellite tracking data Patrick was sending, and Skywalker's live video feed was displayed on the terminal.

The Skywalker images revealed several patches of recently disturbed ground, which could be assumed to be land mines planted by the bad guys around the Wilton ranch. There had been a lot of activity there in recent days, and a variety of vehicles moving in and out of the property – much more activity than could be properly accounted for. The number of individuals varied. Weapons were all over the place, and roving patrols kept crisscrossing the property. For a ranch that had no animals, no crops, and no ranch or farm equipment evident, all this was highly suspicious.

The thruster jump was a little long, but it placed Patrick between two rings of disturbed earth. They had no way of knowing whether he had landed far enough away from whatever was under there to be safe, but the farther away, the better. Patrick scanned the area with his low-light vision sensors. He was about five hundred yards from the house, where all the activity now seemed to be. 'Can't see that roving patrol anymore,' he radioed.

'The nearest patrol is to the east, about two hundred yards,' Jon radioed back. 'You're right in between two rows of something. You should be able to clear the inner row with the next jump. Turn left, head one-eight-zero, area's . . .'

Jon's report was cut off by a burst of heavy automatic gunfire. A row of bullets ripped into the ground a few feet from where Patrick was standing. He hit his thrusters and leaped toward the ranch house just before the next bullets hit. 'Shit, Jon,' Patrick radioed as he landed. 'Felt like a fifty-cal that time.'

'Gunfire's coming from a ditch bearing one-five-five, range about seventy-five yards,' Jon reported. 'The gun must be hidden in a culvert or under a building.' He couldn't see the gun or the shooter from the Skywalker images, but the blasts looked like bright sparkles, and the red-hot bullets were visible as they plowed into the earth.

Patrick turned to his left and leaped. The machine gun tried to track him in midair, so he was able to identify the location of the nest perfectly. It was hidden in a large culvert that ran across a ditch. He landed right on the road over the culvert, then started running down the road toward the house. Seconds later, a huge explosion split the night. He had left an explosive charge on the road over the culvert, blowing the concrete bridge and the machine gunners underneath it into the mud.

'Wait, Patrick!' Jon radioed. 'The road! . . .' But he was too late. Before Patrick could make the leap toward the house, he stepped on a mine planted in the road. The explosion blew him six feet into the air, swerving around and flopping like a rag doll caught in a twister. He landed hard and awkwardly, and lay there motionless.

'Patrick! Do you read me?' Silence. Jon zoomed the Skywalker cameras in and had a clear view of Patrick lying on the ground, still not moving. Moments later, two Jeeps headed from the house across the meadow toward him. 'Patrick! Two vehicles approaching! Can you hear me? Patrick!' Silence. 'If you can hear me, Patrick, wake up!' Jon screamed. 'They'll be on you in thirty seconds!'

Wearing night-vision goggles, three German soldiers dismounted when they were fifty feet from where they thought Patrick lay and approached on foot. At thirty feet they deactivated their image-intensifiers so the muzzle-flash of their guns wouldn't blind them, and fired at the intruder. Then they reactivated their night-vision optics and advanced on him – but no one was there.

A horn beeped behind them. They turned, found themselves staring into the full-bright headlights of one of the Jeeps, and ripped off their goggles in pain. One of them swore, leveled his machine pistol, and fired at the head-lights. It took almost an entire clip to shoot them out.

'You missed me!' shouted an eerie electronic voice. The shooter swung his submachine gun left to track the voice.

'*Nein! Nein!*' came a shout – but too late. The gun-man, still blinded, opened fire across the area where the voice had come from and cut down both his fellow soldiers.

Patrick checked his suit's systems – running perfectly so far, although power levels had been cut in half after the land mine. 'Down to three hours already,' he radioed.

'Thank God you're okay,' Masters answered. 'I copy that. Do you want to withdraw and get a full recharge? I can watch the area and let you know if anyone tries to escape.'

'No, let's press on,' Patrick said. 'I'll try to conserve power every chance I get.'

Inside the ranch house, the two remaining guards heard and saw the gunfire but could not raise their comrades on the radio. '*Patrouille zwei, berichten!*' one of them called. 'What is your status? Have you terminated the intruder? Patrol Two, report!'

'Here's one heading back,' said the other lookout. 'Patrol Three is heading back!' A Jeep was racing back across the meadow, bumping through the furrows. Then he shouted, '*Wo wollen die hin?*' The Jeep was headed straight for the ranch house at top speed. 'It's him! It's the intruder! Open fire!'

The guards raked the Jeep with their submachine guns. A tire exploded and the vehicle swerved momentarily, then kept on its collision course. One of the guards leveled an antitank rocket launcher at it. It exploded, flipped over, and hit one of the outbuildings near the house.

'Where is he?' There was no sign of life in the vehicle and a quick survey of the house and grounds showed they were clear as well. 'We'd better radio the lieutenant,' said one of the guards as he removed the spent magazine and retrieved a fresh one from his ammo pouch. At that moment a helmeted figure flew at them, body-tackling them like a rocket-powered battering ram. In seconds they were disarmed by hammering blows that felt like steel batons, cracking fingers and wrists.

'*Wo ist der Major?*' the intruder demanded. '*Wo ist der Engländer?*'

'*Go to hell!*'

Patrick heard Jon Masters's voice through his radio. 'Hey, I've got several vehicles heading this way, heading east on Grant Line, moving fast! How's it coming?'

'These guys aren't talking,' Patrick radioed back. 'There're a lot of weapons here, including a rocket launcher – I'll bet they match some of those used in the Sacramento Live! shootout. Can you reach the sheriff's department?'

'Already called,' Jon reported. 'I'm going to change position, get farther to the west away from these newcomers. Let me know if you find anything. I'll signal you when you'll have visitors.'

Patrick secured the guards with nylon handcuffs and began to search the ranch area. He hit pay dirt right away. 'Jon, I got something,' he radioed. 'The barn is full of chemicals. Barrels of it. Ether, acetone, thionyl chloride, phosphorous-3-iodide – oh shit, tanks of hydrogen gas, enough to blow half the county sky-high. You better warn the sheriff's department to bring a HAZMAT crew out here – there's enough poisonous stuff here to kill ten thousand people.'

'Copy,' Masters responded. 'On the way.'

Patrick swung around at a sound off to his left. To his astonishment a scrawny little man carrying a nylon gym bag was running as fast as he could down the long main driveway toward Grant Line Road. Patrick caught up with him with a single thruster jump.

'Jeez!' the man yelped. 'Who the hell are you?'

'I'm the one who's putting you out of business,' Patrick said, yanking away the nylon bag. 'Who are *you*?'

'Nobody!' the little man shouted. 'Let me go!'

Patrick rapped him once on his bony chest, and the guy screeched and hit the ground. 'I said, who are you?'

'You broke my chest!' the man whimpered.

'I'll break your head if you don't answer me!'

'I'm Bennie Reynolds.' The man struggled to his feet despite the pain and cried, 'We've got to get out of here!'

'What are you doing here?'

'I work here. I work for Townsend and the Aryan Brigade. Listen, there's no time . . .'

'Townsend?' said Patrick. Christ, the pieces were finally starting to fit together. 'The British terrorist? You mean Gregory Townsend, the weapons dealer?'

'I told you who, asshole.' The guy was sounding panicky. 'Jesus, we've got to get out of here! The barn has been booby-trapped!'

'What?'

'Don't ask questions, stupid – just *run*!' Patrick didn't hesitate. He grabbed Reynolds and hit his thrusters. Even though the guy didn't weigh very much, the leap was only seventy or eighty feet. But it was a spectacular ride for the drug-cooker. '*Hol-ee shit!*' he cackled. 'Awe-*some*! You can *fly*!'

It would take several seconds for the thrusters to recharge.

'Okay, now talk,' Patrick demanded. 'Where is Townsend? Where's the Major?'

'They bugged out maybe twenty minutes ago,' Reynolds said. 'I don't know where they were headed. You went into the barn, didn't you?'

'Yes.'

'Then we're dead unless we can get at least a mile away from here,' Reynolds said. 'For sure you tripped a switch. Townsend has that barn booby-trapped seven ways to Sunday. Hit those jets and let's get the hell out of here!'

'Can't quite yet,' Patrick said. They started down the road as fast as Patrick could half-carry, half-drag Reynolds. He switched over to his secure channel: 'Jon, we're on the move,' he said. 'I've got one prisoner.'

'Copy,' Jon replied. 'I'm heading toward you.'

Patrick called up the GPS tracking device on Jon's location and saw he was around a mile and a half away. He grabbed Reynolds, turned in the direction of the Hummer, and hit the thrusters . . .

. . . and just as he was about to touch down from the first eighty-foot leap, a massive explosion erupted behind them. A delayed-action bomb exploded inside the barn, rupturing the hydrogen tanks and sending up a huge cloud of fire.

They were lifted off the ground by the shock wave and thrown another hundred feet. The concussion from the blast landed them across Grant Line Road in a shallow cow pond and covered them with eighteen inches of muddy water, just as the white-hot fireball rolled over them like a tsunami. The fireball vaporized the six-acre pond, turning it into a blackened hole – but as the water vaporized it sucked away enough of the heat from the fireball to keep the two of them from instantaneous incineration.

337

Then the suit's environmental system kicked in, and – barely – kept enough of the residual heat away from Patrick's skin to prevent his being burned. But he could not protect Reynolds. He covered him with his body as best he could, but when the fireball rolled over them Bennie's clothes burst into flames, the hair on his head turned into white ash, and his skin reddened, then turned dark, then peeled like burned paper.

It was over as quickly as it began. The vegetation as far as Patrick's eyes could see was blackened down to the earth. The ranch house and the buildings around it were gone. On the other side of Grant Line Road, over a half mile away, other buildings were on fire. The ground around him was crusty and smoldering. He did a systems check – the suit was still functioning, although the environmental system was guzzling power at a tremendous rate. He took off his helmet to help it vent excess heat.

'Nice try, flyboy.' To Patrick's astonishment, Reynolds was still alive. 'You almost got me out.'

'Try to relax. I'll get you to a hospital as fast as I can.'

'Never been to a hospital, and I don't intend to go now, buddy,' Reynolds said. 'Damn, now I know how those salmon feel sitting in my skillet.' He looked at Patrick, his face just visible in the faint glow from the fires. 'You look like a good guy, brother. I seen you before, haven't I?'

'Don't know,' said Patrick. 'Maybe on TV – there was some stuff when my brother was in the hospital. Paul McLanahan, one of the cops who was shot by the Major. Is he part of Townsend's organization?'

'Yeah. The Aryan Brigade, they call themselves,' Reynolds said. 'Although they don't do much Nazi shit except when there's visitors.'

That was an interesting tidbit, thought Patrick, filing it away. 'They were the ones who staged that robbery at

Sacramento Live!?' he asked. 'They set up those explosions around Sacramento?'

'Yeah. Townsend ... what a piece of whacked-out work,' Reynolds said. 'Kills two cops to steal enough money to build meth hydrogenators, then gives them away to the bikers, then blows them all up. Squandered hundreds of thousands of dollars. He tells me we can start up production again out here at the ranch, then booby-traps thousands of dollars' more worth of chemicals. One sick motherfucker. I knew I should've stayed away from him.'

'Where is he now? Where can I find him?'

'Don't know,' Reynolds gasped. He was having difficulty drawing breath by now. 'Only place I ever been is right here.' He was looking at Patrick, but his eyes were focused far away. 'Hey, man, I'm sorry ... sorry about your brother an' those cops,' he said weakly. 'I never meant to hurt no cops. All I wanted to do was go about my business . . .'

It was an apology, Patrick realized; the poor guy was trying to make his confession. But Patrick felt only disgust. 'I guess your business is over,' he said, then realized Reynolds had died before he could hear those words.

Minutes later, Jon Masters arrived in the Hummer. He was as excited as a kid in Disneyland. 'Oh man, did you see that explosion?' he asked as Patrick climbed in, turned on the generator, and plugged in the backpack. 'It looked like a mushroom cloud, just like those old photos of aboveground nuclear tests in Nevada, except it was all fire! How close were you to the blast?'

'About a hundred yards.'

'A close shave – awesome!' Jon exclaimed. 'Hey, where's your prisoner?'

'Dead,' Patrick said. 'Didn't you see his body lying

there? He got burned up by the fire after the blast. But he talked before he died – he was the guy in charge of cooking drugs and building the equipment for a group called the Aryan Brigade.' Patrick filled Jon in on what he'd seen at the Wilton hideout.

'It looks to me like it must be over now,' Jon said. 'With his base of operations gone, this Townsend guy must be heading for the hills.'

'I'm not sure about that. Some things that Reynolds said make me wonder. Look – he said that Townsend staged the Sacramento Live! shootout to raise money to build the meth generators. Then he gave the generators away to the gangs – and blew them all up. The deal would have been worth hundreds of thousands of dollars a month. Why would he give all that up so Reynolds could go back and start making drugs all over again? It doesn't make sense. There's got to be some other agenda. And Reynolds said that Townsend and his group don't act like neo-Nazis except when there's someone around from outside their organization. I wonder what that means.'

'It means he's crazy,' said Jon. 'Maybe he thought he'd lose control of the Brotherhood unless he killed them all. Maybe he wanted to make his mark with the cops and the gangs, you know, sort of be the *capo di tutti capi* or something. Or maybe it was some kind of tactic to run the price of meth up on the street, then make his own and make more money. Who knows? Who cares?'

Patrick let it drop. They took Douglas Road west to the east entrance to the Mather airport, which gave them a shorter drive to the old SAC alert facility on the southeast side of the runway. The roads were completely deserted. They turned down the long access road that led to the entrapment gate. As they pulled up, Jon activated his earset cellular telephone and dialed the number for the guard shack so they could open the outer gate, but the line was busy. 'Busy?' Patrick asked. 'That doesn't sound right. You'd better let me . . .'

There was a tap on Jon's window. They turned in surprise. To their astonishment, there was Tom Chandler, the muzzle of his 9-millimeter automatic pressed against the glass. He made a circular sign with the gun, and Jon reluctantly rolled down the window.

'Good evening, Dr Masters,' said Chandler. 'You're out late tonight.' He looked into the backseat and saw a wiped-out Patrick McLanahan sitting by himself. He was in that Tin Man suit Chandler had last seen as he leaped away from the headquarters parking area. 'And good evening, Mr McLanahan – or should I say, *General* McLanahan. You've been very busy tonight, I see.'

'Go to hell, Chandler,' said Patrick.

'Easy, General.' Chandler gestured behind him, and several sheriff's deputies in full SWAT assault gear emerged out of the scrub bushes and surrounded the Hummer. Simultaneously a dozen squad cars with lights flashing and sirens wailing roared down the access road toward them. 'Party's over, boys. You're both under arrest. You have the right to remain silent.' He held up a sheaf of papers. 'I have a warrant to search this facility and take you and the suit. You and the suit are considered a lethal weapon and we can use any amount of force in our discretion in the name of officer safety. We won't hesitate to kill you if you try to resist. Dr Masters, step out of the vehicle. General McLanahan, stay right where you are.'

SWAT officers opened the doors of the Hummer and leveled H&K MP-5 submachine guns at Patrick. The helmet on the seat beside him was taken away. 'Aim for the head only, boys,' Chandler said. 'Okay, General. Do

341

whatever you need to do to deactivate that getup and take it off.'

Patrick had no choice. He removed the gauntlets, then detached the backpack power supply. Chandler grabbed him and hauled him out of the Hummer. 'Hands on the vehicle, spread-eagle.' He began to search Patrick.

'How did you find us, Chandler?' Patrick asked.

'Give me a little credit, General,' Tom Chandler said. 'I may be a desk jockey, but I can still add two plus two.

'First of all, of course, you told the chief exactly what you were going to do – in the hospital after the funeral, when he barged into your brother's room without checking with the doctors. Remember? You told the chief about what you did, the stuff you work with, the gadgets you could supply the department with. The chief probably doesn't remember that conversation, but I do. I didn't do anything about it, though. Even when you showed up in my office, I thought you were just an angry, frustrated relative who had a few too many beers back at the Sarge's Place.

'But that image was so different from the guy I saw when you were getting ready to move your brother,' Chandler went on. 'You looked and sounded like a guy in control. You got Paul out of the hospital right out from under our noses. That took an organization and resources and training. That's when I knew you were much more than an angry brother and ex-bartender. I had my suspicions about you after that, but I expected you to just find a biker somewhere and shoot him with a handgun. But then I did a little checking, hit up my FBI friends, and found out about your military background – even about your stint with the Border Security Force. Now you got my *full* attention.

'You screwed yourself with those two attacks last week,

McLanahan. My lieutenant briefs me on two specific locations that she wants surveillance set up, and a couple of days later a mysterious guy wearing some kind of lightweight body armor shows up at those very same two places and busts them up. Way too coincidental. You got my division bugged? You bribe a few dispatchers? Hell, my detectives are so pissed off these days, they might've *volunteered* information for you. You've menaced this city, McLanahan. You've broken the law.'

'Oh yeah? With who? Murderers, cop-killers, robbers, drug dealers, child abusers . . .'

'So now you become judge, jury, and executioner, right?' Chandler asked. 'You killed a man, McLanahan . . .'

'I did not,' Patrick said. 'I told you, it was some guy dressed in a black combat outfit who spoke German. He had a face mask on, like a commando. The two guys suspected as being part of the Sacramento Live! shootout, with the broken legs, the two you let go – they were Germans too. That's no coincidence, Chandler!'

'These Germans plant the bomb in front of the doorway too?'

'Okay, that was me, but I didn't kill that biker and I didn't try to rape that woman. I saw those drug deals at that house in Rosalee go down just like your surveillance officers did. I saw that child in danger too . . .'

'Oh bullshit.'

'I acted the way any good citizen would,' Patrick argued. 'I acted the best way I could with the resources at my command. It may have been illegal, it may have even been wrong, but it sure felt *appropriate*. I have seen my family torn apart by these creeps and whoever is supplying and feeding all the chaos in this city. Hordes of innocent people have been killed. I had the power to act, so I did.'

'Sounds like a confession to me, boys,' Chandler said.

'Place your hands behind your back.' Patrick did as he was told, and Chandler snapped handcuffs on his wrists. 'Frankly, General, I thought you'd offer a bit more resistance. An Air Force general officer, with his own private security team surrounding us and a special suit that he could've used to snap my neck in half – I expected you to put up much more of a struggle.'

'I want to talk with a lawyer,' Patrick said flatly.

'Good boy – that's the right thing to say,' Chandler said. 'But I think we already got enough to put you away for a very, very long time. Let's go.'

**Office of the Mayor,
Sacramento, California
Monday, 30 March 1998, 0747 PT**

All the local TV and radio stations, plus a number of national shows, went live at seven-thirty that morning Pacific time in the office of the mayor of Sacramento. Surrounding Edward Servantez were the chief of police, the sheriff of Sacramento County, the captain of the police Special Investigations Division, and the district attorney of Sacramento County.

The mayor cleared his throat and began: 'I am pleased to announce that an arrest has been made in connection with the bombings around the state, the recent invasion-style assaults here in the city of Sacramento, and the large-scale meth-lab explosion in south Sacramento County. Thanks to the efforts of the Sacramento Police Department, in particular Police Chief Arthur Barona and Captain Thomas Chandler of the Special Investigations Division, working together with the Sacramento County Sheriff's Department, a new and significantly dangerous menace has been removed from the streets of our city. This arrest may also shed some new light on the wave of bombings, shootings, and gang and drug violence that has plagued this city for the past several months.

'Arrested this morning was forty-one-year-old Patrick S. McLanahan, last known residence and occupation unknown,' Servantez went on. 'McLanahan is the son of retired veteran Sacramento Police Department sergeant Michael Thomas McLanahan, deceased, and the brother of recently retired police officer Paul McLanahan, who as you might remember was seriously injured in the Sacramento Live! shootout with police last December. Also arrested was Jonathan Colin Masters, age thirty-seven, last known residence in Arkansas. Masters is the president of a defense weapons research and development firm. Let me ask District Attorney Scurrah to outline the charges against the accused.'

The district attorney, Julianne Scurrah, continued: 'Patrick McLanahan was booked early Saturday morning into the Sacramento County Jail, charged with second-degree murder in connection with the slaying of Joseph Brolin, a resident of Elder Creek and a suspected illegal-drug maker and dealer,' she said. 'He is also charged with the attempted murders of five Sacramento Police Department officers, three civilians, and one child; four counts of assault with a deadly weapon; breaking and entering; and three counts of malicious mischief with the intent to do great bodily harm and for exploding incendiary devices within the county. Masters has been charged with conspiracy to commit murder and aiding and abetting in the commission of a felony.

'McLanahan and Masters were arraigned this morning in Sacramento Superior Court before Judge Richard Rothchild,' Scurrah went on. 'They both pleaded not guilty. They are being represented by attorneys from San Diego. Bail in the amount of one million dollars was given for Masters; McLanahan is being held without bail in the Sacramento County Jail. Masters must surrender his passport and may not leave Sacramento County.

'If found guilty on all charges, McLanahan will have been convicted on more than three felony charges. If this occurs, the "three-strikes" repeat-offender law would be invoked and he would have to spend a minimum of twenty years in prison, plus a mandatory additional seven years for each conviction of attempted murder against a police officer,' Scurrah concluded. 'He can be found guilty on the lesser charge of manslaughter in the Brolin death. But my office is seeking a second-degree murder conviction and the maximum penalty because of the particular viciousness of the attack, and also because we want to show the people of Sacramento County that we will not tolerate vigilantism. The death penalty does not apply in this case. That's all the information I have at this time. Thank you.'

Scurrah stepped aside and let Servantez step up to the microphones again. 'We are investigating the possibility that McLanahan and Masters are part of a militia movement and may have masterminded the recent explosions in and around northern California and indeed around the entire state, in coordination with other extremist militia groups,' he said. 'It appears that McLanahan was trying to avenge the attack on his brother by planning and executing a series of attacks and assaults on suspected gang members and drug dealers in and around Sacramento. He was apparently using sophisticated weapons and devices developed by Dr Masters, weapons manufactured for use by the military, to hunt down, capture, interrogate, and then kill those who he thought might be involved in the attack on his brother and other police officers.'

Police Chief Barona took his turn at the microphones. 'I cannot comment any more about this case because of the investigation, but I would like to make one very important point: This city, this county, will not tolerate vigilantes. The city and county of Sacramento have some of the finest law-enforcement organizations in the country. We don't need anyone, no matter who or what they are, taking the law into their own hands and disrupting our streets with hatred and violence.

'We are a society of law. We will not tolerate anyone, no matter what his background or personal motivation, tragedy, or reasoning might be, to take the law into his own hands. McLanahan and Masters, if found guilty of the crimes of which they are charged, will be punished to the fullest extent of the law. I urge the citizens of this county not to be swayed by what the two suspects might claim are their reasons for doing what they did. If they broke the law, they should be punished for it. Thank you.'

Sacramento County Jail,
651 I Street, Sacramento, California
Tuesday, 31 March 1998, 0815 PT

A sheriff's deputy led Patrick McLanahan into the visiting room and escorted him to the seat farthest down the row of phone cubicles that connected the prisoners with their visitors on the other side of the Plexiglas barrier. Patrick was wearing a white T-shirt that looked two sizes too small, with the words PRISONER, SACRAMENTO COUNTY JAIL stenciled front and back, baggy blue jeans that looked three sizes too big, white socks, and floppy black canvas slip-on shoes. The deputy walked between him and the row of prisoners seated in the phone cubicles, but this didn't stop several white prisoners from turning to look at him, muttering threats and flashing obscene and gang gestures at him.

Jon Masters was waiting for him, dressed in a suit and tie. When Patrick sat down at the cubicle, Masters looked at him in shock. He picked up the phone on his side. A recorded warning announced that conversations might be recorded. 'Jesus, Patrick!' Jon exclaimed after the recording stopped and the connection opened. 'What happened to your face?'

Patrick gingerly touched the cuts on his swollen, bruised cheeks and mouth. 'Some bikers got hold of me,' he said.

'Are you all right?' Patrick nodded. 'If they can't protect you in there, I'll get the attorney to have you transferred somewhere else . . .'

'I'm in an isolation cell now,' Patrick said.

'Thank God.'

'Isolation means that only one out of every three gobs of spit hits me now,' Patrick said with a wry smile. 'Now they just *tell* me they're going to rip my balls off, instead of actually trying to do it.'

'Patrick, how can you make jokes at a time like this?'

'I'll be all right, Jon,' Patrick said reassuringly. 'Half of them think I killed their buddies, but the other half think that if they mess with me, my friends will go after their families. It's a part of being in the gang – harassing me shows the other members that they're solid. I can handle it.' Jon's face was ashen, as if he could scarcely believe what he was hearing. Patrick pointed a warning finger at the phone, then at the sign behind Jon stating that their conversations could be monitored. 'Have you spoken with Wendy?'

'Yes,' Jon replied, signaling that he understood. 'She's all right. She's real worried about you.'

'How's Bradley?'

'Just fine,' Jon replied. He smiled, then added, 'A lot of folks in your . . . your *family* have contacted me.' He emphasized the word *family*, and Patrick picked it up. 'They're all very concerned and will do anything necessary to get you out of here and clear your name.'

'That's nice,' said Patrick. 'Ask the family to talk with Wendy and reassure her that everything will be all right. I'll be out of here soon enough. I can't wait to tell my side of the story to a jury. Are you meeting with anyone from the legal department?'

'I'm meeting Henry Fowler, the senior partner in the law firm that does our legal, in about an hour,' Jon said. 'They've got all the police reports, and they say we have a good chance of getting all the charges dismissed. He's going to introduce me to the criminal-defense team they've retained. They'll have someone over later this morning to talk with you.' He looked a little embarrassed, then added, 'I brought over the money you asked for last night, but they took it from me. They said they have to log it in. Have you gotten it yet?' Patrick shook his head. 'God, Patrick, this is a nightmare.'

'Everything will be all right, bro,' Patrick said. 'Just tell Wendy and the family that I'm all right.'

'You got it, bro,' Jon said, watching helplessly as Patrick was led away. A big, mean-looking prisoner tried to get up out of his seat as Patrick was passing, bumped him, and screamed an obscenity before the deputies pushed him back down.

There were reporters waiting out in front of the jail, so Jon was led out a rear exit that bordered on the H Street parking garage, and the heavy steel door locked behind him. He made his way warily around toward the front and looked for the company car that was to meet him, but there was no sign of it. The rain started to come down, a dull, chilly mist at first, then heavier.

Man, he thought, life pretty much sucked right now. Patrick was in jail, charged with murder; the Ultimate Soldier project was compromised, perhaps destroyed; and his company was without a leader, drifting aimlessly. He didn't even have Helen Kaddiri to torment him anymore . . .

Helen. It was the first time he had thought about her in many days, and he realized that the thought of her warmed him inside. For the first time in his life, Jon felt truly alone. For all those years before, he had kept himself surrounded, first with academia, then with the government, then with the company. Now all were gone. He needed Helen. He wanted her. Once the idea was laughable, then unthinkable – and now, all he could think about was her.

He pulled out a cellular-phone earset, a tiny device that looped onto the ear and picked up vocal vibrations in the skull for transmitting. He used voice commands to dial her home number in San Diego and got her answering machine. 'Helen, this is Jon,' he said after taking a deep breath. 'I don't know if you've heard all the news lately, but I'm here in Sacramento. I just got out of the Sacramento County Jail on bail. Patrick is being held without bond. We . . .'

He was going to make a full 'report' to her and fill in the circumstances, but he found he couldn't continue – his heart wouldn't let him use the company 'we' again, wouldn't allow him to be so impersonal. 'Helen, I need you,' he said. 'The company does, sure, but I need you more. I need your support, your guidance, and your friendship. I don't know where you are – probably out making a deal to launch your new company – but please, come up here to Sacramento. I'll probably be at the R & D facility at Sacramento-Mather Jetport, the old alert facility. I won't blame you if you don't show up, but please don't leave me now. I . . . I love you, Helen. I probably sound like the biggest geek in the world, but I don't care. I love you. Bye.'

Jon ended the call and put the earset away. A few minutes later he heard a car horn beep across the street. He looked over and saw a hand waving to him. His ride at last. The driver was unfamiliar and the windows were tinted so he couldn't see in, but he crossed the street and went around to the passenger side. He was surprised to see Tom Chandler in the front passenger seat.

'Hello, Dr Masters,' Chandler said. 'Care for a ride?' He noticed Masters's quizzical expression as he looked at the unfamiliar driver. 'This is Officer Williams of my division. I rate a driver today, and he's it. Need a ride?'

'I've got one coming, thanks.'

'Dr Masters, listen, I know what you and Patrick are going through,' Chandler said. He lowered his voice so the driver wouldn't overhear. 'Don't castrate me because I'm doing my job. It would look worse if I showed any favoritism at all. If I let my opinion that Patrick is a hero leak out, I'd be off the case and you and Patrick would have to swim with the sharks alone.'

'You think Patrick is a hero? The other night you thought he was a criminal.'

'I think both you and Patrick are heroes,' Chandler said, 'taking on the dirtbags in this city like this. It shows courage, real courage. But Patrick's in jail, and the city that you and he tried to protect wants to make an example of him. That's not right. We need to get together and strategize. Come over to my office so we can talk. You can call your people from there and tell them where to pick you up.'

'I don't know . . .'

'Hey, c'mon, Doc, I'm doing everything I can on my end to make sure that you and Patrick get every break possible,' Chandler said. 'The DA doesn't have much of a case. They've been hammering me and my guys for hours, trying to find even the smallest piece of incriminating evidence. They don't have it. But now I need your help.'

'Shouldn't I have my attorney present?'

'This is not an interrogation,' Chandler said. 'I'm not going to ask you anything that will incriminate either you or Patrick. You can refuse to answer anything you feel uncomfortable with.' He saw Masters still hesitate. 'All right, if it would make you feel better, you can call your attorney and have him present. But I'm not going to Mirandize you, because this is not part of the investigation. In fact, it's the opposite – I want to talk about ways I can help you and Patrick get out of this mess. Believe me, there are a lot of cops in this town who are very thankful for what you two did.'

'There are?'

'Absolutely,' Chandler said. 'Even if it gets to trial. But they want to hear from you. Will you do this for Patrick?'

'Of course I will!' Jon exclaimed. 'Man, I'm so glad you came by! I thought you were more concerned about making an arrest than helping us.' Jon hopped into the rear seat as soon as Chandler got the door unlocked.

They headed down I Street toward Interstate 5. Just before they reached the freeway, there was a beeping sound. Chandler turned around and saw Masters retrieve what looked like a Cross pen from his pocket. 'Is that your pen beeping, Doctor?'

'My pager,' Masters said with pride. 'My own design.'
He checked the tiny LCD display on the barrel. 'It's my
driver. Probably wondering where I am. I'll give him a
call and let him know where I'll be.' He retrieved his
cellular-phone earset. 'What I do is punch up the phone
number on my wristwatch. There's a wireless connection
between the earset and the watch. The number I retrieve
on my watch is the one that gets dialed. Or I can use voice
commands.'

'What other gadgets do you have back there, Doc?'
Chandler asked.

'Oh, I got a million of 'em,' Jon replied. 'I can . . .'

A car pulled out of the on-ramp from I Street and cut
in front of their car, and with a screech of the wheels the
driver swerved to miss him, blurting out, '*Schweinehund!*'

'Cool,' Masters said. 'Your driver swears in German.
About all the German I know is "*ein Bier, bitte.*"' The
driver shot a panicky look at Chandler. 'German always
sounds so mean. A naked woman can be whispering sweet
nothings in your ear in bed, and if she's talking in German
it sounds like she wants to rip your heart out with a fork.
I once heard . . .' Jon stopped abruptly, noticing where
they were. 'Hey, aren't we supposed to be heading north
on I-5?'

'No,' Chandler said. 'Dr Masters, give me that cellphone
and your watch right now.'

'You want to see how it works?'

'No, I want to take them from you,' Chandler said
patiently.

'Why?'

Chandler half-turned in his seat, aiming a SIG Sauer
P226 pistol at Masters in the back. Jon blanched. 'Dr
Masters, you are either a very good actor or just about the
most naive and scatterbrained Ph.D. I've ever met.' Jon

handed over the earset cellphone, his wireless transceiver wristwatch, and the pager pen with shaking hands. 'We are going to meet up with some friends of mine. They would very much like to talk with you.'

Jon looked at the driver's eyes in the rearview mirror. 'I suppose they're German-speaking friends, right? Maybe with a guy who speaks with a British accent?'

'I think you're finally getting the picture,' Chandler said. 'Swing around in the seat and put your hands behind your back. I don't think my friends would want you to know where we're going.' Masters did as he was told, and the SID captain reached back and snapped handcuffs on him.

'Why are you doing this, Chandler?' Masters asked. 'Why are you working for the bad guys?'

'Simple, Doc: money,' Chandler replied. 'It was an offer I couldn't refuse.'

'Oh yeah – those gambling debts,' Masters said. 'What were they – thirty, forty grand?'

'So you *did* have my office bugged. The department doesn't even have enough money in the budget for us to sweep our offices of listening devices. Yes, the last time I ever bothered to total 'em up, forty thousand in gambling debts was about right. Add in a few thousand in back alimony and child support, some maxed-out credit cards, an apartment, car, an allowance for my girlfriend in Las Vegas . . .'

'Don't forget Kay in Granite Bay,' Masters said.

'Oh, she's low maintenance compared to Edie in Las Vegas,' Chandler said casually. 'Anyway, even a year of my salary wouldn't bail me out of this mess, assuming I cared to get bailed out at all – not to mention the fact that I'd join a lot of real hard-timers in prison if any of this ever came out. *That's* why I'm doing this, Masters.

And it all goes away today. Just deliver you and the suit to Townsend.'

'You've got the suit too?'

'Of course I've got the suit – it was locked in *my* property room,' Chandler said. 'My new employers want you to show them how to use it, perhaps modify it to fit Townsend himself. Let's face it, McLanahan is not exactly of average dimensions. I'm sure he has the strength and the endurance to wear it, but let's be honest, Doc, an army of Tin Men like McLanahan would not be much of an army. It certainly would not strike fear into my heart.'

'You are so full of shit, Chandler,' Masters said. 'How can you turn your back on your city and your career? Don't all the years you spent as a cop mean anything to you?'

'Not a thing,' Chandler said. 'In fact, I've worked harder over the last five years than I did in my previous thirty years, and I've seen this city – and this entire state, for that matter – slide down into the crapper faster than I ever thought possible. What have I been slaving away for?'

Chandler was all worked up by now. 'A friend of mine retired after thirty-one years on the force. He gets up to receive his plaque from the city and they've mis-spelled his name and service dates on the plaque. Then he gets home and he's the victim of a home-invasion robbery. He goes into a coma and dies two weeks later. No recognition from the city, no tribute, not even flowers for his gravesite. I stood over his damned grave and I saw myself staring up from that hole in the ground. I decided right then, no way I was going to check out like that.'

'Your friend checked out as the unfortunate victim of a violent crime,' Masters said. 'You'll check out as a traitor who sold out.'

'At least I'll check out grabbing for the brass ring, instead of having it shoved up my ass,' Chandler said.

'Real mature attitude,' Masters said. 'You ever stop to think that I might not help you out at all?'

'Dr Masters, you won't be helping *me* out, you'll be helping *yourself* out,' Chandler said. 'I get my money when you get delivered to Townsend. Whatever happens to you then is up to him and you. The colonel is an honorable guy . . .'

'Oh *sure*. Is he the one with the British accent who tied up and threatened to kill Patrick's wife and child, or is he the one who got two cops killed and several others wounded in the Sacramento Live! shootout?'

'He may be ruthless to his enemies,' Chandler retorted, 'but he stands up for his friends. He's assured me that if you do what he says, he'll let you go free. You keep breathing, and you're free to build more Tin Man suits and beeping pens and earset cellphones and whatever the hell else you build.'

'And you call *me* the naive one,' Masters said. 'You're worm food the second the suit and I get delivered. Then as soon as this colonel bozo figures out how to use the suit, I'm toast. And if he starts using the suit, the entire city of Sacramento could be toast. You know it and I know it. I've just accepted the fact that I'm going to die today, Chandler. You still think you're going to have some naked bimbo on your lap tonight. Give it up. You got the gun. Kill that German guy driving the car, and let's get back to town. You tell your side of the story to the cops, you get immunity from prosecution, and . . .'

'Nice try, Doctor,' Chandler said. 'But I've already received a down payment for my services, and I can't disappoint Colonel Townsend. I advise you not to disappoint him either. Do what he says and you'll live through this. Act like a hero, you'll end up dead, and your technology will be in his hands anyway.'

Research and Development Facility, Sacramento-Mather Jetport, Bancho Cordova, California later that afternoon

The visitor picked up the phone mounted on the outer fence outside the research facility that Sky Masters, Inc. was leasing. It rang a few times, then: 'May I help you, ma'am?'

'Yes,' the visitor replied. 'I'm Dr Kaddiri, Helen Kaddiri. I'm supposed to meet Dr Masters. I'm not sure where he's staying or where he is. Can you help me find him?'

'Of course, Dr Kaddiri,' the guard said. 'One moment, please.' He buzzed open the outer entrapment door to let her in.

As Helen walked toward the guard room, the security guard picked up a walkie-talkie and radioed, '*Kontrolle, Wache drei. Eine Dr Helen Kaddiri ist hier. Was sind Ihre Anweisungen.*'

'*Lassen Sie sie rein,*' came the response a few moments later. '*Sie soll warten.*'

'Okay,' the guard responded. He opened the ID port. 'May I please see a picture ID and your company ID badge, Dr Kaddiri?' She still had her badge – she had no intention of surrendering it before her resignation was legally finalized – and she handed it to the guard with her driver's license. He did a cursory check, then gave them back. He pressed the button to unlock the revolving security gate. 'Thank you, ma'am. Please step through the gate. Someone will meet with you right away.'

Helen stepped through the gate and was greeted by a good-looking man in a suit and tie. 'Dr Kaddiri?'

She did not recognize him. 'Yes, I'm Helen Kaddiri. I am the corporate vice president of . . .' She stopped, realizing he didn't have a Sky Masters ID badge. 'Who are you?'

'I'm Captain Thomas Chandler, Sacramento Police Department,' the man replied. 'I am the officer who assisted in the arrest of Dr Masters and General McLanahan the other night.'

'Can you please explain what's going on?'

'Of course,' Chandler said. 'Did you bring your car in? Is there anyone else with you?'

'I left the car outside, and no, there's no one else with me,' Helen replied. 'I didn't know if I'd be leaving right away. Where's Jon?'

'He's out on bail, as you know,' Chandler said. They walked toward the semi-underground research facility. 'He and his attorney are assisting me in my investigation of your company's activities here.'

'Then I don't think I should be talking to you,' Helen said. 'Anything I have to say to you should be with the company's attorney present.'

'Dr Kaddiri, I know what you, Patrick, and Jon are going through,' Chandler said. 'I'm here to help them.'

'By arresting them?'

'I think both of them are heroes. I had to arrest them because it's my job. But even though they're guilty of most of the lesser charges against them, I can make sure they get the most lenient sentence possible. But I can't do it alone.'

'But shouldn't I have our attorney present?'

'This is not an interrogation,' Chandler said. 'I'm not going to ask you anything that will incriminate either

Jon or Patrick. You can refuse to answer anything you feel uncomfortable with.'

Kaddiri still looked apprehensive. 'If you don't mind, Captain, I'd like to meet up with Jon and our attorney first, before I talk with you,' she said warily. 'He didn't tell me where he was staying, only that he . . . wanted me here, with him.'

Chandler nodded, looking into Kaddiri's eyes. 'He mentioned that he'd called you,' Chandler lied. 'He thinks a great deal of you.' He paused, then added, 'Obviously you think very much of him too, or you wouldn't be here.'

'We've had our differences,' Helen said, 'but . . . yes, I guess that's true.'

'That's nice,' Chandler said. 'That's *very* nice.' They passed two men dressed in black battle-dress uniforms and carrying submachine guns, but Helen barely noticed them, or that they weren't wearing Sky Masters ID badges either. 'I'm not sure when Jon was going to be back,' said Chandler, 'but we'll just go up to General McLanahan's office inside and wait for him to call. If he isn't coming back, we can take you to his hotel. Please, this way . . .'

Sacramento County Jail,
651 I Street, Sacramento, California
later that evening

The Sacramento County Jail in downtown Sacramento was a fairly new, modern facility. Each of the four inmate floors had a common area, surrounded by twenty-four cells, each holding up to six prisoners depending on its capacity. Each cell had a steel door with a large, thick glass window in the center, and an unbarred narrow window looking outside. A guard tower overlooked the entire floor. An exercise room and medical holding facility were on the fifth floor, and booking and administrative offices on the first. The common area served as the dining hall, indoor rec room, and meeting hall.

The dynamics of the downtown jail made for a tense atmosphere. It was where prisoners were held from the time of their arrest and arraignment until they were convicted, after which they would be transported to the larger Rio Cosumnes Correctional Facility in Elk Grove to serve their sentence. All the prisoners at the downtown jail were thus innocent in the eyes of the law, and mostly innocent in their own eyes as well. Many came from violent or oppressive environments, often of their own making. They were fresh from the hurt, ignominy, indignity, and betrayal of the arrest and the cold indifference of arraignment, and were now faced with the arcane babble of legal proceedings and the uncertainty of their future while the trial process creaked along.

That tension was pervasive even in peaceful, so-called normal times. But there was nothing normal about what was going on in Sacramento County these days. Within the confines of the jail, the threat of retaliation and escalating gang violence following the deaths of the Satan's Brotherhood members sent the level of fear sky-high. It was just as pervasive among the jail authorities, who increased the number of guards, dogs, and weapons to compensate, and in a snowball effect generated still more fear.

Actually, today had been a fairly quiet day for Patrick, When he was in solitary, he was more or less out of the minds of the bikers, neo-Nazis, white supremacists, and other wackos who were looking to kill him. When he was out among the other prisoners, he kept his distance, with more or less success. Usually one guard was assigned to watch over all the isolation inmates and try to prevent trouble.

The common area on each floor of the jail had ten steel star-shaped tables fixed to the floor, with five fixed chairs at each table. Hot meals were prepared in the kitchen, then placed on paper plates on fiberglass trays and wheeled out to the common area on large carts. Utensils were cardboard. Prisoners selected a meal, either vegetarian or nonvegetarian, a beverage, and a dessert, then found a seat.

Except for sick or very violent prisoners, there was normally no preplanned segregation of any kind in the jail. The prisoners did their own segregating – blacks sat with blacks, whites with whites, Hispanics with Hispanics. There was usually enough available seating at meals to allow the members of rival gangs to be seated apart. But even when space was relatively tight, the prisoners knew that meals were not the time to get into a fight. Besides, despite the dangerous tension level, the jail was not a hard-core facility. These were prisoners awaiting trial, not yet convicted and sentenced. Most of them minded their own business and stayed out of trouble.

Patrick took the first available tray; he didn't want to appear picky or slow the line for those behind him. He poured himself a cup of water, grabbed a carton of milk from a large tub of ice and a brownie from the dessert counter, and found a seat between two older-looking guys. The meal was what they called Salisbury steak: a piece of indeterminate meat floating in a puddle of slimy gravy, along with sodden boiled carrots, reconstituted mashed potatoes with more gravy, and a slice of white bread that had to be one or two days old but had been steamed into a semblance of freshness. The two guys on either side of him glanced at him but said nothing.

Everything on the plate tasted pretty much alike, which really characterized life in jail, Patrick thought. In a way, it reminded him of pulling strategic nuclear alert years ago: your life regulated by horns, bells, whistles, shouted voices, and the PA system; the sameness of everything, from the food to the uniforms; the regimentation; and most of all, the lack of freedom. Of course, there was no real comparison. But it was remarkably easy for Patrick to put his mind back to those days when, for seven days every three weeks, he was a virtual prisoner of the Strategic Air Command jailers, serving an unwanted but self-imposed sentence in support of the laws of nuclear deterrence. He had always passionately hated alert, hated the wasted time and wasted resources, and he found it ironic that he was relying on those memories to help keep his sanity now.

He left half of his plate untouched, finished the brownie, and drank up the milk and water. Seconds weren't allowed, so he looked around for someone who might want his leftovers. The two old characters next to him declined. He asked the other guy at the table, 'Hey, want any more?'

'Leave me the fuck alone,' the guy spat. Patrick was sorry he'd said anything. The man was big, lean, and tall, with cropped salt-and-pepper hair. He looked as though he'd been beaten up – his nose was broken and twisted and his face bruised. There were tattoos on his arms – and not tattoo-parlor ones but prison tattoos, made by inmates with sharpened ballpoint pens . . .

. . . and one of the tattoos, the biggest one, on his left arm – was a Satan's Brotherhood tattoo. Oh *shit* . . .

The biker was hunched over his tray, enveloping it with his arms as if protecting it from a thief. This was a good time to get the hell out of the common area, Patrick decided. He got up quickly. 'Hey!' the biker snapped, fixing wild, psychotic eyes on him. '*You!* Who are you?'

'Nobody, chief,' Patrick said.

'The fuck you are,' the biker said. 'I know you. I hearda you. You're the guy who was goin' around killing Brotherhood.'

The two old guys scattered as fast as they could. The biker got to his feet, eyes burning. Patrick looked up at the guard tower, but the guards up there were busy. 'Listen, chief,' Patrick said, 'you've got it wrong. I didn't kill any Brotherhood members.'

But the biker exploded like a volcano. '*Die, mother-fucker!*' he screamed, and launched himself at Patrick. He tackled him to the ground, rolled on top of him, pinned his arms, and pummeled his face. '*This – is – for – the – Brotherhood!*' he shouted with each blow of his fists.

By now the other prisoners had joined in the fray. 'Get him!' they shouted. 'Kill the cocksucker! Kill him for the Brotherhood!'

Patrick felt something warm on his face, and through his blurry eyes saw blood all over the biker's fists and shirt. Then the biker wrapped his huge hands around Patrick's neck. In a daze, Patrick heard a whistle blow and the PA system blare out something about a lockdown. Then the biker squeezed harder. He felt a hand on his throat, another on the side of his head, then a sharp push – and everything went dark.

Chapter Four

Chapter XXII

Mount Vernon Road,
Newcastle, California
Wednesday, 1 April 1998, 0905 PT

Jon Masters awoke to blackness. He found his hands and feet handcuffed to what felt like a chain-link gate, and a thick hood over his head. He had been stripped naked. He had a colossal headache, a result of the gas they had used to put him asleep, and he could smell vomit on the inside of the hood.

He lay there for what seemed like hours. Then he heard a door open and footsteps approaching him. '*Guten Morgen*, Dr Masters,' said a voice.

'You must be one of Townsend's goons,' Masters shouted. 'Let me go, jerk-face.'

A blow from a leather whip struck him across the face. 'You will call me Major or sir,' said Bruno Reingruber. 'You will conduct yourself like a man and not a comic-book character in my presence. Your situation is already dire enough without the added unpleasantness of being punished for rudeness.'

'Fuck you,' Jon said. 'Let me go right now! *Help! Someone help me! Help!* Some goddamn German guy is going to kill me!'

'*Sehr gut*. Have it your way, *Herr Doktor*,' Reingruber said. Several pairs of rough hands grabbed Masters, unfastened his handcuffs, and forced him facedown onto the concrete floor. The handcuffs were refastened behind his back, and he was lifted up and shoved into a metal drum. As icy water poured over him, he cried out in shock. It filled the drum to the level of his mouth, and a grilled lid was snapped onto the drum.

'We know from experiments the Third Reich did during World War Two that a human can survive immersed in water like this for about an hour,' Reingruber said. 'Of course, their subjects were concentration-camp prisoners, probably in far poorer physical condition than yourself. We shall be back in an hour and see how well you did.

'You should also know that we shall be exploring the spectrum of physical, psychological, and emotional torture. We shall learn together, we and you, of your fears, your nightmares, your weaknesses, and your thresholds of pain and stress.'

'Why are you doing this to me?' Jon cried through chattering lips. 'What do you want?'

'Why, Doctor, you may feel free to tell me anything that you might think I would like to know,' said the Major. 'But you are being punished because you seem to have this macho image of yourself that will undoubtedly prevent us from dealing with each other in a civil manner. You need to accept that this attitude is counterproductive and will not do.'

'Hey, you kraut bastard, face me like a real man!' Masters screamed. 'Screw you!'

'Oh, and one more fact that I thought should be brought to your attention,' Reingruber said. 'I have learned through my sources that your friend and colleague Brigadier General Patrick McLanahan was killed yesterday in the Sacramento County Jail.'

'*What?*' Jon Masters cried out, raising his head in shock and crashing against the lid. As he rebounded underwater, he inhaled a great snoutful of water, coughed, and fought for breath. 'Patrick is *dead*? How? . . .'

'Apparently he angered a fellow inmate who happened to be a member of the biker gang he attacked.'

'You mean the one *you* attacked!' Masters screamed. '*You* killed those bikers! And they've killed Patrick because of you? Oh God, *no*! . . .'

'Most unfortunate,' Reingruber said in mock sympathy. 'We are informed he is being cremated the day after tomorrow. If you cooperate, perhaps you may still have time to pay your last respects to your friend.'

'Wait!' Jon cried out. 'You haven't asked me anything! You haven't told me what you want! *Wait!*' But Reingruber had already departed.

Jon screamed for help until his throat turned hoarse. He could not straighten his legs, but he pressed up against the lid with his head as hard as he could to force it open. It didn't budge. If that wasn't going to work, the important thing was to cope with the cold. He could handle it. Sure, it was cold now, but eventually his body heat would warm the water enough to prevent hypothermia. He swished back and forth like a washing machine, and sure enough, the sting in his legs and arms started to go away. The sonofabitch, Jon thought, he's not going to beat me! Townsend's goons might be cold-blooded terrorists, but they weren't the sharpest knives in the drawer.

If he stopped struggling, he found he could breathe slowly and more naturally while keeping his face above water. Perfect. No point in trying to escape; it wasn't possible. Don't panic. Relax. He closed his eyes, dreaming, remembering trips to Guam, to Australia, to southern California . . .

He woke up with a scream, then gurgled as water geysered out of his throat. He tried to take a breath and found his lungs filled with water. He panicked, fought the arms trying to hold him underwater.

'Easy, young man, easy,' said a soothing voice. He opened his eyes. A kind-looking gray-haired man was looking at him. 'Don't panic. I'm a doctor. I'll help you.' The doctor's hands pressed on his stomach, and great quantities of water poured from his mouth. He coughed, and found he could breathe again.

'Is he going to be all right, Doctor?' a British voice asked.

'Yes, yes,' the doctor replied. 'He wasn't under very long. The cold water slowed his breathing and heart rate, so there should be no brain damage.'

'We are just in time – you are very lucky, Major,' said the British voice, which then spewed out a stream of invective in German. Jon turned his head. Reingruber was standing at attention, his face impassive. 'Get out of here before I throw *you* in that barrel!' Then the Brit stooped over Jon. 'Are you all right, Dr Masters?' he asked, concern etched on his face. Jon's teeth were chattering too hard for him to respond. 'Get those blankets, Doctor, *now*.' He wrapped Jon in two large blankets, sat him up, and gave him a cup of chicken broth.

'You're . . . you're Townsend, aren't you?' Jon asked at last, warmer now. The doctor was hovering nearby, and periodically checked his heart rate.

'Yes, Doctor.' Townsend saw the distrust, then the fear, building in Jon's eyes. Jon looked at him hard, and what he saw in his face was pity and apprehensiveness. 'Don't worry,' Townsend said. 'Major Reingruber is gone . . . for now.'

'Let me go,' Jon pleaded. 'I swear I won't tell anyone about you guys. I'll pay any ransom you want, anything. Just let me go.'

The doctor spoke up: 'Let's not talk about that now. What you need, young man, is rest.'

'Of course.' Townsend gave Masters a reassuring tap on the shoulder. 'We'll speak later,' he said as he left.

'That was Gregory Townsend, wasn't it?' Jon asked the doctor. 'The international terrorist?'

The doctor scoffed. 'Oh, sure. That's what the various governments and tabloids have labeled him,' he said, 'a terrorist, like Carlos the Jackal or something. Nonsense.'

'Really.' Jon narrowed his eyes. 'That's bullshit. This is an act, a ploy to get my confidence. You're butchers, all of you, like that Reingruber asshole.'

At the mention of Reingruber's name, the doctor blanched. 'Take care, Dr Masters,' he said. 'Major Reingruber *is* a dangerous man, very dangerous. Colonel Townsend keeps him on a very short leash, but he is unpredictable. Be very careful around him.'

'And Townsend is Mother Teresa's sainted uncle, I suppose?'

'The colonel saved your life, young man,' the doctor said. 'He came in just in time and saw what Reingruber had done. You could have drowned.'

'I fell asleep? Hypothermia?'

'Yes. You were in the water for about ninety minutes, and possibly three to four minutes underwater. Thankfully, your heart and breathing rates were already slowed down to next to nothing. Colonel Townsend dragged you out of the water and performed CPR on you until you came to.'

'Oh shit,' Jon exclaimed. The world's master terrorist and arms smuggler saved his life? This was unreal – crazy – yet it had to be true. He had certainly been moments away from drowning. He looked at the physician, baffled. 'And who are you?'

'Dr Richard Faulkner, internal medicine,' the physician said. He extended a hand. 'Recently of the Dana-Farber Cancer Institute . . .'

'Boston?' Faulkner nodded. 'I'm an MIT grad. Where'd you go to school?'

'Dartmouth Medical School. Before that, Dartmouth College. I . . .'

'You're kidding! I went to Dartmouth too! What in the world are you doing here?'

'Gregory . . . Colonel Townsend . . . did me an extraordinary favor years ago,' Faulkner said. 'My father was in deep with loan sharks to pay off medical bills for my mother. They threatened to kill me, my sister, and my mother if we didn't pay up. Gregory stepped in and got the loan sharks off my father's back. In return, I help him whenever I can.'

'But . . . but Townsend's a killer, a terrorist . . .'

'Never,' Faulkner said. 'I know what's said about him, but I promise you it isn't true. He's a professional soldier. He wants to do his job. Unfortunately, he has a tendency to get in with the wrong elements – Major Reingruber is an example. Reingruber's the enemy here. This entire state would be in flames were it not for Gregory.'

'That's sure as hell not what I heard about the guy.'

'Don't believe the falsehoods, young man,' Faulkner said. 'But you do need to watch out for Reingruber. He'll be very angry now that Gregory has reproved him in front of you. Gregory will protect you, but you have to trust that this is so and you have to be watchful. Do you understand?' Jon nodded. 'Good. Let's get you out of here and into some warm clothes.'

Still puzzled and uneasy, Jon tried one more plea. 'Why don't you just let me go?' he asked. 'It could be set up. We could make it look like I conked you on the head . . .'

'No way. Major Reingruber would kill me for sure,' Faulkner said. 'No. Our best chance is with Gregory, believe me. I trust him with my life. I have reason to. We'd better get out of here before Reingruber catches us alone.'

Faulkner helped Jon out of the back room and into the central part of the building. The place resembled a small warehouse, with rooms like small offices opening off the main area. They glimpsed Reingruber in one of the rooms, cleaning guns. He got to his feet when he saw them, his rage at Masters evident in his eyes, but he did not come out. Faulkner led Jon into a small windowless room equipped with a cot, blankets, a floor lamp, and a couple of chairs. 'You'll be safe here, Jon,' Faulkner said. 'The door locks.' From a pocket under his jacket he pulled out a newspaper conspiratorially. 'Here,' he said. 'Hide this under the blankets. You don't want Reingruber to know you have it. I've got to go.'

'That bastard will come after me . . .'

'I'll be right outside, and Gregory is nearby,' Faulkner said. 'Don't worry. Again, you can rely on us. Gregory'll get you out of this in fine shape, but you're going to have to do as he says and place your trust in him. Do you understand? Will you do that, Jon?'

What choice did he have? 'I'll try, Doc.'

'Good. Lock the door after I leave. You must open it when they demand entry, but you'll have *some* privacy.'

Jon locked the door instantly, then sat down on the bed and wrapped himself in the blankets.

This is crazy, he said to himself. Reingruber is a madman. Even if what Faulkner said about Townsend was true, what kind of jerk was he, hanging around wackos like that? He'd saved his life, for which he was grateful, but it was baffling nonetheless. Still, he had the two of them to keep the psycho away from him, and they certainly seemed to mean it.

He unfolded the paper carefully. It was today's pages 3 and 4 of the *Sacramento Bee*, tattered but still readable, with late-breaking details on the explosion in Wilton. As he read, he froze. He could not believe what he was seeing.

The coverage spelled out what it described as the Tin Man's reign of terror. Patrick McLanahan had killed several Wilton residents, whom he suspected of being terrorists. He had misidentified the house as a hideout for meth cookers and terrorists when it was actually rented out by an itinerant farmer, his family of three kids, and his brother's family with four kids. He had killed several of them, including three children, then set an explosive charge on a propane tank outside, causing the huge explosion.

Jon was stupefied. Their intelligence had been perfect, impeccable, accurate – yet, there it was in black and white: They had made a terrible mistake and eleven people had died because of it. There was a Reuters account, an Associated Press piece about the attack. And there was a big article from the *Bee* news service about Patrick's death in the Sacramento County Jail, characterizing it as a kind of 'suicide by inmate' – Patrick had apparently sought out a Satan's Brotherhood prisoner and taunted him into the attack that led to the retaliatory killing. The story suggested he was so schizoid that he thought he still had the suit on – was invulnerable – when he attacked the inmate, proclaiming his innocence all the while. The body, it ended, was to be cremated and the remains taken to an undisclosed location.

Jon folded away the paper and sat on the bed, his face a mask of horror. Eleven innocent people had died at their hands. They were murderers.

*   *   *

'He's falling for it,' said Faulkner. With Townsend and Reingruber, he was watching Masters on a closed-circuit TV monitor, broadcast via a pinhole camera in his room. 'It was a great idea to have the computer print it out on newsprint. And can you believe how he took in all that crap about me being a doctor from Dartmouth? Now I'm his goddamn best friend. Still, I don't see why you don't just beat the information out of him, Colonel. He's as sensitive as a pansy.'

'Because he will faint at the slightest injury and be quite useless to us,' Townsend replied. 'The tank wiped him out. And drugs will only dull his mind, and we need that mind to be as sharp as possible. No, physical or chemical techniques will not work. This is the way to proceed. Scientific genius though he may be, he is obviously not trained in misinformation, propaganda, or interrogation-resistance techniques. He is reaching out for a friend, and he has found one in you, and soon in myself.

'His internal clock should be running on *our* timetable soon – that was programmed when we convinced him he was in the water for ninety minutes, not the fifteen it actually was. And as soon as that occurs, it will be easy to get the information we need.' Townsend walked over to the rack and examined the BERP suit hanging there. 'You have not succeeded in discovering how it works?' he asked Faulkner.

'I discovered how to plug in the power and turn it on from the outside, and how to keep it recharged,' Faulkner said. 'There are sensors inside the helmet that activate functions that are displayed inside. But I've got to figure out how to break the code. Well, we can probably get it from him. The way it's going, you'll have him babbling like a kid and squawking like a parakeet in no time.'

'There's no certainty about that,' said Townsend sharply. 'These misinformation and psychological techniques are not foolproof. I am relying on *you* to break the code and activate that suit. Masters can then fill in the pieces. You had better get back to work. We'll discuss our next scene with Masters when that is done.'

He turned to Reingruber. '*Gute Arbeit, Herr Major.*'

The major clicked his heels and bowed.

'Status of the target?'

'Still under full security, Colonel,' Reingruber replied. 'Departure has been delayed because of the explosion at the ranch. Security has been increased slightly, but not with any specially trained forces.'

'We may have to implement Phase Three of our plan after all,' Townsend said. 'We must be sure the targets are not in ferry or decommission configuration. The weapons systems must be in maintenance preload status or else we may not be able to upload all the weapons we require.'

'I understand, *Herr Oberst.* Our informants are keeping close scrutiny on the targets at all times. The weapons systems remain in full maintenance preload status, and are not expected to go to ferry status until just prior to departure.'

'Very good,' Townsend said. 'Keep me advised. Have you been able to get me confirmation on McLanahan's death? Is it accurate that he was killed by a Satan's Brotherhood member in the Sacramento County Jail?'

'It is accurate, *Herr Oberst.* It has been confirmed. The county coroner pronounced him dead this morning, and a state justice-department official also examined the body as well.'

'But not an independent report? I had hoped for word from an outside source, Major,' Townsend said. 'Well, we cannot spare the manpower or risk discovery. But it does not seem he was an important factor in any case – without the suit, simply another desk-bound engineer.'

'I do not understand why we are wasting any time with Masters and his suit, sir,' Reingruber said. 'It is not essential to our purposes.'

'Because it represents another profit opportunity for us,' Townsend said. 'You need not worry, Major. It will not interfere with our timetable. Masters and his contraption are distractions; at best, the suit will prove to be useful. Your task is to keep careful watch on the targets and advise me as soon as they are ready.'

County Morgue,
Sacramento County Coroner's Office,
Stockton Boulevard and Broadway,
Sacramento, California
the same time

'Welcome to hell, General.'

Patrick McLanahan opened his eyes, blinking through the pain. He saw Hal Briggs's face beaming at him. 'Where am I?'

'Dead,' Briggs replied. 'How do you feel?'

'Dead.' Patrick touched his face gingerly and winced at his broken nose. Briggs helped him sit up on the table. 'What happened?'

'What happened was either the most elaborate ruse ever created, or the strangest set of circumstances I've ever witnessed, General,' said another voice. Patrick was startled to see Sacramento Police Chief Arthur Barona standing next to him. 'I'm still trying to make up my mind which is which.'

'You're at the county morgue, Patrick,' Briggs said. 'We set the whole thing up after we listened to your wiretap tapes and heard Captain Chandler talking to Gregory Townsend – that British guy who confronted you . . .'

'Townsend got to *Chandler*?' Patrick said.

'Looks like it. He found out about Chandler's gambling debts, and he got Chandler to grab Jon Masters and the suit. No one's seen Masters since he was released from jail yesterday morning. He never met his assigned driver.'

'Police security cameras photographed him getting into a car,' Barona added. 'We couldn't identify the driver or the passenger in the car, but we think it must have been Chandler – we haven't been able to contact him. I notified your legal team of Dr Masters's disappearance, and they contacted your guys Briggs and Wohl at the facility out at the airport.' He looked at Briggs and Wohl suspiciously and said icily, 'Colonel Briggs then told me of his plan to spring you from the jail.'

Patrick looked at Briggs, who grinned. 'Hey, nobody tries to frame my friends. What we decided was to give the chief your wiretap tapes. Then we let him know of my plan, and he got the sheriff on board. We had Sergeant Wohl dress up as a biker – how'd you like those tattoos? – and we planted him on your floor to "kill" you.'

Patrick felt his nose again. 'Good job, Chris. Very realistic.'

'My pleasure, sir,' said Wohl, looking pleased with himself.

'With a little help from some theatrical blood and a mild nerve agent that slowed down your breathing and heart rate enough to pass you off as dead, we got you out of there,' Briggs finished up. 'But Jon's disappeared. If he's in Townsend's hands, that's bad news – we've got to find him and Chandler.'

'We can find Townsend,' Patrick said. He struggled shakily to his feet. 'He probably took all of Jon's gadgets away from him so we can't use them to locate him, but we can use the suit's tracking system to locate *it*. Assuming Jon stays near the suit.'

'I still find it hard to believe any of this,' Barona said. 'The suit Jon Masters created makes the wearer almost invulnerable. He's part of your team. Why would he go off with it to a guy like Townsend, who's got some kind of secret organization? He's a madman – he was associated with Henri Cazaux. And if it's his operation that's attacking the city and the motorcycle gangs, for what purpose? What's he up to?'

'We don't know yet,' said McLanahan. 'I was told that Townsend and his so-called Aryan Brigade are not what they appear to be, but my informant died before he could tell me more than that. He's a dangerous bastard. It's urgent to locate Jon; that's where we'll find Townsend. Hal, I need one of your Pave Hammer tilt-rotors out at McClellan. What's their maintenance status?'

'They haven't started yet,' Hal said. 'They're just finishing work on the F-117 Night Hawk stealth fighters out there. Whatever you need, you got.'

'I want one MV-22, armed and ready to fly,' McLanahan said. 'I'll mount a locator unit to find the suit. Once we pinpoint it, we'll send a Skywalker reconnaissance drone overhead to scope out the hideout, then hit it.'

'Hold it, hold it!' said Barona. 'What are you jokers talking about? First of all, McLanahan, you're not going anywhere, especially not on some secret armed aircraft.

If you disappear, my ass is in deep trouble. Second, I can't allow you to use any of these men, these *commandos*, to stage an operation in the state of California without coordination and permission of the proper authorities. Third . . .'

'You can stop right there,' McLanahan said. 'In case you haven't figured it out yet, Chief, *we're* in charge of this operation, and we're going to do whatever it takes to get out friend back, and that suit. If you continue to tell us what we can't do, we'll be happy to lock you in a nice cozy room in some undisclosed location until we're finished. Or, you can cooperate.'

'Don't you dare threaten me, mister,' Barona said. 'I'm risking my career to help you. But I can't stand by and watch you take the law into your own hands.'

Patrick considered it for a moment; then: 'All right, Chief. We'll cooperate as much as possible. Tell us what you want us to do. But you need to know I will not allow anything or anybody to get in the way of this rescue. That's firm.'

Barona nodded. He spelled out what McLanahan needed to do so that this could look like an officially sanctioned joint law-enforcement operation. Then they all went on the phones to the various agencies, sometimes literally begging for cooperation and clearance. Patrick hung tough, and eventually they got what they needed.

'One more thing, McLanahan, and all of you,' Barona said sternly. 'I need results, and I need them right away. My ass is already on the line for you. We could have prevented all this if you'd brought me the wiretaps on Chandler earlier. I'm going to have to explain not only why McLanahan is not in jail, but why he's not dead as well. I'm going to give you twenty-four hours to wrap this caper up, and then I'm going to the district attorney and attorney general, tell my story, and let the chips fall where they may. If that's the way I end up, I guarantee you I'll do everything in my power to fry you all. I'll come away with an embarrassing bloody nose for trying to cooperate with you – but you: You'll all be in prison.'

Research and Development Facility,
Sacramento-Mather Jetport,
Rancho Cordova, California
Thursday, 2 April 1998, 0649 PT

Those brutal sons of bitches, Tom Chandler thought. *This* he'd never anticipated. Someone needed to teach those assholes a lesson.

When Chandler had heard that some woman was here to see Jon Masters, he figured it was his wife or girlfriend. He'd make up an excuse, maybe flash his badge, and send her on her way. When it turned out she was a high-ranking company officer, he shifted gears: She might prove useful for putting the pressure on, make a pretty good hostage, someone to help guarantee their safety until they made their escape. But Townsend's men had different plans for her, once they too learned she was the corporate vice president, and they notified Townsend in Newcastle.

Chandler had listened to the sounds of Kaddiri's cries echoing through his closed door from the chief-engineer's room across the corridor until he could stand it no longer. He was barred from the scene, but it took no imagination to work out what was going on. He broke communications silence, picked up the telephone, and called the Newcastle number.

'Hey, Townsend, I am not going to be your god-damn wet nurse for another day.' He was calling from Patrick McLanahan's office. Outside the office, several of Townsend's people were hunting through the computer files at the workstations. But the heavy-duty work was going on in the office opposite, where two of the soldiers were busy working not on computer workstations, but on Helen Kaddiri.

When Townsend learned that the woman Chandler had captured was the company's vice president – that this was the organization that had developed the astounding weaponproof suit – he had given orders to postpone the evacuation of the R & D center. If threats, torture, or bribes succeeded in presuring Kaddiri to unlock the company's extensive computer files, he would have access via the Internet to thousands of companies and government agencies all over the world. One password from Kaddiri – that was all it would take – to open many of the West's most critical engineering and research files: data on weapons, aircraft, new designs in the pipeline, intelligence information. And there it would be, at Gregory Townsend's fingertips.

'Your soldiers are going to kill Kaddiri if they keep this up,' Chandler warned. 'For Christ's sake, pull them out of there.'

Townsend was furious. 'You are not in charge, Chandler. I am! I must have access to those computer files before we evacuate. I need access long enough to change the password or enter in my own back-door password.'

'We can't wait. This is Masters and McLanahan's company. Look at the charges against them! I can hold off the sheriff's department and DA investigators only so long,' Chandler warned. 'In case you've forgotten, I'm out of my jurisdiction. What do we do when more investigators show up? And Masters has government military contracts here – we're likely to have the FBI and the Defense Investigation Service here any minute.'

'Then I'll turn Kaddiri over to you. *You* get across to her the grave situation she's in. You get her to cooperate. Tell her anything you want, but *get that password.*'

'You're going to kill her anyway, aren't you?' Chandler asked.

'Once I have what I want, Kaddiri is free to leave,' said Townsend. 'I prefer not to kill women, but I will do anything necessary to protect my organization. Now *go*!'

Chandler slammed down the receiver. Bullshit, he thought. Kaddiri was going to die – and probably so was he – the second they got access to those files. In fact, Kaddiri was far more valuable to Townsend than he was. He had twenty thousand dollars waiting for him in a Cayman Islands bank account – not nearly enough. For another hundred thousand it had seemed worth the tricky effort of keeping the DA and the sheriff's department out of the facility, but now that he'd actually seen Townsend in action, he realized he wasn't likely to live to get his hands on the money. Past time to get the hell out.

He dialed the number for the Sacramento office of the FBI. It rang once, then a voice with a German accent came on the line: 'Who are you trying to call?' He slammed down the receiver. Shit! Townsend's men were monitoring all phone calls from the security office. His life span was even shorter than he expected. He had to get a message out to somebody, *fast*!

Looking at the phone at McLanahan's desk, Chandler saw a button marked WENDY VM. He picked up the phone and hit the button. It was a direct computerized link to

Wendy McLanahan's voice-mail system – it could not be intercepted or cut off by the security office. He spoke fast into the recording. 'This is Tom Chandler. I'm at the Sky Masters research facility at Mather Jetport. Townsend's men are trying to break into the company's computers. You'd better get someone out here, right now, or Helen Kaddiri is dead. There are twelve of Townsend's men here. They're . . .'

The office door burst open. 'You!' shouted a German soldier. 'Stop! Hang up that telephone immediately! Orders from *Oberst* Townsend!' He complied. There was a submachine gun pressed against his face.

Time had just about run out.

Mount Vernon Road, Newcastle, California the same time

Townsend hung up the phone after speaking with his lieutenant in charge at the Mather site. Sure enough, Chandler had tried to call someone right after he got off the phone with him. He ordered the lieutenant to cut off all communications from the R & D facility except for secure radio communications, and to place Chandler under arrest. He had outlived his usefulness. He would dispose of him before long.

It was just about time to complete the final phase of this operation and get out of the area.

He went into the mess hall. Reingruber was waiting for him, ready to give a report, and Richard Faulkner came over and sat down. 'How are you progressing, Faulkner?' Townsend asked. 'We need to be able to operate that suit now.'

'Not quite yet, Colonel,' Faulkner replied. 'But Masters is falling into line very well. I think he is cooperating fully.'

Reingruber agreed. 'It does appear that he has turned into a proper little soldier, sir.'

'Small doses of you and large doses of me do seem to be working,' Townsend said. 'But it is going much too slowly. I want a demonstration outdoors in two hours, Major. If Masters is not ready, you will ask the reason for the delay – *forcefully* ask. Then I will pull you out before he turns into a blubbering infant. That will put the pressure on. That suit must be working for us before the final phase of our plan is put into motion. Get in there now, Faulkner.'

After Faulkner left, Reingruber warned Townsend: 'We may be running short on time, sir. Our informants tell us that the targets are entering final inspections prior to buttoning up. Sign-offs could be completed by this afternoon or tomorrow morning. The targets could be ready to depart within twenty-four to thirty-six hours.'

'No better estimates than that, *Herr Major*?'

'I am sorry, sir,' said Reingruber. 'Security is still very tight, especially with the National Guard troops. The normal security forces appear to be deployed the same, but the forces outside the target area have increased.'

'Very well then, we will put the Phase Three contingency plan into action at once. Assemble your men, Major. H-hour will be at zero two hundred hours local time. Instruct your men at the Sky Masters research facility to start confiscating all the materials they can carry and rendezvous with us here immediately. Have them bring Kaddiri with them – and execute Chandler just before they depart.'

'Very good, *Herr Oberst*,' said Reingruber. 'We will be

ready to go in two hours. It will be a glorious operation. And what about Masters, sir?'

'We may have use for Dr Masters in the future; his psychological reprogramming has been very successful. Bring him along too.'

Townsend walked over to the room where Jon was working on the suit. He was eating breakfast. Faulkner was wearing the suit, experimenting with its mobility. Jon put down his coffee cup and stood at attention. 'Good morning, sir,' he said.

'Good morning to you, Dr Masters.' Townsend extended a hand, and Jon shook it, formally bowing his head and standing until Townsend had seated himself. Reingruber passed by the open door and Townsend saw the fear in Masters's face. 'Has the Major been bothering you, Doctor?'

'No, not really,' Masters replied. 'But I'm always afraid he's going to hurt me. He keeps watching me, and he speaks to some of the men while they're working with me. It's as if he's plotting to hurt me and make it look like an accident.'

'You need not worry about him. Stay close to me and it will be all right,' Townsend said. 'I am the one in command here.'

Jon seemed reassured.

Townsend was pleased. They had organized the psychological dismantling of Jonathan Masters well. Reingruber had had another session with him yesterday afternoon, after the water drum, pressuring him to tell how to work the electronic suit. Masters did a creditable job of resisting the threats, but the pressure took its toll. Reingruber barely even touched him, but he was terrified. When Townsend appeared, he was ready to run into his arms like a child.

From then on, he confided in Townsend, describing his inventions to the point of forgetting who he was talking to, where he was, and the fact he was a captive. Before long, he began to explain the intricacies of the suit – the real evidence of a successful indoctrination, Townsend decided. He and Faulkner had made him feel included, liked, respected. He was eager to please them in return. The belligerent John Wayne attitude was gone. He agreed to let Faulkner wear the suit, and got up before dawn that morning to start working with him, explaining all its systems.

'How is everything progressing?' Townsend asked. 'I understand Dr Faulkner is having a little trouble with the suit.'

'It's going well, sir,' Masters said. 'Richard's a fast learner and he's patient.'

'But he doesn't seem to be learning to use the systems as well as I'd hoped.'

'It takes time,' Masters said. 'The coordination necessary to use the eyeball sensing menu system is complex. It may take another day or two. But we should be able to try a test outdoors tomorrow morning, perhaps even with live ammunition.'

'We really need to do it much sooner than that. We have very little time to waste. Can you set it up for early this afternoon?'

'I'm not . . . yes, sir. We'll make it work. Sir . . .'

'Yes?' Townsend said patiently.

'I wondered – have you reconsidered perhaps having the suit fitted for you? It will take some time, but I think I can do it.'

'Perhaps later, Doctor,' said Townsend. 'Now get back to work.'

Masters jumped to his feet, snapped to attention, and

hurried back to Faulkner, who was about to try on the gauntlets. The helmet lay on the table; it would come next.

As Townsend walked off, one of Reingruber's lieutenants came running up, out of breath. Reingruber was following, as angry as Townsend had ever seen him. *'Wir haben ein Problem, Herr Oberst,'* the lieutenant said.

'What is it?'

The lieutenant held up a portable receiving unit. 'This. We did a routine electromagnetic security sweep this morning. We found this.' A needle on the receiving unit was oscillating across the scale. 'It is a high-power omni-directional UHF satellite uplink,' the lieutenant explained. 'A tracking beacon.'

Townsend didn't need to be told more. 'Get your men assembled and out the door immediately!' he ordered Reingruber. He drew his Calico automatic pistol and went back into the room where Masters was working with Faulkner.

Masters saw his livid face and froze. Faulkner, oblivious, raised his arms proudly. 'What do you think, Colonel?' he said. 'I get a shock every time I get hit, but the sucker works.'

'Oh, it works, all right,' Townsend said. 'Very clever, Doctor. Pretending to be brainwashed so you could get your hands on the suit and activate some sort of tracking beacon, correct?'

Jon Masters positioned himself behind a confused Faulkner. There was no point in dissembling. 'Listen, Townsend,' he said, 'I spent enough years with *real* military guys to know when I'm being brain-drained. Hell, if the only way to survive was to let you think you screwed with my head, it was worth the try.' He looked at Faulkner mockingly. 'And *you* a Dartmouth grad? Not in a million years, loser. A child could see that newspaper was phony.'

Townsend raised the automatic. 'Well, your friends are too late to save you, Doctor,' he said. 'And they're too late to save your friend Helen.'

Jon blanched. 'What did you say?'

'Did I forget to tell you?' Townsend asked. 'Yes, Dr Helen Kaddiri is a guest of mine. An unexpected bonus. She will be my insurance policy. If your friends try to come after me, she will die. As for you . . .'

An enormous blast shook the room and the wall behind Masters crashed down. The concussion threw the three men to the floor, and as the sound of the blast subsided they heard heavy rotors coming close. Masters curled himself up behind Faulkner, as if willing himself to become even smaller than he was.

'You bloody bastard!' Townsend shouted. He lifted himself on one arm and pulled the trigger on the Calico, but the shots went wild as heavy cannon fire erupted outside. Townsend fired again, raking the floor with automatic gunfire. The suit protected Faulkner, and Masters behind him, until one shot hit Faulkner in his unprotected head. Another missile hit the building, then another volley of heavy-caliber cannon fire.

'*Herr Oberst!*' Reingruber shouted. 'Helicopters! We must get away fast!'

Townsend leaped to his feet, reloading a fresh magazine into his autopistol as he fled. 'Remember, Doctor,' he shouted, 'I have Kaddiri. Tell your friends to back off or she dies!'

The MV-22 Pave Hammer tilt-rotor aircraft swept over the rolling wooded terrain. The pilot had activated the helmet-mounted targeting system, which directed the 20-millimeter Hughes Chain Gun onto a target when he turned his head and pulled the trigger. The targeting system also gave him a virtual targeting reticle for the MV-22's pylon-mounted laser-guided Hellfire missiles. Once he designated a target by looking at it and pushing a button, the targeting computer locked on to the target and illuminated it with a laser beam. One push of a button, and a Hellfire missile leaped off the Pave Hammer's weapon pylons, followed the beam of laser light, and scored a direct hit.

'They're scattering!' the MV-22's copilot shouted. 'I see a helicopter lifting off to the northwest, and several vehicles heading west. Do you want me to go after them?'

'No!' McLanahan shouted. 'I want to get Jon Masters first! Set it down by the building where the tracking signals are coming from.' Minutes later, the MV-22 had transitioned from airplane to helicopter mode and set down a few dozen yards from the main building on the isolated Sierra Nevada-foothill ranch.

The first ones off the MV-22 were California Highway Patrol SWAT officers, who surrounded the landing pad and moved out to secure the landing zone. This was done deliberately. It was highly illegal for the federal government's Intelligence Support Agency to run any operations within the United States, but it could fly support missions for state or local law-enforcement authorities. As long as the ISA was in a support function only, its men could fly and fight inside the United States.

Lieutenant Colonel Hal Briggs led the way into the main building, armed with his .45-caliber Uzi submachine gun. Right behind him was the commander of the California

Highway Patrol Special Weapons and Tactics Detail, Deputy Chief Thomas Conrad, followed by a sergeant representing the Placer County Sheriff's Department's SWAT team. Gunnery Sergeant Chris Wohl and Patrick McLanahan followed behind, guarding their rear. Three more four-man squads of SWAT officers fanned out across the ranch and began to search the grounds, but there were no signs of resistance. Afraid of booby traps, Briggs recalled the teams as soon as they completed their sweeps.

To Briggs's amazement, he found Jon Masters running through the main house, darting from room to room. 'Jon!' Briggs shouted, lowering his weapon. 'What in hell are you doing?'

'I've got to find a phone! I've got to find a phone!' he was screaming. Briggs grabbed him and held him tight. 'Let me go, dammit! . . .'

'What in hell are you talking about, Doc?'

'Helen! They've got Helen!' he cried. 'We've got to find her!'

'Jon!' Patrick McLanahan shouted when he caught up with them. 'My God, Jon, are you all right? What's that about Helen?'

'They got her,' Jon told him. 'Townsend and Chandler grabbed her. I don't know how, I don't know where, but they've got her.'

'We'll find her,' Briggs said. 'Don't worry. We'll scour this whole state until we . . .'

'No! You can't!' he shouted. 'Townsend said he'd kill her if we tried to interfere!'

'That's exactly why we *must* go after her,' Briggs said. 'They'll kill her anyway. We've got to find her before they try to harm her.'

'*No!*' Jon shouted. 'We can't take the risk! Oh God, it's all my fault. I called her after I got out of the jail. I told her . . . told her I wanted to see her. She must've come to Sacramento.'

'Jon, we'll do everything we can,' Briggs said. 'We'll save her if it's at all possible. But you've got to be prepared for the possibility that she's dead. I'm sorry, man – I promise we'll do everything we can . . .'

Patrick's earset communications beeped. 'McLanahan.'

'General, this is Sky Masters Security Operations Center,' said the caller. Patrick recognized the voice; it was the chief of the company's security division at their headquarters in Blytheville, Arkansas. 'I'm patching an urgent call through to you from Dr McLanahan.' There was a beep; then: 'Go ahead, Dr McLanahan.'

'Patrick?' Wendy asked.

'Wendy, are you all right?' Patrick asked. 'Is Bradley all right?'

'We're okay, Patrick,' Wendy said, but he could hear the fear in her voice. 'Listen: A few minutes ago, I got a message on my voice mail.' The company voice-mail system automatically notified the recipient via nationwide pager when a message came in. 'It was from Tom Chandler, that police captain from Sacramento PD.'

'*What?* Chandler called *you*? What did he say?'

'He said he was out at the research facility at Mather,' Wendy said. 'He said someone better get out there right away or Helen was dead. He said there were twelve of Townsend's men out there, going through the company's computers.'

'Helen at Mather? We'll get right on it – thanks, love.' Patrick turned to Briggs. 'Get everyone on board, Hal, *now*. Chandler and Helen Kaddiri are out at the alert facility at Mather.' Hal radioed his tactical ground crews to return to the MV-22, then notified the cockpit to get ready for liftoff. 'Jon, where's the suit?'

'In the room over there,' said Masters, and brought Patrick over to where the body of Richard Faulkner lay. They stripped off the suit, hoisted the body on board the MV-22, and were airborne moments later.

Research and Development Facility
Sacramento-Mather Jetport,
Rancho Cordova, California
a few minutes later

'*Ja, Herr Oberst!* I understand. We will be airborne in fifteen minutes!' The senior officer hung up the secure cellular phone, then got on his handheld radio and ordered everyone to the helicopters and prepared to repel attackers. Then he dashed to the main administration offices and the room where Helen Kaddiri was being interrogated. She was still conscious, but barely, strapped to a chair with a hood placed over her head. She did not look as if she had been injured, but the lieutenant knew there were many ways of torturing a prisoner without leaving visible signs. The screen of the laptop computer on the desk beside her showed lines of error messages, indicating the unsuccessful attempts to gain access to the classified Sky Masters files.

'Get her to the helicopter!' the lieutenant ordered. 'Take that computer too!' He drew his sidearm and headed across the corridor to the senior engineer's office, where the renegade police captain Chandler was being held. His orders were explicit: to execute him immediately.

He unlocked the door and stopped in his tracks. On the desktop, lying faceup, was the body of Thomas Chandler, his hands still handcuffed behind his back, his eyes open and staring up at the ceiling. A streak of black-and-red crossed his neck, and a pool of red spread out across the desk. The dirty work had already been done for him, probably by the guard assigned to watch him – it was a violation of orders, since no one had given the order to kill Chandler until now, but the lieutenant wasn't going to complain. He turned toward the admin section and brought his handheld radio to his lips . . .

Chandler brought the metal chair down on the German bastard's head as hard as he could, and slammed it again and again until he was dead. The trick had worked. He had used a hidden handcuff key to get out of the handcuffs – he had several of them hidden on him and knew how to use them even with his hands behind his back. Then he had opened up the color ink-jet printer in the office and spread the ink on his neck and the desktop to make it look as if his throat had been slit.

He picked up the officer's pistol and ran out. Through the engineering offices, a security door opened on an upsloping concrete ramp that led to the flight line, the same covered ramp that SAC bomber and tanker alert crews used to run to the flight line and their waiting planes. Chandler didn't know what was going on, but it was sure as hell time to get out and he was damned if those Nazis were going to leave with a hostage.

The only way he could possibly redeem himself, he figured, and save himself from spending the next ten years in prison, was to start doing his job.

The German-speaking soldiers had left their posts and run to the flight line in front of the half-underground R & D facility, where two surplus UH-1 Huey helicopters were waiting for them, rotors turning. When Chandler emerged from the tunnel, he saw two guards no more than fifty feet away, half-carrying, half-dragging Kaddiri through the alleyway between two hangars toward the waiting helicopters. He took cover just inside the doors to the ramp, raised the pistol, aimed, and fired.

The soldier on the left cried out and fell, clutching his lower back. The other turned toward Chandler and opened fire with his submachine gun, but the shots went high and right. Chandler fired several rounds to throw off his aim, then threw himself back into the tunnel as bullets pinged off the outer security doors. Lying on his belly, he peeked out the doors. The soldier had propped up Helen, who looked semiconscious, using her as a shield while he checked his comrade.

'Helen! Kaddiri!' Chandler shouted, his gun poised to fire. 'Get up! *Now!*' He was afraid she would be too weak to act, but she heard him and had enough strength to roll free of the soldier's grasp. Chandler dropped the second soldier on his first shot.

He ran to her. 'Come on!' he said. 'I'm going to try to get you away!'

Heavy machine-gun fire rippled the ground not five feet away from them, shot from one of the helicopters on the flight line. Chandler fired two rounds toward the helicopter, picked Kaddiri up, and ran for the rear of one of the hangars. Placing her on the ground behind the hangar, he tried to make a run for one of the submachine guns dropped by the soldiers who had taken Kaddiri, but a burst of gunfire drove him back to cover. Two soldiers had dismounted from the helicopter and were headed straight for them. Chandler took aim and fired but his gun clicked empty. He threw it away, looped one of Kaddiri's arms up over his shoulder, and ran down the ramp behind the hangars. It was their last, their *only*, chance.

*   *   *

'I've got one of the helicopters lined up!' the pilot of the MV-22 Pave Hammer tilt-rotor aircraft called out on interphone. 'Give me permission to shoot!'

'*No!*' Jon Masters shouted. 'Helen might be in one of those choppers!'

'Put me right over the lead helicopter,' McLanahan radioed. 'Target the second helicopter's tail rotor with the cannon. Try to keep it on the ground, but don't hit it!'

The MV-22 was flying about sixty miles an hour in helicopter mode as it swooped across the two parallel runways at Mather toward the R & D center. Patrick knew their altitude, about thirty feet above ground, and their speed. He relied on his experience as an Air Force bombardier for the rest.

As the MV-22 swept in on its targets, Patrick stepped out through the left crew door onto the left main landing gear sponson and steadied himself against the left weapon pylon. At just the right moment, he let go and flung himself out into space, jumping right down onto the spinning rotors of the first UH-1 Huey helicopters.

He looked like a doll tossed from a speeding car onto a busy freeway when he hit the rotor disk. He landed right-shoulder-first onto the left side of the rotor, but the BERP suit protected him from being sliced into hamburger. His body skipped across the rotor disk, hitting again on the blade tips just forward of the cockpit canopy before being thrown a hundred feet into the air.

The helicopter's blades bounced like palm fronds in a hurricane. One blade snapped and flew off into space; the others dipped so low that they struck the ground and then the tail, snapping off the tail rotor. Unbalanced, the entire main-rotor assembly cracked off the hub and shattered. The transmission screamed into high rpm's, then it too shattered and disintegrated. The transmission burst into a globe of shrapnel, shelling out the turbine engine with a huge explosion.

Patrick landed up against the steel post of one of the facility's ballpark lights. He knew he was alive because the ferocity of the electrical surges through the suit had set his entire body on fire. He writhed in pain and tried to relax his muscles, let the energy move through him and dissipate; but the more he tried to relax, the harder the waves of electricity came.

It felt like hours before they stopped. He didn't dare move at first, thinking he was sawed into pieces. The vision of those rotor blades rushing up to his face was imprinted on his eyeballs. But when he opened his eyes, he saw hangars, lights, and gray cloudy skies. He was alive.

He got to his feet and looked over the R & D facility flight line. Soldiers were streaming out both crew doors of the disabled Huey, some holding injured comrades. The MV-22 Pave Hammer tilt-rotor was directly over the second one – it could fire straight down with its chin-mounted Chain Gun, but no one on board the Huey could shoot straight up because they'd be shooting through their own rotor disk. The second Huey's tail rotor began to disintegrate as 20-millimeter rounds chewed it to pieces, and in seconds it was unflyable.

Soldiers began firing at the MV-22. 'Hal! You're taking ground fire!' Patrick shouted into his helmet radio. 'Get out of there *now*!' As the MV-22 moved away, Patrick hit his thrusters, aiming straight at the soldiers firing on it. He plowed into them going full speed, knocking them over like an out-of-control truck.

Then he heard shouts of '*Halt!*' in German through his omnidirectional microphone – and cries of 'Help!' in English. He hit his thrusters in the direction of the cries, jumping across the ramp behind the second hangar. He could see two soldiers chasing someone and recognized the running figure of Tom Chandler, carrying a woman down the fenceline behind the hangars. The soldiers had fired a warning shot in the air, but Chandler wasn't stopping. One of them raced after him as the other knelt down and began to line up his shot.

Patrick hit his thrusters again but discovered they hadn't recharged yet. He ran toward the kneeling soldier, shouting, 'Chandler! Gun! Behind you!' with his electronically amplified voice. Chandler turned, pushed Kaddiri to the ground next to the fence, and raised a pistol. At last, a 'Ready' indication. Patrick hit his thrusters and speared the kneeling soldier with his flying body just in time. The other soldier had thrown himself on the ground when he saw Chandler's gun, trying to find cover.

Patrick got to his feet, made sure the one he had downed was out cold, and yelled 'Stop!' at the second soldier. But he was too late. Chandler went down just as Patrick reached the guy and put him out of commission.

Patrick went over to Helen, lying where she had fallen when Chandler dropped. She looked semiconscious. 'Helen! It's Patrick! Are you all right?'

She opened her eyes. 'Patrick?' she said groggily. 'Patrick! I . . . I think I'm okay.' She turned her head toward Chandler. 'He saved my life, the son of a bitch. How is he?'

Patrick checked him over. He had a bullet in his upper chest and left shoulder. 'Not good,' he said. He tore off one of Chandler's pant legs and stuffed the cloth into his chest wound to stop the bleeding. They heard the sirens of approaching police cars and fire trucks. 'We're going to have to get him out of here. And you need to be checked over too.'

The MV-22 had swooped over the R & D facility, firing at soldiers on the ground, but now it touched down on the ramp behind the second disabled Huey. Patrick carried Chandler out onto the ramp, with Helen hobbling beside him, just as the Sheriff's Department and California Highway Patrol cars and county fire trucks roared up. The officers ran out, weapons drawn, and aimed at Patrick. 'Put him down,' they ordered. 'Hands in the air!'

'Hold on, hold on!' It was the commander of the Highway Patrol's SWAT team, Thomas Conrad, who ran up, followed by Masters and Briggs. 'Let him go, boys. He's one of us.' Then he pointed to Chandler, still in Patrick's arms. 'But not that man. He's under arrest. Get him to the hospital but keep an officer with him at all times. And this lady needs medical help too. But hold it just a sec . . .' Conrad went over to where Chandler was lying, withdrew something from his pocket, and put it in Patrick's right hand. 'Here,' he said. 'You deserve this a hell of a lot more than he does.'

Patrick looked at it. It was Chandler's gold captain's badge.

Jon Masters was focused only on Helen. He took off his jacket and gently wrapped it around her. 'Oh God, Helen,' he kept saying. 'Are you all right? Oh Helen, I'm so sorry . . .'

'I'm okay, Jon, I really am,' she reassured him, smiling at him weakly. 'I . . . I must look like hell, but I'm not really hurt.'

'You look beautiful to me,' he said. 'But you've been through hell, and we need to get you to the hospital right away.' The paramedics moved him out of the way and helped Helen onto a gurney. As they began to wheel her to the ambulance, she reached out a hand and grabbed at his sleeve. 'Don't leave me, Jon,' she said.

He took her hand and walked beside her. 'I won't, Helen,' he said. 'Never again.' He realized he was deliriously happy. 'You crazy kid, you're still in love with me.'

'Yes, you crazy kid,' she replied happily, 'I'm in love with you.'

Research and Development Facility,
Sacramento-Mather Jetport
several hours later

Hal Briggs thought it was the weirdest sight he had ever seen. There sat Patrick McLanahan in the chair in his office at the R & D facility, taking sips of coffee and working on the computer – with a cord running from him to a wall outlet. Of course, he still had the BERP suit on. But *weird* was the word, like Patrick was some kind of futuristic half-man, half-machine, both parts getting refreshed at the same time.

It had been a very long day. After the shootout with Townsend's men, the R & D facility had been overrun with sheriff's deputies, then Highway Patrol investigators, then FBI and ATF officers. Since Townsend was so fond of using booby traps, the whole facility had to be evacuated while the place was searched. Then the interviews began, one agency after another gathering statements from all of them. Additional security units were on the way from Sky Masters, Inc.'s facilities in Las Vegas, San Diego, and Arkansas to secure the Sacramento facility, but until they arrived the place was being guarded by Sacramento County Sheriff's Department deputies, augmented with National Guard troops.

'Out of the twelve soldiers that Chandler said were here,' Briggs said to Patrick, 'we got seven, Sacramento County Sheriff's got one, and Folsom police got another one. That leaves three unaccounted for. Not a bad day's work.'

'It's not them I'm worried about – it's Townsend and Reingruber I'm after,' Patrick said, seated at his terminal. He was fingering Chandler's seven-pointed gold star thoughtfully.

'Unfortunately, I think the only way we're going to learn what he's going to do next is to wait,' Briggs said. 'He's probably got a dozen more hideouts in the area that we don't know about. He could be anywhere. If he were smart, he'd be long gone.'

'No,' Patrick said. 'He's after something here. This whole caper of his never made any sense. First he's into armed robbery, but he only hit one place. Next he's into drugs, but then he blows it all up. He raids this place, but it looks like this was just a target of opportunity. He's an arms smuggler and dealer, not a drug dealer. What's he *doing* here?'

'Nothing against your hometown, partner,' Briggs said, 'but there ain't a helluva lot here. You've got Intel, HP, Packard Bell, Aerojet, and a couple of other high-tech companies, and you've got the state capital. Except for a couple of bases outside of town, all of the military bases here are closed or will be closed soon. There's nothing here.'

'Henri Cazaux was involved in some pretty elaborate schemes to cover his real objectives,' Patrick pointed out. 'Maybe Townsend is doing the same thing.'

'But what? Cazaux was supposedly out to avenge himself on the United States and the US Air Force for screwing up his twisted little head when he was a kid,' Briggs said. 'You think Townsend wants revenge on Sacramento? What for? That doesn't make sense.'

'Makes as much sense as anything else he's done,' McLanahan said. 'Unfortunately, it doesn't help us figure out what he's going to do next or help us catch him.'

'Hey, I say let's leave it up to the FBI now,' Briggs said. 'My bosses at ISA are screaming their heads off, asking what the hell I'm doing flying support for the local yokels. No one has any sense of humor anymore.' Patrick kept flipping through computer records. 'What are you doing there?'

'Just trying to figure out what Townsend's men were looking at. They were obviously accessing all our Internet stuff, trying to find a way to access our company network, looking for passwords, downloaded messages, journals, notes, that sort of thing. I should be able to backtrack and find out what they were looking at.'

'Say what?'

'They were looking for clues about where users stored their passwords,' Patrick explained. 'Remember when you could look around the doorsills and inside desk drawers around any combination safe in the Air Force and find the combination to that safe? Guys had trouble remembering the combination, so they wrote it down near the safe itself.'

'Now, *that's* stupid.'

'Stupid but commonplace,' Patrick said. 'Computers can do the same thing, but they do it electronically. You just need to know where to look.'

'Can you see if they broke in to your system?'

'The security offices in Arkansas should be able to tell us that when they do a security audit,' Patrick said. He called up several Internet-access programs and browsers. 'Judging by how much they hurt Helen, they weren't able to get in.' He paused, lost in thought. 'They were definitely looking at the engineers' individual Internet-access applications, looking for stored passwords. The company prohibits storing passwords and our applications don't allow it, but some guys get careless or lazy and program them in anyway, using macros.'

'You lost me, man,' Hal Briggs said. 'That computer stuff is for the birds. Give me a gun and a chopper any day, and I'll solve all the problems of the world.' But curiosity got the better of him, and he peeked over Patrick's shoulder. 'You got something?'

'Not about our network, but something else,' Patrick said. 'This is an Internet browser program, for accessing articles on the World Wide Web – that's the global network of computers, all linked together. Browsers save pages in files called caches, which allows the pages to load faster. You can look back through the cached pages and see what they were looking at. Pages accessed from secure sites aren't cached, but articles accessed over nonsecure sites are. Look at this.'

Hal studied the screen. 'That's weird,' he remarked. 'What's CERES? The name of a town? You think that's where Townsend is?'

'No,' Patrick replied. 'CERES stands for California Environmental Resources Agency. They do studies on the use of land, water, air . . . holy shit, look at this.'

'I'm lost, Patrick,' Briggs said, shaking his head. 'This is more environmental stuff. The Bureau of Reclamation? Why would they be looking up all this?' But Patrick flipped to the next cached page on the browser, and he started to understand. 'Hey, that's the dam right near here, right?' he asked. 'Folsom Dam? What's all this about?'

'Never mind!' Patrick shouted. 'Get the MV-22 ready to fly right now! We've got to get out to the dam!' He hit the print button on the keyboard, printed out a copy of the diagram, and raced out onto the flight line.

Near Folsom Lake, twenty-five miles northeast of Sacramento, California a few minutes later

'This is the forensic-summary report on the Gate Number Three rupture back a few years ago at Folsom Dam,' Patrick said on interphone. He and Hal Briggs were sitting in the rear of the MV-22 tilt-rotor aircraft, heading northeast toward the large concrete dam. 'The support structures on one of the spillway Tainter gates broke and sent half the volume of the lake into the American River. The river canyon contained the water from that break . . .'

'So you think Townsend is going to blow up these Tainter gates?' Briggs asked. 'Heck, why not just blow the dam itself?'

'The dam is concrete, probably thirty feet thick. How much dynamite would it take to blow that wall?'

'Probably ten thousand pounds of TNT.'

'It would probably take a lot less trouble and explosives to duplicate the 1995 accident and blow those struts on the Tainter gates,' Patrick said. 'That forensic report they downloaded from the Internet spelled out exactly where they could set the charges to dislodge those gates. And if more than two or three of those floodgates let loose, with a nearly full dam it would cause a massive flood downstream. Christ, it could wipe out a half-dozen towns along the river and inundate most of downtown Sacramento. The lake is near capacity right now from all the rains and runoff.'

'But I still don't get it,' Briggs said. 'Why do all this? Is he just plain crazy?'

'I don't know,' Patrick replied. 'But we've got to stop him first.'

'You ever think about the possibility that this might be a trap?' Hal asked. 'What if he planted that information on the computer so you'd find it and chase him out there? What if this is another diversion?'

'We've got nothing else to go on, Hal,' Patrick said. He put on the suit helmet, activated the BERP system, then clicked open the radio commlink: 'Drop me off at the top of the dam,' he said to the pilot over their command channel. 'Then get as close as you can to the face of the top of the dam. Watch out for power lines.'

'We've got the power lines on radar,' the pilot reported. The MV-22 used a millimeter-wave radar that could detect power lines as small as a half-inch in diameter in time for the pilots to steer over or under them.

The big aircraft settled into a hover just ten feet above Folsom Dam Road atop the huge concrete dam. Patrick, fully suited up, jumped out of the right-side cargo door. He could see the level of the lake on the northeast side of the dam – it was just a foot from the top, 465 feet above mean sea level. No doubt about it: If the dam let go, it would create a monumental disaster for miles downstream on either side of the American River.

Patrick landed on the road, climbed over the guard-rail, and jumped down onto a catwalk. The catwalk ran across the top of the spillways, eight steep concrete chutes that plunged 340 feet down into the American River gorge. All the spillways appeared dry, with no more than small rivulets of water running down the steep faces. That meant that the entire discharge from the lake was being diverted to the hydroelectric turbine chutes to make electricity.

Right below the catwalk were the tops of the eight Tainter gates. The Tainter gates were huge curved steel doors fifty feet high and forty-two feet wide, with support struts in the middle that attached the gates to trunnion pins on each side; the pins were mounted on the concrete supports on both sides of the spillway. Each gate had two large chains, resembling huge bicycle chains, that lifted the gates when necessary and allowed water to flow down over the spillway to relieve hydrostatic pressure from the reservoir side of the dam.

From the catwalk, Patrick could look down the back of the Tainter gates at the chains, using the infrared scanner visor on his helmet. Everything looked normal. He ran down the catwalk and inspected the top of each gate. Still nothing. 'I don't see anything yet,' Patrick radioed to the MV-22. 'You guys see anything?'

'Not yet,' Briggs replied. The pilots were using the infrared scanner in the nose turret to scan the face of the dam. 'We're getting as close as we can, but those transmission lines will keep us at least two hundred feet from the dam. We'll see if we can slip in between the lines and the dam, but it'll be tight. We've got dam inspectors and National Guard on the way to secure the dam. Their ETA is about fifteen minutes.'

'Copy,' Patrick answered. 'I'm going to have to go down

the face of these gates, Hal. The way they're designed, blowing the chains would prevent the gates from opening.'

'Roger that,' Hal acknowledged. He was rereading the computer printout as the MV-22 began to maneuver over the transmission lines. 'According to this forensic report you got off the computer, when that gate let loose back in 1995, it was friction from one of the trunnion hinge pins on the sides of the gate that caused the strut braces to buckle. The braces hold the gate against the spillway opening. Once they bent, the water pressure and the weight of the gate just pushed the gate out. Check the struts on each gate. If I was going to blow anything, that's where I'd set the charges.'

'Copy,' Patrick said. He looked over the edge of the catwalk. There was another catwalk forty feet below him, at the same level as the trunnion pins on which the Tainter gates pivoted. Patrick considered trying to jump down to the lower catwalk, but if he missed, it was a three-hundred-foot fall down the face of the dam to the river below. 'Hal, come back to the top of the dam and pick me up,' Patrick radioed. 'It's too far to jump to the lower catwalk.'

'On the way,' Hal replied.

Patrick hit the thrusters and jumped easily to the road above. He saw the MV-22 climb and start toward him, maneuvering easily over the transmission lines. With remarkable speed and agility for a bird its size, the huge tilt-rotor aircraft moved smoothly toward the road.

Then a streak of fire arced across the sky from the lower catwalk and plowed directly into the right engine. The engine disintegrated, a shaft of fire blowing downward from the right rotor as burning fuel streamed out and was caught in the rotor wash. The MV-22 dipped down below the rim of the dam. Patrick heard the left engine spool up to full military power, and the bird veered right, missing the lower catwalk by just a few feet.

'Will!' Patrick screamed into his helmet radio to the pilot. 'Pull up!'

'We got it! We got it!' one of the pilots radioed back – Patrick couldn't tell who it was because the voice was so high and squeaky. But it didn't look as if he had control. As he watched, the aircraft slipped to the right, barely missing the power lines across the gorge in front of the dam, and dropped.

But the MV-22 had a crossover transmission system that allowed power from one engine to drive both rotors, and as it fell down into the gorge, power was coming up on both rotors. What started as a barely controlled crash quickly turned into a powered glide. It was still going down but the pilot was back in control. Just in time, the pilot pulled back on the control stick and flared the aircraft as it hit the water a few yards from the rocky shoreline. It skittered across the rocks, spun around facing upstream as the dead right-engine nacelle struck the water, and came to rest on the edge of the shore, with the right wing and right-engine nacelle dipping into the American River.

'We're okay! We're okay!' Hal radioed. 'We're evacuating the aircraft!'

Patrick's relief gave way to a rage that rose up out of his chest and flooded his brain with hatred. He was past thought or calculation – he reacted. He used his helmet's infrared scanner to pinpoint the location of the terrorists on the lower catwalk – one of them was still holding the red-hot rocket launcher so spotting them was easy – and he hit his thrusters. He bounded over the railing on the

408

road and soared out into space, aiming for the terrorists in the darkness nearly a hundred feet below.

His aim was perfect. He landed on his chest and face right on top of the guy holding the spent rocket-launcher tube. He went down hard, but so did Patrick, who then crashed over onto the catwalk. The electrical surges coursing through the suit startled him with their force. Screaming in the effort to clear his head, he reached up to grab the handrail of the cat-walk . . .

. . . and the bullets struck him in a high-speed drumming on his back, then his helmet, then his chest. Within seconds, two terrorists, in front and behind him, emptied their thirty-round magazines of 9-millimeter automatic-weapon fire on him. The suit kept him safe but electrical pulses nearly overwhelmed him. He struggled to his feet as the gunmen reloaded fresh magazines and opened fire again. A warning flashed in his heads-up display – he was already at reserve power levels from the long fall from the road, followed by all the bullets at such close range. He ran forward and grabbed the gunman in front of him, head-butting him, crunching his jawbone, and knocking him out – and was hit square in the chest by a LAWS man-portable antitank rocket, fired from about fifty feet away down the catwalk. He was blown thirty feet back, up and over the catwalk's safety railing, and onto the number five Tainter gate.

Patrick opened his eyes after several long moments and checked the systems in his armor. The check did not take long: The report on the heads-up display simply read EMERGENCY. That explained why he wasn't feeling any feedback shocks from the suit: It no longer had enough power to electrocute him. The infrared-scanner visor was dead, so he retracted it. The environmental system was shut down, and he felt as if an elephant were standing on his chest. He managed to roll onto his hands and feet, desperately trying to get his balance back. But he was alive, goddammit, *alive!*

A hand grasped the bottom of his helmet and jerked his head up and back. He grabbed the hand, but found he didn't have the strength to pull it free. Then he felt the point of a knife right under his sternum.

'Well, well, General McLanahan,' said a voice with a heavy German accent. 'We meet at long last. I am Major Bruno Reingruber. I understand you have been looking for me for some time now. Unfortunately, our meeting will be shortlived. I am sorry I was unsuccessful in killing your brother or your friend Dr Jon Masters, but killing you will compensate for those previous failures.'

Patrick swung at Reingruber with his free arm, but the blows had no effect. 'It seems your armor is no longer functioning,' Reingruber said. He slowly pressed the point of the knife against the suit and up toward Patrick's chest, a fraction of an inch at a time. 'If my man's report is true,' Reingruber went on, 'your suit will not activate if it is not struck. In that case, we will do this nice and slow . . .'

The knife pierced the fabric. Environmental-system-conditioning fluid gushed forth. 'He said not to be fooled, that this is some kind of coolant in the suit and not blood, *ja*? But a little more, and the Tin Man will not disturb us ever again.' The knife point pierced the suit, the cotton undergarment, then pressed against his chest. Patrick cried out. '*Auf Wiedersehen*, General.'

Through the stars clouding his vision, Patrick activated the heads-up display in his helmet. He canceled the EMERGENCY readout and called up the status display. All systems were shut down. Everything was dead . . .

The knife penetrated the skin . . .

No, not every system was down. The thruster gas accumulators were fully charged. Patrick coughed inside the helmet as the pain intensified. Just as the knife started to pierce through the skin to muscle, Patrick summoned up the last volt of power left in the suit, braced his feet squarely against the number five Tainter gate, and activated the thrusters. They pushed Patrick, with Reingruber clutching him, up off the gate, over the lower catwalk, and out into space.

Reingruber screamed as they plummeted three hundred feet down the spillway and into the American River. In his terror, he kept a tight grasp on Patrick the entire way down, and it was *his* body that absorbed the brunt of the impact with the icy-cold water.

The strong current running from the hydroelectric power plant swept Patrick downstream. There was enough air in the helmet to breathe, although cold water was leaking into the suit through the knife puncture. The weight of the backpack power unit dragged him under, but scrabbling desperately, his fingers found the releases for the spent unit and he freed himself of it. His helmet burst above the surface. He kicked and paddled and found he was strong enough to keep his head above the water, so he unlatched the helmet and pulled it off. Cold, damp air never tasted so sweet. The cold water filling the suit was starting to numb his legs, but he was breathing, and he was alive.

Now, where was the nearest shoreline? He heard a shout: 'Patrick! Over here!' It was Hal Briggs. Spotlights lit up the river, and they turned right on him. Somehow Briggs had managed to see the fight up on the catwalk, and to find Patrick in the swirling river. Rescue teams came after him, and minutes later, Sacramento County Sheriff's deputies and California National Guard soldiers dragged him out of the water and began first aid.

'Check the dam, Hal,' Patrick said through chattering

teeth. His face was white, and his hands, lips, and legs trembled uncontrollably. 'Have them check the dam!'

'They're doing it right now, Patrick,' Briggs said. They were carrying him into a minivan ambulance that had pulled down the American River Bike Trail to the river's edge. 'They already got a couple of the charges. You were right, man – Townsend was going to blow up the gates on the dam.'

'Tell them to find Reingruber,' Patrick said urgently. 'If I survived that fall, he might have too.'

'Don't worry about it, Patrick,' Briggs said. 'You're done for the night. Let the National Guard and FBI . . .'

Bright flashes of light lit the sky behind them, followed seconds later by loud booms, the noise of cracking steel – and the sound of rushing water.

'Explosions on the dam!' someone shouted. In the glare of the searchlights illuminating the huge concrete dam, they could see pieces of the Tainter gates tearing off and flying into space. One thirteen-ton gate popped off the wall of the dam and fluttered through the air like a playing card tossed into the wind. A shaft of water shot through the opening like a massive lateral geyser.

Boots scrambled on rock and gravel, car and truck doors slammed, and the vehicles raced up the access road and away from the river just as the torrent raged over everything in its path.

Watt Avenue and Elkhorn Boulevard, Sacramento, California
a short time later

'What we're looking at, ladies and gentlemen,' said the radio announcer, 'is a terrorist disaster of monumental proportions. Four of the eight gates of Folsom Dam have apparently been blown apart by terrorists. Here's what we know so far: Police and FBI were at Folsom Dam after receiving information about possible sabotage of the dam. This is linked to the shoot-outs reported out at Mather Field earlier today. Sheriff's-department bomb squads removed several explosives from the dam but were not able to reach all of them before the remaining charges were detonated, apparently by a timer or by remote control. Eyewitnesses at the dam saw several explosions; some described them as demolition charges. The dam has all but ruptured at this point. We repeat, Folsom Dam has suffered a major accident and has ruptured. Outflow from the dam is in excess of one hundred and fifty thousand cubic feet per second, over twenty times the normal outflow, and is spilling over the banks of the American River Canyon.

'All residents living within two miles north and south of the American River are being ordered by the state Office of Emergency Services to evacuate the area immediately,' the announcer went on. 'This includes all residents of the cities of Folsom, Rancho Cordova, Fair Oaks, Gold River, Carmichael, and West Sacramento. In the city of Sacramento, evacuations are being ordered for all areas south of Arden Way east of the Capitol City Freeway, and south of El Camino Boulevard west of the Capitol City Freeway. In addition, all residents in areas north of Kiefer Boulevard, north of Fourteenth Avenue to Highway 99, and the entire downtown district north of Broadway are ordered to evacuate.

'At this time the flood surge has reached the western edge of the city of Folsom and is now approaching the Gold River and eastern portions of Rancho Cordova. It is spilling over Nimbus Dam and the fish hatchery. The Rainbow Bridge in Folsom has collapsed, and the Negro Bar and Hazel Avenue bridges are threatening to weaken or even collapse. In Folsom, all areas north of the river appear safe so far, but south of the river in low-lying areas the destruction is extensive. Old Folsom and indeed all areas south of the river and north of Blue Ravine Road are under at least four feet of water. We do not have any estimates of loss of life at this time, but the explosions came with no warning. The Aerojet-General rocket plant is underwater, and the safety and environmental hazards are very great. There are reports that tanks of rocket fuel and propane gas are adrift in the floodwaters and could present a highly dangerous explosion hazard.

'The flood surge is moving at a rate of approximately five miles an hour, and is expected to reach the city less than three hours from now. Evacuation orders are mandatory and will be enforced by California National Guard troops. Highway 50 and Folsom Boulevard have been closed east of Watt Avenue, so everyone should travel either north or south on major surface streets away from the American River and stay off Highway 50 and Folsom Boulevard. California National Guard units will be blocking off the freeway to aid in evacuations, so please do not use these thoroughfares. We repeat, all residents of flood-prone low-lying areas within two miles of the American River are ordered to evacuate immediately, and residents within five miles of the river are urged to evacuate as a precaution.'

The passenger in the front seat of the California National Guard Humvee turned off the radio as the vehicle approached the Elkhorn Boulevard gate of McClellan Air Force Base in the north part of the city of Sacramento.

Three more Humvees followed. The gate was a madhouse as security guards scrambled to keep track of the vehicles streaming in and out. The four Humvees took their place in a long line of military and civilian trucks trying to enter the base. Under the press of traffic, the security guards began waving all military vehicles through with cursory checks of ID cards, and the Humvees entered without difficulty.

One of them split off and headed east on the base, stopping at the security headquarters and the central communications facility, then going around the west side of the base to the power transformer farm near Roseville Road. The others headed north around the runways toward the hangars on the northwest side. Again, one split off, dropping off four soldiers in full-camouflage battle-dress uniforms and combat gear at strategic locations on the access roads leading to the hangars. There was virtually no security anywhere on the base except for the southeast side, where air rescue and relief activities were beginning to gear up in response to the rupture of the dam and the anticipated flooding of the city of Sacramento.

Gregory Townsend and eighteen of his soldiers dismounted from the remaining vehicles and ran to the edge of the security fence around the four target hangars. When all his units were in position, Townsend issued the order to go. Explosions destroyed the base's central communications facility, and more explosions at the power transformer farm on Roseville Road cut off power to most of the base. This did not affect power inside the target hangars, but it deactivated the security systems surrounding them, slowing down any response from elsewhere on the base. Then he blew open the security gates and headed for the hangars.

There were eight of them, but Townsend had targeted only the four on the west side and assigned four soldiers to each hangar. On his signal, they entered the hangars simultaneously by blowing open the outer doors, then rushing inside, neutralizing the Air Force guards, and mopping up the remaining armed resistance.

The guards in the hangars had managed to sound the alarm, but the base's central communications system and security-police headquarters never received it. Still, Townsend knew that before long someone would realize they were missing a scheduled security report or check-in, and there'd be some form of response. But with the frantic preparations for coping with the flood rapidly approaching Sacramento, he calculated he had at least an hour's leeway. His men could easily deal with any roving or curious security-police unit that happened by in the meantime, and an hour was all he needed. His men set to work on their final objective.

The complex on the northwest side of McClellan Air Force Base had changed hands many times over the years. Back in the 1950's and 60's, the area had been used to decontaminate spy planes that were flown over American, French, Russian, and Chinese aboveground nuclear-weapons explosions. In more recent years, flight-test squadrons built and tested new air weapon systems there, such as the 4,700-pound GBU-28 'bunker-buster' bomb used to try to kill Saddam Hussein as he hid in his deep underground shelters in the 1991 Persian Gulf War.

In addition to the classified weapon and flight-test work done there, the complex had another secret activity: It contained a small but full-scale nuclear reactor, which produced gamma rays used for NDI, or nondestructive inspection, of military aircraft. Although magnetic eddy current fields, X rays, lasers, radar, and plain old eye-balls were still useful in detecting cracks and fatigue in aircraft structures, they weren't reliable or adequate for the new crop of composite 'stealth' aircraft, so gamma-ray inspections were developed to check these planes without having to disassemble them first. Fifteen years ago, McClellan Air Force Base had been the first aircraft-maintenance depot in the world to use gamma rays for aircraft NDI, and it was still the main nuclear NDI facility in the free world.

And the latest clients ready for their annual nuclear NDI inspection were sitting right there before Gregory Townsend and his soldiers: four F-117A Night Hawk stealth fighter-bombers. All four of these odd-looking planes, with their multifaceted, pyramid-shaped fuse-lages, short pointed wings, and thin, highly swept tails, were Gulf War veterans, each having performed more than thirty missions in the heart of stiff Iraqi air defenses without a single casualty. Although they could carry only five thousand pounds of ordnance – usually two two-thousand-pound laser-guided bombs – and were more than fifteen years old, they were still in good condition. And because they were virtually invisible on radar and invulnerable to most modern air defense systems, they were four of the deadliest warplanes on earth . . .

. . . and they now belonged to Gregory Townsend.

While several of his soldiers began to refuel the planes and brought over ground power 'start carts,' Townsend and three of his other men, all trained combat pilots, stepped up the special access ladders designed for the F-117 stealth fighters, opened up the cockpit canopies, and got to work preflighting their aircraft. The preflight checks went quickly. Because the Night Hawks' cockpits were so cramped and uncomfortable, they were designed

417

from the outset to be highly automated, relegating the human on board to being a system monitor rather than a pilot.

Besides, these pilots were not concerned about getting the planes ready to go to war. They simply had to make sure they had enough gas to fly a few hundred miles to an isolated airstrip in southwestern Nevada, where more fuel was waiting. A thousand miles at a time, and the aircraft would eventually end up in South America, where eager international arms merchants and foreign countries were waiting to start the bidding on the auction of the century.

On a signal from Townsend, all four F-117 engines were started inside the hangars themselves, in preparation for taxiing. There was no concern about the exhaust damage – it didn't matter what the hangars looked like after they left – and none of them bothered with flight-control or engine checks. The F-117 Night Hawk stealth fighter was inherently unstable in all flight axes – there was no such thing as 'dead-sticking' an F-117 to an emergency landing. The aircraft needed at least one flight-control computer and one engine to fly. If it lost more than that, the pilot had a single option: eject. But a foreign government such as Libya, Iran, Iraq, or China would still pay hundreds of millions of dollars for an F-117 stealth fighter even with only one engine or one flight-control computer.

'Report ready to taxi,' Townsend ordered. When the other three pilots reported, the four hangar doors were manually opened. Guards stationed themselves in front of the hangars and along the taxi route, prepared to repel any security forces that might come along. Each was armed with an M-16 assault rifle fitted with an M-206 grenade launcher for fighting off heavy response vehicles or trucks. 'Release brakes now,' Townsend ordered.

At that moment, the pilot of the number four F-117 moving from the westernmost hangar saw a blur of motion off to his right. A soldier in full combat gear and helmet appeared out of nowhere directly in front of his hangar, carrying what looked like two large duffel bags. He dropped both bags on the tarmac, then reached down with his left hand and threw one of them under the nose gear of the aircraft. *'Nein!'* the pilot shouted. 'What are you doing? Clear the way!'

Then the pilot looked again and realized that these were not duffel bags being thrown under his wheels – they were *bodies*! Soldiers' bodies. This . . . this stranger was throwing bodies under the wheels to prevent him from taxiing! 'Warning! Intruder alert!' he called. 'I am stopped! I can't move!'

'Unit four, go to full power!' ordered Townsend, who could not see what was happening from his cockpit. 'Taxi immediately! All other units taxi at maximum speed!'

The number four pilot shoved his throttles up to full military power, trying to taxi over the bodies of his dead comrades. But the intruder had disappeared under the nose of the F-117 and seconds later the pilot felt four hard bangs. The aircraft shuddered and dropped. Before the pilot's stunned eyes the intruder reappeared, one of the dead soldiers' sidearms in his hands. He had shot out several of the tires.

The pilot pulled the throttles to idle, opened his canopy, and jumped out of the plane. He watched as the intruder calmly walked over to the number three aircraft. Then he crouched down to get the M-16 assault rifle slung across the body of the soldier under his left main gear, checked it, loaded a fresh magazine, and fired from a range of fifteen meters. There was no way he could miss – yet the man did not go down. He turned around to look at the pilot even as the shots struck him, then continued on his way.

It was him, the pilot realized. The Tin Man. He was alive! He had been killed in the dam explosion but he was *alive*!

The Tin Man reached the number three F-117 and fired several rounds into the left main landing-gear wheel. The outside tire popped, but the inner tire kept the plane moving. As the plane's pilot watched in astonishment, he saw the helmeted figure leap fifteen meters across his windshield and land on his left wing.

Atop the engine inlets were blow-in doors, which provided additional inlet air to compensate for the reduced airflow through the large main inlets caused by the radar-absorbing mesh screen covering them. Before the pilot's eyes, the Tin Man dropped the empty pistol into one of the open blow-in doors on the left engine. Sucked into the engine, it shredded the first-stage compressor blades in a matter of seconds, and the disintegrating remnants shot out in all directions, puncturing fuel and hydraulic lines and blasting apart the entire engine and part of the left fuselage.

The number one and two F-117's were taxiing away fast. The Tin Man sped down the right wing of the stricken number three, jumped onto the ground, ran toward the taxiing fighters, then leaped as soon as his thrusters were recharged. He landed right on the canopy of number two, but with nothing to grasp and the groundspeed building up rapidly, he beat on the glass canopy panels. His left fist broke through a side panel with ease. The glass of the forward panels was much thicker and stronger, but several crushing blows broke it too. He reached in, shattered the heads-up display atop the instrument panel, then grabbed for the pilot. 'He is on my

420

aircraft!' the pilot shrieked into his radio, evading the grasping arm.

Unable to reach the pilot to disable him, the Tin Man grabbed the overhead curtain ejection handle on the ACES II ejection seat, then hit his thrusters to blow himself clear of the plane. The pilot shot up through the broken canopy on a column of fire from the rockets in his ejection seat. He was blasted 150 feet into the night sky. His parachute fully deployed, but there was time only for one swing under it before he hit the taxiway. The plane continued straight ahead. But starting the ejection sequence had automatically cut off fuel and power to the engines, so it rolled forward until it hit a blast fence on the north side of the main runway and came to a stop.

The Tin Man got back to his feet, scanning the area with his infrared visor. It was too late to reach Townsend in the number one F-117. By the time the thrusters were fully charged, Townsend had already lifted off into the night sky. The one he really wanted had escaped.

'Well, General McLanahan,' he heard in his helmet radio, which was set to monitor the emergency UHF channel. 'Yours was a valiant effort. But one plane will still make my buyers very happy. Good night, and enjoy what is left of your city.'

But astoundingly there was one last chance. A UH-1 Huey helicopter with CA NATIONAL GUARD markings touched down on the apron directly in front of the security hangars where the F-117's had been parked. It had arrived as planned to pick up a few chosen members of Townsend's assault team, and the soldiers ran to board it. The Tin Man shot across the runways, and as the fully loaded helicopter was lifting off, he jumped up and grabbed on to the right skid, then the belly cargo hook, straddled the skids, and held on for the ride. The pilot didn't even notice the additional weight because the aircraft was already wallowing from its heavy load as it lifted into the sky.

The Huey headed almost directly east, climbing to eleven thousand feet as it cleared the Sierra Nevada Mountains. It took all the Tin Man's strength and concentration to hold on in the frigid night air whistling around him at 120 miles an hour. Two hours later, the helicopter swooped across steep, rocky crags and flew low through a high-desert valley. An airfield came into view. It was surrounded by what appeared to be abandoned military hangars and industrial structures. As the helicopter moved low over a group of wooden buildings, the Tin Man dropped free, using his thrusters to break his fall.

The place had a weird look to it; it was like stepping into an abandoned city. The hangars were large enough to hold the biggest military or commercial aircraft, but they were empty and falling apart. He saw the twisted, rusted hulks of what might once have been an oil refinery or large factory. The ground was covered with cactus, tumbleweeds, and thick dust. There was a long unlit runway ahead, and a very large aircraft-parking ramp lit by blue taxiway lights. The only other lights were on a lone building on the northern edge of the ramp, which had a rotating airport beacon and several radio antennas on top, a few scraggly trees in front, and a fuel truck parked nearby. The Tin Man headed for it.

A sign indicated that the building was a general-aviation fixed-base operator – an FBO – called Tonopah Flying Service. He knew there was a Tonopah, Nevada, a small desert town in the southwestern part of the state, midway between Reno and Las Vegas. This had to be it, and from the look of it, he guessed the airport must once have been a military base.

Moments later, the UH-1 Huey helicopter touched down on the ramp in front of the FBO building and Townsend's terrorists dismounted. Within minutes, the Tin Man could hear shouts in German coming from inside – they were taking over the facility. He peered through a side window and was startled to see a terrified woman cowering in front of a man with a gun.

At the sound of a muted whistling out on the runway, the white runway edge lights snapped on. Then an F-117 Night Hawk stealth fighter swooped down, paralleling the long runway on a downwind leg. He switched to his infrared visor to watch as it touched down at the very edge of the runway, careened down it, and stopped just in time at the north end. Then it turned off on the taxiway, swerved around as soon as it had room to maneuver on the aircraft apron, and taxied right back onto the runway, now heading south. The fuel truck drove out in its direction.

The Tin Man's first concern was the hostage, not the F-117. No one was in sight when he sneaked to the front of the building and looked through the glass door, which meant that the gunman had to have taken the hostage inside the office behind the short counter. He dashed inside, hit his thrusters, and jetted directly at the office door. It crashed in, and he discovered it had come right down on the terrorist himself, knocking the gun he was holding out of his hands. One punch from the gauntleted fist, and the man was out cold.

'You're all right now,' the Tin Man said to the frightened woman. 'But these are terrorists taking over the airfield. You've got to get out of here quietly and call for help. Is there a phone anywhere?'

She nodded. 'There's one behind the building,' she said, her voice quavering.

'Tell the police that the terrorists who stole the stealth

fighters from the Air Force base in Sacramento are here, and they're going to refuel and take off again. Then hide yourself until help comes.' When she left he grabbed the terrorist's gun, peered out the door, and crept outside.

'Hurry up, damn you!' Townsend shouted.

'The pump on this truck is very slow, sir,' the soldier answered. The base obviously wasn't used often, and the Jet-A truck even less.

Townsend cursed again. The guard he'd stationed inside the FBO had missed a second five-minute check-in – an ominous sign. A burst of fire, then an explosion, tore into the Huey. Gunfire erupted from the rear of the FBO building but was silenced moments later. 'Disconnect!' Townsend shouted. 'Prepare to repel attackers!' Silence. Where were his men? He looked toward the fuel truck and saw all four of them lying on the ground. My God – when had that happened? Dammit, he hadn't heard a thing and he was right here!

He had just put on his helmet and finished strapping himself into his seat when a voice came over the UHF guard emergency channel: 'Townsend. Gregory Townsend. Can you hear me?'

Quickly Townsend checked his switches and skimmed through the checklist, but realized it would be suicidal to try to take off. He lowered the cockpit canopy. 'The Tin Man, I presume? Very good of you to see me off, General McLanahan. My men reported that you had been killed by Major Reingruber.'

'Indeed. As you can see, I'm here. But I am not seeing you off. You are going nowhere, Townsend. It's time you paid for all the death and destruction you've caused.'

'I'll tell you what I'll pay for, General,' Townsend said.

'I'll make you the same deal I made before, only better: you and I as partners. With one phone call, General, I can wire ten million dollars into an offshore bank account in your name. Moreover, I'll give you half of whatever we can negotiate for the sale of this aircraft. We should be able to split two hundred, perhaps three hundred million dollars. I make one phone call and it's yours.'

The response was a burst of automatic gunfire. The left main landing-gear tires blew out. Then the nose-gear tires exploded and the aircraft's nose wheel settled into the asphalt up to its hubs. 'You may as well shut 'em down and come on out, Townsend,' said the Tin Man. 'You're going to prison.'

With an angry yank, Townsend pulled the throttles to cutoff, threw open the canopy, unfastened his seat belts, and climbed out of the Night Hawk. He stood directly in front of the dark-clad figure, shaking with rage. 'You miserable cretin!' he snapped. 'You've just thrown away millions of dollars for us both.'

'You're not going to need money where you're going, Townsend.'

'Is that so?' Townsend retorted. 'Tough talk for someone hiding behind an electronic suit of armor. Coward! Why don't you take that thing off and let's have at it, you and me, man to man. Or are you too cowardly for that?'

Stunned, he watched as the figure dropped the backpack power unit off his shoulders. 'Well, well. You do have some sporting blood in you after all, General . . .'

But the surprises were not over. As the Tin Man unfastened and removed his helmet, Townsend saw before him not General Patrick McLanahan but his brother. He could not believe his eyes. 'Good Lord! It's Officer McLanahan! Following in your dead brother's footsteps, I see.'

'Patrick is very much alive, Townsend,' Paul said coldly. 'He survived the fight on the dam. Major Reingruber did not.'

Townsend managed to maintain his composure. 'Be that as it may, Officer, you are here and he is not. And there is still a business accommodation we can make, you and I. It would be worth ten million dollars to me for my freedom right now. You have the stealth fighter and all my surviving men, including the ones who killed your fellow officers in downtown Sacramento. As I understand it, you also have no job now, nothing but an inconsequential disability pension. There are no witnesses out here. One single phone call, and a secret Cayman Islands bank account will be established in your name, ten million dollars in it, all for you. You can go back to being a lawyer, or you can live out your lifelong fantasies in a country where the law can't touch you.'

'I've got an even better idea for you, Townsend,' Paul said. He walked over to one of the soldiers lying unconscious next to the fuel truck and withdrew the combat knife from his leg sheath. 'You kill me, and you keep your ten million dollars and walk away free.'

Townsend smiled a satisfied grin and pulled out his knife with theatrical flourish. 'You are a sporting man, Officer McLanahan,' he said – and attacked with the speed of a cobra.

The fight appeared to be over before it had begun. Townsend feigned a slash to Paul's head, then reversed the knife and brought it down full force on his left shoulder. Paul made no effort to counterattack; he simply raised his left arm in a feeble attempt to block the assault. But he was far too late. Townsend's knife buried itself to the hilt. Townsend laughed right in his face, then tried to remove the knife – and found it stuck fast . . .

. . . and before he knew it, Paul's own knife lashed up and deep into his belly.

Townsend dropped to his knees, clutching his midriff. He watched dumbfounded as Paul McLanahan jiggled the big knife in his shoulder and freed it. There was no blood. Not a drop.

'Ironic, isn't it, Townsend?' Paul McLanahan asked. He removed his gauntlets, opened the suit front, and shrugged off the left sleeve. Underneath was a dull aluminum prosthesis. It moved like a real arm, but it was definitely not human. It was one of the prototype Sky Masters, Inc. prosthetic arms, attached and activated without any cosmetic enhancements. 'I owe you thanks for this,' he said. 'Your bloodthirsty attacks gave it to me. I felt sorry for myself and I told them I didn't want it, but I'm glad they helped me change my mind. What do you think of this, Colonel?'

But Gregory Townsend was a long, long way from being able to answer.

Epilogue